# THE
# CONNECTION

### A NOVEL

## MICHAEL J. SENGER SR.

## LULU.COM

ISBN: 978-0-6151-5598-2

Manufactured in the United States of America
First Lulu Press Edition: July 2007
Second Lulu Press Edition: March 2015

Contact Michael J. Senger Sr. at *msengersr@hotmail.com*

_Thanks to:_

Robbie Byrd
Mary Collins
Melva-Lynn Norwood
Eileen Batson
and Evelyn Mair

_your feedback helped shape the initial manuscript
and encouraged me to complete this project_

# THE
# CONNECTION

**A NOVEL**

**1**

*Saturday, June 1, 1996, 9:30 PM:*

The only light that shone on the gravel road ahead was from the full moon. It was low in the sky and glowed an amber color that would warm and comfort most people as they viewed it. However, Joe was not comforted at all. His mission for the night had not gone well and his passenger was not cutting him any slack. He sat, with the car in park and his headlights off, at the entrance of the gravel road anticipating what was about to happen.

"What are we waiting for? Why did you drag me all the way out here? What is this all about? What do you want from me?"

Amanda fired off question after question, as she had done for the past hour, with little or no reply from Joe. He just sat there staring out the windshield with one hand grasping the steering wheel and the other holding the gun on Amanda. As each question came, his grip on the wheel got tighter.

Joe had done hundreds of deals before. He loved his *occupation*, as he called it. The money, the girls, the travel, the freedom, and all the drugs he wanted. Most of all he loved the respect it brought him. *People I meet are glad to see me,* he thought, *and treat me well. But this girl...*

"Stop it!" he snapped. "Get out of the car," he ordered

waving the gun in the direction of Amanda's door.

The look on her face and her hesitation told him she was not sure what to do and her gazing back and forth from the gun to his face confirmed it.

*She's scared. Is she thinking I'll shoot her in the back as she gets out? What would happen if I did and she died? How long would it be before someone found her way out here?*

"You don't have to do this," she pleaded. "You could just let me go and I won't tell anybody or call the police."

For a few seconds Joe pondered the idea then stated unemotionally, "It's not part of the plan. Get out!"

It was not part of the plan, but neither was her being there in the first place. He replayed the plan in his head, every detail, but could not figure out what went wrong. *How did the cops know?* If the deal had gone right, he would have left the girl outside the restaurant with the drugs in her purse and the money in his pocket. He would be here alone and...looking at his watch...on time.

Her voice was shaky and her bottom lip quivered as she asked once more, "What do you want from me?"

Joe still did not reply, partly because he really did not know what he wanted from her, other than her silence. He raised the gun to Amanda's face.

"I'll use this," he said coldly. "Now get out!"

Amanda turned and grasped the handle to the door and jerked it up. Outside the car, she stood motionless. Joe turned to get out of the car on the driver's side and took his eyes off her for a second. The sound of her shoes hitting the gravel turned his frustration to anger. Instantly, he swung his arm over the roof of the car and pointed the gun at her.

"Stop!" he yelled, but he knew it was no use. *If it were me, I wouldn't stop either*. He pushed himself away from the car, put the gun in his trench coat pocket and chased her.

Amanda could not run very well in her high heel shoes and Joe caught up quickly. He grabbed her by her long brown hair and yanked. Amanda shrieked as her head jerked back and her feet slipped on the gravel beneath her. The momentum of Joe's pace caused him to run into her as she was falling. Both of them went to the ground hard. Amanda landed on her back while Joe fell forward and turned to land on his right side hitting his head on a tree root sticking out of the ground. He winced at the pain that immediately spread through his head and shoulders. It made him even angrier.

Joe stood and grabbed Amanda's right arm with his left hand. He was not a big person, but he was strong. With one quick motion, he jerked her slim and petite frame to her feet. She held the back of her head with her left hand.

"Don't try that..."

Before Joe could finish, Amanda had brought her balled up fist sailing from behind her head with all her might, striking Joe in his right temple above his eye. His head twisted quickly but he did not let go of her arm. With his right hand, he felt the wetness of his temple as blood started to run down the side of his face and his anger got the best of him. He drew back his right hand, clenched it into a fist and with all his might punched Amanda in the jaw. Her head jerked back quickly and her body went limp. Just before she hit the ground, he caught her and carried her back to the car.

He dropped her behind the car and then walked over to the driver's door, reached inside, turned off the engine and pulled the keys out of the ignition. Amanda was still out when Joe returned to the trunk and opened it. The trunk light came on but it gave very little light. There was one thought on his mind, *silence*. He was going to make sure there were no more questions.

"Where is it?"

Joe had to fumble through several boxes left inside the trunk to find the duct tape.

"Got it!"

He rolled Amanda over on her stomach and placed her hands behind her back. Then pealed off a long piece of tape and wrapped both her wrists together. As he went to tape her ankles, he noticed she was missing one shoe.

"Damn. I'll have to go find it."

He finished taping her ankles, but before putting away the tape, he placed a piece over her mouth. "I should have done this when we left the restaurant."

Joe was feeling less frustrated now that he had stopped the never-ending questions, but time was not on his side and he knew it. Looking at his watch again, Joe knew he was seven minutes late, still he had to find the shoe. *No loose ends*. This was going to make him even later. He would have to explain this as well as explain the girl.

"First things first," he grunted as he threw the tape back in the trunk and pushed all the boxes up against the back seat. Bending down, he picked up Amanda's body, dropped her into the trunk then lowered the trunk lid, but did not shut it. Before going after the shoe, he wiped the blood from his face and looked around to make sure no one saw anything.

Ten minutes later Joe was back with the shoe in his hand. As he approached the car, he stopped. A cold chill went down his back and he stood stone still. He thought he heard voices. The sound was low and muffled then quickly faded away. *Who else was out here?* As he reached the car, the voices came again from a distance though he could not tell from where. He peered through the darkness as hard as he could. There was nothing to see. In one quick motion, he opened the trunk, threw the shoe inside and slammed the lid shut. Jumping into the driver's seat, he started the car and headed down the gravel road.

Frightened that more than one person was waiting for him, Joe began to talk to himself. "What am I going to tell him? She wasn't supposed to come with me here. Only I was supposed to meet him. He's going to blow a gasket."

He drove down the gravel road until he got to an open space. It was circular in form and clearly used by folks who had driven down here by mistake, turned around and gone out the way they came. The chain that blocked the only other exit from this point was lying on the ground.

Joe took a deep breath. *He's here.*

The path beyond the chain was only wide enough for one car and a thick row of trees and bushes lined each side. There were no signs displaying an address or a name, nor anything to indicate who lived here. No signs telling others not to trespass. Only the chain and with it down, the invitation was obvious.

Slowly, he traveled up the narrow gravel road. The moon was higher in the night sky now but its light could not penetrate the thick brush. Joe squinted, trying to see what was ahead as the path turned and opened up.

"Ahhh...!"

He slammed on the brakes and stared at the black figure standing in front of the car. The sound of his own heart beating rapidly in his ears made every other noise disappear and he cracked the window to get some air. As he did, he heard the man speak.

"You're late."

Joe breathed a sigh of relief. He shut off the car and climbed out. The road had opened up into a field that led down to the water's edge about fifteen yards ahead. As Joe got out, the only sound he heard were the waves splashing up on the shore.

"Jeeze, I could have run into you. Why are you standing in the middle of the road?"

"What road? There's no road here."

Joe looked down at the ground and realized that the road curved to the left about ten feet back.

"Sorry, boss, I couldn't see anything."

"Never mind. How did it go?"

"You mean the deal?" Joe swallowed hard. "It didn't go so well."

"Really?"

"Yeah, someone tipped off the cops. I was about to do the

deal with the girl. I sat at her table. When I looked up, I saw the cops coming down the road with their lights on. So we took off."

"We?"

"Yeah, me and the girl."

"What happened to the girl?"

"Uh, uh...she's..." Joe bowed his head. "She's in the trunk."

"Trunk?"

"Yeah, she was driving me nuts." Joe explained with his arms waving in the air. "She kept telling me she wasn't buying any drugs, she didn't know who I was and she wasn't at the restaurant to meet me. She went on and on and on until I couldn't take it anymore. So I tied her up and put her in the trunk."

"I see. So why did you bring her here?"

"I didn't know what else to do with her. I figured if I left her and the cops caught her she would spill the beans on us. As I drove here, I began to wonder if we had the right girl, like maybe we made a mistake or something. Then I couldn't let her go. I figured you'd know what to do."

"You were right, Joe, I do know what to do. Show me the girl."

Joe led the way to the back of the car and opened the trunk. The dim light revealed a woman in a tan dress that was dirty and torn. Her hair was messy and tangled with a couple of leaves in it. She had several runs in her stockings. One shoe was on the other laying in front of her. She was awake and looked up at both of them.

"Was there a problem?"

"Well, yeah, she tried to run away," Joe said.

"I see."

\* \* \*

Amanda's vision was blurry and she could not make out whom the second man was. She was sure the first was the lunatic who kidnapped her. The voice of the second man was a little familiar though.

"Do you still have your gun?" she heard him say.

"Yes," said the lunatic.

"Let me have it."

She watched as the lunatic handed over his gun and asked, "What are you going to do?"

The same question ran through Amanda's mind and she wondered who these people were and why they were doing this to her. She tried to focus and see them clearly but the light from the trunk lid was not bright enough.

"I'll show you," said the second man.

Amanda saw the gun pointing at her again but something was different. When the lunatic had pointed it at her she got the sense that he would not use it, but that was not what she felt now. A chill ran through her body and she began to shake as she realized the answer to her question. She tried to speak, to ask for mercy but nothing came out, only groans. Even if she could speak the tape over her mouth would have prevented anything from coming out. Her eyes focused on the gun, then to the second man who was pointing it at her, and then back to the gun.

"Good-bye, my dear," he said politely.

This time Amanda recognized the voice. Her eyes moved from the gun to the face of the man. She recognized him and raised her eyebrows.

BANG!

\* \* \*

Amanda's body went completely limp as blood ran down her forehead.

Joe screamed, "What'd you do that for?"

"Never mind. Help me pick her up."

The two men lifted Amanda's body out of the trunk and carried it down to the pier, which was to the right of the field, and followed it to its end.

"Okay, drop her."

Joe obeyed and they heaved Amanda's body into the river. With little remorse, they turned around and headed back to the car.

"You still have that briefcase I gave you?"

"Yeah," Joe said. "It's in the back seat of my car."

"Did you open it?"

"No, you told me not to."

"Good. You've done well Joe."

The two stopped walking and faced each other.

"Now I want you to drive straight to the airport. When you get there, open the briefcase. Inside you'll find your tickets, some instructions and other things you'll need. You're going on a trip,

Joe. Follow the instructions and I will contact you soon. Don't take anything with you except the briefcase and don't talk to anyone."

"But what about..."

"Don't worry about any of this. I'll take care of it."

Joe turned and walked back towards his car, his thoughts racing. There was no mention of killing the girl, but then there was no mention of bringing her here either. Rationalizing the event he made himself believe that she had become a liability and could not be let go, she knew too much. But so did he. Suddenly he remembered the voices and his eyes scanned the area as he walked. Were there others or was it his imagination? *Are they going to let me live? What's this about a trip?*

When he reached the car, he climbed in, grateful to have made it this far. His right hand was shaking as he reached for the keys and he grabbed it with his other hand to steady himself. Looking over his shoulder he glanced at the briefcase in the back seat and wondered what was in it. Was it really stuff for a trip or something else? He knew they would see him if he checked it here so he decided he would wait until he got out of sight. He started the car, turned it around and left. As he drove away, he glanced in the rear-view mirror and saw two men step out of the shadows. *There were others!*

* * *

The three men watched as Joe drove away. No one said anything until his taillights disappeared in the darkness.

"Myers, follow him and make sure he gets on that plane."

"Yes, sir," Myers said, and disappeared.

"Ted, take me home."

"Yes, sir, Mr. Michaels."

* * *

*Friday, June 7, 1996, 2:45 PM:*

Friends and relatives filled the Chapel of the McCoy Funeral Home. Arrangements of roses surrounded Amanda's casket in front of the platform. Every corner of Amanda's ivory casket had her favorite flower painted on it and on top laid a long array of roses and greenery. The dim lights and the hymns played by the organist helped soften the mood of the room. Twenty-four candles on their own stands lit the platform - one for each year of Amanda Gilbert's life.

Walter Gilbert stood next to the American flag in the foyer of the Chapel. He was a tall man with a small potbelly and short white hair that made him look as if he was in his sixties, but he was only forty-seven. The paisley tie he wore did not match his dark navy-blue suit and it stood out against his white shirt. Because he was color blind, his wife, Doris, always picked out his ties, but she was unable to do it today. To his left was a window that allowed him to keep a watch on his wife and daughter. They sat in the front pew to the right of the center aisle.

Standing next to him, and peering through the window as well, was his long time friend and pastor, Granite Wells. His parents had given him the name Granite because he was so stiff when he was born. Later, after he had been ordained as a minister, his name became a comfort to those to whom he ministered.

Walter felt Wells lean in close to him as he whispered, "How are they doing, Walter?"

"Doris decided to wear a black dress that Amanda had given her years ago, but it's a little small. I can see her fidgeting with it to get comfortable."

They watched as Doris politely greeted a group of friends that came by and engaged in short conversation with each other. After they left, she wiped her eyes with the handkerchief her husband had given her. She did not get up. When she was not greeting someone, her eyes fixed on the portrait of Amanda sitting on an easel next to the pulpit on the platform.

"She is doing well today," Walter continued, "unlike the past few days when she had spent much time alone. She hasn't cried much and I wonder when she will. She's been wandering around the house, not as if she was lost or didn't know what to do but as if she was deep in thought.

"You know how she's always telling people to fulfill their destiny instead of running from it? Well, she believes that Amanda had fulfilled hers and this comforts her in a way I can't understand."

His gaze shifted to Rachel, Amanda's younger sister by three years, who sat next to her mom. Dressed in a black business suit with her thick black shoulder length hair put up in a bun, she was unattractive. Normally Rachel paid close attention to the way she looked, but today she did not seem to care. She only wore enough make-up to cover the dark circles under her eyes; no lipstick, eyeliner or eye shadow. Nothing about her showed how beautiful she could be. Like a mirror image, Rachel did exactly what her mom did as people passed and then sat staring at the same picture of her sister.

Images of Amanda and Rachel as little girls appeared in Walter's mind and he watched silently as they played on the swing set in their back yard and with dolls in their room. He even remembered the tea party they had invited him to.

Wells interrupted the silence. "What about Rachel?"

"Rachel's another story. She's lost her best friend. She's not one to hold back her feelings and has spent days crying. She tortured herself by sitting on Amanda's bed and staring at the pictures on the walls, the doll collection in the curio cabinet and her photo albums. She *is* lost and needs help to get through each day."

Again, thoughts of the girls when they were young came to mind. This time it was the fishing trips they took. Walter felt pride as he remembered how bad they were at first, then, after teaching them, how good they became. There was the time Rachel cast her rod, it went sailing out of her hands, and they spent the next thirty minutes fishing it out of the water. And when Amanda tried to cast her rod while standing in the boat she fell out and they had to fish her out of the water. Years later they could bait a hook and fillet a fish as well as any man could.

Interrupting his thoughts again Wells asked, "Walter, how are you holding up?"

There was a pause before he spoke. Staring through the

window, he could feel his throat tightening and he tried to curb the effect, but it did not work. "I can't believe she's gone," was all he got out before his voice cracked. He swallowed and then continued, "It seems like we were just fishing last week." Pictures from their last fishing trip of Amanda holding a stringer of fish she had caught came to mind and he reflected on it. "You know it's funny, you think you have all the time in the world and then this happens. I was going to call her and see if she wanted to go fishing off the coast next month. You know, take a few days off with the old man. I just didn't get around to it. Then that detective called at nine-o'clock in the morning this past Monday and our world came to a screeching halt."

He wiped his eyes with a tissue and fell quiet again, peering through the window at his wife, daughter and Amanda's picture.

**2**

*Friday, May 12, 2006, 4:35 PM:*

"It's time for us to honor you, the graduating class of 2006. As we call your name, please come up on the platform from the steps on my left, receive your diploma, shake hands with Dean Alterman, pause for a picture, exit by the stairs on my right and return to your seat. Parents and guests please hold your applause until everyone has received their diploma. Thank you. Now will the graduating class please rise."

Graduating students stood in anticipation of their prized moment. As the students were called, Rachel imagined Amanda, dressed in her cap and gown, with her blond hair, walking up the steps and across the platform. She could see her arm held out with her hand open to receive her diploma and she could hear her parents and friends clapping and saying her name with flash bulbs going off. She was lost in the event.

\* \* \*

Walter, his wife, their family and friends, had been waiting for Rachel for twenty minutes while she took pictures with classmates. He watched as the grounds around Cassell Coliseum buzzed with activity. Everywhere he looked, families and guests surrounded students, who were dressed in caps and gowns, with cameras clicking and flashing in their faces. Pictures with family members, classmates, professors and the speakers were important. It was a once in a lifetime event that could not go without being captured on film. Remembering the awkward attempts his wife and he had made in the past to capture the achievements of their children, Walter decided to hire a professional to do it for them.

"Rachel will be along in a minute," said Mark the photographer as he walked up to the Gilberts carrying his two Nikon cameras. Mark was a young thin man with short sandy blonde hair who was also a graduate student at Virginia Tech. "She's just finishing up a couple of pictures with her friend. We already have shots with her classmates, the staff and the speakers. When she comes over I'd like to start by taking pictures of her with just her parents and then we can add the rest of the family and then friends."

"It sounds like we're having a wedding."

"Walter, stop. You know this is a big day for Rachel. It has been hard work for her to overcome all those hurdles, finish her studies and earn her Ph.D. She didn't give up like she wanted to, remember?"

Walter only nodded at his wife. He was not complaining, only trying to be funny, but he knew he could not explain this to her. His daughter *had* been through a lot and he was so proud of her. Words could not express what he felt, so he said nothing.

"Here she comes," Doris said. "Now don't be negative,

Walter. We don't want to spoil her day."

With his eyes rolling back in his head Walter said, "Yes, dear."

* * *

Rachel knew her smile went from ear to ear. For years, she had worked to get to this day and now that it was here, she did not want it to end. A flood of memories from the ten years she had spent here at Virginia Tech. sidetracked her urge to run to her parents. Her steps were in cadence with the memories as they came and it seemed, to her, as if she was walking in slow motion. As she walked, she held down her cap with her left hand so it would not blow off. Her black gown furled in the breeze like a flag and her gold tassel bounced like a ponytail behind her.

The memories stopped and Rachel dwelt on one idea that had not yet totally materialized, though it was beginning to come into focus. Like an arrow piercing the air as it flew, sure to find its mark, coming ever closer, the *whoosh* growing louder with each closing inch. *I completed all my courses. I didn't quit. I went the distance.* The *whoosh* was almost deafening now. *I earned my degree, my Ph.D.! Thonk!* It hit. *I did it, Dr. Gilbert!*

When she reached her parents, she wrapped her arms around both of them and gave each of them a hug and a kiss. "I love you both so much," she whispered in their ears. "I've never been so happy."

With a hesitation in her voice as if she was choking back

sobs, Doris said, "We love you too."

Walter added, "And we are so proud of you," as he locked eyes with his daughter holding her face in both his hands.

A spontaneous duet erupted from both her parents breaking the moment, "Congratulations!"

This was the cue for the rest of her family and friends to join in. Congratulations came from all around as she hugged and kissed everyone. Some cried, some laughed, some shook hands and hugged her tightly, while others gave kisses and embraced her with great affection. She knew what this day meant to them and watched as they breathed a sigh of relief. For the past ten years, the family held its breath wondering if the death of her sister would permanently hinder her from ever achieving any goal. Today, they all got their answer and it was good to see them breathing again.

Mark chimed in and began positioning people for pictures. Rachel did not rush, she allowed herself to observe each moment, each face and its expression. There were things that the camera was not going to catch and she wanted these memories tucked away for future reference.

Positioning people took time, but Rachel did not mind the wait. She cherished each moment as if it was the final decorating of a cake. Years ago the ingredients were mixed as she started her studies at Virginia Tech. Each class, each assignment during each year added another ingredient. Then came the time to beat the mixture and get all the lumps out to create a smooth batter. This process started when Amanda was murdered and continued for years. There was a point when she felt the batter would never smooth out, that the lumps would not go away. Finally, they did and she was able to put the batter in a cake mold and place it in the oven by returning to school and finishing. The cake was made and today it was being frosted and decorated. Each moment was another rose on the cake.

"I believe I've gotten everyone," Mark said proudly. "Are there any other shots you'd like me to get?"

"There's one more," Rachel announced. She turned to her mom. "Did you bring it?"

Doris walked over to the wall next to the steps where the portrait of Amanda was leaning, it was the one the Gilberts had made for her funeral. She picked it up, uncovered it and brought it over to Rachel.

Holding the picture in front of her, Rachel softly said, "Mark, please take a picture of me with my sister."

Amanda introduced Rachel to the field of psychology. They both studied at Virginia Tech. under the same professors. They were best friends. However, the pair was split when Amanda, instead of starting her last year, moved to Richmond to try a teaching position and never finished her degree. Before she had a chance to decide which she liked best, she was murdered.

Looking at the portrait and then back at Mark, she added, "This day is for both of us."

Fifteen minutes later, they were all leaving the parking lot beside Cassell Coliseum and heading up Washington Street to leave the campus of Virginia Tech. along with everyone else. The steady flow of traffic made the normally five or six minute trip to Bogen's an undetermined length of time. Bogen's Steakhouse was Rachel's favorite place to eat and she knew a feast awaited them there.

As she sat in the back seat of her father's car, Rachel watched the slow moving line of cars in front of them. She glanced at the portrait of her sister which drew her thoughts back to the line of cars parked on the road next to the grassy hill where Amanda was buried. It was an indication of something ending, an end of a friendship with a school that brought her back from despair after her sister's death. There was no chance to say good-bye to Amanda, but there was still a chance to say good-bye to her school.

"Dad, I know you're hungry..." Rachel started.

"Yeah," he said with anticipation.

"I'm going to miss this campus. I've spent so much of the past six years here...and ten years in all. Would you mind if we drove around the Drillfield one last time? Besides, it doesn't look like this traffic is going to let up quickly."

Looking at the line of cars in front of him, he replied, "Of course, dear, I'd be happy to."

Walter took the left at Kent Street and drove the short distance to the Drillfield. As they took their tour, memories of professors and papers, research and sessions with students flowed through Rachel's mind. *I entered this school unaware of how cruel life could be and during my journey, I found out.* The unnecessary and senseless death of her sister almost kept her from continuing her journey, but she found help through those that worked here. *They brought me back and helped me finish my journey.* When asked by others what she learned from her time here, her response was always the same, comfort.

With their tour finished, Walter turned to leave the campus by way of the Alumni Mall. This is the main entrance into the campus from North Main Street. Halfway up the Mall Rachel turned to look out the rear window to see it all one last time.

She whispered to herself, "Good-bye and thanks."

At seven-thirty, Rachel and her parents entered Bogen's. They walked through the entryway, into the second floor dining area before Dave saw them, and came over to greet them. Dave was a short middle-aged bald man, very thin and impeccably dressed, who made every guest feel like royalty returning to their castle. He was graceful and sincere in every way.

"Congratulations," he said to Rachel as he gave her a hug.

He shook hands with Walter, gave Doris a kiss on the cheek, and then escorted the three of them into the banquet room decorated for the occasion. As they entered, all of the guests clapped for Rachel. Looking around she noticed the streamers and balloons that were hanging from the ceiling and the life size cardboard figure of Freud standing behind a seat.

"I figured since you spent so much time studying his work, he ought to be invited to the party," Dave explained, and they all laughed.

Over his shoulder, Rachel saw a server who had followed Dave with a tray of filled champagne glasses. Dave passed a glass to Rachel and to her parents. Then he took the last glass for himself.

"I'd like to propose a toast." He waited until everyone was up.

"To Rachel Gilbert, a fine woman from a fine family, whose radiance captures the hearts of all those who come in contact with her. May your life be filled with joy, may your work be satisfying and may those you help find their way as you have."

"Here, here," everyone said and they all drank.

"Thank you, Dave," Rachel said softly. Peering at all the faces in the room looking at her, she suddenly felt a sense of strength she had not realized before. It was another arrow finding its mark. "All of you have been so supportive of me over the past years. I could never have made it without you, so I toast to all of you." She raised her glass to all those in the room and then took a sip.

Again, everyone drank.

As the server took the glasses, Dave led Rachel and her parents to the buffet, "Let me show you what we have prepared for you."

Throughout the night, guests came by to personally greet and congratulate Rachel. Just before leaving, Admiral Orin Garry stopped by. Garry was a big man in every way. He was retired from the JAG Corps and had his own private legal practice in Richmond. He was a long time friend of Rachel's dad but she never knew how they had met. Both served in the Navy but she was not sure if that was the connection. Garry had told a story once or twice about a sailor accused of assaulting an officer that he had to defend and she wondered if the sailor was her dad, but never asked.

The Admiral was never seen without a cigar in his mouth and Rachel marveled at the fact that he was not even holding one. He knew how much Rachel's mom hated them and politely restrained from smoking at the banquet.

"Congratulations, my dear," he said in his deep James Earl Jones-type voice. "This is quite an achievement."

"Yes, it is. Thank you."

"Where are your parents?"

Rachel had been talking with so many people that she had not even noticed that her parents had gotten up to mingle with the guests.

Looking around, she said, "I'm sure they're around somewhere."

"I wanted to say good-bye to them."

"Are you leaving?"

"Yes. It's a long drive back to Richmond. So, what are your plans now?"

"Well, I'm staying with my folks until Tuesday. Sunday's Mother's Day and Monday's my dad's birthday. Mom has planned a party."

Chuckling, Orin said, "Yes, I know. I'm not able to attend. I've got a case that requires my attention."

"I'm sorry. I know Dad will miss you."

"Yes, thank you. What I meant was, what do you plan to do with your future?"

"Oh! Well, I'm in the process of looking for a job. I hope, when I return to Richmond, I'll have some responses to the number of resumes I sent out. Dr. Claire, from the Sheltering Arms Hospital, the place where I did my internship, said she would talk to her administrator to see if there is something available there. In the meantime, I'm tightening up my dissertation getting it ready to publish, I hope. My work with the trauma patients at the hospital was a great resource while writing it."

"Sounds like you have a plan. Good. If you need any references or any legal help, you know where to find me. Make sure you run any contracts by me first, okay?"

Saluting, Rachel said, "Yes, sir, Admiral." Then she rose, came around the table and gave him a hug and kiss good-bye.

"Please tell your parents I said good-bye."

"Sure thing, Admiral."

"Good-bye, Doc."

She watched as Garry walked out of the banquet room. He did not have one foot fully planted on the floor outside the room before he placed a new cigar in his mouth. Garry always treated her like a daughter. He had no kids of his own and his wife had left him while he was still in the Navy. Thinking life had given him a raw deal; Rachel wondered why he was not resentful. As he stepped out of the restaurant, he stopped. Through the glass windows, she saw him light his cigar. He took a long drag and exhaled slowly. Then he walked down the porch and disappeared around the corner.

Just then, Rachel's parents returned. Once again, Rachel gave them both a big hug.

"Thanks again, Mom and Dad."

* * *

*Saturday, May 13, 2006, 3:27 AM:*

Suddenly, gasping and sitting straight up in bed, her eyes and mouth wide open, Rachel took a few seconds to realize where she was. With the help of the night-light plugged into the wall by her bed, her eyes slowly began to focus. She was safe in her old room, in her parent's house. It was *just* a dream. Looking at the clock on the nightstand, she realized she had been asleep for a little over two hours. The dream came in bits and pieces – out of order – nothing made sense. The only thing real was the fear and sense of panic it created. Beads of sweat ran down her forehead. She dropped her head into her hands and closed her mouth and eyes. "Oh no," she softly said, "not again."

Once she had calmed down, she got up and walked down the hall to the bathroom. She stood staring at herself in the mirror, thinking, remembering. This was not the first time this dream had invaded her sleep. Each time, the dream came as fragments, never a full flowing story, but she knew where it came from. It had started right after Amanda's death and continued for several years. During those years, it kept Rachel from continuing her studies, but the help she received tamed it. Not having the dream for several years left her believing it was gone, never to haunt her again - until tonight. She splashed cold water on her face, dried herself off and headed back to her room.

As she passed Amanda's room, she stopped and looked in. Enough light came through the window from the streetlight that she could see that most of the room was the same as it always had been. Memories of bouncing on the bed, pillow fights, discussions about boys and experimenting with make-up came to mind. They had great times together. Slowly she walked over to Amanda's bed and laid down on it. She wrapped her arms around the pillow and softly cried herself to sleep.

# 3

Walking out of the John Marshall Courts Building and into the covered entryway, Caleb felt the cool, light breeze. Although the air conditioning was on, his purpose for being there had him so riled up that he didn't notice any air movement at all. Now that it was over, outside, in the breeze, he was relaxed enough to notice little things like the temperature. He took off his camel-colored sports coat and reached into the right back pocket of his jeans for a handkerchief to wipe his brow. Replacing it, he wished it were as easy to wipe away the memories of the past eighteen months and his visits to this courthouse.

Next to him, Richard Libbie, his lawyer, seemed undisturbed by anything that had happened over the past eighteen months and was unaware that there even was a temperature existing anywhere. Standing six inches above Caleb's five-foot eight-inches in his charcoal-colored Armani pinstripe suit with exposed French cuffs and silk tie, he looked like an ad for *Whose Millionaire Is He Anyway.*

"After a year and a half of working through this thing, I didn't expect it to be over that fast," Caleb said.

Matter-of-factly, Richard explained, "Pronouncing a couple divorced is a simple thing once all the preliminary cases are out of the way."

"Every time we came here for something it took forever. Either something was missing and had to be found or there wasn't enough information and one of us had to get more or we couldn't reach an agreement. It was always something. I can't believe it has taken eighteen months to get to today and then it's over in a matter of minutes."

"Part of the problem is the system; it's just not what it ought to be. Another part was your wife and her lawyer. They could never come to an agreement on what they wanted. At first, I think the judge wanted to give them every opportunity for a fair separation. I believe he would have done the same for you had the roles been reversed. Then I think he just got tired of it and forced them to make up their minds. If he had not done that, this would not have happened today."

"Still," Caleb admitted, "I wish it had not happened at all."

When they reached the steps that led down to Clay Street, they stopped. Caleb noticed the people walking on the sidewalk below, all of them going somewhere, with some purpose, oblivious to his eighteen-month plight. Somehow, even though he had been living alone for all that time, a feeling of loss grew deep inside.

"I'm alone again," he said, "I can't understand what it is that makes me unable to stay married."

Richard put his hand on Caleb's shoulder, "I don't know what happened with you and your first wife, but this time your wife left you."

"Left me?" Caleb looked at Richard as if he had been in another world through the whole thing. "Jena didn't leave me. She got caught up in that cult thing and chose *it* over me. That's all."

"She made a choice and it wasn't you, Caleb. She left you and that's the way you need to look at it."

"Yeah, she made a choice, but what made her choose it over me? That's what I really want to know. The first time, when I divorced Sally, I thought I was doing the right thing; I couldn't stand arguing all the time. I thought it would be best to be apart, I was wrong, but this time I feel like I did everything right and gave Jena every chance. I swore I'd never be divorced again and here I am, *again*."

"Time will heal your hurt, Caleb."

He knew Richard was trying his best to comfort him, however, it was not part of Richard's character to be empathetic, and after all, he *is* a lawyer.

"I've got to meet another client at my office in fifteen minutes. Are you going to be okay?"

"Yeah, I'll make it home."

"I didn't mean," Richard paused with a puzzled expression on his face. "Do I need to *worry* about you?"

Surprised at his question and then realizing how what he had said must have sounded, Caleb replied, "No, no. I'm sorry. I didn't mean to sound like that, forgive me."

"Okay, then," Richard said reaching out his hand.

Returning the gesture, Caleb agreed, "Okay, then."

"I'll mail you a copy of the final decree." Richard let go of Caleb's hand. "Congratulations, it's over. Go home."

Richard disappeared down the sidewalk on the other side of the entryway before Caleb started down the steps. He cleared the last step and headed up Clay Street, crossed Eighth Street, then Seventh Street, and walked through the courtyard between the Food Court and the Coliseum. Entering the public parking garage beyond the courtyard, he took the elevator to the third floor, to his car, which he had only parked there an hour ago.

He started the car and sat thinking, *go to work or go home?* For a couple of minutes he argued with himself about which he should choose. It was like one of those cartoons where the angel appears on one shoulder and the devil on the other. His eyes went back and forth as if he could actually see them.

"The responsible thing to do would be to go to work," the angel said.

"Aw, forget her, go home and nurse your sorry soul," shrieked the devil. "You've been through enough. You deserve it."

Back and forth, they went at each other. Back and forth, Caleb's eyes went until...

*Honk, honk,* sounded the horn from the little Toyota truck in front of him.

"Are you leaving or what?" the person in the truck yelled.

Raising his hand, as if to say, *"I'm sorry,"* Caleb put his Chrysler Sebring into drive and pulled out of the space. Barely had he gotten out of the space when from his rear view mirror, he saw the truck dart in.

"People today have no respect for others. They just don't care. I'm going home!"

Traffic was not a problem at this early time of the day. Thirty minutes after leaving the parking garage, Caleb pulled into the corner parking space in front of his Copper Mill apartment. The large oak tree next to the parking lot cast a shadow over the entire space. *So, all I have to do is come home early to get the shady spot,* he thought.

After collecting his mail, he entered his end unit apartment; seven hundred square feet with one bedroom which had a walk-in closet, a kitchen, a dining room, a living room with a fireplace and a covered patio with a storage room. The rental staff told him that the previous tenet never used the kitchen so the appliances were almost new. Caleb spent most of his time at work and had no real life to speak of, since before the separation. Therefore, the appliances would probably remain this way for the next tenet.

He dropped the mail and his keys on his desk, which separated the living room from the dining room. Throwing his jacket on the back of the L-shaped sectional in front of the desk, he dropped himself onto the couch, closed his eyes and rubbed his face with both hands.

The apartment was very plain because he did not have much interest in decorating. It was pretty much the same as it was when he moved in. Without Jena's income, he could no longer afford the house they lived in and sold it. He moved what furniture would fit into the apartment and the rest he either gave away or used at the office. He left the walls bare, no paintings or artwork anywhere. The only indication that he had any culture at all was a clay statue of the hand of God giving Eve to Adam, a wedding present he could not part with. In his mind, a decorated home was a haven, a place to come to and be rejuvenated, but this was not a home, just a resting place between meaningless days.

A mixture of emotions ran through his heart and mind like a carousel spinning out of control with no caretaker operating the controls to shut it off or slow it down. All he could do was hang on and hope it did not kill him. *Pain, anger, remorse, bitterness, fear*...each carousel character had its name... *disappointment, puzzlement, insecurity, frustration*...and he was riding all of them. When he opened his eyes, the vision went away, but not the feelings. In his chest, the carousel seemed to wreck, beating against every rib and making it hard to breathe.

In front of him, on the glass coffee table was his Bible. He grabbed it by the binding and flipped through the pages not really looking for anything, it had just become a ritual to him. Getting to the end, he slammed the book shut and stood up with it still in his hand. He placed the Bible on the top shelf of the bookcase that lined the back wall of the dining room as he walked past the desk heading towards his bedroom.

In his room, he undressed down to his boxers and threw his clothes on the bed, then headed back across the hall. The shower was nice and hot and, even though the vent fan was on, steam filled the bathroom. The forceful water pressure sent a stream of water through the nozzle that penetrated the muscles in Caleb's head, neck and shoulders. Soon he began to relax, but his mind did not disengage. Memories of the past seemed to flow as fast as the water. His thoughts drifted off to that cold December morning, seven years ago, when Jena Owens walked into his office...

She was a thin woman with short curly auburn hair covered with a light tan knitted cap with three small rows of pink near the rim. Her skin was pale and the cold made her cheeks and nose red, but her eyes warmed her face. They were perfectly sized, light brown, with long lashes and he could not stop staring into them. She wore a pink scarf around her neck, a pink trench coat and pink gloves.

"Hello, I'm Jena Owens," she said pulling off her gloves.

"Hi, I'm Caleb Prescott," he answered as he rose to shake Jena's hand. "Please sit down. What can I do for you?"

Pulling off her cap and sitting down, she continued, "I have a small pottery supply shop on Tomlynn Street."

The attraction was obvious but he could not say exactly why, only that she was different. He watched her eyes and mouth as she spoke each word, pulling in every detail of her face and enjoying the moment.

"Almost every day I see your trucks pulling out of the parking lot of this building. I need someone to deliver my supplies. I've been doing it myself with my cousin's help but I have to close my shop when I leave, which means I'm missing customers. I need help."

If being attractive and different were not enough, being a damsel in distress was. He instantly pulled out a blank contract and began filling in the blanks. Without finding out more about the need, he agreed to the job...

The scene in his head switched to the next day when his partner, Jeff Birch, found out about his deal with Jena. Caleb was at his desk in his office when Jeff came pouncing in. They were about the same height and weight and could have been twins had it not been for Jeff's red hair and freckles. Reaching across Caleb's desk, Jeff planted both hands on the front edge and leaned over the desk almost in Caleb's face.

"Caleb, how could you sign a contract without me looking at it first?" he demanded.

"I'm sorry, Jeff. You're right. I wasn't thinking."

Jeff backed off a bit and stood up, "Do you know what we will be picking up?"

"Pottery supplies."

Jeff scowled, "What kind, Caleb?" Pacing in front of Caleb's desk he continued, "Are we picking up bags of clay or already made pots or both?"

"I don't know," Caleb said sheepishly.

Softening his tone and standing still, Jeff asked, "How are they packaged?"

Knowing that he had not done what he should have, Caleb sat with his head hung feeling guilty for letting his friend and partner down.

"I don't know."

"Where are we delivering them to?"

Caleb leaned back in his chair, avoiding Jeff's eyes. "I don't know."

There was silence for a moment, then Jeff took a seat in one of the chairs facing Caleb's desk.

"She must have been pretty," he finally said.

Caleb's eyes lit up as he raised them to look at Jeff and sat straight up. With a spark of energy, as if someone gave him a new set of batteries, he became animated.

"I'm so sorry, Jeff, I just couldn't help myself. She *was* beautiful and in need. She just melted my heart."

"Its okay, buddy, I understand. I'm happy for you. I'll give her a call and find out all the necessary information, then you can go by and check out her operation. That'll give you the chance to ask her out."

Caleb liked the sound of that.

"One more thing, Caleb, from now on how about I do the contracts and you do the follow up?"

Caleb did not like meeting customers. He would rather be the behind-the-scenes person, so he agreed.

Once again, his thoughts changed course, to the day Jena and he got married. He could see her in her delicate laced strapless gown with the long train.

"God has brought us together for a special purpose, Jena," he whispered into her ear as they danced their first dance during their reception...

As quickly as this vision had come, it left, replaced with the day she left. She was wearing a tie-dyed T-shirt with a peace sign on it and jeans with rips in the knees and back pockets missing. Both hung on her small frame, which was a result of becoming anorexic.

Caleb remembered feeling lost and alone as he watched her load her two bags into her Honda Civic and drive away with no good-bye or even a wave. He wanted to hide or disappear. Later on, when Jeff came by to check on him, he did not talk much.

"Maybe she just needs some time to sort things out," Jeff said, not being very convincing.

Caleb did not reply, instead he sat on his couch, silent, staring out the sliding glass doors that led to the patio.

Changing the subject, Jeff offered, "I tell you what, I'll come by in the morning, pick you up and we'll go to church together, then..."

"Forget it!" Caleb snapped, "I'm not going to church tomorrow or next week or ever again. I've had it with the church and cults and confusion. I just want to be left alone." He stormed into his bedroom and slammed the door.

The sound of the door slamming changed the scene to the courthouse and the judge slamming his gavel onto the wooden block on his bench, declaring Caleb and Jena divorced.

A cold sensation washed over his body as the water heater emptied itself of hot water and Caleb was jolted back to reality. Quickly turning off the water, he opened the shower curtain and grabbed a warm towel from the warming rack on the wall above the toilet. His only thought, as he dried himself off and stepped out of the shower onto the towel on the floor, was *I'm a failure,* and he said it out loud. At that moment, his legs went numb and he sat down on the edge of the tub. Days, weeks and months of emotions, held back because it was not the right time or it might have been embarrassing, all came at the same time. The carousel wreck found its way out and he dropped his face into his towel and sobbed.

Forty-five minutes later Caleb was in his boxers again sitting at his desk going through the mail. He pulled the newspaper ads out first and tossed them into the wastebasket between the desk and the wall to the right of the desk. Next, he looked through all the junk mail. The credit card applications he tore in half without even opening them and tossed them in the trashcan as well. Then, he pulled out two postcards. The first was from the Post Office explaining the new hours for the Glen Allen branch and its annex. Before he could read the second postcard, the phone rang.

An exasperated voice chided, "Caleb!"

"Jeff, is that you?"

"Yeah, it's me. I've been trying for an hour to get you over the radio with no luck. Do you have your radio with you?"

"Uh...yeah." Caleb squinted his eyes as he said this knowing what was about to happen.

"Do you have it on?"

Pausing, he did not want to say the obvious but he couldn't really lie and get away with it either.

"No, Jeff, I don't have it on."

"Man, I knew it. How many times do I have to tell you to keep your radio on! It was your idea to buy these things so we could communicate and you never use it. What's the sense of spending the money on them if you're *not* going to use yours?"

Caleb had heard this lecture six times in the last five weeks since they had bought the radios but it had not helped him get into the habit of leaving his on. The lecture was not finished and he knew it. The next part was always worse than the first and he prepared himself for it.

"Now, why did we buy these things?" Jeff asked in a parental tone. "Come on now, tell me why."

"Okay, we got them so we could communicate if you were out of town. In case an order came in that you could do on your way back or if there was trouble."

"That's right, and whose idea was it to get these?"

"It was mine."

"Thank you."

*Here it comes*, the worst part of the whole thing. He hated this more than the scolding, but Jeff was his friend and was right, so he endured the humiliation.

"Now, pick up your radio, Caleb."

Caleb reached for his radio on the desk. He had selected this style because it looked like a cell phone. It had two buttons on the left side, one for volume and the other to use when you wanted to talk. The second button had a lock feature to lock the talk button down so you could talk without interruption. There were times they had to read contracts over the radio and it was too cumbersome to try to read, flip pages and hold the button on the radio down at the same time. On the right side was the power switch.

"Do you have it, Caleb?"

"Yes, Jeff."

"On the right side of the radio is a switch. To turn the radio on you slide the switch up towards the top of the radio. Do you understand?"

"Yep."

"Okay, we are going to practice. Please turn your radio on."

Caleb switched the power switch into the on position. The display screen quickly lit up as the radio chirped.

"Good, I heard it come on. Now, turn the radio off."

The display went blank as Caleb switched the radio off.

"Now that you know the difference between the two settings, let's turn it back on."

Caleb turned the radio on without saying a word. The display came on and the radio chirped again.

"How about we leave it there now, Caleb. You'll never miss my calls and you can still plug it in to charge while it's on."

"I don't like the chirping."

Jeff, who seemed surprised that Caleb said anything, stuttered, "You...you...never said anything before. Is this sinking in?"

Jeff took Caleb through a few steps and soon Caleb's radio was no longer chirping, instead it would vibrate, which Caleb preferred.

There was a pause before Jeff changed the subject. "So how are you doing? Is it over?"

"Yeah, it was over this morning. It was quick, not like everything else."

"I know you are probably not up for company, but I'd like to take you to dinner."

"Okay."

"Benny's?"

"Benny's it is," Caleb agreed.

"I'll pick you up at six-o'clock. We can get there early, before the crowd."

Jeff was obviously joking, it was Tuesday and Benny's was always slow on Tuesday nights. After hanging up, Caleb returned his attention to the mail.

The second postcard was an advertisement that caught his eye. One side was a light green color with the title, *"The Connection"* at the top in dark green with a light gray shadow. It words were underlined by a picture of a coax cable that had a male fitting at the end. Below the title were pictures of couples, some close up and others full length. The back of the card explained how this service brought people together. It touted that they had the most in-depth application process of any Internet dating service, the best record for matching people, and claimed that seventy-six percent of all their matches got married and are still together. Lastly, they offered the first month free. Dating was the last thing on his mind and without really looking; he tossed the postcard at the wastebasket and focused on the rest of his mail.

\* \* \*

It was now two-thirty in the afternoon and Rachel had just finished straightening up her room. Her bags were downstairs. She gave the room one more glance over to make sure she had not forgotten anything.

She picked up her purse and the portrait of Amanda and headed downstairs.

As she entered the kitchen, her mom asked, "You ready to go?"

"Yeah, I guess so."

Doris stopped washing the dishes and dried her hands with the apron she was wearing. She walked over to meet Rachel and put her arm around her shoulders.

"You sound sad, dear. You don't have to go you know."

"Thanks, Mom, I know." Rachel looked into her mom's eyes and tried to change her tone. "I'm anxious to find out if I got any replies to the resumes I sent out."

"Your bags are loaded in the car," Walter announced as he entered the kitchen from the garage door.

"Thanks, Dad. Well, I guess it's time. Thanks again for everything you guys did for me this weekend. Mom, I hope you enjoyed your day."

"Yes, dear, I did enjoy my day."

"Dad, did you enjoy your party?"

"Thank you dear, I did very much. I will really enjoy playing with the Wireless Weather Station you gave me."

"I figured that on the days when you're not working at the weather station you could keep track of things from home."

"That's very thoughtful Rachel, thanks."

"Before you go, Rachel," Doris said as she walked out of the kitchen, "we have one more surprise for you. We thought you might want to display your diploma. So we had it framed for you," and she handed it to Rachel.

"Oh Mom, Dad, what would I do without you."

Rachel waved good-bye to her parents as she backed out of their driveway and headed down Country Club Drive to South Main Street. When the light turned green, she took a left onto South Main Street and followed it to Route 460, which would take her to I-81 and the long drive home to Richmond.

To accommodate her internship, Rachel moved to Richmond for the last two years of her studies. She took her remaining classes at the branch of Virginia Tech. in Richmond.

Not being a materialistic person, Rachel did not spend much time acquiring things. Sitting in her passenger seat were the only two material things that meant anything and everything to her – the portrait of her sister and her framed diploma. As she left Blacksburg, her ear-to-ear smile returned.

It was four-o'clock in the afternoon when Rachel stopped in Charlottesville to stretch her legs and get a Pepsi. She had just gotten back in her car when her cell phone rang. It was Annie. She could tell because she had set Annie's ring tone to be the song "Tomorrow" from the musical. Annie was a nurse at the Sheltering Arms Hospital in Richmond who worked with Rachel during Rachel's internship.

"Annie, hi."

"Hey, Rach. How ya doing?"

"I'm great. I'm on my way back home. How are you doing? How are things at the hospital? How's Prometheus?"

"I'm doing fine. The hospital hasn't changed since you left

and your turtle's out of food. How did the graduation go?"

"Did you get more?"

"I'm doing that as we speak."

"Thanks. The graduation was awesome. I enjoyed every minute of it and of course my parents out did themselves. They invited everyone we ever knew to come to Bogen's."

"I'm so sorry that I couldn't make it. I would have loved to see you receive your diploma."

"Thanks, Annie, but I know you were tied up at the hospital. Besides, who would have taken care of Prometheus?"

"True about your pet. As far as the hospital, this is what you have to look forward to." Annie chuckled. "Listen, do you have any plans for Thursday afternoon, say around three-o'clock?"

"At the moment I don't. I don't have any plans at all right now, but I'm not home yet. For weeks prior to leaving for Blacksburg I sent out resumes. I'm hoping when I get home I'll have a response from someone."

"I hope you do too. The thing is the girls and I wanted to give you a little party since we couldn't be with you and we were hoping to do it on Thursday. The small conference room is open from three to five and I reserved it for us. Do you think you could make it?"

"Annie, for you, I'll change all my plans to make sure I'm there. You guys are so sweet to do this. Thanks."

"Great," shouted Annie over the phone with so much volume that Rachel quickly pulled the phone away from her ear and rubbed it to chase the ringing away. "I'll let everyone know and we'll see you on Thursday."

"Okay, Annie. I'll see you then."

"Drive safely."

Rachel put her phone back in her purse, closed the door and started up the car. Her black Lexus GS430, a gift from her father when she moved to Richmond, started with a roar as she held down the accelerator. She let up on the gas, put the car in drive and hit the pedal once more. She took off so fast that her head jerked back.

"That Annie, she's a nut," she said as she got back on the road.

* * *

Jeff had the innate ability to know what time it was without looking at his watch and could tell exactly how long it would take to do things. He never liked being late. At six-o'clock on the nose, Jeff was knocking on Caleb's apartment door. Caleb, who could not live without a clock in every room, was still putting his socks on when he answered the door.

"Do you want to walk or drive?" he asked as he opened the door and then hopped back into his bedroom while still putting on his right sock.

With a chuckle in his voice, Jeff asked, "What difference does it make?"

"If we are going to walk I'll put on sneakers...," Caleb yelled from his room, "...and if we drive I'll put on my loafers." Caleb could not avoid being practical, it was as much a part of him as his eye color. He would weigh each of his options to make sure the choice he made, made the most sense. Even when he tried not to be practical, he would weigh whether it was a good idea or not given the current situation.

"Let's drive. It's warm and humid." Jeff said.

"Loafers it is!"

Two minutes later Caleb walked out in blue jeans, a green Polo shirt and loafers over his bare feet.

Pointing at Caleb's feet Jeff inquired, "What happen to the socks?"

"Don't wear them with loafers," Caleb said matter-of-factly. "Let's go."

Jeff had left his red Jeep Wrangler running with the air conditioner on, to keep it cool. They climbed in and were off. Within minutes, they pulled into the parking lot of Benny's. Benny's Restaurant and Tavern had been Caleb and Jeff's hangout for the past three years since it opened. Outside, the building was red brick with large windows that had green awnings over them. Above the main entrance was the neon Benny's sign that glowed green at night. The roof was also green. Inside were two areas. The left side was the dining room and the right side was the bar. The carpet was green as was the tiled ceiling. Benny was not Irish but Caleb and Jeff always thought he was trying to be.

Caleb held the door for Jeff. "Have you brought your new girlfriend here yet?"

"Nancy would rather eat in than eat out."

"Welcome to Benny's," greeted the host. "Two for dinner?"

"Yes," both Caleb and Jeff said.

She grabbed two menus and led them to a booth in the back corner of the dining room. "Your server, Katie, will be with you shortly."

While Caleb and Jeff looked over the specials listed on the inside cover of the menu, Katie arrived. They both ordered sweet tea and she left. While she was gone, they discussed what they should have. They settled for the soup and salad special: Tortellini soup and Fajita salad. When Katie returned with their drinks, she took their order and disappeared again.

Caleb watched as Jeff searched the room. There were only a few other guests; a man in a suit in one corner and a couple of older women in another. Neither was close to them and apparently it made Jeff feel comfortable to talk.

"Are you glad it's over?" he asked.

"I am and I'm not. I'm glad that I don't have to see that courtroom anymore, hear the judge's and lawyer's voices anymore, or read any more documents. On the other hand, as long as it was still going on there was a part of me that hoped Jena would change her mind and we could go back to the way things were."

Katie interrupted quietly by placing a basket of fresh sourdough bread on the table and gave each of them a small bread plate. When she left, Jeff continued.

"What are you going to do now?"

"I don't know. I feel like such a failure."

Caleb knew how desperate this sounded but inside he was beginning to believe it was true. Being divorced twice was not the only thing that made him feel this way. There were a couple of times, two years ago, when Caleb had made terrible mistakes in the books for their company. He and Jeff had spent several weekends sorting through old records and reports to fix the books. It almost cost them their business. Jeff never spoke of it and Caleb never forgot. Then he tried to go back to school a year ago. The problems with Jena started shortly afterwards and he could not focus on the class work, so he dropped out. Six months later, he dropped out of the choir at church because of conflicts with the leader.

"Everything I've tried to do over the past few years seems to be falling apart. I can't seem to stay on target with anything."

"The business seems to be doing well," Jeff assured.

"Yeah, but I think it's more because of you than me."

"Caleb, you're being way too hard on yourself. It's true you've had some down times, but it won't last. You'll see, time will distance you from the pain and you'll be out there dating again."

"Dating," Caleb chuckled. "You know I got a postcard today for an Internet dating service. They say they have the best record for matches and most of them get married and stay together."

"There you go, that's something you should check into."

"No, I wouldn't know what to do and I feel so inadequate at trying to date."

"Come on, Caleb, you're young, a business owner, okay looking, you could find someone nice."

"It's not just about finding someone, Jeff, it's about being someone."

After Caleb finalized his first divorce, he spent a lot of time alone. One day, while driving past the Monument Heights Baptist Church, he stopped at the light at the nearby intersection. It was a warm spring day and through his open windows, he watched the church members having a picnic on the grounds. There were hymns playing over a set of outdoor speakers and the setting brought him back to the days when he was a kid and his parent's church had these same picnics. The members looked happy and he so wanted this in his life. As the light turned green and the traffic moved, the visions of the church disappeared, but the desire for what they shared did not.

The following week, Caleb found himself attending their Sunday morning service. The text for the pastor's sermon was from Matthew, Chapter 11 and Verses twenty-eight through thirty.

"Come to Me, all who are weary and heavy-laden and I will give you rest," the pastor read. "Take My yoke upon you, and learn from Me."

Caleb felt a tug. He surely was weary and bore a heavy weight, but he could not understand how a yoke could teach someone.

Addressing the congregation the pastor explained, "Now, you're probably asking yourself, 'How can I be taught with a yoke?' Well, when you walk your dog you put him on a leash to keep him safe. He lets you because he knows he can go for a walk with it. Without it, he cannot do what he wants. The leash also keeps the animal from running away, chasing something or going where he shouldn't. The leash becomes a training tool. In time, the animal learns. Now we aren't dogs, but the yoke that God places on us, if we let Him, will keep us safe and train us as well."

This made sense to Caleb and he decided that he would give God a chance again. After attending a few more weeks, he joined a Sunday school class and met Jeff. They clicked quickly because the two looked so much alike except for their hair color and Jeff's freckles. They liked the same sports, music, types of food, were in their mid-thirties and from Richmond. Both wanted to be business owners, although neither had a desire to be confined to an office every day. Six months later, they came up with the idea of a delivery business. They researched it, planned it out, checked out their competition, and one year later opened N'Route, their Richmond, Virginia based business. They were partners who had gone through a lot together and it strengthened their commitment to each other and made them feel as if they were brothers. They had been friends for ten years, so when Caleb got serious with his words and feelings, Jeff listened and did not speak.

"I've lost my focus of who I am. So much of what we do defines who we are."

Just then, Katie returned with their soup and salad. "Is there anything else I can get you," she asked politely.

"No, we're fine," replied Jeff.

Caleb continued once Katie had left. "I'm not talking about just work, I'm talking about what we do with our lives, our purpose. I don't know what my purpose is anymore. When I taught classes at church or sang in the choir or helped with the teenagers, I felt like I was contributing something. I wasn't just taking, but I was giving back. All the time Jena was there looking elsewhere. I wasn't enough; we were not partners in our beliefs. Now, I feel as if I have nothing to give and even if I did, I have no credibility anymore. Who's going to listen to or believe a two-time loser? We talk about how God is forgiving and that we all do things wrong, but what we really want is for everyone to always do what's right, especially if you're a leader. God is forgiving, but His flock is not."

"I can't say I understand how you feel," Jeff admitted, "but I can see how deep it runs in your soul and the struggle you are having with it."

"When you are faced with failure, not just failing, but the idea that you are truly a failure, where do you go? What holds meaning, purpose and hope for you? I know there is a truth and I search for it in everything. However, when I think I've found it, I wonder if what I found is yet another lie or illusion. So when I think of dating my mind haunts me with questions. Who is she really? What does she want? What do I want? What am I willing to settle for? Struggling to believe in myself is hard enough; I don't need to add to it by trying to date."

Caleb stopped talking and started to eat his soup. Jeff had already finished his soup while he listened to Caleb. There was silence for a moment as Jeff moved his soup bowl out of the way and pulled his salad plate closer to him. Caleb kept working on his soup.

"Caleb, I know that you are hurting, and I'm not making light of that fact at all, but I want you to think about this. While all you have said is true, you forget one thing. God has not let go of you and He still has a purpose for your life even if you can't see it. There are new chapters to the book of your life that haven't been written yet. You need to move forward and let those chapters be written. Let God reveal His plan. This is what faith is all about. Trusting in what you cannot see."

Caleb sat quietly thinking about Jeff's words. The moment hung like a dense fog covering the streets of London. He had heard Jeff's words and felt the weight of them, but he could not really make out how this should play out in his life.

* * *

Rachel pulled into her apartment complex a little after six-thirty. Traffic at the exit from I-64 to Broad Street tied her up a little. It is a congested area with businesses, shopping malls, restaurants and apartments. Most hours the traffic was heavy but during rush hour, it almost did not move.

Her first stop was the mail hut. On the other side of the pond from the mail hut was Rachel's building and she could see her rear apartment on the second floor. She hurried back to her car and drove around the pond to her building.

Rachel traveled light. She had one small suitcase on wheels, which she pulled out of the trunk after she parked and an over-the-shoulder bag. With her purse over one shoulder and her bag over the other, she tucked her diploma, the portrait and her mail under one arm and dragged her suitcase with her free hand. She scaled the steps to the second floor and her apartment. Once inside, she released the suitcase and leaned against the door. *Why did I let them talk me into a second floor apartment? When I leave, Dad's going to have to hire those movers again.*

On the dining room table was a brown paper bag and a note from Annie. It simply read *Feed him.* She dropped her purse, the shoulder bag and the mail on the table and then carefully placed the portrait and her diploma on it. For several moments, she gazed at her diploma.

"I can't believe I did it."

Once again, an arrow was approaching. *I have the ability, the power to do what I choose. Whoosh! I am somebody! WHOOSH! I am on top of the world! THONK!*

She walked into the kitchen and poured herself a glass of water. On the counter in front of her, she noticed the blinking light on the answering machine and pressed the message button. The mechanical voice announced that she had two new messages. The first call was from Annie.

"Hey, Rach, I wasn't sure if you were home yet. I'll try you on your cell phone."

Rachel deleted the message and moved on to the next. It was her mom.

"Hi, dear, call us when you get in. We want to know you made it home safe. We enjoyed your stay so much. Love you."

Rachel deleted this one as well and the machine clicked off. Disappointed that no one had called about her resume she sat at the dining room table to sort through her mail. She pulled aside the ads to review them later but did a quick glance to see what kind of sales were going on. Next, she separated the bills. "I'll deal with these tomorrow." Sifting through the remaining mail, she looked to see if any of it might be a job offer. One envelope caught her eye. She pulled it out and read the return address, A. E. Research. The name was unfamiliar so she went to her desk to check the list of companies to which she had sent resumes. Maybe she had forgotten this one. A. E. Research was not on the list.

"Another piece of junk," she said as she threw the envelope back on the table.

Nothing else looked promising and Rachel gave up her search. She headed back to her bedroom with her suitcase in tow to unpack and call her mom.

**_Wednesday, May 17, 2006, 8:42 AM:_**

"Wait a minute, Joe, I think you're forgetting who you're talking to."

"The name is Brian, B-R-I-A-N, and I'm not forgetting. You're forgetting I'm taking all the chances out here."

"Okay, _Brian_, but you're not the only one taking chances. Do you think its easy finding ways to get past Customs, the Feds and the police?"

"I thought you were supposed to be good at it? What happened in Miami and New York?"

"I agree, Miami and New York were unfortunate and sloppy on my part, however, I have a new plan, Brian."

"What now?"

"I have a new exchange set up at the coast that our suppliers have already been introduced to. I'm in the process of acquiring a new delivery service to transport the product from the coast to Richmond."

"Man, you're taking a lot of chances putting this in our own back yard."

"You see, Brian, you _are not_ the only one taking chances.

You need to relax and trust me. I've got it all under control. Just keep doing what you've been doing and I'll contact you as soon as all the arrangements are made."

When the buzzer from the intercom on his desk rang, Michaels spun his high-back leather chair around to face it. He knew his secretary would only interrupt if it were important.

"Mr. Michaels, sir."

Pressing the talk button, he answered, "Yes," and released the button.

"I'm sorry to interrupt you, sir, but the status meeting is going to start in fifteen minutes. You wanted me to let you know when you had fifteen minutes left."

Pressing the button, Michaels said, "Thank you, Stella." He released the button once more, spun his chair back around and walked to the floor-to-ceiling glass windows behind his desk. Looking out over the city, he wrapped up his conversation on the phone.

"Sorry about that, Brian. I have to attend my weekly status meeting. Do you have any other questions?"

"No, I think that's it."

"Okay, I'll call you when everything's in place. Good-bye."

Michaels continued to watch people scurrying around on the streets below after he hung up, like an eagle sits perched atop a high tree eyeing its prey below. The streets of Richmond were Michaels' playground and the people were his toys.

His charm and good looks were the first things most people noticed about him. He was a tall slender man in his late thirties with short black hair that he kept well trimmed and it always seemed perfect no matter where he went or what time of day it was. His face was soft with light green eyes and a comforting smile. The wealth came from his family and he wore it well, the best clothes that money could buy and a personal tailor. Wherever he went, he caught people's attention and this gave him an advantage over them. *Image is power*, he thought; *let them see one thing, unaware of something else going on.*

Michaels managed time well. He had allowed himself these few precious moments to contemplate his existence and those of Richmond for his purposes, but it was time to move on. Sitting at his desk again, he focused on preparing for the meeting.

Michaels' fourteenth floor office was as elaborate as he was from the solid mahogany wood desk to the animal heads and skins on his walls – supposedly bagged by him. With eleven hundred square feet of space, it was more like a small house than an office. It even came with its own bathroom complete with a shower and walk-in closet. Included was a cleaning crew that cleaned and polished the tile and brass. Mirrors hung everywhere in the office, most of them surrounded by very expensive frames. On the shelves and tables were items gathered from travels around the world. The furniture included a sofa bed, which Michaels often used; loveseat and chairs, ottomans, bookcases, coffee tables and curio cabinets, all the best money could buy. There was even a wet bar that Michaels cherished. It belonged to his father who left it to him as part of his will. The only picture in the office was one of his father, Sir Conrad Allen Michaels, above the wet bar. From the looks of his office, no one else was important to Michaels.

Hunting seemed out of place for Michaels. He gave the impression that he was someone who would fight for the protection of animals rather than hunt them for sport. Those he allowed to enter his haven on the fourteenth floor often were confused when they saw the animal heads and skins. They would express their surprise to find out that he would actually go hunting. Michaels used this confusion to his advantage. He always kept people wondering about him.

His father taught him the art of double natures, to keep people guessing. From the twelve years he spent in the military, involved in planning war strategies, to the twenty-six years he spent in the CIA, Sir Michaels had perfected the art of surprise. While his son was in grade school, he started teaching him techniques. Young Michaels would spin tales of having gone on safaris or treasure hunts with his father. His peers would not believe him, but he would always show up the next day with some trinket or picture that would somehow prove him right. Of course, these trinkets were things his father had collected and the pictures he created on his father's computer. Later, when cancer no longer allowed Sir Michaels to teach young Michaels, the training stopped. However, by that time, Tripp Jason Michaels had established himself as a master artist like his father and worked along side him at the CIA.

Once, while studying some war maps and papers found in a raid on a German scouting party, Michaels' father, then Lieutenant Michaels, decoded a plan to assassinate the Royal Family. He passed it on to his superiors who were able to foil the plan. A grateful Queen rewarded the Lieutenant by knighting him in a formal ceremony. From then on, he became Sir Conrad Allen Michaels. His friends called him *SCAM* and he lived up to the name.

Michaels checked his schedule for the rest of the day, reviewed his file on projects in process and his notes on the new business all in eight minutes. He stood up and put on his jacket, picked up the files he was just perusing and headed off to the boardroom. The walk to the elevator, the ride to the sixteenth floor and the walk to the boardroom took six minutes. When he walked in everyone invited was already there, as he liked it. *Power is what people respect. Make them wait knowing nothing starts without you. That's power.* He picked up his glass of water from the beverage counter next to the door and walked to his seat at the head of the long oval conference table. All eyes followed him and he knew it. *Power!* One minute later, at exactly nine-o'clock, he nodded his head to the facilitator to start the meeting.

George Kahn had been the facilitator for the past seven years. He did his job well. He was a *yes-man* upon whom Michaels could depend. Michaels knew the rest of his staff knew this about Kahn and did not like him because of it, yet when push came to shove, they all did the same as he did. It amused Michaels because he knew how much it bothered them that Kahn was a constant reminder of this fact at every meeting.

Kahn was not a big man and he had a voice that was a little more tenor than most preferred. It was hard to listen to him for any length of time. Michaels believed that this fact aided in keeping the length of the board meetings to an absolute minimum. Kahn started the meeting as soon as he saw the nod from Michaels.

"This meeting will now come to order," he said as he banged his gavel on the little wooden block in front of him. "First order of business is to identify who is in attendance."

For the next five minutes, each person attending the meeting spoke their name, one at a time, as they went around the room so the stenographer could record it.

Halfway around the table, as each department was giving their status and requests, there were no surprises. Everything reported was what Michaels had expected. Patiently, he watched and waited as the round continued anticipating the reaction the Security report would generate. He was well aware of the incident and he wanted to see if any of his staff showed signs of also knowing about it. Modern technology, video conferencing was no match for staring someone in the face. Their expressions would tell him two things, there was a leak in his Security department or someone on his staff was involved. Either one would quickly be dealt with. Finally, Kahn asked for the Security report.

"Security, Mr. Myers. We have added several more guards around this building and at some of our out-of-state offices. We have also beefed up our computer security systems. Last week someone tried to hack into our system and leave a virus. Our senior technician, Ian Clark, caught it. Yesterday, an unknown man was taking pictures of the inside of our building and the rear loading area. He was inquiring about the company occupying the fourteenth, fifteenth, and sixteenth floors. One of the building guards got his license plate number and we are running it through our computers to identify him. There is no need to be alarmed at this point, but do notify your people that security has been increased. Knowledge of who is in the building, especially after work hours, is going to be very important. Let your people know if they intend to stay after six-o'clock PM they need to notify the front desk security guard."

Kahn recited his well-worn phrase once more, "Thank you, Mr. Myers. Questions?"

Looking around the room, the expressions told Michaels that this was news to everyone. There was no leak and none of his staff seemed to be involved. He made a note to discuss this matter further with Myers later as he wondered; *what would someone be after and who was that man?* No one asked any questions and Kahn did not address it either, he simply moved on. "Human Resources."

"Human Resources, Mr. Durran, no changes."

Before Kahn could repeat his mantra, Jane Madison raised her hand and spoke. "Mr. Michaels, for weeks we have heard from the Human Resources department that there has been no change. Three months ago, I turned in a request for additional help and yet I still have a vacancy and my current staff is overworked. When am I going to get the help you promised?"

Madison had worked for A. E. Research since it began as the head of the Psychological Research department; she had several degrees in psychology and once headed up Social Services departments for several states including Virginia, which is where Michaels had found her. She was not a very attractive woman, a little overweight, short curly brown hair, a square face with a long nose and penetrating black eyes. She was average height, about five-six, but was tough looking and you could not help but picture her on a Harley motorcycle wearing a black leather jacket with skull and crossbones on it. Madison was one of the few people that did not cower around Michaels. She always shot from the hip and was not afraid to let people know where she stood. Her staff worked about twelve hours a day in the office plus several hours a week outside the office. They were the support team for the Internet dating system, The Connection, operated by A. E. Research, among other responsibilities. Their work had been piling up and Madison had requested three new researchers. Michaels promised her one.

Throughout the entire meeting, Michaels had not said a word. His eyes followed each person as they spoke and he made a tremendous amount of notes on the papers he had in front of him, but he never said anything. Now all eyes were on him. Everyone knew Madison's reputation and she was calling him on the carpet. Even the biggest and toughest man in the room knew not to do this. The silence was deafening.

"Ms. Madison," Michaels said softly but firmly as he looked past her. "I assure you the position *will* be filled within the next day or two. I do not promise what I do not intend to bring about. Understood?" He spoke this with a condescending tone as he shifted his glare from past her to right at her eyes.

Madison glared back and replied, "Yes, sir."

For a few seconds the staring match continued until Kahn fulfilled another one of his purposes as facilitator, which was to move past conflict. Quickly, he regained control of the meeting and pressed on. When Madison's gaze quit Michaels, he looked at Kahn and smiled.

The head of the financial department finished off the S&R round with his report and Kahn announced a quick break. Everyone got up except Michaels. Some went to the restroom while others helped themselves to refreshments. Michaels finished writing some notes and then filed them away in his projects file. He pulled out his new business files and reviewed their contents once more. Ten minutes later, with everyone seated again, Kahn was bringing the meeting back to order.

"Again, thanks to everyone for their patience during the S&R time. Now it's time for new business and I yield the floor to Mr. Michaels." Kahn turned to Michaels and smiled.

On the table in front of him were three file folders, each marked with the A. E. Research logo centered on the cover. The first two had the word *Confidential* stamped in red over the logo. During the break he had studied them once more and arranged them in a specific order that he felt would generate the necessary reaction from his staff. *Power, control, lead them where you want them to go.* These were his thoughts as he prepared. Now it was time for the delivery.

"We have three new challenges, ladies and gentlemen," he announced as he opened the first of the three folders. "The first involves our Cottonwood Lake facility. It seems that some very curious campers stumbled onto our operation there and are threatening to expose our experiment. For now, they have agreed to keep quiet. However, we need to make sure that if they don't, no one will ever believe them."

Looking up, his eyes met the eyes of the Military department head. "Sergeant Pense, these men were ex-Green Beret. Your team will check into their military background and see what we can use to discredit them. Stella will send you their names."

Pense scribbled a note on the pad in front of him and replied, "Yes, sir."

"Mr. Frenzo." He addressed the man on Pense's left. "Your civilian department will investigate these men and dig up information about them. Who do they know and who knows them."

Before Frenzo could reply, Michaels' eyes moved across the table. "Ms. Madison, your group will check medical records and see what you can find. Have they ever been to a shrink? Do they have any conditions?"

Shifting quickly again, he addressed the public relations department head at the other end of the table. "Mr. Seacart, your group will investigate what others may know around the campsite and surrounding communities. Did they tell anyone or is anyone else curious?"

"By next Wednesday," he concluded, "I want a plan put together and presented."

Scanning the faces of those around the table, he knew that he had hit his mark. Most of the work done here is secret and he knew having that threatened would generate anxiety. He was right. No matter what he said from this point on their anxiety would keep them focusing on what was happening at Cottonwood Lake. It was a necessary distraction.

"The second project is more typical of the type of things we do on a daily basis." Addressing the Government department head, he explained, "I have a list of several names here of individuals who will be running for government offices within the next few years." He passed the list around the table to Mr. Allegany. "Have your people do the necessary research on those people, their public as well as private practices and beliefs."

Researching politicians was a normal occurrence at A. E. Research and Michaels believed this would not distract from the anxiety of the first project. This is why he placed it second. Nevertheless, he did have a hope that this project would add to the anxiety.

Allegany reviewed the list and chuckled, "I'll get on it right away, sir. I actually know some of these folks."

This response annoyed Michaels. The list included names of people known for having very radical opinions. He wanted Allegany to bring up this point, to question the validity of the sources that produced the list, to create curiosity in the minds of the rest of the group, but he did not. Creating a secondary source of anxiety for the group was his intent, to draw attention away from the third project. Allegany's reaction did not create the added anxiety, which caused Michaels to decide to move swiftly through the last project. He wanted it to seem almost insignificant.

"The last project involves discrediting a faith healer by the name of Albertson. He's from Jamaica and is smuggling drugs to his followers through his tent meetings. No one has been able to trace how he is doing it, though. Proving that the drug smuggling *is* happening and discrediting Albertson, as usual, will proceed without it appearing that the government is involved. There is constant pressure placed on the government, from local to federal, to stay out of the church or religious practices. It is a politician's hot potato, no one wants it, but it will not go away. We will use The Connection to seek out a candidate for the task. I'll have the criteria to you, Ms. Madison, by morning."

Michaels finished speaking, which was Kahn's cue to open the floor for questions. For a moment, there was silence as the department heads and assistants all exchanged glances at each other. Then several hands went up. Michaels fielded each question with the same caution he gave his delivery. He was pleased that the questions related to the first project.

Twenty minutes later, the meeting was over and Kahn dismissed the group. Michaels had already positioned himself near the door, as he always did, to greet folks as they left. He was a shepherd and this was his flock. He shook hands much the same as a minister did after his Sunday sermon.

As Madison was about to leave, Michaels grabbed her arm. Startled, she looked at his hand holding her arm and then at him.

"Sir?" she inquired, looking at his hand again.

Michaels released his hold and addressed her without meeting her stare. "I have a specific person in mind for your group. I have followed her career and studies. She has just completed her Ph.D. and is looking for a job. Durran has already contacted her and we are awaiting a reply, that's why there is no change in his report."

"Thanks for clearing that up," Madison replied.

"I believe this faith healer project is the perfect opportunity for this new person, Ms. Madison."

"Sir, with all due respect, this new project sounds a bit too complex for a trainee."

"Ms. Madison, I assure you, this new person is not a trainee. She has more credentials to do this task than you have."

Her puzzled look told him she had heard what he said, but he was not sure she caught his drift. Madison was never his favorite person. There were too many confrontations and she was becoming bolder. He wanted her gone, but had not found the right way or time to make it happen. She started to say something, stopped and then offered, "I'm looking forward to the help, Mr. Michaels." Turning, she headed out the door.

"Have a nice day, Ms. Madison," he said to her back.

After everyone had left and the room cleared, Michaels walked over to the windows. Peering out these windows and looking out over the city was a source of joy for him. Beyond the Federal Reserve building, he could see Canal Walk and Riverside Park. He watched the cars cross over the Robert E. Lee Bridge and the boats going down the James River. This was his world and he stood watch over it. In the tinted window, he could see his reflection and he watched himself for a few seconds, and then smiled. He was satisfied.

\* \* \*

Sleeping in late was a luxury that Rachel had not had in a long time. She was getting up early either for school or for work and the weekends did not offer any relief. Once Rachel made up her mind to finish her degree, it became her sole focus. Now it was over and so was her internship, which meant she needed a job. Her hopes of a response from her resumes felt dashed and there was nothing to get up early for this morning, except hunger. While waiting for her cinnamon raisin bagel to toast, Rachel sat down at her table and sipped the coffee she had just poured. In front of her lay yesterday's mail and the letter from A. E. Research. Once more, she picked it up, read the return address, turned it over and opened it.

Dr. Gilbert,

Congratulations on your recent achievement. Earning your Ph.D. proves that you have both the determination and the ability that we, at A. E. Research, are always searching for.

Rachel heard her bagel pop up in the toaster and went to get it. A few minutes later, she returned with the bagel on a plate and some napkins. She sat down, took a bite out of her bagel and continued to read.

We are one of the top research firms in the nation. Our corporate office is located here in Richmond, Virginia and we have satellite offices throughout the world. Our clients include the United States Federal Government, forty-seven state governments, thirteen different countries, law firms, hospitals, financial institutions, and many more. Our services range from simple public feedback to in-depth research on a variety of topics.

Rachel paused to consider what she had just read. The lack of details and the fluffy wording made her wonder what kind of research this firm did. Before she could continue, her phone rang.

"Hello."

"Dr. Gilbert?" asked the woman on the other end. She had a soft tone in her voice, which made her sound very young.

"Yes, this is Ms., um..., Dr. Gilbert."

"Good morning, Dr. Gilbert, I hope I'm not disturbing you."

Rachel thought about this statement for a moment and realized she was about to say that she was not being disturbed when in fact she really was; she was interrupted. The thought went through her mind that she did not *have* to answer the phone, so the interruption was really her own fault and not that of the young woman.

"Hello, are you still there?"

"Oh...excuse me, what can I do for you, Ms.?" Rachel waited for the woman to give her name.

"Yvette, Susan Yvette."

"Ms. Yvette, what can I do for you?"

"I'm Kyle Durran's administrative assistant. He is the head of the Human Resources department at A. E. Research. He sent you a letter several days ago and wanted to know if you had received it."

Rachel looked at the bottom of the letter for a name, *Kyle Durran, Head of Human Resources, A. E. Research.*

"Did you receive the letter, Dr. Gilbert?"

"Yes...in fact I was just reading it when you called. I've been out of town for several days and only returned last night. I haven't finished reading the letter."

"The letter is an invitation to meet with Mr. Durran so that he can present you with a job offer."

"A job offer?"

"Yes, ma'am. I was calling to see if I could schedule the meeting for tomorrow morning at ten-o'clock. Would that work for you?"

"Well, I haven't finished reading the letter. Don't you think I should before I schedule a meeting?"

"If you're not interested after you finish reading the letter you can call back and cancel the meeting."

Rachel realized that Susan Yvette must have been very young, maybe this was her first job, and she was trying to follow her orders. Her task was to call and schedule a meeting and that is just what she was trying to do. It did not matter that the letter had not been completely read and absorbed or that a conscious decision had not yet been made as to whether or not this was a direction Rachel wanted to pursue. No, the only thing that mattered was that she could report to her boss that a meeting was set up just as he requested.

Curiosity took over. *I do need a job and here is someone offering me one. However, who are these people, how did they know me and why do they want to offer me a job? From what I read, their client list is impressive and they knew about my degree.* It was unlike her to accept something without knowing all she could; still she could not pass up the adventure in front of her. Besides, she did have the option to cancel. Scanning her mental day-timer for tomorrow's plans, she knew she had to make the party with Annie and the girls, but nothing else came to mind.

"I think ten-o'clock will work just fine, Ms. Yvette.

However, I would like your number in case I do need to cancel."

Ms. Yvette rattled off her phone number and the address of the office. She informed Rachel to bring the letter with her and prepare to spend one to two hours with Mr. Durran. Before hanging up she added, "Please call before five-o'clock this afternoon if you are going to cancel because that's when I leave. Thank you, Dr. Gilbert."

Rachel returned to her bagel after hanging up and taking another bite, continued to read the letter. It went on to say that A. E. Research was well respected and had an excellent reputation. They hired only the best and the brightest. This is why they were contacting her, desiring to offer her a position in their Psychological Research department.

This was it, the payoff for all the hard work. It was not the trauma work she had expected or even therapy work like what she had practiced in school, but it was a start. A place where she could use all that she had learned to help others. To make a difference, to matter, to bring about change, to finally be able to make sense of things for others, this is what she could not do for herself after her sister was murdered. This took more than she had and now she could help others who are where she was. These thoughts filled Rachel with excitement and she raised her arms in the air and yelled, "Yes!" As she looked down at the table again, she saw her framed diploma. She picked it up with one hand and with the other she grabbed her coffee mug. "Here's to you," she toasted. "I can't wait until tomorrow."

# 5

*Thursday, May 18, 2006, 9:10 AM:*

A last minute check in the mirror and Rachel was out the door. It was a clear sunny day and the temperature was about sixty-five degrees with a slight breeze. Excited and full of energy Rachel quickly bounced down the steps to the parking lot and over to her car. In her purse, she carried the letter from Kyle Durran and the address of the A. E. Research's office. As she started the car, Rachel noticed the time on the clock in her dash, nine-twelve. She had given herself more than enough time to drive downtown. *Being too early shows a sense of being too eager, while being late shows a lack of consideration.* This was something her father used to say and it was on Rachel's mind as she tried to plan her route. She decided to take Broad Street to I-64 and ride it into town. Getting off onto Broad Street again and taking it up to Eighth Street would bring her over to Eighth and Main. At this time of day, she knew the traffic would be light and give her enough time in case she got lost. She arrived with fifteen minutes to spare.

After parking on the fifth floor of the parking garage attached to the Merrill Lynch building, and taking the parking deck elevator down, she walked around a corner and entered a large open lobby. The walls were marble and the floor was a high gloss tile that reflected the walls and made the lobby look taller than it really was. To her right were the elevator banks that led up to the offices. The floors numbers each bank led to were hanging on the wall outside each bank. On her left was a long security desk with several monitors and two uniformed guards. Behind the guards, hanging from the ceiling, was a security camera pointing down at the desk and the elevator banks. Beyond the desk and the elevator banks was an open area with art deco benches made of marble, like the walls, with seat cushions covered in leather. The lobby was nice but plain, with a few potted plants, benches, and a couple of rugs decorating it. She expected it to be a lot fancier.

On the counter at the security desk was a sign that read, *Visitors Please Sign In.* One of the security guards, a short black woman with a serious tone, addressed her.

"May I help you?"

"Yes, I'm here to see Kyle Durran. He's with A. E. Research."

"Yes, ma'am, please sign in." The guard pointed to the sign-in log. As Rachel signed the form the guard held out a security badge and pointed to the elevator bank to the left. "His office is on the fourteenth floor."

"Thank you," Rachel said as she clipped the badge on her jacket pocket.

Feeling confident in her navy blue business suit with a Sheltering Arms pin on her lapel, a gift given to her when she completed her internship at the Sheltering Arms Hospital, she headed for the fourteenth floor. Over her shoulder was her purse and in her hand was a new day-timer, a graduation gift from her mom's best friend, Edna. Prepared she headed for her adventure.

The elevator doors opened to a small foyer on the fourteenth floor. To her left as she got out of the elevator was a large lobby and in the center of it was a circular desk with a high counter. The front of the desk had the name A. E. Research in large gold letters. The young man behind the desk looked up and welcomed her as she approached.

He smiled and said, "Welcome to A. E. Research. May I help you?"

"Yes, my name is Rachel Gilbert and I'm here to see Kyle Durran. I'm a little early; my appointment is at ten-o'clock."

Gesturing to the couch on his left the young man instructed, "Please have a seat and I'll let him know you are here."

She took a seat and watched as the receptionist dialed a phone number and explained that Ms. Gilbert had arrived.

"Ms. Yvette, Mr. Durran's administrative assistant will be with you in a couple of minutes," he said and quickly added, "Would you like some coffee?"

She declined and the receptionist went back to his duties. Looking around she noticed the two arrangements of sofas and chairs on either side of the reception desk. Each arrangement had a coffee table in the center of it and an oval rug that ran under the table and the furniture. On the wall behind the reception desk was a large framed picture of Richmond at dusk. It was not yet dark in the picture but there were several office lights on in the buildings. In the background was a full moon beginning to rise with its reddish-orange color. It gave the feeling of the end of a good day when folks are ready to go home, which seemed an odd image to portray for an office, but then maybe they were trying to say that every day here ends as a good day. Underneath the picture was a brick enclosed flowerbed that ran the length of the wall. At each end grew a dwarf banana tree. Between them, spaced about a foot apart, were several different kinds of hostas with large green and white leaves. In-between the hostas were colorful pansies and behind the flowers was a waterfall that trickled softly. Everything in the lobby screamed "Relax" and she became aware that it was working. That is until Ms. Yvette walked up.

"Dr. Gilbert, I'm glad you could make it. Please follow me."

By the time Rachel picked up her purse and day-timer, and rose, Ms. Yvette had already turned and headed back the way she came. The girl was as young and pretty as Rachel had envisioned during their brief phone call the day before and her lack of formalities reflected her youth. No polite greeting or handshake, instead they started with a race, which Rachel was obviously losing. She walked quickly, to catch up and only did after rounding a corner and finding Ms. Yvette standing at a conference room door, waiting.

"Please have a seat and Mr. Durran will be right with you."

There was a single table with four chairs in the room and the walls were bare except one that had a white board hanging on it. The front wall and door were glass. She watched Ms. Yvette walk away and then selected the chair on the far side of the table so she could see through the glass wall. Placing her day-timer on the table and her purse on the floor next to her seat, she watched as people walked by without even noticing her. So far, she was not impressed and began to wonder why she had even agreed to come. A few minutes later a middle-aged man in a black suit walked in.

"Dr. Gilbert, hi, I'm Kyle Durran," he said as he reached out his hand. "It's so nice to meet you."

"Hello and thank you."

She thanked him partly because of his welcome and partly because of the formality, which she appreciated.

He took the seat across from her, laid two file folders on the table and opened the top one.

"Dr. Gilbert, the reason why I sent you the letter and asked that we meet is to offer you a position with A. E. Research, as you know. I know that you have just received your Ph.D. from Virginia Tech. and..."

"Yes and *how did* you know about that?" she interrupted.

"Oh...well...we are partnered with a number of institutions around the world. We ask them to let us know when they have a graduating student with high marks and potential. These are the ones we approach, such as yourself, and in return we help support the institution. It takes a lot to search for candidates these days and we have found that this is one of the best, and the most economical, approaches for finding qualified people."

Satisfied with his answer, she let him continue. Before he did, he pulled out the bottom folder, which had her name on the front. He turned it around to face her and slid it across the table slowly for her to read.

"We have outlined the offer in this folder. It explains more about A. E. Research, our corporate structure, what your position's responsibilities will be, and your reporting hierarchy. It goes over your compensation, benefits, bonuses and vacation packages. There is also a section with answers to frequently asked questions. I would like you to read the offer and give me your feedback. I'll answer as many of your questions as I can and for those I cannot, I'll find someone who can."

Flipping through the folder she explained, "I think I'm going to need some time to go through this information."

"Oh, of course, I didn't mean to insinuate that you needed to do this right now. First, I would like to get to know you better. Could you tell me more about yourself, your family and what you've been doing for the past few years?"

Closing the folder, Rachel sat back in her chair and looked over Durran trying to size him up; nothing about him stood out. He did not have a big nose or exaggerated features of any kind, like being too heavy or too thin. He was very polite and looked at you when he talked to you. Nothing about him gave her the need to be cautious and yet she found herself not really trusting him. She did not interview well and she knew it, but it did not seem necessary to make a first impression since an offer had already been drafted and given to her. Questions ran through her mind.

*Why spend the time getting to know me after you offered me a position? Usually an employer gets to know you first and then offers you a job if they like you or think you're qualified, however, neither has been established as far as I can tell yet. Maybe Durran is just being pleasant and has already made up his mind based upon my transcripts.*

"Dr. Gilbert, are you okay?"

"Oh, yes, thank you, I was just wondering where I should start."

"How about starting with your family."

"Okay..."

For the next thirty-five minutes, Rachel told Durran about her family in Blacksburg, attending Virginia Tech., doing her internship at the Sheltering Arms Hospital and graduating this past Friday. When she did not focus on her suspicions, she was able to talk freely and comfortably. Soon, both were sharing about experiences from childhood and college. It had been a little over an hour since they started when Durran looked at his watch.

"My, how time flies," he said as he looked up at her again. "I know you haven't read the offer, but are there any questions I can answer for you right now?"

She did not hesitate. "Yes, what is A. E. Research all about?"

"I'm glad you asked. A. E. Research or *Alternative Entity Research* researches the possibilities of alternative practices. We are involved in many different aspects of public and private life, political and civilian life and foreign and domestic life. We look at issues and research the possibility of doing things differently, such as changing laws, involving different kinds of people, seeking out new ideas and their logical conclusions, and things of this nature. It's kind of hard to explain because of the many different facets of what we do." He hesitated for a minute as if he was remembering something. "Take, for example, the psychological area where you'll be working. Ask yourself this question; would there be a benefit to giving mind-altering drugs to patients traumatized due to the loss of a limb? If the drugs allowed them to overcome the trauma quicker and caused them to believe they could do anything they set their mind to, could they be retrained quicker and more easily? If they could, think of how this would cut insurance costs and medical expenses, not to mention getting people back to work sooner. These are the kinds of ideas or scenarios we engage in."

"Well, that example is certainly a lot to swallow."

"It's just an example, but one that we would have to study and research both the good and bad in it. If it turns out to have negative consequences then we have avoided needless expenses and time. On the other hand, if it proves to be very valuable, then we can spend our time and money wisely."

"I see, so A. E. Research is a giant think tank?"

"You could say that, but it would only be scratching the surface of what we do." He looked at his watch again and became hurried. "I hate to rush, but I do have another appointment. Can I answer any other questions?"

"No, let me go over the offer first. Would it be okay if I took a day or two?"

"By all means, go ahead. I must tell you though, there are others. However, you are the most qualified and the most desired for this position. We do need to move quickly on our part, but I don't want to rush you into anything. Please take the time you need. I would like you to call me by the end of the day tomorrow just to let me know where you stand." He pulled one of his business cards out of the inside pocket of his jacket and held it out. "Please call me if you have any questions."

She stood up as Durran did and shook his hand as he extended it.

"I'll have Ms. Yvette show you out. Thanks again for coming. I hope you decide to join our team. Either way, it was very nice meeting you."

When he turned and walked out of the room, she picked up her things, including the folder. When she walked outside the conference room, Ms. Yvette was waiting.

Once again, Rachel played the catch-up game with her and lost. By the time she made it back to the reception area, Ms. Yvette was standing there with her finger pointing to the elevators. Disappearing down another hallway she said, "Thanks for coming. Have a nice day."

One more glance at the receptionist, who looked up and smiled at her before returning to his work and Rachel entered the elevator foyer. She pushed the down button. While she waited, she pondered the question Durran had raised about the trauma patients. *What if?*

When she got home, she dropped her purse, the day-timer and the folder on her dining room table and kicked off her shoes. She poured herself a tall glass of iced tea and took it and the folder over to her loveseat to relax. This was the brightest spot in her apartment. Next to the loveseat was the sliding glass door that led to the patio. The two floor-to-ceiling glass doors let in a large amount of light, which is why she enjoyed reading in this spot. She sat down and brought her feet up along side her. After setting the glass on the end table, she opened the folder and began to read.

Important documents always seemed hard for her to read and she had developed a process to help her get through them thoroughly. First, she would skim over the titles in each section gleaning what she could from them, searching for a clue as to what the sections were about. Second, she would go back and skim each section almost speed reading it, to gain some insight about the topic. Next, she would take a break from the document and do something else to distract her mind. Lastly, a short time later, she would come back to the document and read it in detail. This process always helped her gain a complete understanding of the material. She had tried other ways, but none as successful. Her way made for long nights during her education and it did not leave time for fun or dating, at least this was her excuse. Fifteen minutes later the first two steps were completed and she was ready for her break. A phone call to Admiral Garry would be her distraction.

Garry's receptionist told her that Mr. Garry was on the phone with another client but would be off soon. She chose to hold and listened to a collection of classical piano arrangements playing through the earpiece of the phone. This brought back memories of visiting Garry's home when she was young and seeing the Baby Grand piano in Garry's living room, which he played for them at the urging of her mother. It seemed strange to her that a big man like Garry could play such an instrument with such grace and emotion. The music changed to that familiar deep voice.

"Rachel, how good of you to call. How are you?"

"I'm well, and yourself?"

"I'm fine. How was your father's birthday party?"

"It was nice. He enjoyed it and was very surprised. He did say that he wished you could have been there."

"I'm sure you explained why I couldn't. Well, I must say I didn't expect to hear from you so soon, is everything okay?"

"Admiral, I have a job offer..."

"Wonderful," Garry interrupted. "With whom?"

"It's with a company called A. E. Research. Have you ever heard of them?"

Garry took a moment to reply. "Can't say that I know anything about them. Are they here in Richmond?"

"Yes. Their corporate office is in the Merrill Lynch building on Eighth and Main. I had an interview there this morning with a Kyle Durran, who is the head of their Human Resources department. He gave me a packet with the job offer in it. I was just going over it and wondered if we could meet so you could look it over."

"I'd be happy to do that for you. Let me check my calendar." Another pause. "I have a meeting tomorrow out your way at eleven-o'clock in the morning. We could meet for lunch afterwards."

"Where would you like to meet, Admiral?"

"Are you familiar with the China Buffet restaurant on West Broad Street near Hungry Spring?"

As they hung up, she felt at peace. Admiral Garry was like a second father. He did not have children of his own and for some reason he connected with her and watched over her as if she was his own. Thinking back to her first memories of him, she could not remember being told how he and her father had met. What mattered was that she had someone watching out for her here and back in Blacksburg. How many people could say that?

She finished her drink and got up to refill it. Returning to the loveseat and repositioning herself, she moved on to the task of reviewing the job offer in detail.

At two-o'clock Rachel finished her review. She leaned back in the loveseat, took a long stretch with her arms in the air and glanced up at the clock on the wall over the television set across from her. "The party!" She quickly cleaned up her mess and headed for her closet to change for the party with the girls. Twenty minutes later, she was out the door again on her way to the Sheltering Arms Hospital.

The adjacent building next to the hospital was where she had spent three years working while she did her internship. It was an old habit and without thinking, she parked her Lexus in front of it and headed up the walkway. When she reached the doors, she realized she was in the wrong place. Annie's office and the small conference room she had booked for the party were in the main hospital building on the second floor of the South Wing, nicknamed the *Woman's Wing*. Leaving her car where it was, she quickly walked back across the parking lot, up the steps and into the lobby of the Woman's Wing. On this side of the building, she had entered on the second floor and quickly walked past the reception desk, around the corner and halfway down the hallway to a room marked *Small Conference Room*. She did not see Annie or any of the other girls out in the hallway and there was no noise coming from the other side of the closed door, which made her wonder if she missed them or had the wrong time. Her excitement had turned to concern. Cautiously she knocked softly on the door as she slowly opened it. The room was dark and her concern turned to disappointment. Flipping the light switch, she expected to see a completely empty room with all signs of a party cleared away, but what she saw renewed her excitement – balloons! She opened the door wider and stepped inside to a cheer of "Surprise!"

Annie, a short heavy woman with a cute face and short sandy-blond hair, who adored Rachel, reached her first and gave her a bear hug. While they worked together, they were like sisters. They went everywhere together and helped each other out with their individual jobs. Annie kept a watch on the patients that Rachel worked with and Rachel took care of some of the nursing duties for these patients for Annie. Their arrangement helped Rachel to be more effective with her patient's therapy.

"Were you surprised?" Annie asked as she released Rachel and stepped back.

"Yeah, I thought I missed you guys or had the wrong day or time. I'm so glad I didn't. It's great to see you all again."

Annie moved aside and one by one, the other girls came up and gave Rachel a hug. As they greeted her, she noticed that the chairs were lined up against the walls of the conference room and the table was covered with all kinds of finger foods and drinks that surrounded a sheet cake in the center. The writing on the cake read *Congratulations, from your Sheltering Arms Sisters.*

Announcing, "Okay, let's eat," Annie handed a plate to Rachel to start the line around the table and then closed the conference room door.

The last person to greet Rachel was Dr. Lauren Claire, a short thin woman in her late forties with curly brown hair whose voice was always soft, calming and sometimes hard to hear in a crowd. She had worked with Rachel for several years and had known her longer than Annie had. They had a doctor-patient relationship and were friends. Lauren waited until there was a lull in the party and then asked Rachel if she could speak with her outside. Rachel agreed and followed her outside the room with her mind focused on one thing, a job opening.

Across the hallway was a door that led out onto a terrace with shade trees and flowerbeds around the edge. In the center were metal tables and chairs.

"I always loved this spot," Rachel expressed as she looked around. "I remember working with patients out here because it was quiet and away from the busy hospital halls."

"It's a perfect place to talk," replied Lauren.

They chose the table farthest from the door and sat down.

"I really enjoyed your graduation and the party afterwards. Sorry I couldn't stay longer." With a tone of concern Lauren asked, "So, how are you doing?"

"I'm fine, Lauren."

"We have not talked for about three weeks now and I was wondering how things are going. How's your sleep? Have you had any nightmares?"

"Every time we meet you ask me about the nightmares. When are you going to believe that I'm okay?"

"Rachel, although the absence of something may indicate that it is no longer a problem, it is not always the case. Cancer patients go into remission and then it returns. My concern is that you haven't completely worked through the issues that caused the nightmares in the first place. We didn't get to finish our work and this always leaves me worried about things returning, that's why I like to touch base each time I see you."

"I'm sorry, Lauren, I didn't mean to be rude. I hadn't had a nightmare...until this past Friday night."

"The night of your graduation?"

"Yes. It was a long day and I had been up late the few nights before. I had some champagne at the party afterwards and it was also a late night. It was early morning when I had it. I don't remember much except that it was short and in pieces. I've not had another since and prior to that, as you know, I haven't had a nightmare in three years."

"Was it like the others?"

"Like I said I can't remember. I'm not putting you off, I really can't remember. I do remember feeling scared though, not from the dream, but that they might be starting again. Later I realized that it was just exhaustion."

"Maybe. Too much stress could bring on a nightmare, even good stress like you were having. Did you have any physical symptoms?"

"No, not this time, it was just the dream. I'm okay, really, I am."

Lauren looked away for a moment and stared at a pigeon that had landed on the railing. It cocked its head several times as it watched them and then flew away.

"I tell you what, I'll stop bothering you each time I see you about the nightmares if you promise to tell me when you have them."

Lauren's words made it sound as if the healing process had not taken place and the dreams would return. Rachel did not want to hear this and didn't believe this to be true so she corrected her.

"You mean *if* I have them."

"*If* you have them. Is it a deal?"

"It's a deal."

Rachel held out her hand for Lauren to shake, which she did. This was not what Rachel thought Lauren was going to talk to her about so before leaving she had to ask.

"Lauren, did you find out anything about a position here for me?"

"Oh, I'm so sorry for forgetting..."

"*Forgetting?*"

"Yes, I checked on the position right after we talked three weeks ago. It was strange, the position had just been announced at our weekly meeting that morning and I went straight to the administrator's office right after we talked that afternoon, but when I got there, he told me the position had been filled. He didn't tell me who filled it and I never saw a new face, but the requisition was removed. According to the administrator, there is nothing else available right now. I'm sorry. I'll keep my eyes and ears open and if something comes up I'll talk to him right away."

"Thanks, Lauren."

"Shall we return to the party?"

"Absolutely," she said trying to hide her disappointment.

* * *

Caleb did not even notice that Pastor Reynolds was standing in his office doorway. He had not heard the doorbell or his receptionist telling the pastor to go on back. There were three piles of papers in front of him. The first were bills that needed to be paid. The second were shipments that needed scheduling for the upcoming month and the third were receipts that needed to be approved before the receptionist could enter them into the computer. He was focused on all three stacks and trying to process it all at one time.

His phone interrupted his concentration. As he reached to pick it up, he dropped his pen on the floor. After bending over to pick it up and rising, he jumped when he saw the figure in his doorway. Recognizing who it was, he relaxed. The phone rang a second time. Reynolds did not speak but raised his hands as if to say, "Don't let me interrupt."

"I'll just be a moment," Caleb said raising the index finger on his right hand and picking up the phone with his left. "Yes?"

It was his receptionist asking about putting through a call from a potential new client.

"Forward it to Jeff's line so he can leave a message, please," Caleb told her and hung up. "Pastor Reynolds," he said as he stood up and came around the desk. "Please come in and have a seat."

They shook hands and Reynolds took a seat in front of Caleb's desk. Caleb turned the other chair to face Reynolds and sat down.

"What brings you here, Pastor?"

"Well, as a matter of fact, you do, Caleb. I have been thinking about you over the past four or five days and I needed to see you."

"Needed to see me? About what?"

"It's just something I have to do. You see, a long time ago I started having things happen to me. I would think about someone for no apparent reason one day and then they would come to mind again the next day and then the next and then the next. I thought it was strange at first and then I realized it was a sign from God that I needed to go and see that person. I didn't do this at first and I later found that the people I thought about were going through some tough times either physically or emotionally. I realized it was God's way of telling me that I was needed somewhere. This time it's you. I'm here to help."

"Help? Help what? I don't need any help, I'm fine."

"Are you, Caleb?"

"Yes, I'm fine."

Caleb's voice got a little louder and expressed his irritation. Reynolds tried another tactic.

"How's your business doing?"

"It's fine. There's no problem there either."

Once again, Reynolds shifted gears.

"I remember when you sang in the choir at church. Your face seemed to glow and you were full of excitement. You had so much energy that the kids you worked with thought you were a lot younger. You know they came and asked me how old you were and wouldn't believe me when I told them."

"They were great kids," Caleb said as his voice softened and he looked down at the floor.

"Mrs. Parrot asks about you all the time. She misses you and so do a lot of others. Does Jeff ever tell you about the folks at the church?"

Caleb raised his head again and his irritated tone returned. "Jeff and I have an agreement, I don't ask him about the church and he doesn't tell me about it." He stared at Reynolds and wondered what he wanted.

"Look, Caleb, I'm not here to upset you. There are still people who care about you and want to know you're okay. We'd like you to come back to church, to your family."

"Pastor, I don't have a family anymore. It's clear that no one wants me. No matter how hard I try to be what others need me to be, I always seem to fail. I'm a failure. The people in the church took what I gave and didn't give back. I asked several men to pray for me, to check up on me and see how I'm doing spiritually, emotionally...but none of them did. I was selective, I chose those that I thought would take me seriously and they still didn't do it. Everyone was shocked about Jena and me, but no one saw it coming. No one took the time to get to know us as friends. We were there all the time. We went to people's homes, had dinner with them, worked along side them at church stuff and yet no one really knew us. For almost nine years, I attended that church and no one really knew me. It wasn't because I wasn't available it was because no one really cared. They got what they wanted and that was all that mattered. I'm through with the church, Pastor. I'm not coming back."

Reynolds' face expressed disappointment and Caleb wasn't sure if it was for him or for the failure of his flock.

"I know that I haven't been at the church as long as you, Caleb, and I've felt the same way on occasion, but I'm trying to change things. I'm sorry that it appears it's too late to help you, though."

He was right, the damage was done and bitterness had sunk in. Caleb was well aware of this, but did nothing to avoid it. He reasoned that it did not matter since he wasn't going back.

"Caleb, I'm very sorry that our church has failed you, including me. However, the God that created both of us hasn't failed you. I understand if you don't want to return to our church, but I want to encourage you to find a church family that can help heal your pain. I can suggest a few if you'd like."

Caleb realized that he might have been too harsh with Reynolds and began to feel guilty. Reynolds had always been nice to him and tried to get to know him. By the time Reynolds had arrived, Caleb and Jena had begun their downhill slide. Eight months after Reynolds arrived at Monument Heights Baptist Church, Caleb was leaving.

"Thanks for the offer, Pastor. If I decide to change my mind I'll call you."

Reynolds stood up to leave and Caleb followed him. As they reached his office door Reynolds turned to say one last thing. "Caleb, the incidents I told you about, the ones where God was telling me there was a need, there *was* always a need. God was faithful in his urging. I'm here because God sent me. I believe there is a need even if you're not aware of it. Be watchful, my friend."

Caleb thanked Reynolds for his concern and his visit and glibly promised to watch for signs of trouble. He walked Reynolds to the front door and watched him walk down the steps of the front walkway. The sun was shinning right into the front door and Caleb had to shield his eyes with his hand. He saw Reynolds descend the steps before the sun blinded him and when he covered his eyes and looked again, Reynolds was gone. He looked up and down the street wondering where he had gone. There was no car parked in front of the building and besides if Reynolds had gotten into a car surely he would have heard it start up or at least seen it drive away. Reynolds had to have parked on the side of the building or out back. If he was, Caleb should have seen him walk around the side of the building, but he did not. Caleb ran through the office to the back door. Once outside again, he looked around for Reynolds and still did not see him. He ran to the side of the building and there was no Reynolds. He was nowhere. He had just vanished.

# 6

"Would you like to order something special or just do the buffet?" Garry asked as the host seated them.

"Let's do the buffet, I'm starving," Rachel said.

"Great, two buffets please," Garry said to the server who invited them to help themselves.

Rachel and Garry walked to the buffet filled with all kinds of Chinese goodies and loaded their plates. When they returned they started in right away. They were halfway finished before they started talking again.

Garry asked, "How did you hear about this A. E. Research?"

"I received a letter from them while I was in Blacksburg last week and found it on Tuesday when I got home. I thought it was junk mail and almost tossed it, but the research part of the name caught my attention and I got curious, so I opened it. While I was reading it, I got a call from Durran's assistant who wanted to schedule a meeting. It's the only offer that I've received, so I thought I'd look into it."

The server walked up to fill their water glasses and while she did, they took the time to continue eating. As the server walked away, Rachel pulled out the folder Durran had given her and handed it to Garry.

Garry stopped eating, wiped his mouth with the napkin from his lap and opened the folder. He was used to all kinds of formal documents and was very adept at reading through them quickly. Rachel watched as he turned pages and gave an occasional grunt. It amazed her to see someone do something so easily that was such a chore for her to do. It took her almost two hours to do what Garry was sitting there doing in mere minutes.

Fifteen minutes had gone by before Garry closed the folder. He had flipped back and forth through it several times, cross-referencing the information in all the sections. Laying the folder on the table, he took a few more bites before starting to speak.

"It's a wonderful package they're offering you, my dear."

"That's what I thought when I read it, although it took me a lot longer to come to that conclusion."

"I don't know anything about this company and that could be good or bad. They may never have been in trouble and that's why I've never heard of them. Anyway, the offer is sound and I don't see any loopholes or problems with the document. Their charter sounds very interesting and so does their client list."

"Would you object to me taking a position there?" Rachel was looking for some reassurance even though she had already decided that it was a good opportunity.

"No, I would not have any objections based on what I've read, however, I don't know anything about them. Would you like me to do some digging and find out more?"

Rachel was a little disappointed that Garry was non-committal. The offer did not include a timeframe she was committing to so she knew she could always quit if she found out something about the company that she did not like. She did not want to offend an old friend, but she did need a job and this one looked good.

"I think it would be great if you could check into them. In the meantime, I think I'll accept the job and see what it's like from the inside."

"That sounds fair enough."

With business out of the way and their plates empty, they both returned to the buffet for a second round. When they returned to their table, the conversation switched to family.

"So, how does it feel to have your Ph.D.?" Garry inquired.

"It doesn't feel any different except that it's over. I don't have to attend classes, take tests, or do projects. In addition, my dissertation is done! Now it's time to put it to use. I'm so looking forward to helping people like I was helped."

"Your parents must be very proud of you."

"Yes, they are. They've invested a lot of time and money in me. I'm still trying to think of a way to repay them."

"I'm sure there is no need for that, my dear," Garry said. "Parents rarely want anything in return for what they do for their children. They just want to see them happy."

"I must say, I haven't seen my parents as happy as they were at the graduation for a long time. They always seem to be in their own world. They don't go out much or do anything."

"What about fishing? Your dad loved to fish. He would take you guys all the time when you were little. When is the last time he went fishing?"

Rachel hesitated for a moment and then finally said, "Daddy doesn't fish anymore," with tears filling her eyes. "The last time he went was with me about three months before Amanda died. He wanted to go fishing with her, but never got around to calling. He was so mad at himself for that. He thought that if he had called they might have scheduled their fishing trip for the weekend she was killed and it wouldn't have happened. The day after her funeral, Dad was out back in the shed where he kept his fishing equipment. When I went out to check on him I found him on the floor of the shed crying. He had broken every one of the fishing poles and they were lying on the floor all around him. He never went fishing again."

"I'm so sorry, Rachel, I didn't mean to bring up bad memories."

"That's okay, Admiral," Rachel said as she dried her eyes with her napkin.

"Well, now that you have a Ph.D. and a job, what about a man? Any prospects?" Garry tried to lighten the moment.

Rachel chuckled and returned the napkin to her lap. "No, there's no one on the horizon. I've been too wrapped up in getting my degree that I haven't even thought of dating. I figure that I'll wait a bit until I'm secure in my job and ready for additional challenges."

"Challenges? You make it sound as if it's another degree."

"Yeah, I know," Rachel said, chuckling again. "It's just that

I'm not ready to trust too many people just yet. I'm getting better, but I'm not there yet."

"I understand. You just go on and do what you need to do and don't let anyone push you into something you are not ready for, including an old hard head like me."

"Thanks, Admiral, but you're not a hard head, and if we could pick our own godfathers, I would want you to be mine."

Rachel reached across the table, grabbed Garry's massive hand and squeezed it. Garry placed his other hand over Rachel's and patted it lightly.

"It would be an honor," he said.

Lunch was over and Garry had walked Rachel to her car and opened the door for her. Before she got in, she gave him a hug and a kiss. As she drove away, she looked in the rear view mirror and saw Garry pull out a cigar and light it. She could not help but feel sorry for him that he didn't have a daughter of his own or even a wife to care for him. He was alone, but he was always a rock for her and her family. She made a mental note to ask her father how they had met the next time she talked to him.

As Rachel pulled out onto Broad Street heading home, she opened her cell phone and dialed the number for Kyle Durran. The familiar voice of Ms. Yvette came over the phone.

"You have reached the office of Kyle Durran. We are unavailable at the moment. If you would like to leave a message for Mr. Durran please press one, otherwise press two for Ms. Yvette. We will return your call as soon as possible. Thanks and have a nice day."

Rachel figured this message must have been written out for the young Ms. Yvette because the politeness was unlike her and she sounded as if she was reading it. Rachel pressed the one button on her phone and heard the beep to leave a message.

"Mr. Durran, this is Rachel Gilbert, I have gone over your offer in detail and I'm very pleased with it. I would like to accept your offer and make plans to start on Monday if that's okay with you. I look forward to hearing from you. Thanks for this opportunity."

Rachel left her home and cell phone numbers at the end of the message and hung up. The familiar ear-to-ear smile returned on her face as she drove home thinking, *I'm on top of the world.*

* * *

Caleb had sorted through the same stack of bills three times still not finding the one he just had in his hands a few minutes ago. He had laid it down and then looked up something on his computer, when he went to pick it up again it was gone, or so he thought. All week Caleb's concentration was a little less than coherent. Several times, he found himself staring at the same document and rereading it repeatedly still not knowing what it was. The staff had to repeat things two or three times to him before he got what they were saying. Nothing was gelling. His usual sharpness was gone and in its place was a dull void. It was like being lost in a maze where every turn brought you back to where you started.

"Hey, buddy, how's it going?" Jeff said as he stood in

Caleb's office doorway.

Caleb looked up with a blank expression on his face, "What?"

Jeff walked into Caleb's office and shut the door. "Caleb, I've been watching you for the past twenty minutes," he said as he sat down. "You've been working on the same piece of paper, reading it, putting it down to look at the computer, losing it, finding it and then rereading it again. I can tell you are not getting anything accomplished. You look lost and the staff is asking about you. I know this is unlike you and I'm figuring that the only explanation for it has to be the divorce. What do you think?"

Caleb looked up and out the glass walls at some of the staff who were walking by his office. "What are they saying?" he said looking back at Jeff.

"Never mind. I think you need a break. Why don't you skip out early today and stay home all weekend. Go do something fun for yourself. Then maybe on Monday you'll feel better."

"Take a break?" Caleb snapped as he looked back down at his work. "I'm fine, Jeff. Maybe a little tired, but I'm okay. I don't *need* a break."

"Yes," Jeff said firmly and then his voice softened, "you do, my friend."

Caleb looked up again and stared Jeff in the eyes. He could tell from Jeff's face that he was not angry, just concerned. Caleb knew this look he had seen it before. Both of them had their own way of skirting around issues they did not want to deal with, but both of them had the same way of confronting each other, direct and to the point with a soft stare. Long ago, they had both agreed to respect this look and not to abuse it. They would only bring it out when needed. Jeff needed it today and Caleb gave in.

"Okay, Jeff, you're right. I've been reviewing this same bill for almost forty-five minutes and I still don't know what it's for." Caleb dropped his pencil on the desk and sat back in his chair. For a few seconds he rubbed his face with both hands and then laid them on the armrests. "All week it's been hard for me to concentrate on anything. I didn't expect to be affected by this divorce as much as I am. After eighteen months of separation, you'd think enough time had past that it would just blow by, but it's not. I feel more alone now than I did before the divorce was finalized, even though I was still alone. Does that make any sense?"

"Yeah, buddy, it does. Why don't you go home? You need time to get over this. There is a wound that needs healing and you need to take care of it or it will not heal."

Caleb knew his friend was right. Jeff always knew how to get Caleb to see the real need in his life and not avoid it. He trusted Jeff and Jeff knew it. Since they had first met, nothing had come between them that ever made them doubt the intentions of the other.

"Thanks, Jeff. You're a good friend. I think I'll go home. Do you mind covering for me with the staff? I'm going to slip out the back so I don't alarm them."

"No problem, buddy. I'll redirect their attention. You get some rest and call me if you need anything. I'll check on you tomorrow, but I don't want to see you in here until Monday, okay?"

"Sure thing."

They shook hands and Jeff walked out of Caleb's office. A few seconds later, he was calling the staff together up front for a quick meeting giving Caleb a chance to slip out the back door.

It was still early afternoon with a few scattered clouds in the sky. Caleb did not really feel like going home, besides there was nothing there for him to do. He had given up all his hobbies and lost his passion for most everything else. There were no shows on during the day that he cared to watch on TV and he had run through his collection of DVDs three times already in the past twelve months. Caleb was not sure what to do with his time and as he pulled out of the office driveway onto Westwood Avenue heading towards Broad Street, he decided to take a drive. For two hours, he drove around town. First he headed south and then back up to the east side of town and eventually back to Broad Street to make his way home.

It was later in the day now and traffic was getting heavy as people were heading home from work. Caleb was getting hungry. He had not eaten lunch and decided to stop at Benny's for dinner. As he drove he thought about the fact that nothing seemed appealing to him anymore. He had no one to share his life with and this made everything less desirable. When Caleb pulled into the parking lot at Benny's it was already full. The Friday night crowd was starting early. He found a parking space and was about to shut off the car when he saw a couple grasp each other's hand and walk up to the front door. They stopped and stepped aside to let another couple leave. Caleb watched the leaving couple as they walked to their car. The man opened the door for his apparent wife and closed it after she was in. Caleb's gaze shifted as he heard a young man yell

"Hello" and run up to a woman standing by the front door. When he reached her, they embraced and kissed. Caleb could take it no more. He put his car in reverse, pulled out of the parking space and drove away.

Instead of driving across the street and going home, Caleb came up with another plan. He headed for the Short Pump shopping center and the Regal Cinemas. Maybe a movie would cheer him up. He quickly scanned the list of movies on the marquee and decided on an action movie – *Poseidon*. He purchased his ticket and went in. At the concession stand, he got a hotdog, small popcorn and a small Coke. When he walked into the theater, he found it almost deserted except for one couple in the back row. Caleb avoided making eye contact and sat several rows in front of them. He ate his hotdog thinking; s*urely, this movie will not remind me of anything.*

It was not long before Caleb found his thinking to be wrong. One by one, as the theater filled up, couples came from everywhere. Some were young, others older, still others even older, but they all had one thing in common – they were with someone. Caleb stayed and watched the movie and when it was over, he watched as the couples all left. He was the last to leave. Outside, as he walked to his car he saw some of the same couples walking together or getting into cars. He stopped and watched them wondering if he would ever be happy again. Then he wondered if the couples he saw were really happy. He had been married to Jena for three and a half years and thought they were happy, but it was not real. Maybe what he saw was not either. Suddenly Caleb's wondering turned to anger and disgust. He climbed into his car and drove away. *There is no happiness.*

# 7

Caleb had been up for hours. The previous night had left him dealing with a myriad of emotions that exhausted him far more than any delivery job he had ever done. After coming home and crawling into bed fully clothed, he slept for twelve hours straight. When he awoke, he felt more alive than he had in weeks. He had an ample amount of energy and still no outlet to release it. It was an overcast day and the temperature outside was a little cool so he decided to go for a run. Running was something that Caleb used to love to do. He had won several medals in track and field competitions in high school and college. As time went by and he got busier, he stopped running as much. After his separation from Jena, he quit altogether.

As he stepped outside and breathed the cool fresh air, he felt a sense of nostalgia and remembered his races and the medals he had won. His parent's cheers made him feel proud. Mostly he remembered that he had accomplished something. Quickly the memory faded into defeat as he saw himself being divorced twice and no one beside him cheering him on. The emotions from the previous night started flooding back as Caleb started to run. First he tried to ignore them and just focus on the road as he ran, but the thoughts would not go away. He was running in and out of the cul-de-sacs that made up the apartment complex and his attention kept being drawn to cars coming in and out as he swerved to miss them. He changed his path and followed the main road that led through the complex. As he ran, he kept his head up and focused on the scenery. The sky was clearing up and the distant clouds where fluffy white and gray. There was a breeze blowing that swayed the trees back and forth like a rocking chair and this made Caleb relax.

After forty-five minutes, Caleb was back home sweating and breathing hard. He thought about how much harder it was to run now than it used to be and he felt old. Once inside he headed for the shower. An hour later, he was wearing a pair of shorts and sitting on his couch looking out the window at a beautiful day with no idea of what to do. In front of him, on the coffee table, were the remains of a sandwich he had made for himself and eaten, and an empty bag of chips. In his hand was an empty glass of tea with two half-melted ice cubes at the bottom. For several minutes he was frozen in time, no movement and no sound, until a drop of condensation from the glass fell on his leg snapping him back to the real world. He wiped off his leg with a napkin and cleared off the coffee table taking everything to the kitchen.

In the kitchen, he noticed the garbage can was full so he pulled out a large trash bag from the pantry and opened it. After placing a new bag in the garbage can, he picked up the trash bag and headed for the other trashcans in the apartment. The first stop was his desk. He stooped down, grabbed the can, and emptied it into the larger trash bag. As he went to replace it, he noticed something on the floor leaning up against the wall. It was a green postcard. He set the can down and picked up the card. He flipped it back and forth looking at both sides; it was the Internet dating postcard he had thrown away. It had missed the trashcan and fallen between it and the wall. Caleb looked at the front of the card again and reread the back twice. He started to throw it in the trash bag until something made him hold on to it and bring it up to his face to read once more.

"Try something new...with a guarantee." He had not seen this line before. It was in small print at the bottom of the card, but it caught Caleb's attention as if it was the only thing written on the card. He thought back to something Jeff had said about writing new chapters of his life.

"Try something new," he said to himself as he stared at the words on the card. "Maybe *it is* time to try something new."

The next thing Caleb knew he was sitting at his desk and turning on his computer. Excitement raced through his body and he found himself talking to the computer.

"Come on...hurry up...you're too slow."

The hard drive light on the PC came on as well as the power light on the monitor. The hard drive started whirling as the computer tested the drive and the monitor came to life. Within minutes, Caleb was logging on to *The Connection*.

Caleb watched as the screen filled in with a hunter green color and music began to play. At first, the music was soft and barely audible. Then from the depths of the screen came a black dot. It moved from side to side and began to get bigger and faster until it looked like a worm trying to crawl from the back of the screen to the front. The music followed suit and kept pace with the worm. Within seconds, the worm became a video cable with a male fitting on the end. The music got louder and faster. The cable closed in on the front of the screen and then ran parallel to the screen going from left to right. As it moved across the front of the screen, the words *THE CONNECTION* appeared and when the cable reached the right side of the screen it stopped. The music hit its final crescendo and stopped as well. Below the cable appeared two buttons. One read, *First Time Visitor and the other read, Member Entrance.*

Caleb made his selection and the screen filled with the same pictures that Caleb had seen on the postcard and four boxes labeled, *First, Middle, Last* and *Sex-M/F.* Caleb entered his information. The screen started changing again and a sexy woman's voice spoke to him.

"Hello, Caleb Andrew Prescott. Welcome to *The Connection.*" The screen filled in with several lines asking for personal information; address, city, state, phone number and so on. The voice came back, "Let's start by getting to know each other. First, we will start with information about where you live. Please fill in each of the boxes on the screen with the appropriate information."

Caleb obliged the voice and entered what the voice wanted. At the bottom of the screen was a button marked *Continue* and he clicked on it. The screen changed again and displayed three buttons. The first was marked *Credit Card,* the second *Bill Me* and the third was *Special Offer.*

"Thank you, Caleb. Now let us move on to your payment options. If you received a postcard from *The Connection,* click on the special offer button and enter the code written in the bottom right corner of the back of the postcard."

Caleb grabbed the postcard and turned it over to find the code. He clicked on the special offer button and a green box appeared under the button. Caleb entered the five-digit code from the card and the box disappeared. The music started again and the screen went blank except for the hunter green color. A few seconds later an image of a faceless man faded onto the left-hand side of the screen. To the right of the figure was a list of male character traits; eye color, hair color, height, weight, etc. Then the voice returned.

"Okay, Caleb, lets find out what you look like. Please answer the questions on the right with the appropriate information and let's see if we can draw your picture."

Caleb, intrigued by the thought that by answering a few questions this system could draw his picture, jumped right in. As if playing a video game, he answered the questions and the faceless image came to life. His eyes and hair changed to the color of Caleb's. The facial features began to take on the shape of Caleb's. The height and weight proportions seemed to mirror his own and Caleb stared in amazement. As he answered the last question, his face almost went white. If he had been standing, he would have certainly fallen to the floor. There on the screen looking back at him was himself.

"It's good to see you, Caleb," the sexy voice from the computer said.

"How is this possible?" Caleb asked aloud. It was beyond imagination. There was not enough detail in those questions for a program to draw such an accurate image of him and yet there it was staring back at him.

"When you are ready to move on just click the continue button," the voice said.

Caleb realized that the programmers, who built this site, were smart enough to know that this section was going to stop people in their tracks. Impressed by what they saw they would hesitate, so the programmers gave them the time they needed. The voice did not give the impression that it wanted him to move on quickly. It was allowing him to take in everything until he was ready for more.

*What could possibly be next?* He moved the mouse and clicked on the button to continue.

The questions disappeared but the image remained. New questions appeared asking about favorite colors, movies, sports and activities. It asked about hobbies and clubs in which he participated. There were questions about the kind of books he read; TV shows he watched; religious beliefs and political preferences. It seemed as if the questions went on forever. For almost an hour, Caleb found himself answering these questions. Some of them, he thought, were too strange for a dating service to be asking, like the one about things that influence you to take action or inquiring as to what it would take to make you do something illegal. Just about the time he was getting tired of answering questions, the voice returned.

"Caleb, let's shift gears and do something fun!"

The screen cleared once more and a few seconds later a faceless image of a woman faded in where Caleb's image had been.

The same kind of questions about physical features appeared on the right with a few differences, some additional questions specifically targeted about women.

"Now, Caleb, let's find out what your match looks like," said the voice. "Just like before, answer the questions with the appropriate information and see what you're looking for."

*Wow! What an idea! To actually see an image of the type of person I'm attracted to.* Hooked, he watched the image appear as he answered each of the questions. A few times, he changed an answer just to see how the image would change. It was so real, so life like, as if it was a real person's picture. *But how could this be?*

This time at the bottom of the screen, there were seven buttons. The first six were labeled *1* through *6* and the seventh was labeled *Continue*. Just as Caleb noticed these buttons, the voice told him about them.

"Each of the numbered buttons you see allows you to save the answers you just gave. You can create up to six different versions of your match image. We will use the images to search our database for the person or persons that match your selections. When you have chosen as many as you wish then click on the continue button."

Caleb created four different images and saved them. Then, with a sense of apprehension, he clicked on the continue button. The screen faded out once more and the music returned. The search had begun. Again, the screen filled with images of people that scrolled across the screen in random patterns while a box across the bottom displayed the progress of the search. The voice returned.

"Please sit back and relax, Caleb, while we search for your match. This could take a few minutes. While you wait let me share a few facts with you. First, we are the largest Internet dating service of its kind. Second, we are very discreet. No one will ever know that we matched you with them unless you make the first move to contact them. And lastly, we have a seventy-six percent success rate, not only in finding matches but in those matches having lifelong relationships."

The voice paused for a moment as the progress bar was nearing one-hundred percent. Then it continued. "Our search is almost done. Get ready to see your matches."

The progress bar disappeared, the screen went blank and the music stopped. A second later seventeen female faces displayed on the screen in four rows; three rows of five and one row of two. Once again, the voice gave instructions.

"Okay, Caleb, meet your matches. Click on an image and read all about her."

Caleb moved the cursor over the first image and clicked the left mouse button. The image zoomed out until it covered all the rest. Her profile displayed to the right of the picture. At the bottom of the screen were four more buttons marked, *Send a wink*, *E-mail her*, *Save in Hot list* and *Exit*. Caleb clicked on the exit button and watched as the profile disappeared and the image shrank back to the size of the others. Caleb was looking at the seventeen images again.

He had been sitting at his computer for over an hour and a half already and had not noticed the time slipping by. One by one, he opened each of the profiles and read them, surprised at how similar they all were. Excited and curious he was quickly lost in his task.

* * *

Rachel sat at a desk on the second floor of the Innsbrook Library staring at the computer screen. Research at the library allowed her to get out of her apartment and it gave her more than just the Internet to search. Several reference books lay open on the left side of the desk piled on top of each other. On the right side lay a small pad with a few notes scribbled on it - the results of the past three hours of searching.

This branch of the public library was very familiar to Rachel. She spent a lot of time here doing research while in school and working at the hospital. It was located on a back street surrounded by several office parks and away from the heavy traffic. The branch was small with two floors. The second floor housed a good-sized business reference section and a computer system that stored all kinds of records. The first time Rachel came here, she was doing research on the Sheltering Arms Hospital. She was beginning her internship and wanted to know more about the hospital, their staff and their practices. One of the librarians directed her to the business section and showed her how to use the computer system and find the necessary reference material. Over the years, she had become an expert at research. However, today she did not feel like one.

Researching the history of A. E. Research was no small task. Using Google searches brought up several different organizations with the same initials, such as; Architectural Engineering Research, Aerospace Engineering Research and Animal Ecology Research, but there was no listing for the company that she had interviewed with. Next, she tried looking through a reference book that listed the names of companies started in the Richmond area within the past thirty years. Here she found what she was looking for.

A. E. Research (Alternative Entity Research)
707 E. Main Street Suite 1400
Richmond, Va. 23219
Established: November 12, 2000

Rachel jotted this down on her pad. She now knew when they started here in Richmond. She moved this book aside leaving the page open and opened another book. The second reference book was a list of business owners in the Richmond area, but she did not find anything in this book. There was no listing of an owner of A. E. Research or Alternative Entity Research. She set this book on top of the other and moved on. She opened another book listing companies that had changed their names within the past twenty years and found nothing there as well. This book also went on the pile. Next, was a reference book that listed business license purchases in Richmond going back as far as the year 1955. In this book was a listing of a business license purchased on *July 16, 2000* by a *George Acuron, CFO of A. E. Research*. Rachel jotted this down on her pad as well. The last two references books did not give any more help. One was a list of companies that owed back taxes and the other was a list of companies that were investigated by the Better Business Bureau.

The reference books provided Rachel with two small pieces of information she did not have before, the date established and the license information. Rather, what she wanted was to know who they were, where they came from and what they did. She turned her attention to the computer system again. In the newspaper section, she searched for articles that referenced the name A. E. Research. Again, she had to weed through the list of articles about other research groups with the same initials. She skipped over about fifteen articles and found an article about A. E. Research.

Slowly, she read the article and was shocked to find out that A. E. Research had funded the building of the counseling wing of the Sheltering Arms Hospital. The picture with the article showed the completed building that sat off to the side of the hospital, the very same building she had worked in for years while doing her internship. She pictured the lobby of the building in her mind and searched for a plaque of some kind on the wall indicating who funded it, but nothing came to mind. Next, she envisioned the hallways and elevator foyers. There was nothing there, either. Finally, she pictured the outside of the building and the grounds hoping to remember something in the concrete walkway or a carved stone of some kind, still nothing. Nothing indicated who funded this wing.

Rachel thought this was strange that a company would invest in this kind of thing and not want to have the publicity of it remembered for years to come. Then a thought came to mind. *Could it be that the hospital did not want to advertise this fact? If so, why? The hospital benefited from the wing, why would they not want to thank the people who gave it to them?* She continued to stare at the picture and then she noticed the small print underneath. It read, *Sheltering Arms Hospital Counseling Wing funded by A. E. Research under the direction of CEO and President, Jason Michaels.*

"Did you find what you were looking for?" said a voice from behind Rachel.

Startled, she turned quickly to see the older librarian that had helped her. "Oh, it's you. I was so engrossed in this article that I forgot where I was. You startled me."

"I'm sorry. I guess that means you found what you were looking for."

"Well, sort of. I found out a few bits of information about the company, but not much. However, I found this article about them funding the counseling wing of the Sheltering Arms Hospital. I used to work there and I never knew this."

Rachel had turned to face the computer again and was pointing to the picture on the screen. The librarian was looking over her shoulder at the same image.

"The caption under the picture says that the CEO was Jason Michaels." She turned to face the librarian again. "Do you know of him?"

"No, I sure don't, but I've only been in Richmond for two years."

"Hmmm...I used to date a fella named Michaels years ago, but his name was Tripp. It didn't end well." Rachel cleared her throat, and then, thanked the librarian who headed off to help someone else.

For several minutes, she sat there staring at the picture as her thoughts drifted back to when she was dating Tripp. He was young and full of ambition, always saying he was going to become something and change the world. She wanted to follow him anywhere, but something held her back that she could never quite put her finger on. Then they broke up.

Suddenly, images of a funeral, Amanda's funeral, replaced the thoughts of Tripp and young love. She saw the closed coffin, a last face-to-face good-bye stolen by a bullet wound in Amanda's head, and the sad faces of their friends and family. She remembered the tears shed by her and her parents in the back seat of the limo and the portrait of her sister, which reminded her that she lost her best friend. She swallowed down that familiar lump and sat completely still as if in a trance. She experienced the pain of her loss as if she was right there all over again. Then once again the images changed and she was lying on her bed in her room in her parent's house in Blacksburg. It was late at night about six months after the funeral and she was jolted awake screaming at the top of her lungs. The nightmares had started. Rachel started to jerk in her chair at the library and was about to let out a scream when she felt a sudden jolt. Someone had bumped into her chair and brought her back to reality.

"I'm so sorry," the young man said as he looked down at her. She wondered if he could see the trail of tears and hoped he did not notice. "If you don't mind me asking, are you okay?"

Rachel did not turn to look at him. She sat still holding the sides of the desk with both hands as if she would fall over if she let go. A few seconds passed allowing her to gain some composure before she answered him. "Yes, I'm fine. Thank you."

"Okay then. Again, I'm sorry about running into your chair," he said and then walked away.

Rachel watched him out of the corner of her eye without turning her head or moving in any way. She sat there breathing hard and trying to recover from her thoughts. After a few minutes, she was able to let go of the desk and started to clean up. She logged off the computer, closed all the books and carried them over to the cart by the librarian's desk. Before she placed the pad in her purse she wrote down, *Jason Michaels – CEO*. She picked up her purse and walked down the stairs to the front door.

When Rachel stepped outside the sun was bright and she had to shade her eyes until they adjusted. Standing still until she could see, her thoughts drifted back to the newspaper article. *They built the building that allowed me to continue my education and be what I am today. It must be fate that they offered me a job there. It was meant to be.*

What Rachel had found out about A. E. Research was not much, but it was enough to make her feel better about going to work for them. Her eyes had adjusted and she walked to her car. Once inside, an overwhelming urge hit her and she gave in to it. As she backed out of the parking space and put the car in gear she announced to herself, "It's time to go shopping! I need some new clothes for my new job."

\* \* \*

Caleb received the call from Jeff around four-o'clock and hurried to get ready. He could not believe that he had passed the whole day away reading through profiles of women from an Internet dating service. The trashcan that he had emptied hours ago was still sitting next to the desk where he left it and so was the trash bag. He knew that Jeff would be knocking on the door any minute now - he was never late.

As Caleb walked out of his bedroom carrying his shoes and still drying off his hair, he noticed he had left the computer on and he saw the trashcan and the bag on the floor. He placed the can back between the desk and the wall, carried the bag to the front door and then logged off the computer. He was just slipping on his shoes when the doorbell rang and he looked at the clock on the wall. Four-thirty-five on the nose just as Jeff had said. It still amazed him that Jeff was so precise. Caleb grabbed his keys and opened the door.

"Hey, Jeff," he said as he stepped through the doorway and turned to lock the door.

"Hey, buddy," Jeff said, apparently stunned that Caleb had not invited him in first and was already ready. "What's the hurry?"

"I'm starved. I haven't eaten much all day."

"What have you been doing?"

"I'll tell you on the way. Where are we going?"

"There's a new place up by the Short Pump shopping center called Capital Ale House, which some friends told me about. They said it has great food. I thought we'd try it."

"Sounds great, Jeff, let's go." Caleb was in his car starting the engine before Jeff could say anything.

"It's good to see some enthusiasm from you."

Fifteen minutes later, they entered the restaurant, which was an upscale steakhouse and saloon. The draw was the beer that they sold – seventy-seven different beers on tap and two hundred and fifty different bottled beers. Because they both had an alcoholic parent, Caleb and Jeff did not drink, although all the different kinds of beer fascinated them. The host met them when they walked in and quickly led to a table in the main dining area. The lighting was dim for dinnertime and lit candles were on every table. From their seats, they could look across the room and see the wall where all the beer taps were. Constructed of beer kegs, each keg had several taps in it. They watched for a moment as the bartender went from tap to tap pouring beers for other guests. The place was already beginning to get busy. A server came over, took their order and left them to talk.

Caleb was almost bouncing in his seat unable to sit still. It was not that the seats were uncomfortable, he had been sitting for so long earlier that he was a bit sore. Jeff watched him for a few minutes and then asked what was going on.

"Man, you've been bouncing since we left your place, what gives? Did you take some kind of medicine?"

"No, my seat is sore."

"What?"

"Jeff, you wanted to know what I've been doing all day, well I've been sitting at my computer since before lunch time and my butt's sore."

"You weren't working, were you?"

"No, I wasn't working. Remember that Internet dating

service I was telling you about earlier this week, the one I got a postcard from?"

"Yeah, I remember."

"Well, I thought I had thrown it away and it turns out I missed the trashcan. While I was cleaning up this morning, I found it. I was thinking about what you said about writing my future and trying something new...and...well, I signed up."

"Really?"

"Yeah, the first month was free so I figured if I wasn't satisfied I would just cancel it. Anyway, as I logged on this neat music came on and..."

Caleb went on to tell Jeff all about what had happened that morning and afternoon. He was like the Energizer Bunny. He only stopped to take a breath, even when the server brought their food he kept right on going.

"The neatest thing about it was that all the women it selected were pretty much the same. The only difference was the way they looked." Caleb had finally stopped and there was silence for a moment.

"So the only thing you have to do is choose the one whose looks you like the best, right?" Jeff said, finally able to speak.

"Yeah, I guess that's right."

Caleb had switched from a motor mouth to a placid-thinker. His eyes were looking up towards the ceiling and to the right. Thoughts of what to do next were running through his mind. *Who would I choose and why that one? Then what? I'd send her an e-mail and then what? What if she doesn't answer? How long do I wait? I guess I should have a first, second and third choice. Man, this is like choosing a car or a pet.*

"What are you thinking about?"

"Oh, Sorry Jeff. I guess I zoned out there for a moment. I was thinking of what to do next. I'm not quite sure how to proceed."

"I think you should look over the list, select the one that you feel would be a good match for you and send her an e-mail just to say hi and introduce yourself."

"Yeah, you're right. It doesn't have to be fancy and I don't really have to ask her out, I just want to get to know her."

"That's right."

"Boy, Jeff, thanks so much. If you had not encouraged me I'd be sitting here yawning from being bored all day."

"Caleb, remember the last time we talked I told you that God still has a plan for you?"

Caleb nodded, "Yes."

"Well, this could be a part of it. God could use this service to draw you to the person he wants you to meet for whatever reason. If you keep walking, God *will* direct your steps, but if you stop walking, he can't. It won't hurt to pray about it either."

"Thanks, Jeff. I understand what you are saying, but God and I are not talking much these days."

"I know, Caleb, but He is still listening."

"Okay, if you say so."

Caleb did not want to get into an argument with his friend especially since his friend had taken the time to check up on him. Most of the people from the church had not tried to contact Caleb. A few sent some e-mails at first but Caleb never replied. His guilt and embarrassment kept him secluded. Over time, the only person that stuck by him was his friend and partner. Caleb did not want to alienate him, so he dropped the subject.

They finished their meal with casual talk about the business, employees, plans for the future and who would pay the bill. As they walked out of the restaurant Caleb was reassuring Jeff.

"I'll have a date by Monday morning when I see you again."

**8**

*Monday, May 22, 2006, 8:00 AM:*

"Jeff," Caleb yelled from his car window as he drove into the parking lot at their office.

Walking up to the back door, Jeff stopped, turned and yelled back, "Hey, Caleb." Jeff waited for Caleb to join him. "How was the rest of your weekend, buddy?" Jeff asked as Caleb walked up.

"It was great."

Jeff had already unlocked the door and pulled it open as Caleb walked up. Caleb walked in first and entered the four-digit number on the alarm keypad to turn off the alarm. They both walked down the hall to the kitchen to start the coffee pot.

"Well, what did you decide about the dating service?" Jeff asked.

"I spent the rest of the weekend analyzing the seventeen matches. I reread all their profiles and made notes of the small differences. Then I studied each of their pictures wanting to see if any of them reminded me of someone else. I did not want to get involved with someone who reminded me of my past wives or a bad relationship. It might jinx the whole thing. There were twelve left after this. Next, I went and checked out where the women lived eliminating those that would create a long distance relationship. This shrunk the list down to six who live in the Richmond area. Then I tried to rank them in some kind of order but it felt too weird, like I was making up a Christmas wish list. So I decided to e-mail each of them and introduce myself."

"All six?"

"Yeah, I figure maybe one will answer and that would be the fate factor."

"Fate factor?"

"Yeah, you said that this might be God's handiwork and I figured if it is, he'll pick the one for me."

"Careful, Caleb, don't get cavalier with God's plan."

"I'm not. I know I'm making it sound that way but I'm really not. I sincerely hope that God will choose instead of me. I don't have a good track record."

"Okay, so you treated this like a school project, what happened?"

Caleb looked up at Jeff and simply said, "Nothing."

"Nothing?"

"Yeah, I didn't receive one reply. But the way I look at it is they have not had enough time to receive the e-mail, check out my profile and determine if they want to reply. I didn't get the e-mails out until late yesterday afternoon. It took me a while to go through my process."

"I see. You don't seem to be too disappointed about not having a date by this morning like you said."

"Well, I'm not. Being off the weekend and getting involved

in something new has made me feel alive again. I'm curious about my future again and what's more, I realize that I could have one."

The coffee was ready and Caleb poured a cup for each of them. They heard the chime from the back door that indicated someone had walked in and they knew the staff was arriving. Jeff started to get up and head for his office but Caleb grabbed his arm and stopped him.

"Jeff, I just wanted to thank you once more for making me take some time off. It was a great idea and I do feel much better."

"You're welcome, buddy. Just keep me informed of what happens in your new soap opera."

"Hey, maybe you should try it," Caleb said as they left the kitchen.

* * *

For the past two hours, Rachel had been in the Human Resources office of A. E. Research. Durran had returned her call last week and asked her to show up at eight-o'clock this morning. She arrived a little early and greeted by the same young man at the reception desk with the exact same greeting she had received last week. She wondered if the person was able to say anything else or if he had a small repertoire and it had cycled around to the same point where it was last week when she first came in. A feeling of déjà-vu came over her as Ms. Yvette came walking down the hall. Rachel was prepared this time. She jumped up as soon as she saw Ms. Yvette and before she made it to the reception desk Rachel was already there. Ms. Yvette gave her a puzzled look and then turned to escort her to Durran's office. Rachel was on her heels all the way.

There was much to do this first day. From getting her picture taken for her ID badge to being fingerprinted for office records. There was a corporate video she was shown and a stack of forms she had to fill out. She even met with the head of the security department, Mr. Myers, who went over the security procedures for the building and staff. It was almost noon and Rachel was already getting tired. She had not left the conference room that Durran had taken her to, and one by one people came in and out to talk to her or give her something. She felt like a ping-pong ball in a round-robin contest bounced from one person to another, then to another and back again as the people rotated in and out of the room. Finally, Durran returned and instructed her to gather her things. He was taking her to meet her new boss.

Jane Madison's office was on the fifteenth floor in the north corner of the building. It overlooked Eighth Street, but did not have much of a view. Durran and Rachel met Jane on her way to her office and Durran introduced Rachel. He thanked her, wished her well and left them. Jane invited Rachel to her office and Rachel followed the rest of the way.

"Please have a seat," Jane said as she walked into her office and pointed to the couch on her right.

The couch was up against the glass wall at the front of her office and faced the large glass windows behind Jane's desk. Rachel entered the office behind Jane and quickly took a seat setting her file of papers and her purse on the couch next to her.

"Thank you, Ms. Madison."

Jane walked to her desk and placed the files she was holding on it. Picking up the phone, she looked at Rachel, "Would you like some coffee, I'll have my assistant bring us some." She waited for a reply before pressing any buttons.

"Yes, thank you that would be nice."

After hanging up the phone, Jane walked over to a Queen Ann chair next to the couch and sat down.

"Well, how's your morning been so far?"

"I feel like I've been the baton in a ten man relay race. I didn't expect to be fingerprinted or have to fill out so many forms," Rachel said as she patted the file of papers Durran had given her.

"Yes, I know. When the government is funding your endeavor it seems things go a little overboard."

"Government? Like as in the United States Government?"

"Yes, didn't Durran tell you?"

Rachel shook her head from side to side and was about to speak when a woman walked into the office carrying a tray with a pot, two cups with saucers, a sugar bowl, creamer and two spoons.

"Excuse me, Ms. Madison, here's your coffee."

"Thank you, Elsa."

Elsa placed the tray on the coffee table in front of the couch and left. Jane poured a cup for Rachel, placed a spoon on the saucer next to the cup and handed it to her. Rachel was very impressed that Jane was using real china.

"Tell me, what did Durran tell you about us?" Jane said as she poured her own coffee.

"To tell you the truth he was a little vague. I knew the government was a client, but didn't know the company was funded by them."

"Durran likes to make it sound like they pay us for our work. The reality is they are responsible for most of what you see around you. We currently operate out of this building because it does not advertise that it is government run. Our operation tries to stay out of the limelight so that we can accomplish things that we would not otherwise be able to."

Jane and Rachel both took sips of their coffee before continuing. Rachel took a moment to scan the room. On one side of Jane's office, near the door, was a wall of certificates, degrees and awards. The opposite wall was a floor-to-ceiling bookcase filled with books, pictures, knick-knacks, a stereo and a TV. The windows behind her desk and the wall behind the couch had blinds and curtains pulled open. The office almost had the air of an apartment without a bathroom, kitchen and bedroom.

"So, tell me about yourself. I like to get to know my staff when they first arrive."

"Well, I was raised in Blacksburg with my sister, Amanda," Rachel began. "My mother is a housewife and my father works at the weather station on the campus of Virginia Tech. My sister and I were very close and took up the same interest in psychology when we were young. After several years at Virginia Tech., Amanda started losing interest in school and decided to move to Richmond. She took a job with a middle school and became a teacher's assistant, where she did well and the kids loved her. A little over a year later, she was murdered. That was ten years ago. She was my best friend and I went nuts. I had a hard time dealing with the senselessness of it. She was in the wrong place at the wrong time and was kidnapped and killed. My struggle brought me to the point of giving up on the field of psychology until a doctor here in Richmond helped me get through my grief. I wanted so badly to understand why someone would kill another person for no reason, so I completed my education and earned my Ph.D. My goal is to help others deal with the same kind of things I had to."

Rachel paused, took another sip of her coffee, and watched Jane to see her reaction to what she had just heard. Her face was emotionless. She sipped her coffee as well and let Rachel continue.

"My hope was that I would land a job working for a hospital working with trauma patients. I never dreamed of working for a research company, especially one funded by the government. I've had a lot of practice though and it seems like a very exciting opportunity."

Rachel went back to sipping her coffee. It was Jane's turn to share.

"Yes, it can be exciting, as many things can be depending on how you approach them. There are many aspects of our department and we do a variety of things. Sometimes we're asked to generate a list of questions that can help identify what type of people work for a company or shop at a certain store or buy certain products. We have several departments that will then use those questions, create surveys, and take them to these companies to get their employees to complete them. The surveys get returned, we analyze them and we pass the results on to our management team who reviews them with the client. Our main focus, and the place where you will start, is The Connection."

"The Connection?" Rachel asked.

"Yes. It is an Internet dating website. We use it to learn more about who people are. The information we gain allows us to help other people."

"How?"

"For example, several years ago there was a mayoral race in a small town in the mountains of North Carolina. The current mayor was going to step down due to health reasons and they needed a new one. The only person who announced he would run for the job was known to have connections with the timber industry. It was leaked that this candidate, if elected, would award contracts to several timber companies to come in and cut downs trees along five-hundred acres of land that bordered on a wildlife preserve. The people were afraid that any development would affect the wildlife. But there was no one to run against this guy. The Federal Government got wind of the situation, but they did not want to go in and make choices for these people and have to deal with future cases like this, so they got us involved. Using The Connection, we found a man who wanted to serve in this capacity who was concerned with saving the environment. We helped him set up his residence in that town and introduced him to many of the locals. When time came for the election, his name was on the ballot and he won. A successful conclusion to a potential nightmare. These are the kinds of things we do here."

"I'm impressed. I had no idea a company like this existed. How do you get your information?"

"We have thousands of people working for us in all kinds of areas all over the world who pass information back and forth. We are also tied into networks, cable stations and radio stations around the world. We get information from so many different sources and we hire only the best and the brightest so that this information can be processed in the most efficient and effective manners. Our computer equipment is the best money can buy. Some of the hardware and much of the software that we use cannot be purchased on the streets."

"It all sounds so overwhelming," Rachel said, trying to absorb the massiveness of the operation of which she had just become a part.

"We'll take it slowly. It will take you some time before you are fully up to speed. The fact that you have been hired means someone believes you can do this."

The hairs on the back of Rachel's neck stood up. It was not what she had just heard that caused her to stare at Jane, but the way it was said. Tthere was a tone of disapproval with a slight edge of tongue-and-cheek that sounded as if Jane was challenging her, as if daring her to play the game.

"I assure you, I am a very quick learner and an expert at research. Besides that, I am very knowledgeable in my field." Rachel did not want to seem as if she was throwing out her own challenge.

"I'm sure you are," Jane said.

Watching Jane's eyes, Rachel caught a look that told her she was trying to soften the blow of her previous words.

"I'm sorry. I was trying to pay you a compliment. Perhaps it didn't come out in the right tone."

Rachel shrank back, a little embarrassed, but still cautious. "I'm sorry too. I'm always on the defensive when I meet new people. Please forgive me, Ms. Madison, for being a little too forceful about my abilities."

Jane's expression transformed from a competitor into one of acceptance and respect. Although Rachel was not sure what had just happened she understood that there was more to this little exchange than competition.

"I suppose you should call me, Jane."

This confirmed what Rachel was thinking about something happening and she smiled.

"You're going to be a fine addition to our team," Jane said as she placed her coffee cup and saucer on the tray. She got up, walked over to her desk and picked up a thick folder. When she returned she sat next to Rachel and handed the folder to her.

"This is your first assignment. There is information in there about the need, the people involved and The Connection. Read the file, get familiar with the information and the website and we will meet again tomorrow morning to discuss it in more detail. Agreed?"

Rachel returned her cup and saucer to the tray and stood up following Jane's lead, "Agreed."

"Would you like to see your office now?"

"Office?" Rachel had not thought about this before now. Her

expectation was to sit at a cubical somewhere on the floor with hundreds of others, but as she walked out of Jane's office carrying her folders she noticed that there were no cubicles, only offices.

Jane led Rachel to the opposite end of the floor, to an office on the west side of the building. It was much smaller than Jane's was, with a clear view of the James River. Rachel walked in and placed her folders on the desk.

"Welcome to A. E. Research," Jane said as she reached out a hand.

Rachel took her hand and gave it a firm shake, "Thanks, Jane, it's good to be here."

"If you need anything you know where I am. I'll see you tomorrow morning."

With that said, Jane turned and walked out of the office closing the door behind her and leaving Rachel to take in her new surroundings. She noticed the hook on the back of the door, removed her suit jacket and hung it on the hook. For a few minutes, she walked around the office inspecting the furniture, which was not as nice as Jane's, but was still very comfortable and stylish. The set up was similar to Jane's office. A couch up against the glass wall at the front of the office, a bookcase that spanned the left wall and rose up to meet the chair rail, a desk, large and made of cherry wood, sat almost in the center of the room with its matching credenza against the wall to the right. In front of the desk were two armchairs with leather seats and behind the desk were the usual floor-to-ceiling windows, but these did not have blinds or curtains. It did not matter to Rachel. She had her own office with a view of the river! She opened her assignment folder labeled, *Brian Albertson*.

Ten minutes later a young quirky kind of person knocked on Rachel's closed office door, opened it and poked his head in.

"Hey! You must be the new help?"

Rachel looked up from her reading startled and confused, "Oh, help?"

"I'm Ian Clark," he said as he walked into her office without an invitation, "You are the new help, aren't you?"

Rachel watched him walk up to her desk. He was a short lanky fellow that looked to be in his early twenties, wearing khaki slacks and a light blue polo shirt with a breast pocket that was bulging a bit. On his feet, he wore tan loafers and no socks. His hair was short almost to the point of not existing. He had a cute face but his cockiness did not make him attractive.

"Yes, I'm the *new hire*." Rachel repeated his words wondering how long she would be referred to in this way. "My name is Rachel Gilbert."

"Well, it's nice to meet you, Rachel," Clark said as he extended his hand and sat in one of the chairs facing her desk.

Rachel lightly grabbed Clark's hand, partly because she was unsure of him and partly because he sat down so fast that his hand came out of hers.

"I'm the Network Specialist for this place," he said in a bragging tone. "I'll be setting up your access to the system. If you haven't already found out you won't be able to log on to the system without security clearance and a password. I do this for all the new hires." He pulled a little pad out of the breast pocket of his shirt and pulled a little pencil out of the spiral binding of the pad. "Rachel, is that with a Y or a C?" he asked.

"R-a-c-h-e-l." She spelled it out for him thinking he could not spell at all. "Gilbert, G-i-l-b-e-r-t."

Clark wrote as Rachel spoke. "Thanks," he said when she finished. "I will also need to get a password from you. It can be anything up to sixteen characters, including numbers and special characters." He looked up at her, pencil in hand ready to write as she spoke.

Rachel sat back and thought for a moment, there was only one password she had used for everything in the past ten years. She wondered if she should use it here. Finally, she could think of no reason why she should change. The password had always been a tribute and it would continue to be. She looked at Clark as he sat there waiting. His expression reminded her of a dog waiting for his treat. She could almost picture his tongue hanging out in anticipation. He liked this job way too much. She wondered how long he would sit there waiting and thought about waiting him out to see, but then changed her mind.

"Amanda," she said. "That's A-m-a-n-d-a."

Clark looked at her puzzled. She could tell he was trying to figure out why this name. He started to speak then stopped. His expression changed and he continued, "Okay, Amanda it is. It's not very cryptic, but it'll do. I'll get your level of security from Ms. Madison. My extension is 3476. I should have you set up by late this afternoon, which means by tomorrow morning you'll be able to get on the system. Call me when you're ready and I'll come up and show you how to log on." He placed the pencil back in the spiral of the notebook and replaced it in his shirt pocket. Jumping up he said his thanks and hurried out the door.

"What is it with these guys today?" she said to herself.

Looking down at her desk Rachel saw the folder full of paperwork that she had to fill out for Durran. She had already lost her train of thought about her project folder and would have to start over again. She decided it would be better to get the paperwork out of the way now so she could focus on her project. She sat down and opened the folder containing the paperwork. The title of the document on top of the stack read, "Application for FBI Security Clearance."

# 9

A sense of pride and relief came over Rachel as she walked, unescorted, to her office this morning. There was no race and no one to follow, just a direct route to her new home carrying a box of personal items. The halls at A. E. Research were already buzzing with activity and she was eager to join in, however, she had an important task had to do first – to make her new space hers. Inside the box were special trinkets collected from here and there during her time at Virginia Tech., pictures of friends, her parents and her sister, a collection of books and her framed diploma.

After removing her jacket and pulling the hammer and nails out of the box, she quickly went to work placing things just where she wanted them. She hung the pictures, placed the books in her bookcase and set up the trinkets around the office. The last item out of the box was a picture of Amanda and her taken before Amanda died. Sitting at her desk, she placed the tools back inside the box and removed it from the desk. She set this last picture next to the computer monitor where she could see it when she worked. It was going to be the reminder of her purpose in life.

"I'm going to make you proud," she said to the picture.

Then, seeing the folder for Albertson on her desk, she added as a caveat, "Give me a little time, though."

Next to the phone was a list of extensions for the staff. She found Jane's number and dialed it.

"Jane Madison."

"Jane, hi, it's Rachel. I was checking to see if you were in. When would you like to meet?"

"Have you gone through the file?"

"Yes, and I'm a little confused about what I'm supposed to do with this information."

"Why don't you bring everything to my office. I'll have some coffee brought in and we can go through it together."

"That sounds great. I'll be there in a few minutes."

*Information, or knowledge, alone is not power until you understand how the information relates, and then it's only effective if you understand how to use it.* For years Rachel's father tried to explain this to her from the standpoint of the weather, but she never really grasped what he meant. This morning it was becoming a little clearer. There were many pieces of data, but how did they fit together and what was the next step? *What's the objective, the overall goal here?* These were some of the questions she hoped Jane would answer.

When Rachel reached Jane's office Elsa was already leaving and Jane was pouring the coffee.

"Hey, Rachel. Please have a seat and some coffee."

After seating herself and sipping her own coffee, Jane began, "Okay, let's start with what you've learned."

"Well," Rachel said putting her coffee cup down. "First, Brian Albertson, a faith healer, has been operating in the Richmond area for about four years now. His information says he's from Jamaica, however, there's no birth records or addresses from there. From his picture, he doesn't look much like a Jamaican so I'm thinking he wasn't born there."

"That's a fair assumption," Jane interjected while sipping more of her coffee.

"Second, there are several pictures and reports of meetings between some known drug dealers and Albertson. There is no record of these meetings going on for any length of time and they all happened before or after one of Albertson's tent meetings. This could mean that these guys are interested in what he has to say or they are truly working through him. Along with these, other drug dealers and known users have attended Albertson's tent meetings, but they haven't had personal meetings with him.

"Third, two attempts on Albertson's life have been made over the past two years. In each case, one of Albertson's followers threw himself in front of Albertson to protect him. The followers died to save their leader.

"Lastly, several law enforcement groups have tried and failed to discover how the drugs are changing hands."

"My, you *have* done your homework."

"Well, thanks, Jane, but it's really all here in the file."

"Yes, but you have consolidated it nicely."

"But what does this mean? How can this information help us to expose this guy?"

"Those are good questions and to answer them you'll need to see the problem from a different perspective. Right now, you see Albertson as a criminal who is performing illegal acts. You can't see how to stop him because you see it as a legal issue and you're not a cop."

"Okay, that's true, but how else should I look at it?"

"What would you do if Albertson came to you for therapy?"

"Therapy? For what?"

"For his illness."

"What illness?"

"Now, that's a good question, Rachel. At the hospital, how many people came to you because they believed they had an illness?"

"Well, very few. Most of my work dealt with some aspect of trauma."

"Exactly. To help them you had to understand the nature of the trauma and how it affected them, right?"

"Yes," Rachel admitted not knowing where Jane was going with this.

"It's the same here. To see how to expose the trauma for what it is you first need to find out how it's interpreted by the patient. You need to understand Albertson. Who is he and how does he think? This is part of the research you'll do, however, the biggest help you'll get is from someone who has a passion about exposing him. Someone who is willing to get close and find answers to your questions."

"Who?"

"That's where The Connection comes in. Using The Connection, you'll find a match-subject who will seek out Albertson and learn how to expose him. Your job is to feed this subject the pertinent information at the right time to influence him to do the task."

"This sounds like manipulation."

"True, it does, but it's really not. By knowing Albertson, you'll be able to search The Connection database for someone who wants to do this kind of task but doesn't have the opportunity. We are simply providing him or her with the opportunity. So you see it's not manipulation at all."

The morning had been going well so far. The tension Rachel had felt between her and Jane the day before was gone and their conversation was moving along nicely. However, this last comment brought back the same cautious feelings she had felt yesterday. A volley of thoughts ran through her mind. *I'm being too cautious before I really know what's going on. But I must stay true to my feelings because they have always served me well before. If this place is doing illegal things, why is the government supporting them? However, governments hide things all the time...*

"Rachel, are you still with me?"

"Oh...yes, sorry, drifted there for a moment. This sounds so much bigger than it did when I came in here."

"Like in therapy, if you break things down into small pieces first, each piece becomes manageable. I suggest you start by creating a psychological profile of Albertson."

Holding up the file Rachel expressed, "There's not much

information in the file to work from."

"Yes, I know. Your best bet is to search our company's research files for all you can find on Albertson. When you've gotten what you need we can meet again."

Back in her office, Rachel started a list of tasks. Confusion became the enemy to overcome for now. She knew she did not totally understand all the ins and outs of A. E. Research, but this was not feeling right. Using her ability as a therapist to influence behavior was one thing; this seemed to be using it for the wrong reasons. The fact that the outcome would be something good left her wondering if the end does in fact justify the means.

*Research would provide the answer* she thought, and she went to work. The lack of response from her computer after a few keystrokes reminded her of what Clark had said the day before. She was not looking forward to experiencing him again, though to move forward she needed his help. She picked up the phone and dialed his extension.

* * *

Two things made Caleb smile as Jeff walked into his office and he was eager to share them.

"I can see there's something on your mind, buddy. Okay, spill it."

"Jeff, I've been sitting here for the past two hours working on paying bills and I discovered two things. First, I've been very focused. It's been a long time since I've been able to work on a task for any length of time without building up some anxiety. Today, I've been able to work through all the bills and get them caught up and stayed completely calm. On top of this, the other thing I discovered is that we made more money this past month than we did in March and we made more money in March than we did in February. If this trend continues we might be able to buy a couple of bigger trucks soon."

"Caleb, that's great news. I'm glad to see that both of us are doing much better."

"Of course, it would be helpful if we could pick up some more business."

"Well, let me add to your day. I received a couple of calls yesterday from people who are looking to transport some goods from the coast back to Richmond. I have three deliveries to take to the coast tomorrow and one to bring back on Friday. What do you think about me staying out there until Friday and using the extra time to talk to these new folks and see what happens?"

"I think that's a great idea, Jeff! Do you know much about these folks and their businesses?"

"No, not yet, but by the time I return on Friday I'll know all we need to know."

"Wonderful. Hey, I'm feeling so good, how about I take you to lunch?"

"If you're buying, I'm in."

\* \* \*

She was surprised at the depth of knowledge that Clark had and the ease at which he shared it. He was different today, or was she the different one; it was hard for her to tell. He was not so mysterious or scary today. What made the change? Whatever it was was not important, she was logged on now and searching through the massive amounts of information A. E. Research had stored in its computers.

Among the newspaper files she found the same article she had found at the library plus many others, all of them expressing the many positive things that A. E. Research had done for the community and the country. Again, she felt the conflict inside her start to build and she had to push it back down. It was the wrong time and place. *A. E. Research is doing good things; I just need to learn more before passing judgment.*

There were too many articles on Albertson to read on the computer. She needed to print them and go through her routine to absorb the information. She watched the video files and then saved them on her computer as well as the additional pictures she found.

According to the videos, Albertson was developing a large following. Some of the people interviewed believed he could do miracles and heal people from all kinds of lifelong ailments. Respected religious leaders believed him to be a fraud. Law enforcement officers claimed he had not broken any laws and he had the correct permits for his tent meetings. He seemed to be legit.

Several hours later after reading through the articles and reviewing the videos again, she found herself staring at his picture. "Who are you?"

*Interaction was always a key to working with a patient at the hospital. The expressions on their face or their body language helped to know them, not to mention what they could express verbally. But to understand someone from things others said about them was totally foreign. What's true and what's not? Whose information is tied to their own agenda?*

The task was running away from her again and she had to push down her feelings and curb the questions in her mind. *Pieces, must keep it in do-able pieces. Psychological profile first.*

Turning to her computer, she paused for a moment to take in the picture of Amanda and her. Even though not physically there, Amanda's image had a comforting and calming effect on her. Opening up her word-processor program, she started a new file. In it, she listed all the facts she knew about Albertson and what conclusions she could come to from them. As an afterthought, she added a section about what others thought about him. She saved the file with the name *Psych-Profile-Albertson.*

Without even noticing, the day had slipped away from her. It was not until Jane was standing in her doorway that she realized what time it was.

"Hey, just dropped by to see how things are going."

"Oh, hi, I guess okay. I've been working on the profile for Albertson. It was easier to do at the hospital where the patient was there to ask questions. I've been able to put together a limited profile with the information I've found."

"That's great. How about we meet tomorrow afternoon at one-o'clock to go over what you have?"

"Sure thing, Jane."

Jane started out the door and stopped abruptly, then walked back into Rachel's office.

"One more thing, you'll need to create a profile on The Connection for yourself."

"A profile for me? Why?"

"Each researcher creates a dummy profile. This way, as they locate their match-subject, they can communicate with that person to gain more information about them. The key to making this all work is getting as much information as possible."

Once again, Jane headed out the door and stopped. This time she poked her head back in and added, "By the way, don't use your real name either." With that said, she disappeared down the hallway.

*A dummy profile? For me? But not my real name? Play the matchmaker and be the match too?* This was getting much larger than Rachel could have ever believed and she longed to be back at the hospital where life seemed simpler. Nevertheless, it was not an adventure like this.

Pulling out a pad and pen, she started writing down female names that came to mind. She wrote several names down and scratched them out because they just did not seem to fit her. Frustrated, she sat back in her chair and looked around the office as if a name were on the wall somewhere. Scanning across her desk, she saw the picture of Amanda and her. For a moment, she stared at Amanda's eyes for a sign of approval. Through a connection only found between sisters as close as they were, she got her approval and wrote *A-M-A-N-D-A*.

This action sparked a memory sensor that transported her back to the kitchen of her Blacksburg home where she watched her father answer the phone. At first, he seemed puzzled and confused. *Who was he talking to?* Then the fear that captured his eyes told her something terrible had happened. He sank to the floor with tears rolling down his face and she knew someone had died.

Quickly the memory changed to the McCoy Funeral Home prior to everyone getting there. Draped over the closed coffin Rachel wept for her sister wanting to see her once more, to say good-bye, to have one last hug.

Another scene change and she was standing in the doorway of the shed in the backyard of her home. On the floor in front of her, was her father sobbing and repeating, "It's all my fault." His cherished fishing poles lay broken in many pieces on the floor next to him.

Fast forward and she is sitting in her living room with her parents as the detective is explaining that they have exhausted every lead and have no clue who the killer was or where he might be. The case would remain open, but there was little hope it would be solved.

Unconsciously, while these memories played out, Rachel's hand moved the pen over what she had just written. Touched and sadden by the memories, tears began rolling down her cheeks. The memories disappeared and she was back to reality when a single tear fell on her hand. Conscious of where she was and what had happened she looked down at the pad and was surprised at what she saw; *A-N-█-N-█-A*.

Clark surprised her when he poked his head in her office. "Hey, you still here?"

Startled, but keeping her face staring down at the desk, she quickly tried to compose herself.

"Are you going to stay any later?"

Rachel could not look up or answer him yet.

"Because if you are the guards at the front desk need to know."

Feeling composed, she looked up at him but did not say anything. When she met his eyes she could tell he was concerned.

"Are you okay?"

"Yes, I'm fine. It's been a long day and I'm just tired."

"So you're not staying?"

"No, I'll be leaving shortly."

"Okay. Well I'll see you tomorrow."

Clark disappeared as quickly as he came without waiting for a response. *Youth and manners just don't go together* Rachel thought as she looked down at the pad again. A few seconds later, she looked up, out the glass wall of the front of her office and down the hallway, which Clark had just gone down. Looking back down at the pad, she smiled and wrote *C-L-A-R-K* after the name *A-N-N-A*.

"Anna Clark," she whispered and then nodded her head.

Dropping the pen and picking up her purse, she headed to the door. She pulled her suit jacket from the hook on the back of the door and stopped to look back in her office.

"Anna Clark."

Satisfied, she turned out her light.

**10**

"Ladies and gentlemen," Michaels said after Kahn yielded the floor to him. "I would like to thank you for the quick and extensive work you have done pertaining to the Cottonwood Lake dilemma. You have come up with an excellent plan of containment, so congratulations. Please keep me updated through e-mails as things progress."

Rising to take his usual position at the door, Michaels gave Kahn the cue to end this week's status meeting and dismiss the guests. Like a trained dog, Kahn went to work.

Once dismissed, the department heads and their assistants filed out past Michaels as he shook hands and patted shoulders. Spotting Madison, he called her over to him.

"Ms. Madison, how is your new staff member doing?"

"She is doing well, sir. Thanks for the help."

Hesitating and expressing his discontent with a scowl, he scolded her. "Ms. Madison, you know as well as I do that your comment tells me nothing. Has she caught on to her job? Is she proving capable? Does she have reservations? These are the types of questions I expect you to answer for me."

"I see," she answered with a smile, clearly enjoying the conflict.

Angered at her seeming insubordination but pleased she accepted the challenge; he fired back at her. "So tell me, Ms. Madison, how *is* she doing?"

"Sir," her smile widening, "she has proven capable and has taken to her task quickly with little reservation. I am meeting with her often and each time she progresses. I hope this satisfies your curiosity."

"Indeed it does," he said through slightly clenched teeth. Realizing that she had won this volley, he tried intimidation. "Would you be offended if I paid her a little visit, just to meet her and welcome her?" Meeting new employees was never something Michaels did or even wanted to do. He only wanted to interact with those that attended his weekly meeting, so he knew this would throw her off guard.

With the smile gone and slightly fumbling for words, she replied, "No sir. I...I...have no reason to be offended. When...would you like to come by?"

He left her hanging with a wink. "I'll let you know when I can fit it in. Thanks."

* * *

Releasing the pressure valve on the pallet-jack, Jeff dropped off the final load of medical testing kits heading for Egypt and returned to the truck to secure the pallet-jack. Climbing down out of the back, he saw Pete, the civilian supervisor in charge of the shipping warehouse on Walker Airfield. Although Fort Monroe was an Army training base, like many military bases civilians were hired from nearby towns, in this case Hampton, Virginia, to fill the non-military positions.

Jeff grabbed the clipboard he left sitting on the floor inside the truck, checked off and initialed the total number of cases delivered and handed the clipboard to Pete.

"I just need your signature and I'll be out of your way."

Taking the clipboard from Jeff and signing his name at the bottom of the shipping invoice, Pete asked, "Jeff, you up for a drink?"

"Man, Pete, I'd love to, but I've got one more delivery to make before my day is over."

"You heading back today?" Pete handed back the clipboard.

"No, I'm staying until Friday. I've got a shipment to pick up on Friday and tomorrow I've got new clients to meet. In fact, you might be able to help me. I'm supposed to meet a man named Ymir Waldemar. He's a foreman at the Newport News Dry Dock. Ever heard of him?"

Pete paused for a minute and then asked some of his people if they knew of Waldemar. All the faces were blank and no one responded. "Apparently he's not well known. I've got a man out sick who used to work at the shipyard, I'll talk to him tomorrow if he comes in and I'll give you a call."

"Thanks, Pete."

"Hey, if you're staying in town why don't we get together

for dinner and that drink?"

"Sorry, Pete, my last stop is going to take me up to the Newport News International Airport. My staff booked me in a hotel around the corner from the airport and I'll have to spend the evening putting contracts together in case things work out tomorrow."

"Okay, Mr. Important! I'll catch you next time."

Jeff chuckled, shook hands with Pete, handed him his copy of the invoice and then climbed up into the cab of the truck. He regretted not being able to have dinner with Pete because Pete always made him laugh. Although they always talked about drinking, they never did. Pete was a recovering alcoholic and Jeff had been one of the few friends Pete had that helped him get sober. However, he had to stay focused on the potential new clients. This could be the break he and Caleb needed to move their business to the next level and he was not about to let anything distract him from his task.

As he drove off the Army base, he waved at the guards at the front gate following Ingalls Road heading for Mallory Street and I-64 that would take him northwest to the Newport News airport.

* * *

The meeting with Jane had gone well. They talked about many things including Albertson's profile. While Jane shared her views and ideas, Rachel made numerous notes. Even though they had only known each other for a short time, Rachel was feeling connected with Jane and hoped Jane felt the same.

After a long lunch, Rachel spent some time updating Albertson's profile and created a profile on The Connection for Anna Clark, which took up most of her afternoon and as the day was winding down, so was she. For the past thirty minutes, she had been reviewing her notes on the next couple of steps when her phone rang.

"Psych. Research, Rachel Gilbert speaking."

"Rachel, hello."

"Admiral Garry, how nice to hear your voice."

"Am I disturbing you?"

"Of course not. Nothing is too important to not talk to you. What's up?"

"Well, I did some checking like you asked and I wanted to fill you in on what I found, or rather didn't find."

Curious, but not worried, Rachel asked, "What did you *not* find?"

"I asked around about Michaels and no one seems to know or has ever heard of him. A few colleagues do know some of the board members of A. E. Research, but don't know much about the company, other than that they do research for many different kinds of clients. I checked some records and found some of the same information you had already found, but not much more."

"You sound disappointed, Admiral."

"Somewhat, yes. This guy, Jason Michaels, doesn't seem to have much of a past. I can't locate where he's from or what his background is. There isn't even a traffic violation on him. If he's got a home or apartment it's not listed under his name, although I did find out that A. E. Research owns several homes around Richmond. He might live in one of them. There are some classified records on him, and I don't have the authority to get access to them, not without some legal cause."

"So what are you saying, Admiral?"

"What I'm saying is, this guy is almost a ghost, like he doesn't exist. This could mean one of two things. The first possibility is that he is totally connected to the government in which case they, for some reason, don't want people to know who he is. Maybe for his protection, maybe for theirs. The other possibility is that he is connected with some very influential and wealthy people who also don't want him to be known. These people could be criminals, such as the mob, or they could be legit, such as financial tycoons. Either way, there are some powerful people who are going through a lot of trouble to make sure no one knows too much about this guy."

"Admiral, are you saying that I'm in some kind of trouble? If I am, what about all the others that work here and have for years?"

In the back of her mind, she started wondering if Garry was taking this *watching-over* bit a little too serious. It seemed as if he was overreacting. This was not like the Admiral Garry she knew. He was always calm in the center of a storm and nothing ever seemed to scare or worry him.

"I'm not suggesting anything at this point, only that there's more to this than it seems like up front. Are you able to talk about what you are working on?"

"Well, no. I have several government clearances to do the

research I'm doing, but I'm not allowed to share this information with anyone outside of the company."

"Are you uncomfortable at all with what they have asked you to do?"

Rachel spent a few minutes thinking about her answer to this question. She knew she had reservations at first but things seemed to be progressing in a way that did not leave her uneasy about her tasks. The interaction had not started with the match-subject yet and she was not sure what she might feel at that point, however, for now, things seemed okay. There was not much use in getting an old friend all worked up over nothing so she convinced herself and him that there was nothing to worry about.

"Everything here is just fine, Admiral. I'm actually enjoying the interaction I'm having in a world outside of school and the hospital."

"You know I trust your judgment, dear, but I want you to keep your eyes and ears open and be careful. If you become scared or suspect anything wrong you call me right away, okay?"

"Yes, Admiral, I will."

"And if you come up with any additional information on Michaels that you want me to check out, let me know. I'll touch base every few days just to see how things are going."

"Thank you, Admiral, but you don't have to."

"I'd feel much better if I did."

She heard Garry hang up his phone, but before she hung up, she heard a number of clicks as if several phones were hanging up or the phone had come unplugged. She checked the wire under her desk to see if it was loose. It seemed secure but she pulled it out and plugged it back in just in case. Putting the receiver to her ear, she heard that familiar dial tone and assumed everything was fine now. *I must have kicked it with my foot.*

* * *

Michaels hung up the phone on his desk while Myers hung up the extension at the wet bar. Both were silent after hearing the conversation between Rachel and Garry. As Myers took a seat in front of the desk, Michaels walked over to the bar and poured a drink for the two of them.

"Myers, how much do you know about this lawyer, Garry? Is he a potential threat?"

"He's a has-been lawyer, sir, who had his glory days in the Jag Corps. Other lawyers didn't want to come up against him and his clients were pleased to have him represent them. He earned several citations and even wrote a book on Navy Defense Strategies. However, most of his fame was lost when he defended a drunken sailor who assaulted his commander. The sailor swore there were words but no punches. However, the commander had him locked up and, according to the sailor, sent several other sailors to his cell to teach him a lesson. No one but Garry believed the sailor. The commander was well known and on his way up the ladder. At the trial, Garry produced another sailor who testified that he saw the men beating up the first sailor in the cell. The commander lost his command and his goons where dishonorably discharged. After that, no one trusted Garry, so he retired and started his own law firm here in Richmond. He does not take high profile cases anymore and keeps himself in the background, but he's very thorough and he can't be bought."

Michaels quipped, "You didn't answer my second question." He handed Myers a tumbler of scotch and took a seat across from him. "Is he a threat?"

"Sir, I'm hard pressed to answer that question. Is he a threat to us losing this Gilbert girl? Maybe. Is he a threat to our organization? I don't believe so. We've made sure that all information about you and this company is classified so no one can access it without your approval. I don't see how he could interfere with our work."

For a few minutes, Michaels thought about what Myers had said. Myers had a history of judging people correctly; he had a sixth sense about it. However, Michaels also trusted his belief that no one is to be trusted all the time no matter how many times they have been right in the past. There was no room for resting on one's laurels.

"Myers, do you know what's intriguing about a fly in your soup, other than the obvious?"

Myers was taking a sip of his scotch when Michaels asked this question and it caught him off guard. "No," he said through coughs from choking down the drink.

"The fact that something that's not supposed to be there somehow got there. Although you may feel Garry is not a problem, I do. Make sure someone is following him and report on the things he's doing, especially on what research he does. I want to know about every ghost he's chasing."

* * *

It was an early evening dinner at a small restaurant about fifteen miles southwest of Richmond. Rachel sat there staring at her sister, who sat across from her, wondering why she chose this place. Amanda was engrossed in checking the place over. She kept looking at her watch and looking out the front window and around the room as if she was expecting someone.

Rachel tried to talk. The words formed in her head and her mouth moved to speak them, but no sound came out. *Why?* She could hear them clearly in her head. Again, she tried, and again there was no sound. She looked for help from Amanda who was still too occupied with looking around to notice the problem Rachel was having.

Behind her, Rachel heard the bell tied to the front door's doorknob. She knew someone had walked in. She could also tell because Amanda stopped looking around for a moment and stared at the front door. Whoever came in walked past them to a back table and sat down. Amanda went back to her scanning.

Still unable to make a sound and now waving to get her sister's attention, Rachel became very concerned that her sister was not even acknowledging that she was there. *How rude! What's happened since you moved? You had better manners back in Blacksburg.*

Amanda focused on the front door again as another person walked in. She did not recognize him either and resumed her scanning. However, this person, a young man in a trench coat, stopped at their table and spoke. *His* voice made sound.

"Hey, are you Amanda?"

"Who are you?"

"I'm the guy you're supposed to meet." He took a seat.

"How do you know I'm meeting someone here?"

Rachel tried to ask the person what his name was, but still there was no sound coming out of her mouth. There was something familiar about him and she wished he would turn to look at her so she could see his whole face.

"I know you're meeting someone here because I set up the meeting. I'm Joe. You sent me your picture so I would know what you look like. You're Amanda." He pulled out a small picture from his inside coat pocket and showed it to Amanda. "I think we should talk outside."

"Outside? Why? About what?"

Joe grabbed Amanda's arm and started to lift her out of her seat, which she protested. Rachel tried to scream for help. Still nothing came out. Suddenly Joe stopped and glared out the front window. Rachel turned around and saw what stunned him. Coming up the road were flashing blue lights from several police cars.

"Damn, the cops!"

"Cops..." Scared and grateful at the same time, Amanda barely got the words out before Joe yanked her up and led her towards the back of the restaurant.

Once again, Rachel tried to scream for help, but it was no use. Her voice just was not there. She went to stand to help her sister and found that her body would not move either. A tremendous feeling of helplessness came over her and tears welled up in her eyes. In her mind, where things worked, she screamed out her sister's name, however, in the real world, something terrible had happened – she was paralyzed.

"My car's out back. We can get away clean without them even seeing us."

"I'm not going with you, I don't even know you." Amanda started to pull Joe's hand off her arm, but he strengthened his grip.

Rachel sat there urging her sister on in her mind. Willing her to fight back and not let this stranger take her. Pleading with those sitting at the other tables to help, but no one did. They just watched as if it were a movie.

"You *are* coming with me because I'm not leaving you here to rat on me." Quickly Joe moved to the back of the restaurant with Amanda in tow as she yelled for help.

No one came to her rescue. Rachel wondered what was taking the police so long to get there. She turned to see them still coming up the road with their lights flashing and sirens blaring. Still they made little progress at coming closer to the restaurant. She turned back around, once again willing someone to help. It was too late. Amanda and Joe were gone. Closing her eyes, she screamed, in her mind, at the top of her lungs until it seemed her chest would explode. No one heard a word.

Seconds later, the police were barreling through the front

door screaming for everyone to not move and put their hands in the air, which startled Rachel and made her jerk.

"NO, NO, NO!" she screamed as she opened her eyes.

In a split second, Rachel realized two things. First, she could hear her voice and second, she was sitting straight up in bed shaking. Looking around she took in her surroundings letting her mind catch up with her emotions. She was home, in her apartment, in her bedroom. *Oh my God! It was just a dream!*

Her dreams of Amanda had never been in this much detail nor in so long of a sequence. In the past, they were always clips in random order, none ever seeming to shed light on the others. This was entirely new. What did it mean? When the dreams had first started, it did not take long before Rachel was unable to function on a daily basis. As her mind wandered back to that time, a sinking feeling started to grow in her stomach. She drew her knees up to her chest resting her head on them and wrapped her arms around them.

**11**

*Thursday, May 25, 2006, 3:18 PM:*

Caleb sat back in his chair exasperated by the schedule in front of him. Repetitive tasks always bored him and making schedules for deliveries was his weekly responsibility. Since Caleb had the more analytical mind, Jeff agreed to let him handle this part of the business.

Each week threw out its own challenges. Last minute shipments would come in that required him to rearrange the schedule. Drivers would call in sick and others would have to double up or Caleb and Jeff would have to fill in. Trucks would break down and shipment times would need altering for drivers to share trucks or use a rental. Caleb wondered *was there ever a week when everything went as planned.*

As nice as that would be to have happen, this week was not going to be it. Earlier in the day, Caleb had spoken to the mechanic who told him that the truck would not be ready until Monday because a part was on back order. Before Caleb could check on a rental truck, one of his drivers called in with a broken wrist, which he sustained while playing softball the night before. With Jeff out until Friday afternoon, Caleb was trying to fill in the gaps and make the schedule work. He was just thinking *I hope nothing else happens* when Tina, his receptionist, knocked on his open door.

"Hey, Tina, what's up?"

Holding up several pages she announced, "I just got this fax for Jeff. I know he's not back until tomorrow. I thought you ought to see it."

"Why? Is something wrong?"

"Well, I don't know. It's a shipping order from the coast for a company we don't have a contract with." Tina handed the fax to Caleb.

"Really?" Caleb flipped through the pages. "Maybe Jeff's made some progress."

"You want me to leave it on his desk?"

"No Tina, thanks. I think I'll give our boy a call."

"Okay," Tina said as she started to walk away.

Calling out before she disappeared, Caleb asked, "Tina, could you do me a favor and call Miller. See if he's available for a delivery or two tomorrow. Thanks."

Caleb pulled his radio out of the holder on his belt and blankly looked at it. It had been six weeks since they purchased these radios and he had not made a call yet. Jeff used it more than he did. Opening the top drawer of his desk, Caleb pulled out the small instruction booklet, but before he had a chance to open it his radio was vibrating.

Pressing the talk button, Caleb answered, "Go ahead."

"Caleb! It worked! You have your radio on! Will wonders never cease..."

"Well, they're ceasing here, my friend."

"What's up, buddy?"

Caleb did not want to dump on Jeff, especially since he was out there getting new business. "I'll tell you in a minute. First, tell me how you are doing and how things are going out there."

"I'm doing fine and things are going great. I've picked up two new clients."

"Really!"

"Yep. I've got two signed contracts in my hands.

Getting new clients was not an everyday occurrence and when it happened, Caleb always felt like he did when they first opened their doors. He got the same adrenaline rush.

"All right! Tell me about them."

"Okay, the first is an import/export business who ships all kinds of Chinese knick knacks into the states. They have a warehouse in Richmond where they store everything before mailing it out to their customers. The shipments are too small for a large company and they're not consistent. The good news is we won't have to make special trips. When we are out here we can pick up whatever they have so scheduling won't be tough."

"Man, am I glad to hear that," Caleb exclaimed.

"I thought you would. It also helps that the second contract will bring us out here every week which makes the first even easier."

"What's the second one, Jeff?"

"The second's a little off the wall, Caleb, but hear me out before you say anything. Okay?"

They had shipped some very strange things in the past, from dead animals for labs to live fish for aquariums to specialized manure for farmers and Caleb wondered what could ever be so strange that Jeff would act this way.

"Okay, I'm listening."

"The second company is shipping *Holy Ointment* from the dry dock in Newport News to..."

Jeff paused and Caleb waited to hear where this stuff was going. It was just like Jeff to get himself caught up in some religious quest.

"It's going to..."

Again Jeff paused, which made Caleb very uncomfortable. *What could possibly be so hard to say?*

"Come on, Jeff, spit it out."

"They're going to Brian Albertson."

"Albertson!" Caleb screamed. "Are you mad? Have you flipped?"

"Caleb, you said you'd hear me out first. Calm down and let me explain."

"Fine. This better be good."

"Okay. I know that this is the nut that caused Jena and you to split up and it is the last contract you'd ever want to have. Believe me, I had no idea when I met with Waldemar that he was involved with Albertson. Had I known, I never would have met with him. However, you won't believe this deal. First, we get paid C-O-D. When we drop off the load there's an envelope there with cash in it. We'll never have to wait for the payment with these guys. Second, they're paying us five thousand a pallet and we can haul as much as we can hold."

Caleb was completely silent. It was true that he never wanted to see or hear about Albertson ever again, let alone be delivering to him. It was also true that cash flow was a constant problem they had to deal with and using a larger truck would allow them to deliver a larger quantity. None-the-less the whole thing did not feel right.

"What about a paper trail, Jeff? I don't want to be involved with anyone that's not willing to keep records."

"I know, Caleb. I told them the same thing and although they are willing to pay in cash, they want us to have invoices printed up. In fact, they are going to fax shipping orders to us each week letting us know how much they have to ship. We can take all or part of what they have."

"Well that explains the fax I have."

"Fax, what fax?"

"We just received a fax from the coast, right before you called. I couldn't make sense of it and I was about to call you when you called."

"Man, these guys work fast. What's the fax say?"

"Well, best I can tell, they have eleven pallets ready to go and want them delivered by this Saturday."

There was a pause and Caleb knew Jeff was calculating how much space he would have left in his truck after tomorrow's scheduled pick up.

"I'll have enough room for eight pallets. Who's the contact on the fax?"

Caleb searched through the pages looking for a name, but could not find one. "There's no name here, Jeff."

"I guess I'll call Waldemar and see if he's okay with me just taking the eight."

"Wait a minute, Jeff. You're talking as if we agreed to do this job."

"Well, what do you think? It's a great opportunity, right? The way I figure, we can lease a larger truck and use it each week to do the coast runs and this contract will pay for the truck in no time."

A chill ran through Caleb's shoulders. Suddenly he thought about what Pastor Reynolds had said and he wondered if this was going to lead to trouble. *The money would make a difference and help bring us where we want to go, besides Jeff is thorough and wouldn't do anything to jeopardize the business...should I tell Jeff about what Reynolds said?*

"Caleb, you still there?"

"Yeah, Jeff, I'm here."

"Well, buddy, what do you think?"

"Jeff, it sounds great, but I'm not comfortable with it."

"Is it because of Albertson?"

"I don't know, maybe. Part of me says it's a big break for us and we should go for it. Another part says..." Caleb let his words trail off as he thought about what to say next. "Jeff, I trust you and right now I'm not so trusting of myself. If you think this is a good deal then I'm with you, but on one condition, I don't want to be a part of these deliveries. Okay?"

"I understand, Caleb. I'll handle all these runs and since I'm going to the coast anyway, it won't be a problem. I'll call Waldemar and let you know what he says. This may bring me back later than I thought tomorrow, are you okay with that?"

"Yeah, that's fine. I wasn't planning on you being back until late anyway. Max still has the broken truck and says it won't be ready until Monday. Taylor broke his wrist playing ball. Tina's calling Miller and if he's not available I'll be out all day tomorrow filling in."

"Hey, buddy, I'm sorry about that. I wish I was there to help."

"You are helping by bringing in new business. By the way, congratulations on the new contracts."

"Thanks, buddy."

Feeling sorry for himself, Caleb said, "I guess I'll give up on going on a date tomorrow night."

"You had a date?"

"No, but I was working on it."

"How's your new interest going?"

"I've been spending every night going over profiles and sending out e-mails. Each day there is a new list of girls and I go through my process of weeding them out and then sending a note. So far, I've not received anything. I'm a little disappointed, but I'm not ready to give up yet, although I'm not as excited about it as I first was."

"Buddy, you'll see, things are going to turn around soon for you. Hang in there. I need to go so I can call Waldemar. I'll give you a call later."

"Okay, Jeff, we'll talk later."

They both hung up and Caleb sat staring at the fax in his hand. A mix of emotions went through his mind as if he was on the carousel again. *Reynolds, Albertson, Holy Ointment, Jena, Jeff, The Connection, no dates...God, what have I gotten myself into?*

\* \* \*

"Martha, what have you got there?" Garry asked his receptionist as she walked into his office holding a large brown envelope.

"Well, sir, I don't know. A thin gentleman just walked in and asked me to give this to you right away and then left."

Puzzled, Garry gazed at the envelope, as did Martha. There was no postage on it and no return address. In fact, it was not addressed at all. Garry's name was the only thing written on the envelope. Turning it over and opening it Garry pulled out several eight-by-ten photos. The first two were pictures of the lobby of an office building. The third was a loading dock attached to a parking garage. The forth was of the Merrill Lynch name on the marble outside the Merrill Lynch building downtown.

Several thoughts ran through Garry's mind as he tried to make sense of the pictures. When he saw the fifth picture he dropped the stack and ran for the front door. Martha followed him as they ran out onto the sidewalk in front of their office. Garry looked up and down the street and told Martha to do the same looking for the man who dropped off the envelope, but he was nowhere.

"Sir, what's wrong? What's in the envelope?"

Back at his desk, he showed Martha the fifth picture. It was a picture of Rachel in the lobby of the Merrill Lynch building.

"This could only have been taken within the past few days," Garry said with an angry tone. "What's this about?"

Pointing to his desk, "Sir, look, a note," Martha said.

Garry flipped the folded note open and quickly read it, "Hopefully I've got your attention. Let's meet."

"Who's it from, sir?"

Garry ignored the question and continued to read. "If you agree, leave your office now. Turn right when you get outside and walk to the corner. If you do not leave within the next five minutes, I'll know you are not interested. You can keep the photos." Garry added, "It's unsigned," for Martha's benefit.

Quickly, Garry put everything back into the envelope and handed it to Martha.

"Martha, listen to me carefully. I want you to stop everything you're doing, take the phones off the hook, lock the front door and then as clear as you can remember, write down a description of the man who dropped off this envelope. Then I want you to call Fletcher. Tell him what just happened and bring this stuff to him. Then go home. Do not come back here until I call you and let you know it's safe. Do you understand?"

"Sir, you're not going to meet this guy are you? That's insane!"

"It might be, but if I don't something could happen to Rachel. I can't take that chance. You do what I told you. I'll be fine."

Garry sent her out of his office and closed the door. From the filing cabinet next to the door, he pulled out a small tape recorder. While he moved around preparing to leave he recorded what had just transpired and what his intentions were. From the center drawer of his desk he pulled out a small caliber handgun and tucked it into his jacket pocket. The last thing he took was a second cell phone, just in case. Before grabbing his keys, he popped out the tape from the recorder and replaced it with a blank one, then headed out of his office. As he walked past Martha's desk, he handed her the first tape.

"Make sure Fletcher gets this tape as well."

"Sir..."

Garry met Martha's stare and could feel the fear she felt. They had worked together for a long time and been through a lot, but nothing like this had ever happened before.

"I'll be fine, really. Don't take long and make sure you lock up. I'll call soon."

A minute later Garry was outside looking around to see if he could spot the person watching him. He could not. He turned to his right and headed to the corner as instructed. When he got there, a cab pulled up. The rear door opened and a rather large man inside invited him in.

"C'mon, get in."

\* \* \*

It felt good to be alive and part of something that would help people, especially if it put the bad guy behind bars. Somehow, this might atone for the fact that they never found Amanda's killer. It might ease the pain a bit and maybe even satisfy the soul. She could show Garry that he was worrying too much and that A. E. Research was doing good things for people. This was her home, her company, her life and although Jane was very pleased with her work so far, Rachel was even more pleased.

The search request she had initiated was still running, trying to match up the criteria she had entered. After several days of meetings with Jane and hours of research, she completed the match-subject profile. Now all that remained was to see whom The Connection would choose. As a child filled with anticipation before Christmas, she watched the progress bar slowly move across the screen, preparing to display the faces of those it had chosen. In some ways, it felt like a game and Rachel had to tell herself how real and serious this was, but the little girl inside her kept returning to her fun.

Finally, the progress bar disappeared and the screen displayed its matches, five men. Rachel deduced that a woman could be sidetracked by Albertson's flare and this caused her to search only for men.

Before using The Connection's analysis help tools, Rachel pulled up each of the five profiles and read them. They all seemed the same other than their location and physical features. Two lived outside of Virginia and another lived in Arlington. The remaining two lived in Richmond. Using her own reasoning, Rachel ranked each of the five to see who she thought would be the most plausible candidate. The two outside Virginia would have to make special arrangements to even meet her let alone come to Richmond to engage Albertson. They went to the bottom of the list. The one in Arlington would have the same traveling issue but might have some relationships in Washington that could help. He went to the top of the list. Of the two in Richmond, one had gone through a divorce recently and would probably not be up to the challenge. She labeled him number three and the other number two.

Rachel wrote down her results and then started the analysis tool running. It would also review the subjects and rank them. She felt confident of her logic and satisfied with her ranking. The computer was sure to match her choices. Again, there was a time of anticipation while she watched the progress bar move.

Above the bar were the five pictures and Rachel studied each of them as if trying to gain some knowledge about each man. For some reason her attention was drawn to the third picture. He had a nice smile but his eyes showed a hidden pain. His expression was a look she had seen many times back at the hospital, a calling card of desperation and confusion. People with this look sheltered a deep wound that they not only wanted to hide, but saw no way to heal. This was a wounded man.

A *ding* sounded from the computer like a microwave finished heating up a meal. The pictures were rearranged into the order the computer had ranked them. In positions four and five, were the two men who lived outside of Virginia and Rachel smiled. The man she had ranked first was in the third position. The two men from Richmond were in the first and second positions with the man with the wounded eyes in first.

Shocked, Rachel printed off the results with the extended explanation and reviewed it. According to the computer, she had guessed right about the two outside of Virginia. It also ranked this issue as a negative for the man in Arlington. His connections in Washington were also a negative because the Government did not want to be involved. The one ranked second was a good candidate but did not have a previous connection with Albertson and the one ranked first did.

This just seemed to be wrong and Rachel had a hard time accepting the computer's ranking. She needed more information before she would be ready to concede to this machine. Clicking on the first man's picture again and pulling up his profile she read his name once more, *Caleb Andrew Prescott.*

"Well, Mr. Prescott, let's find out who you are."

One more click and the computer searched for all the information it had on Prescott. Five minutes later, the printer spat paper. The clock on her wall showed it was ten till five. It was getting late and the thought of stopping here was making her anxious, she needed to continue. Then it came to her.

"Security," said the deep voice on the other end of the phone.

"Hello, this is Rachel Gilbert with A. E. Research on the fifteenth floor. I'm going to be working late and I wanted you to be aware that I'm still in the building."

"Is anyone working with you, ma'am?"

"No, sir, just me."

"Okay, I'll log you in as staying. Please call before you leave to let us know you are leaving."

"Sure thing."

"Thank you, ma'am."

The distraction was not long enough for her to relax so she turned to her computer and started a new file. She named it *Psych-Profile-Prescott*. For fifteen minutes, she entered all the factual data about him that she had and then closed the file and turned off the computer. With her door closed and the hum of her computer silenced, she was now ready to continue with the last step of her routine.

"Okay, Prescott, let's see if you *are* the best candidate."

# 12

"I guess I haven't adapted my thinking to A. E. Research's way of looking at things. The logic I used was on target, I thought, but it seems the computer and I don't see eye to eye. After reviewing the information the computer used and its reasoning I had to admit that it made a better choice than I did."

"Not a better choice, Rachel, but a more informed choice. The computer takes into consideration every piece of data it's given. It doesn't forget things or overlook them. I'm not criticizing at all, just stating a fact. We tend to dismiss things as not important, overlook things or forget them. That's why we had the analysis tools built into the system."

Earlier in the week Rachel would have gone on the defensive after hearing what Jane had just said, today she understood it to be what it was, an explanation.

"So tell me," Jane continued, "what do you think of the computer's choice?"

Rachel said jokingly, "First, let me say that the computer cheated, it had more information than I did. However, after going through the information I can see why Prescott would be the better selection. Having his marriage broken up by this faith healer would give him an incentive to expose the guy."

"Exactly, and more than likely, if he had the chance and the correct information, Prescott would jump at the opportunity to get even."

Suddenly the uneasiness from the first of the week returned and her facial expression must have shown it.

"Rachel, what's wrong?"

There was no way of hiding what she felt and yet she was not sure if the timing was right to share this. It had not even been a week yet, but she believed that Jane and she had made enough progress that Jane could be trusted. The limb was in front of her and the choice to go out on it was hers to make. It would be hard to back out now and risk the connection already built between them. To move forward was going to take a leap of faith that Jane would understand. Trusting her feelings, she decided to move forward, to go out on that limb. Her only hope was that Jane did not own a saw.

"Jane, I'd like to share something with you that I've only shared with a couple of people. It's about getting even." Rachel took a deep breath and let it out slowly before continuing. "I told you about my sister being murdered and...well, I had a hard time getting over it. For years, all I could think about was getting even with the man who murdered her, but they never found him. Years of therapy and counseling told me that I had to let go of this desire so that I could move forward, but I couldn't. I would envision what I would do to him if I ever met him face to face. I even wrote him a letter to get out my anger. While these things are supposed to help release the pent up emotions, for me they just enhanced them."

Rachel paused for a moment feeling a sharp pain in the palm of her hands from her tightly clenched fists. She took in another breath and slowly released it. Jane continued to be still, respecting Rachel's need to share this secret. Feeling more relaxed, she continued.

"It wasn't until I met Dr. Claire at the Sheltering Arms Hospital and shared this with her, that I was able to change. Something about the way she talked to me was different from all the other doctors. She didn't try to change me, rather she helped me to follow through with the thinking I had, taking it to its logical conclusion. Once I got to the end of that road, I realized that I was afraid to let go of my anger towards him and face the real pain of the loss of my sister. At that point, I was able to understand what was happening to me. It was as if Dr. Claire gave me my mind back."

Rachel watched Jane's face for a sign that she understood her point, and although Jane was nodding her head, it was not enough to convince Rachel that she had successfully expressed her concern. She was going to have to say it plainly, to get it out, which had been the one thing she feared since she left her therapy and she never had to admit it to anyone, until now.

"What I'm trying to say...is...*this is going to come out wrong and sound silly*...since I left the hospital my biggest fear was that I would regress back to the desire for revenge. As I heard you talk about getting even, the hairs on my neck stood up, my stomach started to turn and the fear returned. I could feel myself standing outside that door. All I have to do is open it and I'm back where I was before."

There was a deep longing inside her at that moment to hear Lauren's voice again and receive comfort from the doctor who became her friend. It was unclear what she would get from Jane who sat silent almost staring past her. Then Rachel noticed that her eyes were shining as if they were tearing up. *She's been affected by what I said. There is a connection between us!*

"At some other time," Jane said as she stood and moved towards her desk for a tissue, "I'll share a story of my own with you." She paused to wipe a tear away. "Now, however, would not be the right time. You have experienced and shared something very deep and I won't disrespect it by telling you something about me. I will offer you this: opening the door you talk about is a choice. Though you might make that choice in a moment of emotion, it is still a choice, which means you also have the ability to leave the door shut. This is where the character of a person plays in. Things may push you to do what you don't want to do, but not doing them anyway takes character. When you are faced with that choice you will know what your character is really like."

Tears welled up in Rachel's eyes as she realized that she had a new friend. Someone who knows what it is like to hurt and suffer, and understands how it separates people. She knew for sure, there was a connection between them now and Jane could be trusted. Jane offered her the box of tissue as she returned to her chair and resumed the topic of work.

"Now as for Mr. Prescott, I think it's time for him to meet Anna Clark."

"Meet Anna Clark? Excuse me?" Rachel was not sure what Jane was getting at.

"I think it's time for Anna Clark to e-mail Mr. Prescott and find out what he is like. Get to know him and then go out with him."

"What! WHAT?"

It took a little while to accept the fact that she would have to contact someone to help do this task, but the idea of dating him never entered her mind.

"Rachel, how else are you going to confirm if he is the perfect match? Remember, this has to be something *he* wants to do or else we're coercing him."

"Are you telling me I'm going to have to go out on a date with this guy?"

"Yes, I am. You need to meet him and start a relationship in order to pass the information on to him that he needs. Think of it as a field study. Who knows, you might even like this guy."

Rachel was about to thank Jane, for what she was not sure, when a rush of fatigue came over her. She felt dizzy and started to sway. Instinctively her right hand went to her forehead and her left held her steady by gripping the edge of the couch.

"Rachel, are you okay?"

"Yeah, I think so. I'm just very tired. Must be the new job and all the *excitement*."

"Are you sleeping well?"

"Well...no, I'm not." *Oh no, another thing I'm going to have to share. Why now? Why today?*

"Do you want to talk about it?"

Rachel could see the concerned look on Jane's face and decided after what she had just shared there was no reason to hide this.

"For the past couple of nights I've been having my nightmares again."

"The ones you had after your sister died?"

"Yes and no. They are similar, but not the same."

"I don't understand."

*Spill it girl, she can be trusted. Besides, there's no way to hide it now.* "The dreams I had after Amanda died were like looking through a stack of pictures that were not in order. In the right sequence they told a story I guess, however, I never found that sequence. I only saw the pictures out of order and none of them made any sense."

"How are your current dreams different, Rachel?"

"I've had the same dream both nights. It's sequential, like watching a movie. I'm in the restaurant with Amanda when she's kidnapped by some guy, only I never fully see his face. On top of it, in the dream, I'm unable to speak or move until I wake up screaming."

"Have you tried putting meaning to the symbols in the dream?"

"Not yet, I was hoping the dreams were not going to come back and that it was just the stress of a new job that caused them."

"Rachel, I know many people think that dreams are just left over pieces of real life that the unconscious mind throws together when you sleep, but I believe they can be messages meant for us to understand, especially if they are recurring. I encourage you to pay attention to your dreams. You may just find out a few things."

* * *

As the recorded conversation on the tape ended, Garry switched off the tape recorder and looked at his friend. "So tell me, what do you think of all this?"

Fletcher got out of his chair and walked around his office scratching his head. Like Garry, he had been around for a while and served in the Navy. Back then, he was lean and built like Hercules, but years of private life had left him overweight and out of shape. He was no longer the intimidator he was in the Navy boxing ring, but his mind was still as sharp as it was back then. He had left the Navy to work for a private investigating agency and later started his own. When Garry retired into private practice, Fletcher was the only PI he would work with.

Pausing at the window, Fletcher turned to Garry, "You say this man found you how?"

"Apparently, he has a sister who lost a limb a year ago and Rachel was her therapist at the Sheltering Arms Hospital. He'd been hanging around the Merrill Lynch building for a couple of weeks trying to get some pictures of this Michaels guy and was there the day Rachel went for her interview. He recognized her from the hospital. After that, he started following her to see if she had a connection to A. E. Research as well. He took some pictures of Rachel and me, when we met for lunch last week, and then did some research on me. Finally, he was satisfied we had no real connection with Michaels and decided to approach me."

Fletcher pointed at the tape recorder in front of Garry. "And he let you tape that conversation?"

"His goon searched me and took my gun and the recorder. After he explained who he was and what this was all about, he made his goon give them back. He said he had checked up on me and believed that I was not the kind of person that Michaels could buy and he wanted my help. I told him that if he wanted me to help him, he had to let me tape the conversation. He agreed."

"This story about Cottonwood Lake is a fantastic one. That's in Nebraska, right? Do you believe him?"

"I'm not sure what to believe, that's why I'm here."

Fletcher inquired, "How can I help you?"

"I told this guy about you and said I needed you because you could get where I can't. He's okay with that. I want you to do two things for me. First, find out who these guys are and where they come from. Check out the info on the tape and see if it's true. Try to do as much of this without leaving Richmond. If you do, he'll know I'm checking up on him and I don't want that yet. He believes you will be checking up on Michaels, so spend some time finding out what you can on him as well." Garry paused for a moment before adding, "I don't know how connected these guys are or how far they'll go to get what they want, so be careful."

Fletcher walked back to his desk and sat down. As he spoke, he scribbled something on a piece of paper. "This is what we'll do. The information I find on Michaels I'll send to you through normal channels, phone calls, e-mails, postage, etc. What I find on *Mr. Taperecorder*, I'll send to you encoded." He handed Garry the piece of paper. "When you open the e-mail, enter that code and the file will expand itself for you to read. When you exit out it will compress itself so no one else can read it without that code. This means you can't print any of it. If they'll be tracking us they'll see the info on Michaels but won't know what the other stuff is."

"I think we should assume they'll be watching us," Garry said as he stood up to leave.

With a firm tone and a serious gaze, Fletcher replied, "Then I suggest you don't tip your hand."

* * *

Caleb had been home for thirty minutes when the phone rang. He was tired from loading and unloading trucks all day. Because of the broken truck and the disabled employee, he had to run five different routes today. Each was small, but he filled the truck twice, drove all over Richmond, climbed up into and down from the truck seventeen times and was literally worn out. He had no energy for anything but to check his e-mails hoping for some peace and quiet and some good news. However, Jeff had other plans when Caleb answered the phone.

"Jeff, when did you get back and how did things go?"

"Things went very well. I got back about an hour ago. Nancy and I are going to dinner and a movie. Why don't you come along with us and I can tell you about the trip?"

"Sounds like fun, Jeff, but I'm not up to it."

"Why? What's wrong?"

Caleb felt the urge to dump on Jeff for the lousy day he had. He could feel the tension in his neck and the need to release his frustrations, but it was not Jeff's fault, it was not anyone's fault. *Life sometimes just stinks.*

"It's been a long day and I'm tired. On top of that, I was just checking my e-mails and I haven't received one reply from the e-mails I sent out. I'm discouraged, disgusted and just plain down. I wouldn't be good company and I really don't want to be around other couples. You understand?"

"I do Caleb. I'm sorry. It was a little insensitive of me to ask. Get some rest and call me in the morning, okay?"

"Sure thing, Jeff. Have a great time and say hi to Nancy for me."

After hanging up and rubbing his face, Caleb returned to his e-mails. Amidst the many advertising and business e-mails, an unfamiliar one caught his attention. It was titled "Interesting!" and he opened it.

**From:** "Anna Clark" <heterotelic@theconnection.net>
**To:** "Caleb A. Prescott" <caprescott@theconnection.net>
**Sent:** Friday, May 26, 2006 1:17 PM
**Subject:** Interesting!

Hello, Caleb, my name is Anna.

I'm new to The Connection and am amazed at how this thing works. To be honest this is my first time using an Internet dating service and I'm not sure what to expect.

My mate search displayed your picture and I thought you had a kind face. After reading your profile, I was sure you would be an interesting person to meet. However, I'd like to know more about you first, if that's okay?

First, I'd like to know more about where you find yourself at this point in your life, like what philosophies have you adopted, do you have regrets and what kind of goals do you have? Next, I'd like to know more about the business you run. I see that you are divorced, do you mind telling me about it? Also, you didn't indicate a religion. Do you have an opinion on God? Lastly, are there any specific places in Richmond where you like to hang out?

If you reply, please ask me anything you would like to know about me. Maybe this will be the beginning of something new for both of us.

Till I hear from you,

Anna

Included with the e-mail was a picture and Caleb quickly clicked on the attachment to open it. The woman in the picture was very attractive with shoulder length thick black wavy hair. Her pale white skin accented her soft green eyes and her gaze was both mysterious and intellectual which attracted Caleb instantly. His mind told him he was out of her league. She looked sophisticated, high-class with money that probably would not be caught dead around a blue-collar guy like him, let alone a two-time loser.

For some time he looked at the photo wondering why she had not shown up on his list if he had shown up on hers. *There must be something different in what she's looking for than what I'm looking for. I wonder what?* Caleb reread Anna's e-mail three times hoping the answer would jump out at him. It did not. The exercise left him bewildered and reduced to one course of action – to reply.

Although replying to an e-mail that came from The Connection was what he had been waiting for all week, now that he was doing it, it did not seem as easy as he expected. All he had to do was answer some questions and ask a few of his own. Heck, he had answered hundreds of questions from The Connection just to get this far. For some reason this was more difficult because sophisticated Anna had set him up to be interesting; what if his answers proved otherwise? There was pressure to live up to an expectation. It was a performance and if it was not good the curtain would drop with no applause.

These thoughts brought back old memories, images of when he tried to do things for others back at the church and in his marriages, but failed. It was also like performing, like being on display, and it usually did not go well. In fact, he could not remember a time when it had gone well.

*Why in the world am I doing this? It's not going to end well and I'll be hurt for trying one more time. This was a stupid idea and to think I could connect with someone like her.*

A deep sense of failure entered Caleb's head as he realized that this was one more thing he was about to fail at. His fears had paralyzed him and turned the volume up on the negative tapes he had playing in his head. Nothing was going to be accomplished here and as he raised his eyes to avoid the computer screen he caught sight of the one thing in his apartment that carried a positive message for him – the statue of the hand of God giving Eve to Adam.

Suddenly, Caleb thought about the God factor he had joked about with Jeff. *Could this be the hand of God?* With newfound energy and a positive attitude, he started answering the questions.

Before he knew it, he had completed a two-page reply filled with information about him and several questions for her. He sat stunned at what he had accomplished and reread it twice. Before sending it, he reread Anna's e-mail once more to make sure he answered everything she had asked.

Satisfied that he had done his best, he was ready to send the reply. However, he was apprehensive to click on the send button. A phrase, from the end of Anna's e-mail, kept repeating in his mind, one he had heard over and over again this week, that finally gave him the power to move forward – it was time for something new. He told his Inner Critic to shut up and then clicked the mouse button to send his reply.

In an instant all that he had wanted from The Connection had happened, he was changed. A new chapter of his life was starting and it seemed like it was going to be positive. There was a renewed excitement which made Caleb promise himself that this time it was going to be different.

Finished with his task, he powered down the computer and headed off to bed as he stretched and yawned. This caused him to catch sight of his Bible sitting on the top of the shelf where he had left it. Pulling it off the shelf he thought, *I guess it's time to get reacquainted.*

# 13

Several things had Rachel up early this morning. Even though it was clear that the lack of sleep was taking its toll, she could not shut off her thoughts.

She felt frustrated because the dreams had not gone away. They were always the same - being in the restaurant with Amanda watching her being kidnapped, feeling helpless and never seeing the man's face. It continued to torment her. The helpless feeling screamed at her trying to tell her that she was still this way, even today. The faceless man increased her anger about the fact that he could not be found. Each of these wore her down but the bigger attack came from the fact that the dreams were recurring and she had not called Lauren to let her know about them. Already she had broken her promise.

Adding to her frustration was the anxiety of what was about to happen with the match-subject. She had made her e-mail sound as plain as possible while not trying to give any hints away as to her real agenda. Inside she felt dirty. Although she understood what Jane had said about giving someone the chance to do what he or she really wanted to do, it still felt like manipulation and there was no getting past the fact that she was using this person to accomplish a task for her employer. Before A. E. Research, she would have abhorred this idea, but now, involved with it, wanting the good that would come from it, she could not allow herself to think this way.

*Come on, concentrate* she told herself as she made her way around the apartment dusting, just to keep busy. *What's the next step?*

Back at her favorite reading spot, where she started her dusting, she realized she had not accomplished much. *If Mom saw how I dusted, she'd have a cow.* She sat down and peered out the glass doors.

*Would he even reply? Has he gotten it yet? Is it too early to check? No, I should wait until Monday and keep it business. But if he's replied and answered my questions I'll need time to go through them. If I don't check until Monday Jane will probably wonder why. She might think I'm not into this task and pull me off, which would not look good for me. This is nuts!*

"Nothing is going to change anything," she said as she exchanged her soft loveseat for her desk chair. "My checking is not going to change whether or not he's replied. If he has, great, if he hasn't, I'll check again later."

In no time, she logged on to The Connection and received her answer. The message light in the bottom left-hand corner of the screen was blinking. She had a message. Suddenly the room got a little warmer. Her heart started beating a little faster and the tired feeling she had just minutes ago was forgotten. The faster pace of her flowing blood brought with it a new energy level that kicked her mind and emotions into third gear (first and second being getting up and getting moving).

*This could only be from him. I didn't send anyone else a message. Jane? No, she'd call me or use my normal e-mail address. It's him!*

With her palms starting to sweat, she moved the mouse and clicked on the message button. Instantly the screen changed and listed her messages. There was one. It was from him. This knowledge caused her heart to beat even faster, which she felt immediately. Fear mixed with excitement as she moved the mouse once again to open the message. *What would he say? Would he be attracted to me? What if...*

She broke off in mid thought as a young schoolchild sensation wafted over her and the message displayed. It was long, meaning he must have taken the time to answer her questions. Before reading, she clicked on the print button to print out the e-mail. Later, she would use it to update his profile and determine more about him, but for now, it was time to read.

The excitement grew as she read; first, to know that he would reply, then to answer all her questions in such detail, and finally to ask his own questions. This guy was hooked. Realizing this set off a battle of emotions inside her. She was excited and proud that she had succeeded in getting the selected match-subject to be interested and respond. It was an accomplishment that she was sure Jane would be pleased about. However, this guy was more than hooked. He was looking for a partner, a soul mate, and he has been through so much. She was going to deceive him and she knew it.

*Now what? We need to talk further.* Rachel remembered that The Connection was set up to allow matches to chat with each other through the system, which allowed for real time interaction before meeting. *That's the next step!* She clicked on the reply button and started to type.

Hello again, Caleb.

Thanks for your reply; I enjoyed reading it. I'd like to talk further and answer all your questions. I'll be back online at 4:00 PM today if you would like to chat. Hope so.

Till then,

Anna

The schoolchild feeling returned as she clicked the send button. For years she had avoided having a relationship in order to not interfere with her studies and because the ones she had, proved to be harmful. Now, her studies had led her to a job that was requiring her to have one and she realized how unprepared she was. The only thing she had for positive relationship references were crushes she remembered having as a young girl. Yeah, the movies she saw helped to explain and understand relational feelings, but they could not generate the experience for her. In this area of her life, she was severely lacking.

Trying to shake off this feeling, she headed for the kitchen to make herself something to eat. However, there was not much to choose from and the task of preparing something became a task of preparing a shopping list. *Shopping will take my mind off things.* Before heading for the bedroom to get ready to go she glanced at the clock on the wall, *I've got just enough time.*

* * *

The run was a little easier than usual this morning and Caleb wondered why. *Maybe I'm getting back into shape or maybe it's because I slept well last night.* As he wiped the sweat from his face with a paper towel from the kitchen, the real reason became clear to him. He walked over to the computer and without sitting down, switched it on and logged onto The Connection. While he waited for the screen to fill in, he kicked off his sneakers and carried them into his bedroom. He reappeared in his boxer shorts and paused in the hallway to steal a glance at the screen, hoping for the blinking light. It was on.

Putting off his shower for a few minutes, Caleb quickly sat at his desk and opened his e-mail. It was from Anna. A surge of energy came over him and he swore he could do his whole run again with ease. The message was short. She had not answered his questions but she wanted to talk more – online!

Caleb felt satisfied as he sat back in his chair and grinned. It was not what he expected, but it showed promise. Being new to this world, he convinced himself that this was just a new way of doing things and he was excited to try this new approach. The clock on his computer told him he had three hours to kill and without switching it off, he left it and resumed his previous task of taking a shower. *This is going to be a long three hours.*

\* \* \*

Frantic and carrying much more than she should, Rachel rushed into her apartment for the third and last time. She kicked the apartment door behind her closed with her foot as she lunged into the kitchen placing the remains of her shopping on the counter. Spying the clock, which scolded her for cutting this so close, she realized she had twelve minutes left. *First things first.*

Rushing to her computer, she switched it on. While it warmed up and initialized, she rushed back to the kitchen and unpacked the frozen dinners she bought and put them in the freezer. Then, another sprint to the computer and she logged on to The Connection. Back in the kitchen, only the dry goods remained and they could wait. *Six minutes left. Enough time to get comfortable.*

Knowing that she was not going on a date, but feeling like it was one, Rachel wanted to be at her best. She took several deep breaths to relax and release the rushed feelings she had. Then, kicking off her shoes and grabbing a glass of water, she headed for her desk.

At her desk, she went through a few mouse clicks and scanned the list of IDs to see who was online. *It's 3:58 PM and he's not in the list. I made it.*

\* \* \*

*It's funny how a shower and a few hours of idle time can allow so much doubt to creep in.* Caleb sat staring at the computer screen waiting, wanting it to do something without him having to make a move. Just knowing that an outside force was leading him, that was not his own and it could be trusted, would take all the pressure off. Although he knew he had to decide. The past few hours had brought back so many memories of joy that ended in pain and it made him wonder if this would be the same. How could he make this different when he was not sure why things went wrong before?

The clock on the computer ticked and turned to 4:02 PM. An eternity had passed in two minutes. *If I don't log on she'll probably not contact me again, I'll lose this chance. If I log on and tell her what's going through my mind I'll probably scare her off. Once she finds out that I've been divorced twice she'll probably look elsewhere anyway. What do I have to offer someone like her?*

Caleb's heart sank as a raging storm of regrets and failures buffeted him. He sat stone still, hands gripping his desk to steady himself. *How can I move past this?* What positive influence could possibly combat the storm that seemed to be getting stronger? Failure was eminent. What he was planning to do was not going to happen. He was drowning in a sea of despair.

Then, like someone throwing him a life preserver and bringing him back to reality, his eyes saw the one thing in his apartment that would stem the tide. His eyes turned again to the hand of God giving Eve to Adam.

\* \* \*

*Its five after four, where is he? What if he doesn't sign on, what will that mean? Jane and I never talked about what to do if he is not interested. What's the next step? Where...*

A soft *ding* from her computer interrupted Rachel's thoughts. As she scanned the screen to see what had happened, all her negative thoughts disappeared. There it was. What she had been waiting for had shown up – Caleb had signed on.

For a moment, she sat staring at his name in the list. *Now what?* It was the first time Rachel could remember herself setting up a meeting without planning for it. Sidetracked by her shopping and rushing. It was clear that she was now flying by the seat of her pants and uncomfortable with it.

*He's not saying anything. Is he waiting for me? Who should make the first move? He must know that I'm signed on also.* Another minute passed without anything happening. Not wanting to lose this opportunity, Rachel decided to go first. *Play it safe, stay simple.*

Hello, Caleb. I'm glad you made it.

A few seconds later, she received a reply.

Hi, Anna. I'm sorry for being a little late. I had a few visitors that held me up. This is all new to me so excuse me as I get used to it.

Overjoyed that his tardiness was not due to second thoughts, Rachel quickly got engrossed in the exchange.

I understand. It's new to me as well. I have never been married and had put off dating so I could finish my degree and now it's a bit overwhelming.

There was a long pause as Rachel waited for a reply. *What's he waiting for? Maybe I said too much. Maybe his friends returned.*

> I'm not sure how much to share, but you should know that I've been divorced twice. It's not the way I expected my life to go and I'm trying to get past it. I'll understand if this is not what you are interested in.

The sound of pain reached Rachel's core and her natural tendency to nurture kicked in. Suddenly, the exchange went from a business task to a therapy session.

> Would you like to talk about it, Caleb? I'm a good listener.

There was another long pause and she knew he was thinking this over.

> You're the first person who has asked if I wanted to talk about what happened. Most people are afraid to say the wrong thing so they don't want to talk at all. They try to comfort me, but it doesn't work.

For the next forty minutes, Rachel watched as Caleb shared his story. She only interrupted to get clarification. The more he shared the more the battle inside her raged. His pain, although from a different source and circumstance, was as deep as hers was and it was creating a connection between them, deeper then she wanted to admit.

> ...that's when we started having trouble. I begged her to stop going to Albertson's meetings, but she just kept saying that he was helping her to be a stronger person, more independent. She told me I'd feel the same if I would just go with her again. I told her I saw enough the first time and I'm not going back. Three months later, she was anorexic and

so codependent that she moved out. Eighteen months later, we were divorced.

With Caleb's last statement, Rachel's mindset went from therapist back to researcher and she began thinking about how to get Caleb to talk about how he felt about Albertson and if he was willing to get back at him. She was about to ask a question when he began typing again.

Man, I've been typing for almost forty-five minutes! You must be as tired as my fingers are.

Oh, no, I'm not tired of listening, uh, reading what you had to say. I've enjoyed it. You explain yourself well and I can feel your pain. I'd like to keep going if that's okay?

To tell you the truth, I'd rather talk in person. Would you be interested in meeting for lunch tomorrow?

*Lunch! A meeting?* Once again Rachel felt unprepared for what was about to happen. *What if I say no, would I lose this opportunity? I don't want to like this guy. I don't want to hurt him more. We've both been hurt too much!* It was at that moment that Rachel faced the revenge door and slowly turned the knob. *Albertson needs to pay for what he's done...and so does that kidnapper! People like this need to be kept from hurting others.* It did not take long to open the door and step through and once there she knew exactly what she needed to do.

I'd be happy to meet you for lunch, Caleb. Did you have a place in mind?

* * *

When the phone rang, Caleb was just signing off with Anna. He was not sure but it seemed as if her tone changed as they ended. *It's just my friends talking.*

"Hello."

"Caleb! I've been trying to reach you on the radio for hours! Did you turn it off again?"

"Jeff, it's good to hear from you, too."

"Sorry, buddy. It's just that..."

Interrupting, Caleb explained, "Jeff, I'm sorry too. I did have the radio on, but I was rushing last night to get inside and I must have left it in my car."

"It doesn't work if you don't keep it with you."

"I know," Caleb conceded as he rolled his eyes and tried to change the subject. "What's up?"

"I wanted to let you know that I've scheduled a second pick up for Albertson. He wants us..."

Caleb quickly corrected him, "You mean *you*."

"Uh, right, he wants *me* to pick up the remainder of last week's order and all of this week's. I've already rented a larger truck to do the job. I'll be leaving Wednesday morning, will that work for you?"

"I think we'll be alright. You'll be back on Thursday, right?"

"Sure thing. I'll leave Wednesday night and be back Thursday afternoon after dropping off the load."

"Okay with me."

"Good, now, some of the guys from church and I are going to play softball tomorrow afternoon. You want to join us?"

"No, thanks."

"What, you got a hot date or something?"

"Well, Jeff, as a matter of fact I do."

"Really!"

"Yeah, man. I just set it up before you called."

"Did you meet her on that connection thing of yours?"

"Yeah, Jeff. There's something interesting about her. She's not in trouble and doesn't seem to be in need of help, but something in the way she understands things...I don't know, maybe I'm just hoping for something different."

"Hang in there, Caleb, it's going to happen for you, I'm sure."

"Thanks. I'll see you on Monday."

"See ya, buddy. Good luck tomorrow."

As he hung up the phone Caleb's thoughts previewed tomorrow's lunch. Repeatedly he worked through what might happen. Each scenario went poorly. *I'm going to need more than luck.*

# 14

Garry looked up and down the street as he stood in front of his office door. He had not been back since the day the photos came and he had not heard from Fletcher since his meeting with him. If it had not been for the phone call, he would not have been here at all.

The voice over the phone, who introduced himself as Mr. Barnes, was the same as the one on the tape recorder, although Garry was sure it was not his real name. When Barnes told him they needed to meet, Garry became suspicious. He still was not sure this man could be trusted. There needed to be someone watching his back and Fletcher was the only one he trusted. It was strange that Fletcher did not answer his phone. Garry hoped he would get the message in time.

Standing in front of his office Garry expected something to happen. He sensed someone was watching him yet could not tell from where. *Where's Fletcher?* There was no place to go and no one else to call. Rachel's safety was at stake and until he knew she would be safe, he had to go along with what Barnes wanted.

After one more look up and down the street, which revealed nothing more than the first look did, Garry unlocked the door and stepped inside. Before he could close the door behind him, two men appeared out of nowhere. The bigger one shoved Garry further into the office and the thinner one closed and locked the door, peering out the blinds. Garry recognized the larger man as the goon who took his gun and tape recorder. The other was apparently Mr. Barnes.

"Does this office have a back exit?" Barnes asked quickly and in a hushed tone.

There was a sense of urgency in his question and his expression so Garry answered quickly. "Yes, it leads out into the alley behind the deli next door."

"Only one way out of the alley?"

"Yes, unless you go through the deli."

"Let's hope we don't need it."

Barnes peered out the blinds once more and then ordered his goon to check out the office. For the next several minutes, Garry watched as the two men searched his office without saying a word. Then, after shaking their heads at one another, Barnes spoke.

"When's the last time you were here?"

"The day you sent the photos," Garry replied.

"I'm surprised, but it seems they haven't been here yet."

"Yet? What do you mean, *yet?* Who hasn't been here?"

"Mr. Garry," Barnes said. "When's the last time you spoke to your friend Fletcher?"

"Two days ago when I met with him. Why?"

"You haven't heard from him since?"

"No, I told you. What's this all about?"

Garry did not like what he was thinking but he knew there could be no other reason for this guy asking these questions. He braced himself to hear what he already knew.

"Mr. Garry. I'm sorry, but I believe your friend is dead."

Trying to remain cautious, Garry fired back. "Yeah, and what makes you believe that?"

"Mr. Garry. When I told you that I checked up on you, I did my homework. I knew about Fletcher before you told me. We had him followed, partly to see what he would turn up and partly to protect him. We lost contact with our tail and later found him dead in an alley about two blocks from Fletcher's office. If our man is dead, we believe your man is also dead."

"When did you find your man?" Garry inquired.

"Friday evening around six-o'clock. I don't think your man went very far after you met with him."

Garry knew Fletcher. Even though he was not in great shape, he was still hard to overcome. *Fletcher could have killed their tail thinking he was protecting himself. But then why had he not shown up today or called? This might mean that he was dead; however, there might be another explanation.* For now, Garry felt it was prudent to appear as if he agreed with Barnes. If Fletcher was not dead, there was no way Garry was going to give it away if Barnes was fishing for something. Feigning grief over his friend, Garry took a seat and covered his face with his hands.

"Mr. Garry, I'm sorry for your friend, but we must talk."

Uncovering his face Garry returned the condolences. "I'm sorry for your loss as well, but what do we need to talk about?"

"Sir, if they have gotten to your man then they know that we are on to them. It's not safe for you here or for us. We are going to regroup with our partners and suggest you come with us."

"No, no, I can't leave. What about Rachel? I can't leave her here. She's in danger. I need to get her out of there."

"Mr. Garry, you can't do that."

"What? Are you nuts? I'm going to get her away from here."

Garry stood up to leave. He took two steps toward the door before Barnes' goon restrained him. Twice Garry's size and half his age, he was not someone Garry wanted to tangle with.

"Mr. Garry, Rachel is safe as long as she is not aware of what's going on. If Michaels suspects that she is on to him, she'll disappear quickly. She won't be safe anywhere."

"So what do you suggest we do? I'm not leaving her here without someone to watch over her. Besides, if I disappear she'll know something is wrong and that could be dangerous for her."

"You make a good point, Mr. Garry. Let me suggest this, leave a message on your answering machine that you had to go out of town suddenly. Have your receptionist call all your clients and postpone any meetings and court dates. Tell them you'll be away for two weeks. Then stay in a hotel. Do what you need to do to watch over Rachel, but do it quietly. Most of all do not let on to her that there's anything wrong.

"In the meantime, I will return to Nebraska and meet with my partners and determine what to do next. I'll call you when we have a new plan." Pointing to the larger man Barnes added, "Hans will stay here to assist you." He scribbled a number on a note pad from Martha's desk and handed it to Garry. "Do not abuse this! Remember, we will still protect ourselves no matter what. You are a threat to our safety now so we'll keep monitoring you. Hans will help protect you and the girl, however, his first priority is to protect us. Understand?"

Taking the number from Barnes, Garry acknowledged his orders. "I understand."

While Barnes was talking to Garry, Hans peered out the blinds of the front door. There was a commotion outside and Hans turned to face Barnes holding up three fingers.

"Quickly the back door," Barnes whispered.

Garry followed Barnes as he moved towards the back door trying to make little noise. Hans brought up the rear. As they reached the back door, they heard the glass on the front door break.

With a finger lifted in front of his mouth, Barnes whispered, "They're here."

All three quickly left through the back door and ran down the alley. Garry's heart was racing as well as his mind. *Who are these guys and why are we running from them?*

Several blocks away they stopped running and climbed into a white utility van. Hans got into the driver's seat and Barnes joined Garry in the back on the floor.

Between gasps for air Garry asked, "Who were those guys?"

"Probably the same guys who killed your friend and our associate. We believe they work for Michaels. Mr. Garry, are you okay?"

"Yeah, I will be."

Garry had not run for his life since he was in the Navy. He knew the enemy that caused his fear back then as well as the reason. However, the fear he now felt was unlike anything he had ever felt before. He did not know who the enemy was, what they wanted or who he could trust especially if Fletcher was dead.

"Mr. Garry, I have to leave before they find me. I need to report back. Hans will take you home to get whatever you need and then take you to a hotel. Please remember our agreement; all of our lives depend on it."

While he spoke, Barnes changed into a blue jumpsuit and donned a tool belt and hardhat. He said good-bye, left the van and walked to the construction site across the street.

After catching his breath, Garry's thoughts were on Martha. He had to warn her not to go back to the office and to make those calls. He pulled out his cell phone and started to dial.

"No! No calls!" Hans shouted.

"But I need to call my receptionist."

Hans produced his own cell phone from his coat pocket and handed it to Garry. "This, they cannot trace."

For the first time Garry noticed the man's accent. Maybe Hans was *his* real name. He took the phone and started to dial as Hans started the van and drove away.

* * *

Rachel watched as Amanda looked around the room again still searching. Nothing she tried to do to get Amanda's attention worked and now there was a man named Joe, sitting at their table talking to Amanda. She watched in horror as Joe grabbed Amanda's arm and led her out the back door. No one was helping. No one was doing anything except watching. Something had to be done. She had to save her sister. Screaming and moving did not help; nothing happened.

Suddenly Amanda was gone and with the slam of the back door, everything went black. When Rachel opened her eyes, again she was standing outside and behind the restaurant. Still unable to speak or move, she watched as Joe appeared still holding Amanda's arm and leading her to a car.

He commanded her, "Get in," as he opened the passenger door. When she hesitated and tried to pull away, he fetched a gun from his trench coat pocket, which he quickly pointed at her. Again, he ordered her, "Get in!"

This time she complied and got in the car. As Joe ran around the car to the driver's side, the sound of sirens became deafening and Rachel's heart was filled with hope. *They're gonna catch him! She'll be safe now.* Joe put the car in gear and sped away dashing her hopes.

As his taillights disappeared in the night, the police officers, who came barreling out of the back door of the restaurant, looked everywhere, but found nothing. Not even the tracks the car had left in the dirt. Rachel tried to tell them where the car went, but they did not even acknowledge her being there. Once again, she was helpless and closed her eyes to scream knowing no one would hear it.

Things went black again. A second later, she heard voices

and opened her eyes. Focusing, she realized that she was in the back seat of a car. In the front seat, a man was driving and a woman sat in the passenger seat. The woman was upset about something.

"What do you think you're doing? Stop this car and let me out! I'm not who you think I am."

The woman turned to look out the rear window and Rachel saw her face. *Amanda*!

"Amanda, I'm here! Take my hand!"

Over and over Rachel screamed for her sister, there was no reply or reaction from her. Joe did not react either. Helpless like before, all she could do was watch as her sister fired off question after question at the driver. It was clear she was trying to understand what was going on.

Time passed as the car flew down the road but there was no scenery on either side, just blackness. Finally, the car stopped and Joe ordered Amanda out. He leads her to the back of the car, ties her up and pushes her into the trunk.

Tears run down Rachel's face as she pleads with Joe, when he gets back into the car, to let her sister go. With all her might, she tried to get him to see her or hear her, but he does not. He drives on.

Once more, it's black and when Rachel opens her eyes, she's standing behind two men. In front of them is the car with the trunk open. The men are talking but she cannot hear what they are saying. The one in the trench coat hands a gun to the man in a suit. As he does, the man in the suit moves and Rachel can see into the trunk. Inside is Amanda, tied up. Again, Rachel tries to get to her sister, but cannot move. She can only stand and watch as the man in the suit speaks.

"Good-bye, my dear."

*Amanda glares at him. She knows him! She's shaking her head. Through the tape, she's pleading for mercy. Oh God, do something! Save her! Do something! ...*

*BANG!*

*"Ahhhhhhh!"*

Jolted out of her sleep and sitting straight up in bed, Rachel found herself still screaming. Frightened and confused, she could not focus or determine where she was. A cough made her leave her nightmare. Gasping for breath and holding her throat, she finally realized where she was. She yanked the pull chain on the lamp next to her bed to turn on the light.

The illuminated room brought little comfort, as she understood that she had another Amanda dream. Tears flowed down her face from the fear she felt. They flowed for her sister and the fear she must have felt. They also flowed because the dream would not go away and now it went even further.

*Oh my God! The man in the trench coat was Joe! Joe Coffee, the drug dealer I dated years ago. Why would he be in my dream? What's happening to me? Why am I dreaming again? How do I stop it? What do you want from me!*

She collapsed into a fetal position as her sobs became uncontrollable. There was no getting around it now, the dream was back to stay. It was not going away on its own and it was becoming too scary to not deal with. There was no denying it; she needed help. It was time to call Lauren.

# 15

"I'm so sorry, Lauren, that I broke my promise to you. I really thought the dreams were from the stress and that they would go away. I was eating right and getting enough sleep before they started, but now I don't sleep well. I'm afraid that I'll have a dream each time I close my eyes. They are so real and now it's going further."

"Further?" inquired Lauren. "What do you mean by further?"

"The dream went beyond the restaurant last night. I watched as the kidnapper, who appeared to be a guy I used to date, tied Amanda up and then brought her to another man who shot her. I saw it happen. I saw the look on her face!"

"Rachel, I think it's time for you to come see me. We need to get you back into therapy. Are you available this week?"

Rachel understood Lauren's concern. She even shared it, but she was not ready to start up the therapy again. She held the phone tightly as she thought about the years of hard, emotional, scary work that took up so much of her time. She had a job now, a life beyond the walls of the Sheltering Arms hospital and she was not willing to give it up. *I'm past all that, I'm better, I can't go back!*

"Rachel, are you still there? Can you make it this week?"

Lauren would not give up. Rachel had no choice but to agree to meet and try to commit to a therapy schedule.

"I believe," she took a deep breath and let it out, "I can be available to meet you this week."

"Good, I've got two hours free on Thursday morning around ten-o'clock. Can you come then?"

"Sure Lauren. I'll be there."

"Rachel, remember what I said about things returning?"

"Yeah, I remember."

"This time I need you to trust me. It may seem that things are going fine, but if you don't finish the work, there is always the chance it will return. Do you understand?"

Rachel had to agree. "I understand, Lauren. Thanks. I'll see you on Thursday."

Hanging up the phone, Rachel returned to her day-timer and her to-do list. She crossed off the call to Dr. Claire and then added an entry on Thursday at ten-o'clock. Next, she pulled out Caleb's e-mail that she had printed to review it once more before meeting with Jane.

After reading it twice and reviewing the notes she had made about him, she was convinced that he was the right match-subject. Proud of her achievement and looking forward to hearing praise from Jane, she crossed off the second item on her to-do list. Gathering up all her files, she headed for Jane's office.

\* \* \*

Caleb had just returned from getting a cup of coffee when Jeff walked into his office.

"Hey, buddy, how ya doing?"

"Great, Jeff. You're here early."

"Yeah, I stopped by to pick up the dimensions of the pallets for Albertson's stuff. I'm going to go by and check out the rental to see how things will fit inside. But first I wanted to hear about your date. So, how was it?"

"It was...strange."

"Buddy, come on, after all the build up about this service all you can tell me is *it was strange*? What happened? Where'd you go? What was she like? Come on man, details!"

"Okay, okay. We met at Maggianos. I knew she was pretty, but I wasn't expecting..."

* * *

"Caleb?"

"Oh, I'm sorry. Was I staring again?"

"Yes, you were."

"Does it make you uncomfortable, Anna?"

"Well, I'm a little embarrassed by it. I haven't been out in a while and I'm not used to this."

"Okay, I'll try to stop. It's just that I never thought...I mean I never expected...what I'm trying to say is that you're...oh, I'm messing this up."

"Do you get tongue-tied a lot?"

Caleb stopped and stared at Anna again. There was another question about what he is like. She had already asked so many of these types of questions. It was hard for him to describe what he was like. What he thought himself to be was one thing, though people never seemed to see him this way. How they saw him was not what he wanted to share. *Where's the balance?*

"Caleb, you're doing it again."

Caleb shook his head and looked at his plate. "Forgive me. I'm not good at this."

"Do women make you nervous?"

Caleb was nervous. She had too many questions and he was feeling like he was in an interview. Instead of answering, he changed the subject. "Tell me about your family."

Anna took a sip of wine and refolded the napkin in her lap for the tenth time. "I grew up in Blacksburg with my parents and my sister, Amanda. My dad worked for the weather station at Virginia Tech. and Amanda and I went to school there. Amanda died about ten years ago, which was very hard for me. I finished my degree to honor her and help people overcome what I've been through."

She looked up and caught him staring again. He could not help it. While she was talking, he had noticed that other men in the restaurant were staring at her too. They saw the same beauty that Caleb saw and it made him feel privileged, as if he was somebody to be with someone so desired. Anna continued without saying anything about the staring.

"Now that I have my degree I feel I can give back what was given to me. That's why I took this research job. It's an area I'm good at and I thought I'd be able to find ways to help people beyond the normal therapy sessions." She took another sip of wine.

"Sounds like you've had some challenges in your life and your new job sounds, interesting."

"Tell me about your business."

Caleb stumbled over his words trying to explain what it was that he and Jeff did. His mind was not on what he was saying. Thoughts of his inadequacies and her upper-class status kept assaulting him as he tried to make sense of his current life. She ate as he talked and it appeared that she was not that interested, which made it harder for him to speak clearly.

Outside the restaurant, they stood facing each other. Caleb felt sick. He knew he had ruined the night. There was no magic in the air, no sparkle in her eyes; nothing said they would meet again.

"Thanks for dinner, Caleb. It was nice meeting you."

"I enjoyed it." He lied.

They stood there looking around, at the people walking by, the valet driving a car off, the night sky that was clear and cloudless, anywhere, but at each other. Neither said anything more until the valet returned with Rachel's car. One look and Caleb was convinced it was all over.

To Caleb's surprise, the valet handed the keys to him. They both chuckled and he handed them to Anna. They shook hands, said good-bye and he watched her drive off – the story of his life.

\* \* \*

"Shook hands? You didn't try to kiss her?"

"No," Caleb said as he gave Jeff a scowl. "I wouldn't do that."

"Did you want to kiss her?"

"Well, yeah, I guess."

"You guess? Are you gonna see her again?"

"Don't know. Neither of us asked."

"Man, you are right, it was strange. Do you *want* to go out with her again?"

"I'm not sure."

"Caleb! Man what's going on?"

"I'm sorry, Jeff. It's just not as easy as I thought it would be. I just seem to fumble over myself, as if I don't know what to talk about except work. I guess I'm afraid to fail again."

"Buddy, you should try again. Maybe she was nervous as well, you know, first date and all."

"Maybe, and maybe I'm not ready for this."

Caleb paused as he thought about how hard it was to start over, to begin a new life in the middle of life. He was not a kid anymore with a whole lifetime ahead of him. Things could not start the way they used to and mistakes were too risky at this point. Starting over meant making sure and making sure was something he just could not define.

"Caleb, remember, don't force things. Let God guide you, but you have to take steps before you can be guided. If she's not the one, you'll know. Trust your heart and give your mind a rest."

"Easier said than done, my friend. It's a habit I just haven't learned yet."

"It's time to start learning new habits, buddy. Baby steps lead to walking. Got to run. Let me know what happens."

"Thanks, Jeff, I'll keep you up to date."

* * *

"So he actually said he wished there was something he could do to let people know about Albertson?" asked Jane.

"Yes, he did. I knew he was the one right then, reviewing the e-mail was just icing on the cake."

Rachel showed Jane several answers that Caleb had given to her questions that also indicated that he wanted Albertson stopped. They had found their man.

"Great work, Rachel. I must say, I didn't expect you to move so quickly, but in a short while you've made marvelous progress. Congratulations."

Rachel was all smiles as she expressed her thanks, "You've been a big help and encouragement Jane. My success is partly because of you."

"Well, let's not get too far ahead of ourselves. We have a match-subject, but he hasn't accomplished anything yet."

The smile on Rachel's face quickly disappeared. Jane was right – she had not accomplished anything, either. This was only the beginning with the hardest part still to come.

As Jane walked to her desk she continued, "I believe you need to meet with Caleb some more and as you do you'll pass on information that will help him decide to do something about Albertson."

Rachel knew the dates were not over, but she hoped they could be. It was not that she disliked Caleb, but that she did like him and wanted to get to know him better. Easing other people's pain was her mission to repay those who had eased hers. However, this was not going to end painlessly and she knew she would be the cause. If it were just a name and picture over wires it would not be so bad, but here was a real person with real feelings. She could only hope that in the end Caleb would gain enough satisfaction from exposing Albertson that he would forgive her for what she had done.

Jane returned to her chair with a folder that she handed to Rachel.

"What's this?" Rachel asked.

"It's what you will eventually give to Caleb," Jane said with no emotion in her voice and a mournful expression on her face. "Open it."

Rachel gasped as she opened the file. Inside was a stack of photos. The first was of two little girls in dresses lying in a pile of debris that looked like the remains of a house.

"They were eight and ten," Jane explained. "While they played in the family room their dad was high and playing in the basement with matches and propane tanks. The mom said he had been attending Albertson's meetings over the past month before this happened."

The second picture was just as gruesome. A pregnant woman lay on the ground with multiple gun shot wounds.

"She was just passing by when an upset junkie pulled out a shotgun and fired it. He was trying to shoot the person who would not sell him any more drugs and he missed. The guy he was trying to shoot had been seen at Albertson's meetings several times."

As Rachel looked at each of the thirteen pictures, Jane told the story. The results of what Albertson was truly pushing. It was the real story, the real reason he needed stopping. Rachel was speechless. Her only emotion was anger mixed with fear. For the first time, she was getting the bigger picture. The task was much greater than she had imagined and holding the pictures made her realize the danger she was placing on Caleb and herself. It took her a few minutes to form the words and ask the question, but it finally came out.

"Who's going to protect Caleb?"

Jane looked her in the eyes, "That's why we have a security department. Starting Wednesday afternoon, you will be meeting with Mr. Myers, our head of security, each week to fill him in on your progress. He is responsible for developing and executing the plan to protect Caleb. However, we don't want to waste time developing a plan for someone who is not going to accept the task, so you need to get a commitment from him."

"What kind of commitment?"

"You need to pose the question to him that if given the opportunity to do something about Albertson, would he? Or is he just talk? Get the answer to that and Myers can move forward."

Rachel's heart began to beat faster. This was now moving faster and was much bigger than she wanted it to be. *Timing, when?*

"How long do I have to get his answer?"

Again, Jane's voice was emotionless, but her expression showed concern. "Since you're meeting with Myers Wednesday, I suggest you get Caleb's answer as soon as possible. There is no time to wait. When you meet, share what you have to, a little at a time. If you need to, bring up the pictures, show them to him if it's necessary, but make sure it's his idea not yours. Understand?"

"I understand."

For several minutes, they both sat in silence. Rachel was stunned, this was not the world she imagined herself in after graduating. Before leaving Jane's office, she flipped through the pictures once more. Anger and fear gave way to empathy for those that had lost something due to Albertson. Their pain instantly connected them to her as she recalled her own pain. *How many has he hurt? How many are in pain? How many suffered at his hands?* Before the lump in her throat made her nose run, Rachel slammed the folder shut, gathered her things and left without saying a word to Jane. On the way to her office, she could not hold back the tears any longer. With her free hand, she covered her mouth until she rushed through the doorway of her office and closed the door behind her dropping everything she was holding. Slowly, she slid down the door as she sank to the floor and buried her face in her knees.

Her mind raced as she cried. She thought about Amanda, Caleb, the people in the photos, their families, her parents and herself. Each had suffered at the hands of someone else and only those who had could understand how it felt. A voice inside kept reminding her of how helpless she was. It got louder and louder and louder until it blocked out every other thought, until it engulfed Rachel's thoughts. She grabbed her head trying to stop the voice, to shut it off, but it wouldn't go away. It continued to nag and make fun of her.

At that moment, something snapped inside of Rachel and she screamed, "STOP!"

Then silence. No voice, no nagging, only silence. She closed her eyes and took in a deep breath, enjoying the sound of herself exhaling. Then a whisper, *"Fear no more."*

"What? Who..."

Rachel looked around the office, but no one was there. She got up and opened the door. No one. Stepping into the hallway, she saw no one. Turning around and seeing the mess on the floor redirected Rachel thoughts and she began picking up her papers.

As she placed the pictures that had fallen out of the folder, back in, a new sensation came over her. It was not one of hate or anger. It was not fear or empathy. It was determination. It was time to do something.

Laying everything on her desk, she took her seat and logged on to The Connection. *Let's see if Caleb's busy tonight.*

* * *

The day had ended uneventfully, the way Caleb liked it. He had gotten used to his routine and as long as it was routine his anxiety level remained low. However, routine could never replace loneliness and as he entered his empty apartment, once again no one greeted him. His apartment had become a constant reminder of his failure at relationships.

As he settled in, sitting on his couch, his mind returned to The Connection and Anna. He replayed, in his mind, their date trying to determine if there was any indication of her being nervous or that she really liked him, but nothing stood out.

*Why is this so hard? What am I doing wrong? When are things going to go right for me?*

Questions, so many questions with no answers and he was getting tired of them. It made him angry to know that he was powerless to change things and lacked the energy to do something about it. Frustrated and confused, wanting to do something and not knowing what to do, he let his instinct reign. Without thinking about it, he bowed his head and prayed.

"Lord, where are you? Why have you left me to myself? You and I both know I'm incapable of anything, so why did you leave me? What good could come from this? When and where will this journey end? Lord, end this, take me out of this, and restore my heart."

As Caleb opened his eyes, there in front of him, on the coffee table, was his Bible lying open. He could not remember what he had last read, if anything, but several lines were underlined on the page. He picked up the Bible for a closer look.

> Yet those who wait for the Lord
> Will gain new strength;
> They will mount up with wings like eagles,
> They will run and not get tired,
> They will walk and not become weary.

*Isaiah 40:31.* Caleb remembered when he taught on this verse at the church. It seemed like decades ago.

*To wait is to have hope. Like waiting for your parents to pick you up. There is a hope that they will come and because they always have, waiting, hoping, is not hard to do. However, for those whose parents did not always come, it is harder for them to wait the next time. Their hope turns to anxiety.*

*However, no matter which group you fall into, when your parents do show up your hope is strengthened. Those whose parents have not disappointed them don't realize the degree of strengthening, but those who have been disappointed, they know full well what it means to have their hope strengthened.*

*All of us fit into this category of being disappointed if we are breathing. None of us will escape this life without being disappointed. But when we wait and are no longer disappointed, we too will run and not get tired, walk and not become weary.*

It was the one lesson the church leaders requested him to teach multiple times during the year. Now, years later, as he remembered it, it spoke to his disappointed spirit.

*Wait, but still watch. God's timing is not our own. There will be a time when I am no longer disappointed.*

There was no longer a reason to ask why, only when, and this brought a sense of relief to Caleb. There was more going on than he could understand and it was time to let go of trying to comprehend what was so far beyond him. It was enough to wait and watch, like a child watching down the road for the family car and his parents who would come to get him.

Without knowing why, Caleb had moved from the couch to his desk and turned on the computer. Something about watching gave him the need to check for a note from Anna. Quickly, he signed on to The Connection and saw the message light flashing. Opening the e-mail, he began to read.

Hi, Caleb,

I wanted to let you know how much I enjoyed our time yesterday. I'm sorry if it seemed as if I asked a lot of questions. I guess as a researcher its part of the training. I hope I didn't turn you off.
I was wondering if you were busy tonight. If not, maybe we could get together.

Let me know. I'll be waiting.

Anna

Checking his watch, Caleb realized that it was too late to meet tonight and felt sad about it. He wished he had Anna's phone number to call and talk to her, but all he could do is reply to her message.

Anna,

I'm so sorry; I just got your e-mail. I wish I had checked earlier. I also wish I had your number to call you, but this will have to do.

I would love to get together with you again. How does lunch tomorrow sound? My office is not too far from town if you'd like to meet somewhere near your office.

Caleb finished off the message by giving his home phone number, in case she checked her e-mails tonight, and his office number, in case she did not check until the morning. He wanted her to find him. After sending the message, Caleb bowed his head once more, "Lord, thanks for not giving up on me. I'll be waiting."

# 16

Rachel sat at a corner table on the patio of *La Portique* so that she could see Caleb coming. It was a nice day and the patio kept them away from the main crowd. The night had passed without a dream, probably because exhaustion finally took over. Even though rested, she waited with her stomach in knots and her anxiety level high, still trying to get over the images she had seen yesterday and the feelings about dating again. There was every reason to be nervous about this meeting and she could not keep still.

The goal was to leave with some sort of commitment from Caleb. Somehow, she had to get him to express his desire to act against Albertson without her suggesting it and accomplish it within the span of a lunch break or another date tonight. The pressure was great, the stakes were high and she was determined to succeed.

Through the crowd came the man for which she had been waiting. She watched as he walked towards the deli seeking her out. Was it her imagination or did he seem more confident in the way he walked? As he neared, she stood and waved, which caught his attention.

When Caleb approached the table, Rachel, without thinking

about it, wrapped her arms around his neck and gave him a long, firm hug. He returned the gesture. Rachel realized how good this felt. It had been so long since someone held her for no reason and longer still since a man had done it. For a moment, everything else seemed to disappear and she wanted this moment to last forever.

The last time someone held her in an intimate way was with Joe. He wanted to force himself on her and she was not willing to go there. Before Joe, it was Tripp, who was the same and it turned her off. She wanted it to be special with the man with whom she would spend her life. Her friends called her idealistic, but her heart told her it was right. When she felt Caleb pull back, she released her hold on him.

"I'm sorry. I didn't quite expect that welcome. I did enjoy it though," he said.

"It didn't make you feel uncomfortable, did it?"

"No, Anna...well...a little."

"Okay, I'll try to control myself in the future, until we know each other better."

"I look forward to knowing you better, Anna. I'm so glad you called this morning. It's too bad we couldn't get together last night, I was excited about seeing you again."

A waiter interrupted their conversation to ask about drinks. They ordered and took some time to make their meal selection. In no time, the waiter returned, placing their iced teas on the table.

"Anna," Caleb said. "Are you okay? You seem to be nervous. Is there something bothering you?"

There was no denying that she was fidgety and this question

could lead right into what she wanted to talk about but she decided it was too early to get down to business. She wanted to establish a certain trust level first.

"As a matter of fact, there is, but it's not you. I received some bad news at the office that I'd like to tell you about. I want to hold off on it and ask you something first, if you don't mind?"

She looked at him with hopeful eyes wanting him to trust her to get back to his question. If he was willing to wait, she knew he would be willing to trust her with more.

"Okay, ask away, but I want you to know that I'm a pretty good listener also."

Until he said this, she had not realized that Jane was the only person with whom she could share this information. She could not share any of this with anyone else. It would be nice to have someone listen to her for a change.

"Well, Caleb, remember the other day when we were chatting online?"

He nodded.

"You were talking about a faith healer that broke up your marriage."

Again he nodded.

"What was the guy's name?"

"Albertson," he replied. "Brian Albertson. Why, does he have something to do with the news you heard?"

"Well, yes."

There was no better time to spill it. He was ready. The situation had presented itself and he asked. *He's curious*. While the waiter set their sandwiches on the table, Rachel took the time to rehearse how to present the material. When the waiter left, Caleb began to eat his chicken salad as she continued.

"Caleb, my research leads me into many different areas. Yesterday I received some very disturbing news about Mr. Albertson, and frankly, it's hard for me to believe. How much do you know about him?"

"Besides the fact that I hate the guy," Caleb said wiping his mouth. "I don't know much at all except where his meetings are being held. What do you know about him?"

"I read some articles that indicated he had healed people in his meetings and that as far as the police are concerned, he has not broken any laws. However, there are reports that he is distributing or selling drugs at his meetings. If he is, no one has been able to find out how he's doing it."

Caleb looked at her as he continued to eat.

"Yesterday, I saw several pictures of people who were either killed or wounded; each had some connection to Albertson and his meetings. There are people who want him stopped. The police haven't been able to prove anything yet so they leave him alone, and continue to watch him."

She paused for a moment and looked down at her turkey and swiss thinking she had said too much. With the information she had shared, she backed herself up against the wall and wondered how this next question was going to sound. She searched for the right way to say it, to phrase it so it sounded intelligent.

"Don't you think he should be stopped?"

When she looked up, he was holding his sandwich halfway between the plate and his open mouth staring at her as if lost. He was perplexed and she knew it. *Oh God, this is going to end badly!*

"What is it that you do again?" he said with a scowl.

*Whew! Still safe. I can explain this away.*

"Our firm researches guys like Albertson to make sure they're not hurting or swindling people. You wouldn't believe how many of these types pop up all over the country each year and our job is to make sure no one gets hurt, if we can."

*It worked, he's eating again.*

"Must be a tough job, digging up all that information."

"Well, we do have quite an extensive database on some of these guys."

Somewhat relaxed and feeling as if she had avoided a fiasco, Rachel watched for some indication of what he was thinking. There was no preparing her for what he said next.

"Then you probably know that our company is picking up shipments for Albertson at the coast and delivering them here to his warehouse."

Now her mouth hung open. None of her research uncovered this and she was sure Jane did not know or she would have told her. She was losing ground. *If Caleb is making money off Albertson, there is no way he was going to help bring him down. How did we miss this?* There was a little reprieve when Caleb added...

"We've only just started doing this last week. Maybe that's too new for you to know."

"I don't understand," Rachel quipped, with her head shaking

and her eyes closed. "Why would you ship things to him when he's the one responsible for ruining your marriage?"

"Well, first, I'm not doing the deliveries. I told Jeff, my partner, that he had to do them or there was no contract. However, although he was responsible for what happened to Jena and me, that's no reason to not make money off him. It's a matter of economics and one he can afford."

Their conversation was not going where she wanted it to and it seemed that Caleb would never commit. He had finished his lunch, but hers was barely touched and her appetite was disappearing like her chances. *Think, quickly!* Her mind raced for something else to say that would bring the conversation back to him doing something about Albertson. Nothing came to mind. *Oh no, he's checking his watch!*

"Anna, I hate to end our time, but I do need to get back to the office."

There it was; the needle that poked a telephone pole size hole in her balloon. As the air rushed out, Rachel sat there deflated, unable to say anything, dreading the task of reporting to Jane.

"Anna, I hope I didn't make it sound like I condone what Albertson's doing. He's a scum and needs to be taken down. If I had a chance and the know-how, I'd do something, but I don't."

*That was it! He said it! I didn't coax him. He did it on his own! He's in!* In a matter of seconds, her patched balloon refilled to an even greater size than before and it lifted her, literally, out of her seat.

"What I can offer you," Caleb continued as he stood up, "is a way to get the proof about him you're looking for."

Rachel barely heard what Caleb had said. She watched as he moved close to her. This time he was not timid. Not only did he give her a hug, but also as he pulled back, his eyes met hers and slowly he leaned in and brought his lips to hers. It was the gentlest kiss she had ever received and it quickly flowed through her whole body setting off every nerve ending she had.

There was no need for words and she watched as he walked away. Her eyes followed his every step as her nerve endings continued to fire. It was not until he disappeared that the tape recorder she had been using clicked off. Apparently, it had run out of tape.

Knowing she got his commitment, but unsure of how it happened, she packed her stuff and headed back to the office. On her face was the ear-to-ear smile she with which she had become so familiar. *Wait until Jane hears about this!*

* * *

Sitting two tables away from where Caleb and Rachel sat was a man reading a newspaper. Over the edge of the paper, he watched every move they made. Though he could not hear much, he had an idea of what they were discussing.

As Caleb and Rachel stood and embraced, the man's waiter arrived with his check. He quickly signed the check and handed it back to the waiter.

"Thank you, Pedro," he said.

The waiter replied as he took the check, "Thank you, Senõr Michaels." He bowed his head and walked away.

*There is chemistry between those two, which will enhance their task,* Michaels thought. Then he folded up his paper as he watched them part and leave. *This is moving along quite nicely.*

* * *

Halfway back to the office, Caleb came down off the high from lunch, giving way to thoughts of Jena and then to thoughts of Albertson. He wondered why he kept running into people who this man harmed. Worse, why had he allowed Jeff to talk him into doing business with Albertson? *What have we become a part of?*

He knew that Jeff had checked out the product that they were shipping and he trusted Jeff, but there was still a sick feeling in his stomach that told him something was wrong. Jeff had spent time, years ago, going through his own detox program. *He would know drugs if he saw them, wouldn't he?*

Caleb was determined to find out what they were transporting. *Maybe, if it is drugs, it's something Jeff's never seen before.* Then a thought popped into his mind that never would have occurred to him before today. There was never a reason to doubt Jeff before. *Could it be that Jeff knows about the drugs and couldn't pass up the money we were offered? Why would they offer such a ridiculous sum anyway?*

This last thought made Caleb feel extremely guilty. They had been friends and partners for so long and Jeff was like a big brother to Caleb. *How could I mistrust Jeff?* The guilty feeling lingered until Caleb reached the office. *One way or another I'm going to find out the truth.*

Once inside, Caleb inquired of the staff about Jeff's whereabouts. No one had seen him all day. Caleb thought about calling him on the radio, and then decided against it. No, he wanted to find the file on the Albertson shipments first and read it before he talked to Jeff. If Jeff was hiding something, Caleb wanted to know.

Searching Jeff's office turned up nothing. Expecting to find the file in the cabinet with the other contracts, Caleb grew suspicious when it was not there. He searched Jeff's desk but found nothing there, either. As he was going through the desk drawers, Jeff walked in on him.

"Hey…buddy…what'd you lose?" Jeff said cautiously.

Startled, Caleb met Jeff's glare. It was a look Caleb had never seen before; one of hurt, confusion and betrayal. Never before had either of them gone through the other's stuff. That was sacred ground and as close as they were they never stepped over that line, until now.

"If I knew what you were looking for I might be able to help you find it in *my* office."

Jeff's words stung and in that instance, Caleb wished he had waited. Once again, the hand of Albertson had reached out and affected one more person, one more relationship, one more of Caleb's relationships.

"Jeff, you don't understand…this is not what it looks like…" Caleb caught himself and started over. "I'm sorry, Jeff. I got some news at lunch that made me wonder about the Albertson shipments and I wanted to reread the file on them. You weren't here so I looked for it. Do you have it?"

Jeff's sarcastic tone did not change as he answered Caleb. "Yeah, I have it. Remember, yesterday I told you I was getting the dimensions of the pallets. I grabbed the whole file and haven't been back to re-file it until now."

"May I see it, please?"

"Sure, but what are you looking for?"

"Jeff, at lunch I found out that several people had been killed in drug related incidents that seem to be traced back to Albertson's meetings. Some people think he is distributing or selling drugs at these meetings."

"Caleb, just because some people, who are junkies, attend his meetings and then kill some others doesn't mean Albertson has anything to do with it."

"But we don't know that for sure, and we don't know what he's got in those boxes that we are transporting for him. Do you realize what kind of trouble we'll be in if he *is* shipping drugs and we're transporting them and get caught? Our whole business will be shut down!"

"I don't believe this! Caleb, I checked those boxes while I was out there. Remember, we always do this. It's part of our contract before we ship anything. The boxes contained little vials of water with a wax seal on top. I opened a few and check them out."

"What'd you do, open them up and smell them? What does that prove?"

It was clear that Jeff was not taking Caleb's third degree very well and he snapped back quickly.

"I not only opened it and smelled it, but I poured it out, felt it, tasted it and tried to burn it. Even if it was a new kind of drug on the market it would still burn and leave a scent or at the very least, I should have felt something from the taste, which, by the way, I drank the whole vial. It was water I tell you and that's all!"

Caleb had no reply. Jeff was thorough, this could not be argued, but even with all that he did, it was not enough to satisfy Caleb."

"What if they changed vials on you knowing that the ones you tested were just water?"

"Man, I don't believe you. I tested five different vials, each from a separate box, a different box from five different pallets, and they let me make the choices. There are no *drugs!*"

Caleb stood firm in his quest. "Well, I still want to read the file."

"Fine," Jeff agreed as he tossed the file to Caleb. "But you won't find anything in there."

Catching the file, Caleb thanked Jeff and left his office heading across the hall to his own.

"By the way, who did you get this information from?" Jeff demanded.

For a second, Caleb thought about his answer. No matter how he presented it to Jeff, it was going to sound crazy. However, he had just insulted his best friend and partner in the worst way, what could be crazier than that?

"I had lunch with Anna and her research company has been checking out Albertson. Her information indicates that Albertson is involved in drug trafficking."

"And you believe her?"

"I have no reason not to believe her, Jeff."

"You've only know this woman for a few days, me you've know for years and you're taking her word over mine?"

"No. I'm not taking her word over yours. I just want to know more about what we are shipping and who the guys are that are supplying the vials. I want to make sure there is no liability for us."

Jeff had followed Caleb into his office and as Caleb sat down, Jeff closed the door.

"Let me ask you a straight question and I want a straight answer. Are you doing this because you're trying to get back at Albertson for what happened with Jena?"

Caleb met Jeff's glare once more and did not like getting the third degree either.

"I have to admit, there is a part of me that would love to get even with Albertson, but this is not about revenge. This is about protecting our company. This is about survival. Besides, I'm not actually doing anything except asking some questions and searching for answers that will appease my own mind."

"Why? You have never done this in the past. You have always trusted my judgment and me. What's causing you to doubt me now?"

*Ouch!* Jeff had thrown a second dagger and it found its mark. Caleb paused; no words could make this right for either of them, so he chose not to answer the question and continue his research. In his mind, he had reasoned that if he found something, then Jeff would understand and it would be over. If he did not, then he could humbly apologize with a clean conscience knowing Jeff was right. Either way, the truth was going to end the argument. He lowered his head and began to read, leaving Jeff to stew as he left.

\* \* \*

Barely did she have time to drop her stuff on her desk when her phone rang. It was Jane. Apparently, a visitor had dropped by that she wanted to introduce to Rachel.

Her thoughts were on lunch as she headed down the hall to Jane's office. For some reason Caleb was more handsome today than before. He was more confident and sure of himself. Even more romantic, this left her wondering if it would be possible to continue a relationship when this was all over.

Approaching Jane's office, she could see through the open curtains and blinds that a man was sitting in front of her desk with his back towards the door. Jane sat at her desk and rose just as Rachel walked up.

"Rachel, hey. There is someone here to meet you."

There was a smile on Jane's face, but her eyes were not smiling. Something was wrong. Jane was not happy with this meeting. *Why? What's going on? Who is he?*

"Please come in," Jane added.

Rachel watched as the man rose and buttoned his jacket.

"I'd like to introduce you to Jason Michaels, the founder and CEO of A. E. Research."

As Jane said this, Michaels turned to face Rachel and extended his hand. Rachel took a step towards him and followed his gesture until she fully saw his face. After a gasp, which everyone heard, Rachel covered her mouth with both hands and stood motionless.

The smile on both Michaels' and Jane's faces disappeared.

Jane was quick to inquire, "Rachel, are you okay? What's wrong?"

"There's nothing wrong, Ms. Madison," Michaels said lowering his hand. "It's just been a long time since we've seen each other."

"What? You two know each other?" Now it was Jane's turn to be stunned.

"Ms. Madison, I wonder if you would be as kind as to give us a few moments together please."

Nodding her head, she agreed. "Oh…sure, sure." Then left and closed the door.

"Well, I didn't expect you to be speechless," Michaels said as he sat on the corner of Jane's desk. Gesturing to the couch, he invited Rachel to sit. "It's been a long time."

"Yes, it has," Rachel replied. "And if I'm not mistaken, you used to go by the name Tripp. What's the deal?"

"The name? Well, it's simple really. Jason is my middle name. My father believed that it was unwise to use your real name in business; it helps keep your private life private. I just adopted his belief."

"What about when we were dating? You worked and still used your first name. Wasn't I part of your private life?"

"Of course you were. It's just that back then I was young and foolish. I hadn't yet believed the way my father did. You were always important to me and I never wanted to hurt you."

"You didn't? I remember you were upset with me when I broke up with you. In fact, I believe you said you never wanted to see me again and that I would pay for breaking up with you."

Rachel could feel her anger growing and was not sure why. It had been almost ten and a half years since she had broken up with Tripp, what could cause such strong emotions?

"People say a lot of silly things when they're young and hurting. You broke my heart when you left me and started seeing that druggie...Joe"

"I didn't know Joe was a drug addict and dealer at the time and neither did you!"

"I know. The point is I was lashing out from my pain. But people change over time. I've changed as I'm sure you have, right? You're not the same person you were back then, are you?"

Rachel knew there was no way of answering his question without falling into his trap – he had her either way. She despised him for doing this, for bringing her back to the way things were before. He was good at backing her into a corner, then and now. She hated it. There was never a time when she could let her guard down and just be herself. She knew he would corner her during a time of weakness and did not want that to happen. Years later, *nothing* had changed.

"Let me ask you a question. Did you have anything to do with me getting hired on here?"

"Me? No. Our company is always searching for the brightest minds with a lot of talent. You fit the bill, which is why they approached you. Besides, I'm not here much. I spend most of my time in Washington, so these folks operate under strict guidelines with or without me."

"Washington? Wow. So you've become all you wanted to be and followed in your father's footsteps."

"Yes, and I'm proud of it."

"So, do you run things in Washington too?"

"Oh no," Michaels said with a chuckle. "They inform me of the things they want us involved in and I make it happen. Currently, it's this Albertson guy they want to see stopped. Ms. Madison tells me you're making much progress in this area. That's good. I'm looking forward to seeing your results."

Michaels checked his watch and quickly stood. "It seems we are out of time. I have another appointment and need to go. I was early and had heard that you were hired, so I took some time to see an old friend."

Rachel stood as Michaels headed for the door. His path took him next to her and he placed his arm around her shoulders to escort her to the door. Through the glass wall, Rachel could see Jane walking back towards her office.

"It was good to see you, Rachel, after all these years. I hope you will forgive my rashness from years ago and that it will not interfere with us working together."

As Jane opened the door, Michaels dropped his arm and added, "It's good to have you on our team, Rachel."

Rachel stood facing Michaels staring into his eyes, not knowing what to do or say. It was uncomfortable and awkward. Years of memories and emotions were suddenly stirred up again and vying for attention. The stare was not endearing and Jane must have noticed it.

"Is everything okay?" Jane said.

Rachel turned to face Jane, whose expression was one of a kindred spirit, then back to Michaels before answering, "Yes, everything's fine."

# 17

"Come on, Caleb, you know I wouldn't ask you to do this if I could do it myself. I've got a hundred-and-one fever and I've spent the night running back and forth to the bathroom. You know I hardly ever get sick but I've got the flu and I don't think I'll be better by morning. Besides, someone has to pick up the rental today."

"Okay, Jeff. I know you're sick. You don't have to beg. I'll do it, but just this once. From now on, you can never get sick in the middle of the week as long as we have the Albertson contract. Agreed?"

Caleb listened to Jeff hacking on the other end of the phone before he answered.

"Agreed."

"Listen, Jeff," Caleb began, once more trying to apologize. "I know I've already said this twice, but I guess it just hasn't come out the way I wanted it to yet."

Again, Caleb listened to Jeff's suffering.

"I'll let you go. I just wanted you to know how sorry I am that I doubted you."

"It's okay, buddy. I'll talk to you tomorrow."

Even as he hung up the phone there was still a lump in Caleb's throat. Somehow, he still was not able to put into words the deep regret he felt over offending his friend. His guilt caused him to agree to do the Albertson delivery. Jeff was the better man. Even though was unjustly accused, he graciously accepted Caleb's apologies and forgave him. Caleb knew that even if he did a hundred Albertson deliveries it would never make up for what he did.

To take his mind off his guilt, Caleb focused on the to-do list he started before Jeff had called. If he moved quickly, he could accomplish the important tasks and still pick up the truck by four-o'clock. This would put him in Newport News before seven. He could drop off the truck and catch a cab to the hotel. A quiet dinner and a good night's sleep would prepare him for the morning.

Before he could dial Tina's extension to have her change the hotel reservation into his name, his phone rang.

"Tina, I was just about to call you."

"Caleb, I have Ms. Anna Clark on the phone for you. Do you want me to transfer her to your voice mail?"

Caleb did not want to talk to her. She had already caused too much pain and they did not even have much of a relationship. He decided against putting her off and asked Tina to send her through. It was time to end it. Before letting Tina go he asked her to fix the reservation.

"I already did."

"When? How did you know?"

"Well, it doesn't take a rocket-scientist to know Jeff can't drive sick."

"Tina, I apologize, I keep underestimating you."

"Yeah, well, how about showing your appreciation in my paycheck?"

"We'll have to talk about that next week, after I can talk to Jeff."

"I'll put Ms. Clark through."

While Caleb waited for the phone to ring again, he thought through what he wanted to say. He needed to be firm, but not cruel. Anna was not a bad person; she was just trying to do her job. However, her concern was not his and he wanted to keep it that way.

"Caleb, I'm glad I found you here."

"Good morning, Anna."

"Have you found anything?"

"*Found anything?*"

"Yeah, yesterday you said you would see if you could get me the proof I needed. Remember? I assumed that meant you were going to check on the deliveries you are making."

"I remember, Anna."

"Did you check? What did you find?"

"I did check, Anna, and as a matter of fact I found nothing."

"*Nothing? What?*"

"Anna, listen, I spent...no, wasted a lot of time yesterday on a wild goose chase and almost alienated my best friend and partner. I didn't find anything that proves Albertson is what you say he is."

Although Caleb tried not to let his emotions get in the way of what he was saying, he failed. His volume raised and his tone got sharp. He paused to start again.

"Anna, I have enjoyed the time we spent together and I think you're a wonderful person...but I don't think this is going to work out for us."

"I'm sorry to hear you say that, Caleb. I thought things were going okay and that we had a connection because of Albertson, even if it was a negative one. I would like to show you some other information I have on him. Maybe your deliveries are legit, but you should know more about the guy you're doing business with. I could meet you tonight if you'd like?"

"I'm sorry. I really don't want to know more about him, I already hate him enough. Besides, I'm going out of town later this afternoon so I couldn't, even if I wanted to."

For a few minutes, there was silence. He was glad he stuck to his guns, but wondered if she was hurt. There was no question he was attracted to her and would love to have a relationship with her if only Albertson hadn't been the foundation for it.

"Caleb, I just want you to know that I am sorry for what Albertson has done to you. Maybe I focused too much on him because of my job and it was something we had in common. But I want you to know that I am attracted to you and would still like to see you if you want to. I promise I'll never bring up Albertson again unless you ask."

He was still thinking about what to say when she continued.

"Are you going to be back this week? Maybe we could get together this weekend?"

New information merged with old in Caleb's mind as he tried to decide what to do. Here was an opportunity to erase the loneliness, to have someone to share things with and do things. *Could there be a life with her outside of Albertson?* His thoughts drifted off to being so physically close to her yesterday. It filled, if only for a few hours, a void that he had been living with for eighteen and a half months. The scent of her perfume lingered on his shirt the whole day and as he removed it last night, the scent brought back the feeling, even the taste of that simple kiss. His nerves kept him from pursuing more yesterday, but now, with her opening the door, it was his decision to stay or go.

"I'll be back tomorrow, but probably late in the afternoon. I have no plans for this weekend and I would like the chance to start over if you think we can."

"I think we can and I'd like to, also."

Three nights ago, he was dying to get her number. Now, as she gave it to him and asked him to call her when he got back in town, he was not so excited. He knew what he felt and heard what she said, but his trust issue was deeper than he wanted to admit. Albertson was still out there. He was her project and his client. How were they ever going to keep him out of their relationship? This thought remained with Caleb long after he hung up the phone.

* * *

Once again, Michaels stood and greeted each of his status meeting attendees as they left. He stopped Myers this week.

"There are a few things we need to discuss, Mr. Myers. Would you be so kind as to meet me in my office in fifteen minutes?"

Michaels could see the worried look on Myers' face as he agreed.

Fifteen minutes later Myers walked into Michaels' office and took a seat. Michaels met him with a drink and took the seat next to him. There was silence, as they both tasted their scotch. Michaels watched Myers over the glass who did not meet his eyes. After a few sips, Michaels began.

"There are three things I want clarified, Mr. Myers, and I'm sure you know what I'm referring to."

Michaels watched as Myers' eyes moved up and to the right as if trying to picture the three questions. It was time for straight talk and Michaels knew Myers understood this.

"Sir, Ms. Gilbert was unable to follow through with her match-subject. He did commit, but then backed out. Since there was no subject there was no meeting."

Michaels figured as much and was disappointed that Myers did not move beyond the obvious facts. In his mind, the *why* was more important than *what happened* and he could only hope that Myers would do better with the other two issues.

"As far as Fletcher goes, we didn't find him. The tag number we got from the car two weeks ago led us to a rogue who was tailing Fletcher. The rogue put up a nasty fight and, in the end, lost. By the time we entered Fletcher's place, he was gone and we found nothing.

"Garry was also gone when we reached his office, probably out the back. We still don't know who he was with and we never found them either. My guess, Fletcher and Garry are together. Find one and we'll have them both."

Michaels swirled the remains of the ice cubes from his scotch around the bottom of the glass as he absorbed the information Myers had given him. Again, none of what he said was news except the dead tail. The rest was elementary based on what had not happened. As Michaels rose to refill his drink, he took the opportunity to mock Myers.

"It's a pity you can't ask the tail if he knows where the head is. Letting him lose the fight was convenient...for him."

Myers did not react. He sat with his eyes straight ahead watching Michaels' reflection in a mirror.

"You still have not answered my third question."

Myers raised his brow, "Sir?"

"The next martyr? Have you set this up yet?"

"Sir, I thought we had put that off for now? There are still some police and reporters asking questions about the last one."

"Myers, sometimes you surprise me. You know I have all the faith in the world in you but sometimes..."

Again, Michaels watched to see if Myers reacted. It was a test of discipline; Michaels required his top security officer never to act out of anger. He had to be able to think clearly in any situation to insure that he made the correct choice. The dead tail was an indication that Myers was not passing on these requirements, hence the test.

Michaels returned to his seat and gave Myers his orders. "Your men are getting sloppy. Get them in line or get rid of them.

Then find Garry and Fletcher, I don't want them getting any deeper than they are. Next, set up the martyr situation for this Monday night's meeting and make sure the media sees it happen. Lastly, no more mistakes, do you understand?"

Myers nodded as he placed his glass on the coffee table and stood up to leave.

"I'll want a report on where we stand by Friday afternoon, Mr. Myers."

Without turning around to face Michaels, Myers said, "Yes, sir."

Michaels remained in his seat and watched Myers leave his office. In his mind, he ran through a list of names that he had been acquiring in case he needed to replace Myers who had served him well for many years, but it seemed a change was becoming necessary. Unless Myers cleaned things up quickly, there was going to be a new head at the table come next Wednesday.

* * *

Garry paced the floor in his small hotel room. Several times he reached for the phone and stopped himself. It had been a week since he talked to Rachel and the dilemma kept him vividly occupied. An imaginary chess game played out in his head and he watched each move carefully.

Move: *I call Rachel after not calling every few days like I said.*

Counter move: *Rachel wonders if something is wrong.*

Result: *I can't tell her anything.*

Move: *I don't contact Rachel like Barnes wanted.*

Counter move: *Rachel calls my office to check on me and finds out I'm out of town. Then she leaves a message. What if the message contains information about Michaels that she wants me to check on? If Michaels has tapped my phone he'll know and she'll be in danger.*

Result: *I can't let her find out I'm gone.*

Move: *I call Rachel and apologize for forgetting to call as often as I said.*

Counter move: *Rachel knows it's not like me to forget and wants to know what's going on.*

Result: *Back in the same corner.*

Move: *I don't call Rachel.*

Counter move: *She doesn't call me.*

Result: *How do I know if she's okay or not? How long will she hold off from calling me?*

With each move a new problem arose which caused him to backtrack again. The game was getting more and more difficult to play. Then unexpectedly, there was a knock at the door. *The maid?* He waited for the normal announcement, but none came.

Another knock.

There was only one other person who knew where he was. They had arranged that Hans would always call the room first, let it ring twice then hang up and then two minutes later two knocks at the door. This was not Hans.

One more knock and a man's voice, "Garry!"

Garry recognized the voice. *Could it be?* He had hoped and wanted to believe it, but now he was not sure if the voice could be trusted. *It could be manufactured somehow.* There was no place to run and no way to contact Hans.

"Garry! Come on open the blasted door!"

That was too much. There was no way they could have manufactured that sentence or even known that Fletcher could not curse. It was him! He was alive! Garry rushed to the door and opened it.

Quickly, Fletcher rushed in and closed the door behind him. Even for two burly men, a handshake would not do in this situation and they embraced each other with all the affection of two brothers.

"You're okay, I'm so relieved," Garry finally got out.

"I'm fine, but the guy tailing me isn't."

"Tailing you? Who? When?"

"After you left the other day, I headed out to do some research. I noticed this guy tailing me. He wasn't very good at it or he wanted me to know he was there. Either way, I didn't know who he was so I gave him the slip and started following him. I guess he figured I would eventually come back to my office so he went back there to wait. I was just about to jump him when three other guys got to him first. They tried to get info from him, but apparently he wouldn't talk, so they beat him badly, and finally killed him. Next thing I know they're trashing my office, so I split."

"Did you get anything from the guy who was tailing you?"

"Afterwards, I went back to see what I could find, but he was gone and so was his car. Saturday, I checked my messages and got yours. When I arrived at your office on Sunday, I saw the same three men that broke into my place breaking into yours. I headed around back just in time to see you running off with two men. I wasn't sure if you were in trouble, so I followed you. Since they hid you here and hadn't hurt you, I figured you were okay, so I waited until the right time to approach. Man, what is going on?"

Garry grabbed a small suitcase that contained his belongings and headed for the door. "I think it's time for us to disappear and figure this out."

Fletcher led the way. With each sound or movement within a hundred yards of them, he stopped and focused in that direction. They were down the stairs and across the back parking lot in a matter of minutes. Fletcher paused at the row of trees that separated the hotel property from the shopping center behind it where he parked his car. He backed it into the parking space ready for a quick exit. One more glance around the lot and then he gave the order. "Looks safe, let's go."

When Garry got to the car, he flung the suitcase in first and climbed in as quickly as he could. By the time he did, Fletcher had already jumped in, started the car and got it moving. Garry was not the seasoned scout that Fletcher was and he did his best to watch out for anyone who looked like they were going to stop them. Nobody did. They were out of the parking lot and speeding up the ramp to the interstate when Garry thought about Hans.

"Hans! How did you get around Hans?"

Fletcher gave Garry a puzzled look. "You mean the large guy with blond hair?"

"Yeah."

"Right now he's sleeping," Fletcher chuckled. "But when he wakes up he's gonna have a beauty of a headache."

"Yeah, and Barnes is going to be plenty mad at him as well."

Garry paused to think about what to do next. Fletcher was driving as if being chased and Garry turned to peer out the rear window.

"See anything?"

Garry shook his head.

"Good!"

"Where are we going, Fletcher, and why are you going so fast?"

"First, I've got a place no one knows about where we'll be safe to sort this out and come up with a plan. Second, I don't know how much time we've got to disappear. These guys, whoever they are, have connections and I don't want to meet anymore of them today."

Garry agreed and while Fletcher drove, he returned to his game of chess.

# 18

Rubbing the sleep from his eyes and drinking the remainder of his coffee, Caleb sat in the cab of the rented twenty-nine foot truck. In the security booth a few feet away, the guard was shuffling through papers while holding the phone to his ear with his shoulder. The scent of the ocean carried on an early morning breeze and Caleb watched as numerous people scurried everywhere at the shipyard.

*Where are they going and how many of them are actually building ships?* There were rows of buildings that blocked the view of the waterway but he did not see any ships. If this was not puzzling enough, Caleb wondered how shipbuilding and shipping are connected. *Why are Albertson's shipments coming through a shipyard?* It did not making any sense and Caleb's attempts at figuring it out had to be abandoned when the guard interrupted him.

"Sorry for the delay, sir. The paperwork was mislabeled. You can pick up your shipment at bay nineteen. Hang a right through the gate and follow the road around to the last building. You'll see the numbers on the doors. Hand the guys this shipping order and they'll show you where it is."

Caleb took the piece of paper and looked down the road he

was to follow. It was going to be a slow ride because there was so much to avoid. Piles of ship parts and motors and crane sections lay along the sides of the road. One thing was clear, shipbuilders, at least these shipbuilders, were not neat.

"Thank you," he said to the guard and put the truck in gear.

Seventeen minutes later, he was backing up to bay nineteen. No one was there to greet him as he climbed out of the truck. It was a stark contrast to the busyness at the front gate. The bay doors were closed and pad-locked and the only light came from an office at the end of the building. His watch told him he was on time, still the fact that the paperwork was mislabeled and no one was there to greet him made him wonder if he was at the right location. With no place else to go, he headed for the office.

As he reached the steps leading up to the office door, three large men stepped out of the office and headed down the steps. When the man in front caught Caleb's stare he stopped, as did the other two.

His Scandinavian accent was rough and suspicious when he asked, "What you want?"

Caleb, feeling like he was intruding, explained his presence. "My name is Caleb Prescott. I'm from N-Route and I'm here to pick up a delivery heading back to Richmond for Brian Albertson. Here, I've got the shipping order."

For a few seconds the man was silent, as he looked Caleb up and down then reached for the paper.

"Prescott? What happen to other man?"

"Other man?" Caleb said puzzled. "You mean my partner,

Jeff Birch? He's sick and couldn't make it."

"Are we to have new driver each week?"

The interrogation was bothering Caleb and he wanted to be sarcastic, *what difference would it make if there was a different driver each week?* As he looked at the three men staring at him, he decided that it was not wise to antagonize them. "No. Jeff will be your normal driver each week."

The man grunted and said, "I Ymir," as he looked over the shipping order. Finishing his descent he announced, "I open doors. You back truck in and dese mens help you load."

It did not take Caleb long to get back in the truck. As he backed the truck into the bay he kept telling himself there was nothing to be worried about. However, the truth was these men intimidated him. Their size alone made him nervous and the suspicious way they acted made him uneasy. Jeff was better suited for this kind of reception and it made Caleb more determined to never do this again. All he wanted at this moment was to load the truck and leave.

It took an hour to load the truck with two layers of fourteen pallets. Each pallet had two-hundred and sixteen boxes on it and in each box were one-hundred and forty-seven vials of Albertson's healing ointment. A grand total of 889,056 vials. Caleb finished filling out his shipping invoice and headed back to the office for a signature. Ymir met him at the steps again.

"The truck's loaded and as soon as I get a signature I'll be on my way," Caleb said trying to get on the man's good side.

"You check shipment, yes?"

Caleb gave Ymir a puzzled look.

"Your partner say you always check shipment so there be no issues later."

Caleb was speechless. In his hurry to leave, he forgot about checking the shipment. Not wanting to seem incompetent, he said the only thing that would sound logical and hopefully end this confrontation.

"I trust my partner and know that he checked the shipment last week. I have no reason to believe it needs checking again this week. Besides, the packing labels and the shipping invoice numbers all match. I'm sure everything's fine."

Caleb held out the clipboard with the invoice on it and his pen for Ymir to sign. The puzzled look that Ymir gave him turned Caleb's feelings of intimidation into fear. *What's going on here? Something's not right. I need to leave.* Ymir returned the clipboard and Caleb handed him his copy.

The air seemed thicker with the scent of the ocean as Caleb headed back to the truck. This did not go the way he expected, the way most other deliveries went. There was more here than he knew about and he wondered what Jeff went through last week. He was sure Jeff would have told him if something like this had happened. *Were these guys just that uncomfortable with a new driver?*

Caleb sensed the men following him and caused him to rush to the truck. His fear kept him moving instead of turning to look back like he wanted to. He was sure eyes were following him, but he did not want to seem suspicious, as if he knew something more than he did, especially since he did not know anything. Then, as he was climbing into the cab, someone grabbed his arm.

"Hey!"

Caleb turned to see Ymir, which caused his nerves to tense and his heart to race.

"Make sure you tell dem why you don't open boxes. They very strange people and when anyting out of line, dey get upset. That how last company lost contract."

Fear had tightened Caleb's throat. He nodded to Ymir who let go of his arm, then walked away. His hands were shaking as he watched Ymir leave. *Caleb, get a hold of yourself. Start the truck and get moving before anything else happens!*

Twenty minutes later, Caleb pulled onto I-64 heading west for Richmond. His heart had slowed and the shaking stopped but his mind was still racing. He was not sure if his fear was produced by the strange men or things Anna had said or his hatred of Albertson or the fact that he was doing something he didn't want to do just to appease a friend. Too many things were beginning to clash in his mind and he tried to let go of them and calm himself. *At least the worst is over...or was it?*

* * *

By the time Caleb reached the outskirts of Richmond, he was feeling more like himself again and enjoying the music on the radio. The earlier events of the morning began to fade and were almost gone when he turned onto I-95 heading south. Feeling more like one of his normal deliveries, he checked his watch to see how he was doing on time. Just then, a commercial came on the radio that sent a chill throughout his body. It was Albertson, and he was announcing his Tent Meeting for Monday night. Like the flipping of a light switch, Caleb's uneasiness returned.

The closer he got to the Willis Road exit that would take him to Albertson's warehouse, the more he thought about what Ymir had said. *Why would these guys be upset if I didn't open any boxes? Why would they care?* Then something Anna said came to mind, *"...there's more about Albertson you should know." What more should I know?*

As he drove by each exit, Caleb watched the exit signs pass and he counted down the numbers; he was getting closer, but to what? The knot in his stomach was getting bigger and he began perspiring. There was no way to avoid what was about to happen and yet he had no idea *what* was about to happen. Calling Jeff would only make Jeff upset that Caleb was allowing Anna's gossip to affect him. There was no proof that anything was going on and no reason for being afraid, except for a creepy Scandinavian who apparently did not trust Albertson's men either. *Caleb you have to stop letting other people's issues be your own. There is nothing going on here! Let it go!*

Repeatedly, Caleb told himself that everything was fine, even as he turned off I-95 and headed up Willis Road to US-1, but he could not convince himself. No matter what may or may not be happening now, in the present, memories from the past would not keep quiet as Caleb pulled up to the intersection at US-1. The stop light held him third in line in the left turn lane and forced him to deal with the past.

To his left was the location of Albertson's Tent Meetings where he had come with Jena two and a half years ago. It was an old flea market surrounded by a high chain-link fence. This place sat abandoned for years until Albertson started renting it four years ago. Inside the fence towards the back were several small tents surrounding one large tent. In front of the tents was the parking lot. Out front were several ticket booths and a flashing marquee that sat on the corner and taunted him for the entire three minutes he waited for the light to change.

*How could she give in to this junk? How could she choose it over me? We were happy before all this. Nothing separated us. We laughed and cried together. We took walks, had picnics and sang in church. There was life, we were alive then, not dead like we...I am now. What made you trade what we had for this? God, how could you leave me for this! I loved you...*

Like being in quicksand, Caleb's heart began to sink. Each question, each thought, each struggle to find some sense in what had happened seemed to make him sink even further. As he sank, the marquee continued to taunt him, laughing, gloating over his demise and Albertson's success. The emotions were so powerful and the despair so deep that he could not even get mad. The pain from the past two and half years, caused by the separation and divorce from Jena, returned by the hand of a sign that whipped him with each flash until a green light signaled that he had had enough for now.

Pressing on the gas pedal took every ounce of energy Caleb had left. Slowly the truck moved, as if it suddenly became twice as heavy and allowed this whipping to continue for as long as it possibly could. A minute later, the truck was rolling through the intersection as Caleb made the left turn and the Tent Meeting sign was just an image in the side mirror. It had done its damage and the sign continued to flash in victory.

Three short blocks later, Caleb turned left onto Galena Avenue and headed up to the gate in front of Albertson's warehouse. A guard, holding a clipboard, walked out from the hut on the left and stood between the gate and the truck holding up a hand for Caleb to stop. As he stopped the truck, the guard came to speak to him.

"Name."

"Caleb Prescott from N-Route with a shipment for Albertson."

"Thanks, next time just answer the question."

Stunned at this response, Caleb could only glare at the guard. In the side mirror of the truck, Caleb caught a glimpse of another guard holding a long pole with a mirror at the end. He was checking out the underside of the truck.

Pointing his thumb back towards the guard at the rear of the truck, Caleb asked, "What's he looking for?"

"Don't worry about him and I'll ask the questions." The guard never looked up from his clipboard as he was scolding Caleb. "Where'd you come from?"

Nervous, Caleb answered, "Newport News." Checking the mirror again, he noticed that the other guard was gone.

Looking up for the first time, but not at Caleb, the guard with the clipboard pointed to an area beyond the gate. "When I open the gate, pull your truck along side those doors. Turn off your engine and open the rear doors. Wait by the truck until someone comes to help you unload. Make sure you've got the shipping order ready." With that said, the guard turned and walked back into the hut. Ten seconds later, the gate was opening.

Caleb drove the truck through the gate and up to the doors to which the guard had pointed, then parked. *These guys make the shipyard guys look passive.* Each encounter convinced Caleb more that he did not want this contract. *I can't believe they would treat me any differently than Jeff. Was Jeff just not affected by this kind of behavior?* There was too much here that Caleb did not like and more that he knew would never be explained.

As he opened the rear doors of the truck, he had only one thing on his mind. *If I was scared by Ymir and these guys make him look passive like lapdogs, then maybe I should be worried about what Ymir said.* After climbing up into the truck, Caleb looked down the aisle between the two rows of pallets. *Maybe I should open one of the boxes so these guys think I checked the shipment. They wouldn't know whether I did it here or back at the shipyard. Maybe if I did it fast enough I could get it done before they come.*

Caleb looked around to make sure no one was watching and then quickly squeezed down the narrow aisle making his way to the front of the truck. Once there, he grabbed a box from the middle of the top row of boxes on the bottom pallet to his left. It moved easily. Carefully, Caleb slit the tape on the sides of the box with the knife from his pocket. Getting advantage to slice the tape across the top of the box was hard in this cramped space and he gave up his attempt. Putting away the knife, he grasped both sides of the top and gave a small tug. The tape gave but only tore halfway. Tugging again with a little more effort the lips of the box tore apart, but the amount of force he used was too much and unexpectedly several vials flew out of the box. Most landed on top of the other boxes, though a few hit the floor.

From somewhere outside the truck, close, a horn sounded. Frightened, Caleb peered down the passageway knowing that the horn was an indication of trouble. Next, he heard the sound of a garage door opening. They were coming!

Quickly, Caleb scrounged for the tiny vials to get them back into the box. He managed to repack the ones that landed on the boxes, but as he stooped to pick up the ones on the floor, he heard a small crack. Looking down, he saw two vials in front of his left boot. Then, as he picked up his left boot, he saw the remains of the last vial.

Just then the sound of the garage door stopped. It was open. Fright turned to fear as Caleb heard the voices growing louder. He grabbed the two good vials and replaced them in the box. Reaching back down, he grabbed the broken vial. The ointment oozed out of the vial onto his fingers. It was thick and sticky, like honey. *I can't put this back, they'll know.* For a few seconds Caleb froze, not knowing what to do. The voices got louder and fear turned to terror.

"Prescott!"

Someone was calling him. He had to act fast. Putting the broken vial in his pocket and wiping his hand on the seat of his jeans, he rearranged the rest so that the missing space was in the middle layer of the box, then he replaced the box. As fast as he could move, he navigated the aisle until he saw them.

"Prescott, where the..."

"I'm here, in the truck."

The two men turned and looked up at him.

Quickly he added, "I was just recounting the shipment. I'm a little compulsive about these things."

"Yeah, whatever," said the larger of the two men. "Let's get this stuff unloaded." Waving his hand above his head, he signaled the two forklift operators to move in.

The truck was equipped with rollers in the floor that allowed Caleb to roll each pair of stacked pallets to the rear of the truck where the forklift operators pulled them out and brought them into the warehouse. What took an hour to load took only thirty minutes to unload. Caleb climbed down out of the truck as the last pallet entered the warehouse. There was no indication that anyone had seen the open box and as of yet, no one asked about it. *Maybe I worried for nothing. Man, why do I keep letting others scare me?*

"Where's the shipping order?"

Lost in his thoughts, Caleb never saw or heard the large man walk up, but his voice thundered throughout Caleb's body and Caleb's spastic movement made the large man chuckle.

"It's in the cab. I'll get it." Caleb could barely speak. He could not remember the last time he had been this scared, if ever. Then, as he turned to head for the cab, someone yelled.

"Hey, you, Prescott!"

Caleb froze. This was it. He knew they found the open box.

"One of the boxes is opened, what gives?"

Turning to face the second man, Caleb swallowed hard. There was a fearful look in the man's eyes. *What does he have to be afraid of?* To buy time so he could think, Caleb conveniently had a coughing attack. After several coughs and deep breaths, he explained.

"Yes, I know it's open. I opened it. It's part of our contract to inspect each shipment before we transport it. That way everyone's protected."

The two men looked at each other and then at Caleb. Their expressions grew sterner.

The larger man then spoke. "When did you open it?"

Caleb felt confused again. Taking in a deep breath and letting it out slowly, he realized there was no way around the truth. "I know I was supposed to open the box at the shipyard, but I forgot, so I opened it here."

The smaller man got up in Caleb's face and screamed until his face turned red. "After it's opened at the shipyard it's resealed. If any boxes are open when you get here we know someone has tampered with the shipment."

Caleb did not dare move and said nothing. He reasoned that being quiet was the best strategy. The man glared with his coal black eyes and narrowed brow for several more seconds before storming off ranting under his breath.

The larger man commanded, "Get the shipping order."

Caleb returned with the order. The man signed it and gave a

copy back to Caleb.

"I'm sorry for the confusion. I was not aware of the procedure. I promise it won't happen again."

"It better not!"

Caleb watched as the larger man walked back into the warehouse and the garage door lowered. He was stunned at what had just happened. *How could Jeff forget to tell me such an important detail?* Terror began to give way to anger directed at Jeff for several reasons; first, for getting them into this mess, second, for getting sick and third for forgetting to tell him everything. *There's a mouthful I'm going to give Jeff.*

Eager to leave, Caleb ran back to the cab, started the truck and drove it off the lot. Added to all that happened that morning was the fact that these people humiliated him and it fueled his anger. Leaving the warehouse and getting back on US-1 forced Caleb to face the menacing sign once more as he headed back towards town and his office. Still flashing, it continued its taunting and laughing at him, reminding him that Albertson still got the best of him. As he drove past the sign, he pounded the steering wheel with his fist, realizing that his hatred for Albertson was not diminishing, but growing.

\* \* \*

Caleb parked the truck at the office and did not bother to bring the keys inside. He needed to hide, to end this day, to nurse the sinking feelings he had. So much had assaulted him today and he needed a reprieve.

*Once I'm home I should call Jeff. But what am I going to tell him? He won't believe any of this.*

As Caleb drove up Broad Street towards home, he replayed the events of the day in his head trying to make sense of them.

*If Jeff is right and nothing's going on, then what would make these guys act the way they did? Maybe Scandinavians are naturally suspicious? If this were true, why would Ymir warn me about not opening the boxes? No, he was scared, worried that my mistake would come back to haunt him. The man at the warehouse would not have been so upset if this was just a mistake in procedure. Besides, they never even mentioned that a vial was missing...the VIAL!* Caleb reached into his pocket and pulled out the broken vial. "Oh, my God!"

Once again, Caleb's mind began racing along with his heart. Pieces were beginning to fall into place and he suddenly wanted to know what Anna knew about Albertson. If what he was thinking was true, not only would he believe what Anna said, but also he would have the proof that she was looking for.

He wrapped the vial in a towel he kept in the car and raced home constantly checking his mirrors to see if anyone followed him.

* * *

Rachel was returning from her workout at the apartment complex gym. She stopped by the mail hut for her mail and was halfway around the pond when Garry showed up.

"Rachel, get in!"

His exhortation frightened her. "Admiral, what's wrong?"

"I'll tell you on the way, get in."

Rachel rushed around the car and got in.

"How long will it take for you to get a change of clothes?"

"A couple of minutes, why?"

"There's a problem. I'll give you three minutes to get your clothes and then we're out of here."

\* \* \*

Inside his apartment, Caleb quickly locked the door, dropped the towel on his desk and picked up the phone. Three rings later, Anna answered. Before she could say anything, he was rambling.

"Anna, I'm glad your home. I think I've got it. They were trying to hide it, but I believe I figured it out. I need to meet you. You were right!"

Silence was all Caleb heard when he stopped talking. Up until now, his mind raced with thoughts of how they concealed the truth, what to do and who should be told, but the silence stopped his thoughts and his breathing.

"Anna? Anna, its Caleb."

Still no reply.

"Anna?"

After a few seconds, there was a click. Then, several seconds later, there was a dial tone.

* * *

"Admiral, who was that?"

"Not sure. Some guy named Caleb looking for Anna."

Rachel appeared from her bedroom with an overnight bag. "Caleb?"

"You know him?"

"Admiral, there's something I need to tell you."

* * *

*They found her! They know! How? When? Jeff?* Full of fear, Caleb hung up and redialed. "Be home. Please, Jeff, be home. "

The phone rang five times before the answering machine picked up. As Jeff's message played, Caleb wondered if he should leave a message. The recording clicked off, followed by a beep giving Caleb the cue to speak. There was no way he was going to give any more information than he needed to unless he spoke directly to Jeff. As calmly as he could, he left his message.

"Hey, Jeff. I'm back. The delivery was made with little trouble. There was a slight procedure issue you forgot to mention, but I believe I handled it well. Call me when you can. I hope you feel better."

Caleb hung up and began looking around. He never owned a gun because of his fear of them and he did not have much else to use as a weapon if he needed one. He had already called the only two people he trusted. If they were in trouble, calling the police might make things worse. Even if he went to the police, would they believe him? The key was the vial. Somehow, he had to find out what was in it. *How?*

Sensing it was not safe to stay in his apartment and knowing he needed help, Caleb decided to head for Jeff's place. *Maybe he's asleep and turned the phone off so he could rest. It's not unusual for him. He might be home.* He grabbed the towel and headed for the door. Before he could fully open it to step outside, the door flung towards him, which pushed him back into the apartment. Stunned, he gazed at the large man filling the doorway.

"You Prescott?" said the deep voiced man.

Caleb did not strike up a conversation. He made a dash for the sliding glass door. By the time he had the pin out and unlocked the door, the man was on him. Caleb turned swinging his arm to strike the man but the large man caught his arm.

"I don't want to hurt you, but I will if I have to."

Caleb charged the man trying to knock him down, but it was like running into a tree. He did not even budge. In one quick motion, the large man spun Caleb around and placed him in a headlock.

"I didn't come here to hurt you, do you understand? Nod your head if you understand."

Struggling was pointless. The large man had him and there was no escaping. Giving in was giving up in his mind and he was not ready to do that yet. Doing what he did best, Caleb reasoned that it was not wise to go against this giant. So, regretting his capture and the fact that he had no other option now, he nodded his head.

"Good. Now, I'm going to let you go and you are going to sit on the couch and let me explain. Nod if you understand."

Caleb nodded once more.

"I know what you're thinking, but I'm not who you think I am, so when I let you go there is no reason for you to try anything. Understand?"

This time Caleb's nod was not with regret but curiosity. The man released him. After rubbing his neck, he followed the big man's instructions.

Caleb got a better look at the man when he sat down. He was older, not like the big men he had met at the shipyard and the warehouse. His eyes were gentler with no indication of fear or anger.

The large man adjusted his jacket and sat in the chair across from Caleb.

"First, you are Caleb Prescott, correct?"

"I'm not sure I should reveal who I am until I know who you are."

"Fair enough. My name is Fletcher. I'm a PI working for a lawyer named Garry. Do you know this man?"

The man's voice was calm, but the names were not familiar. Caleb just sat there and glared.

"Okay, do you know a woman named, Anna Clark?"

"If you hurt her..." Caleb shifted to the edge of the couch.

"Calm down, no one's going to hurt her. She is how we found you."

"We? Whose we?"

"Mr. Garry and myself. I've come to get you and bring you

to where it's safe."

"I'm not going anywhere with you."

Caleb watched the man stand. *This is not going to go well for me,* he thought. Fletcher reached into his jacket pocket and pulled out a cell phone. He dialed a number and held out the phone. *He's going to grab me when I reach for the phone, it's a trick.*

"Hello. Hello."

It was Anna's voice. Caleb grabbed the phone.

"Anna, its Caleb, are you all right?"

"Caleb, thank God you're safe."

"What's going on Anna? There's a guy here who says he knows you and I'm supposed to go with him."

"Please Caleb, go with Fletcher. He's a friend and he'll protect you. When you get here, I'll explain everything."

There was so much that was uncertain at that moment and Caleb was sure that Fletcher was not going to let him go anywhere else. He had no choice but to go with him.

"Caleb, are you there? Did you understand me?"

"Yes, Anna. I understand."

Tossing the phone back to Fletcher, Caleb admitted defeat, "Guess you win."

"We should hurry, Mr. Prescott."

"Wait, I need to bring something." Caleb grabbed the towel that contained the vial and met Fletcher at the door.

Fletcher walked out ahead of Caleb. When he was certain there was no danger, he motioned for Caleb to come out. Caleb locked his apartment and climbed into Fletcher's pickup.

"How much do you know, Mr. Fletcher?"

"Not much more than you, but between the four of us I'm hoping we can get to the bottom of this before..."

Fletcher backed the truck out of the parking space and then drove out of the complex, never finishing his statement. There was no need to. Of all the questions that ran through Caleb's mind, this one was the only one he could answer himself and he did not want to think about it.

* * *

Garry, Fletcher, Anna and Caleb talked well into the night. Caleb told of his adventure that day and Anna filled in the information she found on Albertson. Garry and Fletcher shared their experiences with Barnes and the story about Cottonwood Lake. Two different worlds with two sets of characters and two different stories but somehow it was all linked together with Michaels in the center.

"The key is the vial," Caleb said. "We need to find out what's in it."

Garry rubbed his chin as he paced the floor. "You're right, my friend, it's the key to the issues here, but it doesn't explain Cottonwood Lake."

"Maybe, if we follow this lead, it will uncover something that does connect it to Cottonwood Lake," Fletcher added.

Caleb walked over to Anna. "Anna, could your doctor friend find out what's in this vial?"

"She might, but..."

Caleb was tired and impatient. "But what?"

"Well, I just can't call her and ask her to check this substance without giving her a reason and I'm not sure it's a good idea to drag one more person into this."

Anna appeared angry. She turned and walked away from Caleb. He watched as she went to the window and peered out into the forest. There was something else going on between Anna and her doctor friend, but he knew they did not have time to work through it. Time was short and they needed to move fast. He turned to look at Garry and Fletcher seeking help. They just nodded for him to continue.

Caleb walked up behind Anna and gently placed his hands on her shoulders. "Anna, I'm sorry. I shouldn't have been short with you. I know that you were trying to tell me about this earlier this week and I blew you off. Now I'm asking you to do something that might get a friend in trouble. It's a lot I know. You're probably scared and if you want to know the truth, I am too.

"I realize that there is more about you I should probably know and believe me, I hope that we get the time for me to find out. But right now we need to..."

Anna turned and met Caleb's eyes. "We need to find out what's in the vial, I know." She lowered her head.

With his hand under her chin, he slowly lifted her face until he was looking into her eyes again. "I will go with you. I will make sure you and your friend are safe."

She nodded and looked up at the ceiling.

Fletcher walked over and handed her his cell phone. Before

dialing, she looked at Caleb, who nodded. "I'll be with you."

The phone rang several times before someone answered it.

"Lauren," Anna said.

She paused to listen to what Lauren was saying.

"Yes, I know it's one-o'clock in the morning, but it's important."

Again, Anna listened to Lauren's response.

"I need a favor."

# 19

Michaels left his perch at the window behind his desk to answer his intercom.

"Yes, Stella."

"Mr. Veiltek is here to see you, sir."

"Thank you, send him in."

Michaels watched as his office door opened and a tall man with very broad shoulders walked in. He was dressed in a double-breasted business suit and donned a military haircut. Michaels invited him in. His stride gave away his confidence, his handshake gave away his strength and his eyes gave away his determination.

"Please sit down," Michaels instructed. "Would you like a drink?"

"No, sir. Thank you, but I do not drink."

"I like you already, Mr. Veiltek."

Michaels poured himself a drink and then sat across from Veiltek.

"As you know, Mr. Veiltek, the head of my security department must demand the utmost respect for him and for me. He must manage his resources well and be a quick thinker. I will not always be there to advise you so you must come to know me and understand the way I think. In this way, you'll be able to make more informed decisions when I am not around."

"I understand, sir."

"Have you fully read the files I sent you?"

"Yes, sir."

"Do you have any questions?"

"No, sir."

"You are a man of few words, Mr. Veiltek."

"Sir, I have found that it is best to stay focused on the task at hand. Too many mistakes happen otherwise."

"I couldn't agree with you more."

Michaels made Veiltek sit in silence and watch as he drank his drink. This man was going to be hard to intimidate, which may prove to be a problem down the road, though right now it was what he needed. Veiltek did not glance away or close his eyes the whole time Michaels was staring at him and that convinced Michaels he was the right choice.

"You'll start with Myers. Find out all he knows and then dispose of him. Meet with his men and make sure Monday night's event is set and ready to go. Are you familiar with the subject?"

"Yes, sir. I've read the file. It will be handled just as you outlined."

"How long do you expect these tasks to take?"

"Myers is not an easy sell. I've known him for years. He'll be tough. However, I will have everything taken care of by Monday morning and Monday night's event will progress as planned."

"Good. I want you available after the meeting Monday night. Once the second issue resolved, you will resume Myers' search for Garry and Fletcher. Do you understand?"

"Clearly, sir."

"If Myers teaches you anything, it should be that my expectations have little room for failure."

"I understand, sir."

\* \* \*

To Caleb, they were carrying caution too far this morning, but he kept his thoughts to himself as he and Rachel climbed out of the third cab they had taken. It was Garry's idea to keep them safe in case someone was following them. After Fletcher dropped them off at a small landing strip six and a half miles northeast of the Henrico County line, they took the first cab to the Hanover County Municipal Airport. Fletcher followed to make sure no one else was following. From the airport, they caught another cab that took them to the Virginia Center Technical Park and again Fletcher followed. Confident that no one was following them, Fletcher gave the signal to take another cab to the hospital while he returned to meet Garry.

It had been a sleepless night for everyone and Caleb wanted to go home and crawl into bed. Yesterday's adventure made his day excruciatingly long and today was not looking any better. With eyes darting back and forth searching for any sign of trouble, they entered the Women's Wing of the Sheltering Arms Hospital precisely at ten-o'clock as Dr. Claire instructed.

"Caleb, wait here while I use the receptionist's phone to call Lauren"

Caleb took a seat in the lobby and watched Anna call the doctor. She had explained that Dr. Claire did not like surprises and required them to call before seeing her. It did not make sense to him since she had already asked them to be there at ten, but he let it go. He was too tired to argue. Several times Anna looked back at him and smiled as she talked on the phone. A couple of times she turned away from him and cupped the receiver as if she was telling the doctor a secret. At one point, it seemed as if they were disagreeing. Seven minutes later, Anna joined him on the bench and three minutes later, the doctor arrived.

"Hello, Anna." She emphasized Anna's name with disapproval.

"Hello, Lauren, this is Caleb Prescott."

"Hello, Mr. Prescott."

"It's nice to meet you, Dr. Claire. Thanks for your help."

"I haven't decided yet if it's nice to meet you, Mr. Prescott. I've known Anna for a long time and drugs have never been part of her life. Now you're here with a wild tale, what am I to think?"

"Lauren, please, Caleb is not a drug dealer or user. It's like I told you last night, he found this vial and we need to find out what it is."

"Dr. Claire, please call me Caleb. I can appreciate your wanting to protect Anna and I can assure you that I have no intentions of hurting her either and I will explain all I know, but first I think it's best for us to talk somewhere in private."

"I'm sorry, you're right. Please follow me."

Dr. Claire led them out of the lobby to a service elevator down the hall. Up on the fourth floor she took them through a back hallway to a rear entrance of the hospital lab. Inside were several technicians working at different stations. Dr. Claire looked around until she spotted the one she wanted.

"Carol!"

A young woman wearing a mask looked over at them.

"Caleb, give me the vial please."

Dr. Claire walked over to Carol, handed her the vial and they spoke for a few minutes.

"Let's go back to my office. Carol will bring us the results."

Without retracing her steps or taking any public routes, Dr. Claire managed to navigate the bowels of the hospital so few saw them before arriving at her office. Caleb and Anna both took a seat.

"Now, how about you start at the beginning and tell me what's going on."

For the next hour, Caleb explained how he met Anna and what they have in common pertaining to Albertson. He shared about his divorce from Jena and his company's delivery yesterday. When he finished they all sat speechless. There was not much else to say until the results arrived.

Several minutes passed by in silence. The knock at the door startled all of them. Carol stood outside. She opened the door slightly, but did not enter.

"Dr. Claire, may I see you for a minute?"

Dr. Claire excused herself and left the room with the

technician. Caleb sat staring at Anna, nervous about what the technician had found or did not find. Two minutes later, Dr. Claire returned.

"Sorry about that. We have a policy that if we find drugs on anyone on these premises they're reported to security and the police. I had to assure Carol that it was not necessary to follow the procedure this time."

"So it is a drug?"

"Yes, uh, Anna. The lab results show that it is hash oil."

"Hash oil? What's that?"

"Well, let me give you a little lesson in drugs, Caleb. First, the dried flowers and leaves of the cannabis plant, of which there are many kinds, is what you smoke. It's commonly called marijuana. Hashish is what we call the resin or sap of these plants. If either of these substances is dissolved in a solvent such as ether or alcohol and then heated so that the solvent is allowed to evaporate, what remains is a concentrated substance call hashish oil or more common, hash oil."

Caleb sat stunned. He was right, but it did not make him feel better or vindicated. *How could Jeff not know about this? It was all lies, everything he said. I trusted him and he lied to me.* A familiar pain returned as Caleb once again felt the sting from a close relationship. Albertson was still winning.

Dr. Claire continued, "The oil can range from a dark brown color to white. The more refined it is the lighter the color and the higher the potency. Honey oil is cheaper to make, but not as potent and it looks like honey, hence the name. That's what you have here.

If you heated it up and inhaled the fumes, you would get a relaxed feeling or a paralyzing feeling if you inhaled a lot. Normally it's packaged in one to five gram vials made of plastic or glass. I'd say yours is more like ten grams."

*But he said it was water. He even drank some!* Caleb needed to know the truth. "Dr. Claire, could someone ever mistake this stuff for water?"

"What? Water? I don't see how. This stuff is normally very thick and sticky. You'd have to be blind without the sense of touch to mistake this for water."

Now Caleb knew Jeff had lied. *Jeff knew what was going on and that's why he accepted the responsibility of doing the deliveries himself. But why send me when he was sick? Why not send someone else who would not question anything?* It still was not making any sense, but one thing was definite in his mind, Jeff could not be trusted.

While Caleb worked through his feelings about Jeff, Dr. Claire was searching through her desk for something.

"Here it is."

"What's that, Lauren?"

"Anna, do you remember when you worked here that the police would send us Alert Notices when they found large quantities of drugs?"

"Yes, but I never saw one."

"Well, I see them. This one came over my desk in the beginning of May. It was a news item from the Jamaica Gleaner about ganja being smuggled into the US through the postal service from Jamaica. Ganja is a Hindi term for cannabis and is often associated with the Rastafarian movement.

"It says in the article that the ganja was mailed in letters and packages to addresses in New York and Miami. They never arrested anyone in the US because the addresses were fictitious, however it goes on to say that the police found a factory in St. James that had two hundred and one pounds of hash oil and two hundred and fifty pounds of ganja. It takes 600 pounds of ganja to make one pound of hash oil.

"I don't know if this is connected or not, Caleb, but I think you might want to contact the police. This is definitely something that's over your head."

"Thank you, Dr. Claire. I believe you're right. May we keep the test results and the news report?"

"Sure."

"Anna, I think it's time we get going."

"Caleb, Carol is on her way back with the vial. Don't you want to bring it to the police as well?"

"Dr. Claire, you have been a big help. Up until now, I was getting a little annoyed with the amount of caution people seemed to be taking. Now I think it's smart that we leave the vial with you. Having the proof and the evidence in the same place may not be a smart idea. When we need it, we'll come for it."

Caleb shook hands with Dr. Claire and headed for the door. He reached out his hand for Anna to join him.

"Caleb, do you think Lauren will be safe?"

"I don't think we would be here, Anna, if Fletcher thought

someone was following us. That means no one is going to come here looking for anything. I think she's safe."

Caleb waited at the door for Anna, who made her way to Dr. Claire hugging her good-bye. It was clear that they had a special relationship and he envied them for it. *What I wouldn't give for a relationship that would not sell me out.*

* * *

"Ms. Madison, may I come in?"

Michaels stood in the doorway of Madison's office like a cat that had cornered its prey. Things were moving along nicely with one exception, he had not counted on the relationship that was developing between Madison and Rachel. She seemed too harsh to connect with someone like Rachel. Her dedication to getting projects done was her biggest asset in Michaels' mind, so he continued to tolerate her until the right time. This morning was the right time.

"Mr. Michaels, I wasn't expecting you."

"Yes, I know. This is what's called a *surprise* visit. May I come in?"

Without getting up from her desk, she replied, "Certainly. Please have a seat. What can I do for you?"

Michaels unbuttoned his jacket and dramatically took a seat in Madison's Queen Ann chair. Pointing to the couch, he invited her to join him. His display of power and arrogance exuded the response he was hoping to receive.

"Mr. Michaels," Madison spoke with indignation. "I can see that you have something on your mind. I'm quite comfortable where I am. Please, get on with it."

"Well, Ms. Madison, I'm not in the habit of pointing out the failures of my staff, however, I have checked around and no one seems to know the whereabouts of Ms. Gilbert. As her supervisor, you should be able to tell me."

His grin went from ear to ear and his eyes looked past Madison to the windows behind her. He knew she believed in professionalism and always looked at you when speaking. To look past her, especially while accusing her of wrongdoing, was an insult beyond that of sitting in her favorite chair. The game was in full swing and Michaels was enjoying it.

"Mr. Michaels, first, I find it very unprofessional of you to be inquiring of my staff where another staff member is. If there is information you need I'd like you to come to me first before talking to any of my staff.

"Second, since part of the job my staff does requires them to do field work, it is not always possible for me, or any others, to know the whereabouts of a given staff member at all times. However, my staff is trained to report in while in the field and document all their time. Ms. Gilbert, who has been performing up to my standards, gives me no reason to be concerned that she is not available at the moment.

"Thirdly, this game you like to play..."

The phone interrupted Madison's rebuke, which disappointed Michaels. He was waiting for this eruption. It started small, but with his help, it was sure to develop into a full-blown shouting match that would end her career. The interruption changed everything and postponed the game until another time.

Michaels could hear a woman's voice on the other end of the line. It sounded excited. He watched as the expression on Madison's face softened.

"Good work, Rachel. I'll see you in forty-five minutes."

As Madison hung up the phone, Michaels watched her indignation turn into a smug confidence. The flare in her eyes was gone and her lips no longer pressed together. Instead they formed a small grin as they parted just enough to reveal her unclenched teeth.

Leaning back in her chair, she calmly said, "You see, Mr. Michaels, my staff *is* well trained and accounted for. Furthermore, Ms. Gilbert is returning with proof that connects Albertson to drugs. Who knows, before long the government may be thanking you for your help and you'll be congratulating my staff and me. How's that for irony?"

Michaels stared at Madison. Inside he was enraged at her ability to come back from the edge of the precipice, but his mind overcame his emotions. She was right about the irony, though she had no idea of the real circumstances behind it. Knowing this, Michaels just smiled.

"I guess that security meeting with Mr. Myers, about protecting Caleb, will take place after all," Madison said.

"I'm afraid not, Ms. Madison," Michaels retorted. "Mr. Myers is no longer with us. Mr. Veiltek is our new head of security. I'll make sure he pays you a visit."

Michaels rose from Madison's chair and buttoned his jacket. "It's interesting isn't it, how we get attached to stupid things like chairs." Before leaving, he stopped in the doorway to add one more insult. "Ms. Madison, having proof of a connection is not the same as having proof of the act. Remember that."

* * *

The Sheltering Arms hospital was not too far from Caleb's apartment, so he suggested that Anna drop him off so he could change and get his car. She went on to her office while he headed to his.

It was a long ride with much to occupy his mind. He was convinced that the Albertson contract should be canceled, even if it cost them money, but he knew Jeff would not agree. Even though there was proof that he was right, he knew Jeff was not going to accept it. *What happens if this becomes an impasse? Not only will a business dissolve, but so will a partnership and a friendship. How will I live with this?*

Facing Jeff was going to be the hardest thing Caleb had ever done. For nine years, they had been friends. They had helped each other through many things but it was not clear if this was going to be another or the end. This weighed on Caleb and caused him to drive ten miles-per-hour under the posted speed limit. Others around him honked their horns for him to speed up and though he tried, he kept slowing down.

Feelings of being helpless and hopeless started surfacing.

Despair was coming, he knew it, he felt it, but he could not deter it. Then from nowhere, an urge began to develop; one that he had not had since he and Jena had met. It grew, causing him to focus on it more and more until the helpless and hopeless feelings drifted to the background of his thoughts.

As he thought about praying, a phrase he had recently heard came to mind, *be watchful my friend. Who said that? When did I hear it?* The phrase played repeatedly in his mind and Caleb focused on it trying to remember the circumstances and significance. Then, as he pulled into the parking lot of his office, it came to him. *Pastor Reynolds, his visit, his concern...he was right!*

Caleb rushed to his office and closed the door, without saying hello to anyone. Quickly, he dialed Reynolds number at the church hoping he was there.

"Pastor, I'm so glad I caught you."

"Caleb?"

"Pastor, I can't explain things right now except to say that you were right. Please just pray for me. I need help and you are the only person I can turn to right now."

"Caleb, I will continue to pray for you, my friend."

"I need to go, but I'll call you back when I can. Thanks, Pastor Reynolds."

Caleb looked up in time to see Jeff enter his office and shut the door. It was time. He could not put it off, but he could not move either. Memories of meeting Jeff, planning the business, opening this office and buying their first set of trucks all flashed before Caleb's eyes as if they were happening at that moment. Suddenly

Jeff looked frail, like a frightened boy who needed help and Caleb's determination faded. He could not destroy one more relationship; he just did not have that in him. He just stared across the hall at his best friend.

When Jeff lifted his head to answer his phone, their eyes met. Instead of the heart-felt connection of two brothers who had not seen each other for years, which Caleb expected, Jeff immediately stormed over to Caleb's office without answering the phone.

"So you decided to come to work, did you."

"Whoa, Jeff, calm down."

"Calm down! Where have you been? I've been trying to reach you since yesterday afternoon. I tried your home and your radio, no luck."

"I'm sorry, Jeff. I kind of had a bad day yesterday and after I got home I left in a hurry and forgot my radio. I picked it up this morning."

"I'll say you had a bad day. Ymir called and chewed my ear off about you not checking the shipment. How could you forget to do that?"

"It was a mistake..."

"*Mistake*? Then you ticked off the guys at the warehouse, according to Ymir, but I haven't heard from them...yet. Then you leave the truck here. I had to return it today and pay another day's rental on it plus a late fee. And to top it all off you decide to take the morning off without calling anyone. Man, what has gotten into you?"

"Jeff, if you'll just calm down I'll try to explain things to you. Please have a seat; I'm sure you're not going to like this."

* * *

"Rachel, are you sure you can trust this lab report? Did you know we have contracts with certain labs?"

"No, Jane, I didn't know about the contracts and yes, I can trust these results. I can't reveal the source without compromising their positions, but I'd stake my life on that report."

"Okay, this gives us a connection, but it doesn't tie Albertson directly to the drugs. We have to see him with it or it being sold or handed out by his people."

"How are we going to get that? I'm not sure I want to get too close to him."

Rachel was uneasy as she sat on Jane's couch watching her pace in front of her desk. There was more on Rachel's mind than Albertson and the drugs. Thoughts of Garry, Fletcher, the tape recording, Cottonwood Lake, Michaels and Caleb sped through her mind and made it hard to concentrate on what Jane was saying.

"The next one is Monday night."

"Uh, excuse me, Jane, the next *what* is Monday night?"

"The next tent meeting."

"Tent meeting?"

"Rachel, haven't you been listening? Albertson's next tent meeting is Monday night. I think you and Caleb should attend and get a firsthand look at what goes on. Maybe you'll find what the police can't seem to."

"I don't think Caleb is going to go for that. Remember, that's how he lost his wife."

"I remember, Rachel. Find a way to get him there."

*Deception and more deception. Will this ever end?* Secrets were beginning to bother Rachel. There was a time when she used her talent to help people unlock secrets that prevented them from being whole and living a full life. Now she was using her talents to keep them and to deceive someone into doing something for the good of others. Somehow, somewhere there was a twist in this thinking that she could not unravel. All she had to cling to was hope that good would come from her actions.

* * *

The long day had finally ended and Rachel sat waiting for Caleb to show up. Along with Garry's plan to start the day, he had given them instructions to end it as well. Of course, this meant Fletcher would be watching.

Rachel sat at the table in front of the reference books at the Atlee Square Regional Library thumbing through a magazine as Caleb entered.

"Anna, how'd it go with Jane?"

"She wasn't as excited about the report as she seemed to be over the phone earlier, but she did think it was good evidence." Rachel could not bring herself to say any more. There had to be a better time to bring up the tent meeting and she decided to wait. "How did it go with Jeff?"

"Well, he listened, but I don't think he heard what I said. He was very upset about what happened yesterday and he's hurt that I'm taking the word of a stranger over his."

"I'm sorry, Caleb; I didn't want to affect your friendship with Jeff. Is there anything I can do?"

"No, I think we both just need some space."

"Caleb," Rachel lifted her eyes to meet his. "Things are not turning out the way I had hoped and well..." She paused as she tried to read him wondering if the feelings he expressed only days ago were still there. "I wanted to know if..."

Caleb finished her sentence. "If I've been thinking about us?" After watching her nod her head, he continued, "Yes, I have. Part of me wants to dive right in and not be cautious. However, my conditioned nature forces me to be careful. Right now, I think we need to focus on Albertson. I don't want a relationship based upon him. After this is over then we can re-evaluate what's there between us."

Rachel lowered her eyes and sat silent.

"That's not what you wanted to hear, was it, Anna?"

Rachel looked up to respond and saw Fletcher outside by his car. "It's time to go." She stood and Caleb mirrored her action.

Each left the parking lot at different times, Caleb first, then Rachel and then Fletcher. The long day was over, but the debriefing was just about to start.

# 20

Caleb woke to the sound of a scream. With groggy eyes, he scanned the living room from the couch where he laid, rubbing his eyes to get them to focus. *Nothing.*

Seconds later Garry and Fletcher appeared at the bottom of the stairs in their boxers and t-shirts. Garry held a flashlight and Fletcher his revolver. Both seemed as confused as Caleb was. After a quick glance at each other, as a team, they ran for Anna's room.

Caleb got there first and flung the door open to find Anna sitting up in bed with her arms wrapped around her knees and crying. Instinct and empathy caused him to rush to her.

"Anna, what happened?"

Holding back her sobs, Anna tried to play down her fear. "Its nothing, I'm fine."

"Did you see someone?"

"No, it was just a dream, nothing more."

"Do you want to talk about it?"

"No. I'm fine."

Caleb pulled back from her and looked at Garry and Fletcher, who just stared back at him and shrugged their shoulders.

"Well, I'm wide awake now," he said as he turned back to Anna. "How about joining me for a cup of tea?"

"I could probably use one," she replied.

"Garry, Fletcher, would you like to join us?"

Garry responded first. "Might as well. I can't go back to sleep now."

Fletcher waved his hand at all three of them and headed back to his room. "It's too early to talk. I'll see you guys in the morning."

Silently, the three of them sat around the kitchen table sipping Earl Grey tea. There was so much to talk about and yet no one broke the ice. After twenty minutes, Caleb wished he had never suggested talking. He was now getting tired and yet did not want to be rude and ask the others to leave so he could crawl back on the couch. Finally, Garry took the lead.

"Fletcher and I have not been able to contact or locate Barnes. We're not sure if he even made it back to Nebraska. Tomorrow, we plan to take a trip back to the hotel where we left Hans and see if we can find a way to contact him. I want you two to stay here this weekend. I'm not sure it's safe to go back to your apartments yet."

"Admiral, I'd like to call my parents and let them know where I am."

"Sorry Ra...uh, Anna, I think it's best to not say anything yet."

"Garry, how long are we going to keep hiding like this? I went to my apartment yesterday to get my car and there was no trouble. Nobody followed us to the hospital and no one followed us here. They're not looking for us."

"That may be true, Caleb, but someone is certainly looking for Fletcher and me. If they know or think you know where we are, they may use force to get you to talk. Until we're sure what we're up against, I suggest you stay here."

"But how long is this going to go on?"

Speaking softly in a volume just above a whisper, Anna said, "Maybe it will be over Monday night."

"What? Anna, what are you talking about?"

"Caleb, there is something I need to tell you. I didn't want to tell you yesterday because so much was going on and I didn't feel right about it. Now I think it might be the key to ending this thing."

Caleb sat quietly, glancing back and forth between Anna and Garry, wondering if there was something else here that he was missing. He could see the same confusion in Garry's eyes and knew this was something only Anna knew. He prepared for another stab in the back.

"Monday night, Albertson is going to hold his next tent meeting. Jane suggested that you and I attend to see if we can see the drugs passed along. I know this is asking a lot, Caleb, but I think she's right."

"Right! What does she know about right? I've been there before and I swore I'd never return."

"Caleb, the vial only proves that drugs are going to the warehouse, but there is no proof he's using them in the meetings. If we can prove this then Jane believes it will be enough to put him away."

Caleb left the table and paced the floor of the kitchen. "I can't believe this. Albertson ruined my life after attending his tent meeting and now you want me to go back again? No way! I'm afraid of what might happen this time." He stopped and leaned over the sink to look out the window. The sun was just beginning to shine its light into the night sky.

Garry finished his tea. Calmly, he addressed Caleb without looking at him. "Sometimes we have to face our fears to find life on the other side."

Caleb turned to see Garry's back. Anna rose from the table and met Caleb at the sink. "Albertson is not going to change my mind. I will still be by your side after we leave."

Oh, how Caleb wanted to believe this; so many had disappointed him before that he built tall walls to protect himself. His thoughts drifted back to the sign that accosted him out front of Albertson's meeting place and the helpless feelings he had. He envisioned Jena as she left him, thin and weak, and Jeff as he sat in his office looking like a helpless little boy. They were all small and defenseless – ants against a giant.

Looking into Anna's eyes, wanting to believe her every word, he saw more than weakness. He saw courage. A courage that brought her from despair over a murdered sister to a survivor who used what she went through to fuel her resolve – David facing Goliath.

It had been years since Caleb sang in the church, but at that moment, the words of a hymn came clearly as he sang it in his head. *We shall overcome, we shall overcome, we shall overcome someday;*

*Oh deep in my heart, I do believe, We shall overcome someday.*

He was ready to tear down the walls. "Okay, we'll go."

Garry rose from his chair at the table and turned to shake Caleb's hand. "You're a brave man, Caleb. Lets talk through this more when Fletcher gets up so that we can have every angle covered."

\* \* \*

**Sunday, June 4, 2006, 6:30 PM:**

"Sir, I'm sorry to bother you at home, but I wanted to give you an update."

"No bother, Mr. Veiltek. Please continue."

"The Myers issue has been resolved. There was no additional information he could provide. I've met with his men and those that were unwilling to adapt to a new way of thinking have been retired. The rest have been briefed on the up coming events and their duties."

"Very good, Mr. Veiltek. I'm pleased with your progress. Is there anything else?"

"Two things, sir. First, Barnes has been located and we expect to have possession of him within the hour."

"Make sure you keep Barnes alive. I want to know everything he knows and then he may prove to be a good bargaining chip."

"As you wish, sir."

"What was the other item?"

"We just received word that Ms. Gilbert bought two tickets to tomorrow night's meeting."

Michaels sat up quickly. This was more than he had hoped. He thought that news of the event would be enough, but the fact that they would see the event firsthand would certainly seal their commitment.

"You're sure it's them?"

"Yes, sir. We checked the credit card that was used, it's hers."

"Did you check where the tickets were purchased from?"

"Sir, the transaction was done over the Internet from a computer at the public library in Short Pump."

"Send some men to see if they can pick up a trail."

"Already done, sir. I expect them to be there shortly. I will call when they report in."

"Thank you, Mr. Veiltek. Already, you are proving more efficient than Myers. Keep me informed."

"Yes, sir. Thank you, sir."

# 21

*Monday, June 5, 2006, 5:00 PM:*

"It's time to go, Caleb."

From the back door where she stood watching him, Rachel could feel the anguish he was going through and spoke softly so she would not upset him. She could only imagine what he was thinking. They had both taken the day off to prepare for this night and yet she wondered how anyone who had gone through what he had could prepare for something like this.

He stood motionless at the railing of the deck, looking out across the vast hillside of trees that hid Fletcher's cabin from the road below. Slowly he turned to face her and when their eyes met, an understanding smile appeared.

"I guess we should get going."

"Are you okay?"

"Somewhat. I've been standing here watching the breeze blow through the trees and realizing how much it resembles my life except for one thing, I have no roots. Nothing has kept me grounded and the wind has had its way with me. More than anything, I want this to change, but I'm not sure how or if it can at this point in my life."

Rachel walked out to meet him. "At the hospital, we would tell our patients that progress comes as we make day to day choices to continue on towards our goal. We don't ask them to obtain a goal but to set one and start moving towards it. Somewhere along the path, they obtain their goal without ever realizing they were close. When we got them to take their mind off the outcome and focus on the journey, the outcome always came as a surprise, usually sooner than they expected.

"What our patients needed was not a judge to measure their progress, but a cheerleader to believe in them and cheer them on. There's no magic in recovery, Caleb. It takes a lot of time, a lot of tears and someone who believes in you." She reached for Caleb's hand and squeezed it. "I believe in you, Caleb."

As they embraced, tears rolled down Rachel's face as she remembered all that she had gone through during her own journey to recovery. Lauren believed in her then and now. Without realizing it, Rachel learned to believe in others from her and that is how she was able to help so many.

Traffic was light until they reached town. The rush for home was in full swing when they pulled onto I-95 heading south. The meeting did not start until seven-o'clock and they had given themselves more than enough time to get there. They made small talk trying to keep their minds off where they were going. When they pulled up to the meeting grounds and the familiar marquee, their conversation stopped.

Caleb paid to park and drove through the gate. "Daniel entering the lion's den," he quipped. "Let's park close to the gate so we can leave quickly if we need to."

Rachel nodded.

A few quick turns and Caleb navigated his car into the third space from the end in the next to last row of parking spaces. "Twenty feet from the gate is good enough. I'm glad you wore sneakers, Anna."

Rachel started to open the car door but stopped when Caleb touched her arm.

"Anna, this may sound crazy and out of place at the moment, but are you religious?"

It *was* a strange question for the moment and Rachel was not sure how to answer. She did not want to do or say anything that might cause Caleb to back out so she gave him a vague reply hoping it would be enough.

"Well, I guess I'm as religious as the next person."

"Then would you mind if we prayed before we went in?"

Rachel felt horrible. Her sense of mistrust had caused her to see the situation in the wrong light. Caleb was not trying to find a way out; he was looking for help to go in. Relieved, but ashamed of herself, she agreed.

Caleb closed his eyes and bowed his head. Rachel followed his lead.

"Father, I'm not sure why I feel the need to pray at this moment, especially since I haven't for a long time, but I know we need you right now. You know why we are here, bless our effort and give us safety. We ask in Jesus' name. Amen."

"Amen," repeated Rachel.

When Rachel opened her eyes, Caleb was staring at her. His expression was peaceful, as if he had accepted whatever was going to happen.

"Thanks, Anna. You ready?"

"Let's do this."

Even though they were a bit early there was a large crowd beginning to form. It seemed as if the entire town had come out tonight, including the media. They walked past dozens of media vans. Many had their antennas raised high in the air, ready to broadcast whatever they found interesting enough to draw viewers, listeners or readers.

"I don't remember this much media attention the last time I was here," Caleb said.

They followed the crowd to the nearest small tent where they got in the Will Call lane to pick up their tickets. After they showed their drivers licenses as ID, the girl in the ticket booth found their reservation on the computer and printed off their tickets. Then she pointed them to the entrance of the big tent and gave them a program.

Another line led to an opening in the big tent. At the entrance were two teenagers taking tickets and behind them stood a massive man wearing a bright yellow t-shirt that looked two sizes too small. *No doubt they're here for security and crowd control* Rachel thought. After giving their tickets to one of the teenagers, each person stopped in front of the men in yellow where they were scanned with a metal detector wand and each woman had her purse searched before they were allowed to enter. Rachel and Caleb waited for their turn.

* * *

Michaels sat in his office behind his desk and peered up at the multiple monitors that lined his wall above the entrance to his office. Most days these screens were hidden behind a fake wall, but during the nights the tent meetings are in session these screens become a window to another world.

On his desk was a panel of joysticks, one joystick for each camera, and he was busy playing with them, taking in every angle he could get. *This is going to be a night I will never forget and neither will Mr. Prescott and Ms. Gilbert. She will finally feel the pain of loss; loss of a relationship, a career and possibilities from both.*

When his phone rang, he was quick to answer it. "Report."

"Sir, I've just been notified that Ms. Gilbert and Mr. Prescott have entered the big tent."

"Thank you, Mr. Veiltek. Is everything ready?"

"Yes, sir."

"Report back when you locate where they are seated. I want to see their expressions when it happens."

"Yes, sir."

* * *

Once inside, Rachel and Caleb found two seats near the exit

and sat to watch others enter. There must have been fifteen rows of chairs between them and the stage, centered at the very back of the tent. Around the stage were five sections of chairs, all similar to their section. The first five rows of each section filled already and the crowd that flowed into the tent was filling in the remaining rows quickly. Judging from the amount of people still standing, it was going to be a packed house.

Two sections over from them was a roped off area for the media. Many already had their cameras and recording equipment set up. The reporters were interviewing audience members who were close by, while the technicians tested their equipment. All around were more of the massive security men. They protected the media personnel and equipment as well as watched the crowd. There were eight around the media, four around every other section and around the stage, one stood every two feet.

"I wonder why they have so many security guys," Rachel stated. "What are they worried about? Does Albertson really need this much protection?"

"Maybe it's more of a deterrent than protection." Caleb said. "Like the show of muscle keeps the peace."

At the front of the aisle next to where they now sat, Rachel noticed a girl dressed in a flowered sundress and wearing a scarf tied under her chin. In her hands, she held a basket and she stopped at each row talking to the people seated there. From a distance, she looked to be in her early twenties but as she got closer, her facial features made her look much older. Though the skin on her arms and legs still seemed youthful, her face looked twice as old with sunken cheeks, dark circles under both eyes, which were bloodshot, and hair that seemed unwashed for weeks.

While the girl worked her way up the aisle, Rachel noticed the elaborate set up on the stage. Several speakers, that stood as tall as men did, fanned out in all directions on both ends of the stage. Above them were several other speakers, hanging from rafters that stretched across the stage. Between the speakers on the rafters were groups of lights pointing in all directions, some at the stage, some at the ceiling of the tent and some at the audience. As she turned to point this out to Caleb, the sound system came to life. It started softly, the sounds of a sitar and flute in gentle harmony, but then the volume grew to a level that would not allow normal conversation. Yelling was the only way to communicate. Rachel winced at the volume and turned to attempt to speak to Caleb. Just then, the girl with the basket arrived.

"Would you like to buy some healing ointment?" she shouted. Her voice was raspy and her hand shaky as she held up a vial of the ointment.

Caleb looked at Rachel and then back at the vial. It was the same type of vial Caleb from the shipment, but its contents were almost clear.

Caleb reached into his pocket and screamed to the girl, "How much?"

"Oh, they're not for sale."

"But I thought you asked if we wanted to buy it?"

"Well, they're free with a donation."

Caleb pulled two five-dollar bills from his money-clip and

gave them to the girl. She dropped the money in the basket and handed the vial to Caleb.

"Now we have real proof, Anna!"

"We need to get it to Lauren so she can analyze it," Rachel said.

"Thanks for your donation," yelled the girl. "Enjoy the meeting and heal well."

As the girl walked away, Rachel's eyes followed her. *There is a lost soul in need. I wonder what hurts so badly that she would allow herself to become like that.* Rachel's compassion connected with the girl – one more person who was lost in a world like Rachel's.

Caleb was tapping her on her shoulder. "Anna, Anna, look at that!"

Rachel turned to see a cloud of smoke forming around the stage. It came out from underneath in small streams and then spread out as it rose to cover the stage until the stage could not be seen. By now, most of the guests had found their seats. The lights dimmed and the music stopped as an announcer spoke.

"Ladies and gentlemen, please find a seat and prepare yourselves for a night that will change your lives. Open your hearts and minds to the possibility that is before you. This night, all your pain and suffering could be healed. Yes, I said all of them and the man who can make this happen, is waiting to meet you. May I introduce...*Brian Albertson!*"

The crowd exploded into a throng of cheers and applause. The cloud of smoke receded back under the stage and Albertson appeared at center stage with his back to the crowd wearing a black cape. Most of the audience members were on their feet and many held their hands to the sky shouting his name as if worshipping him.

"Life!" shouted Albertson.

The crowd calmed and took their seats. Albertson did not speak again until there was complete silence. Softly, the music began to play as he turned to face the audience. With quick motions, he fully turned around; shot out his arms with open hands and spread his legs with a hard pounce on the stage.

"Life...is what you came here tonight for. There is something lacking in your day to day existence and you've come here searching for something more."

This was the first time Rachel had seen Albertson in real life. His medium height was what she expected but he seemed a little heavier than he appeared in his pictures. The curly hair was still there, only less of it and his skin was still pale white. From a distance, he looked harmless, meek and almost boyish. If she did not know better, her compassion could connect with him as well.

"Like Jesus asked the Pharisees when he talked about John the Baptist, 'What did you go out to see?' What have you come here tonight to see? Yes, a prophet with the power to change you and your life."

Suddenly the smoke reappeared, but this time it was coming from everywhere, not just from under the stage. The volume of the music raised and the combination of the two items, the smoke and music, created a trance-like effect. Rachel felt lightheaded and lethargic, like she being transported into another world. It was hard to focus and think. Then, as quickly as it came, it disappeared. The smoke was gone and the music stopped.

Sitting in a chair on stage next to Albertson was an old man wearing shorts. His arms and legs were so thin; you could make out the bones. His hair was white and his face wrinkled.

"I have spent many years in Jamaica studying with the Rastafarians, whose healing ability goes back for centuries. They have taught me their ways and I have brought them here, to the United States, so that you may benefit from them as well.

"While I was there, I witnessed a healing by a Spiritual Mother from Maroon. A man, cursed by an Obeah, a sorcerer, was unable to walk because of his swollen foot, came to her. The medical doctors could not help him, but Madda, the Spiritual Mother, helped him without an operation.

"You see before you a man who is unable to stand because of the twisted cartilage in his knees. He was the victim of a hit and run accident and has been through surgeries that have not been successful. Tonight, full of hope and faith, Eddie has come to have his life changed. Watch and see the power that can change you as well."

The lights dimmed, except for a spotlight on Albertson. He kneeled beside the man and picked up a bowl. From the bowl, he produced a sponge, which he placed over the man's left knee and then squeezed. Fluid ran from the sponge over the man's knee and down his leg. He repeated this process with the man's right knee and then placed the bowl on the floor of the stage. Grasping the man's knees in his hands, Albertson threw back his head and spoke in a dialect that was indescribable. It sounded like Jamaican, but most of the words were unrecognizable.

For three minutes, Albertson went on with his prayer. The man sat quietly with his eyes closed until Albertson stopped praying. Then, as if in pain, the man started to cry out. His shouts were not words but utterances of a man in shock. The louder he got, the more he trembled. Albertson held his knees fast while two security staff came out to hold the man and keep him from falling off the chair. Even though these men were big and strong, they struggled to hold this frail man. Then the trembling stopped and the lights went out.

When the lights came on again, the security staff were gone, the man was sitting calmly in his chair and Albertson stood next to him.

"Now, watch and believe!"

Albertson turned to Eddie and held out his hand, which Eddie took. Slowly, Eddie put pressure on his legs and leaned forward to rise. At first, he was wobbly, but then he found his strength and stood up straight. With his hands raised and tears rolling down his cheeks the man shrieked, "I'm healed! I'm healed!"

The crowd went wild with cheers, applause, and whistles as the smoke and music returned.

Rachel leaned over to Caleb's ear, "What do you think?"

"I don't believe any of this," he replied.

Once again, the room went dark. The music stopped and so did the smoke. The audience calmed down and took their seats once more.

"Anna," Caleb said as he leaned over to her, "get ready.

When the lights go down again, we're going to head for the exit."

"Okay."

When the lights came back on, Rachel turned to check out the exit. She wanted a clear image in her head before heading for it.

Albertson was alone on stage. "True healing," he began, "starts with belief. Tonight, we have in our audience believers and non-believers. The believers see what can be and the non-believers, well, they just don't see."

The crowd began to laugh, which seemed to please Albertson because his grin widened. "It's time to find out who can see and who can't..."

"*ALBERTSON!*"

A man stood up and interrupted Albertson. Most of the media people were in the way and Rachel could not get a look at him, but she heard every word.

"Seeing *is believing*, my friend, and *I see* a man who is going to *believe* in hell in a few seconds!" The man produced a rifle that he aimed at Albertson.

Immediately, the crowd reacted, shrieks came from everywhere as they ran. Those close to Caleb and Rachel, scattered in all directions to avoid being shot and the security guards, who were now running towards the man, were slowed by those that fled. The media cameras quickly turned to capture the event on tape.

Rachel jumped when she heard the *bang* from the gun, her heart racing. She looked at Caleb whose eyes focused on the stage and whose mouth hung open.

The announcer came over the speaker as the lights came up,

"Ladies and gentlemen please remain calm and exit the tent quickly and safely. There is no cause for alarm. The situation is under control."

Someone screamed in horror. Another person shouted, "Someone call an ambulance!" Several people were standing at the foot of the stage. Rachel watched as two security staff escorted Albertson off the stage. Only after he left the stage did she notice the woman lying on the floor. In the distance, she heard sirens.

"Caleb, let's get out of here."

There was no response. Caleb stared at the stage. She pulled his arm and he started to move. Rachel followed, but instead of heading for the exit he headed towards the stage.

"Caleb, that's the wrong way." She grabbed his arm to lead him in the other direction, but he yanked it away and continued slowly up the aisle. Rachel followed.

Most of the audience had cleared away and left the tent. Only a few surrounded the woman. As they reached the halfway mark, the paramedics came rushing in with their equipment. Two police officers followed and cleared the area so the paramedics could work. It was then that Rachel got a clear look at the woman; she had been shot.

"Clear," yelled one of the paramedics.

Rachel watched as the woman's back jerked up off the floor of the stage and fell back down. The machine hooked to her showed a flat line across its screen. Immediately the other paramedic began squeezing a bag attached to a mouthpiece that he had placed over the woman's mouth and nose.

Once again, the first paramedic shouted, "Two-fifty, clear!"

Again, the woman's body reacted and all eyes turned to the line on the monitor, but it was still flat. The other paramedic resumed his task of squeezing the bag while the first adjusted the machine once more.

"Three-hundred, clear!"

One more burst of electricity was sent through the woman's body and it jerked even harder than before, but the line on the monitor was still flat. Everyone watched the monitor as if willing it to change, though it did not. No one moved to do any more. The two paramedics looked at each other and then shook their heads. It was over.

"JENA!"

Rachel turned, as did everyone else, to see Caleb fall to his knees. With tears running down his face, Caleb convulsed on the floor and passed out as if affected by that last shock. Quickly, the paramedics rushed to him and held him down. One produced a stub of ammonium carbonate, broke it and waved it under Caleb's nose. Within seconds, Caleb awoke. He looked around until he saw her, the woman, lying on the floor. Someone had placed a jacket over her face.

"No, Jena," Caleb softly cried as he crawled over to her body. He removed the jacket and held her head in his arms as he cried into her hair.

"She saved him," said a man standing by. "She ran on stage when the man pulled out the rifle and got in front of Albertson. She saved him."

A police officer was standing next to the man. "Sir, do you know this woman?"

"No, sir. I was in the row behind her. I saw what she did. I tried to help, but there was nothing I could do."

"Thank you, sir," said the officer. "Why don't you come outside with me and tell me about it."

"That's my jacket." The man pointed to the jacket draped over the woman.

\* \* \*

Rachel pulled the car to a stop in front of Caleb's apartment. He had insisted on going home and she insisted on driving him. It was a quiet ride except for the directions Caleb had to give.

"Anna, thanks for bringing me home. Let me call you a cab to get you back to Fletcher's."

"No, Caleb. You should not be alone right now. I'm going to stay."

"I'll be fine, really."

"I told myself that years ago, but I was wrong."

"But I am fine, Anna."

"Well, I'll stay just in case an episode arises."

"I won't be much company."

"Now that sounds like a statement from someone who's not fine."

"Okay, okay, you can stay. I'm going to change."

"Do you have any coffee or tea, Caleb?"

"Yes, would you like me to make you some?"

"No, you go change and I'll make it." Rachel smiled and gave Caleb a short kiss on the cheek while she rubbed her hand on his back.

After drinking their coffee, they sat next to each other on the couch. Caleb sat bent over with his elbows on his thighs, holding his cup in both hands, staring straight ahead. Rachel sat next to him with her knees under her, facing him. With her right hand, she softly rubbed his back as she held her coffee cup in her left.

"Caleb, where are you?"

"Huh? What?" Caleb turned to look at her. "Oh, I was just trying to sort this out."

"Sort what out?"

"What happened."

"You mean the senselessness of it?"

"No, I mean the event."

"What?"

Rachel wondered if Caleb was going into shock and denial about the event. He turned to face her on the couch and then explained his thoughts.

"Do you remember entering the tent?"

"Yeah."

"What happened?"

Rachel pictured the event in her mind. "We gave our tickets, were scanned and then we went in."

"Exactly. Everyone was scanned and searched."

"Caleb, what are you getting at?"

"If everyone was searched, how did that man get a rifle into the tent without being seen?"

"You're right, why didn't someone see it? Maybe he slipped it in during one of the blackouts?"

"With all the security they had, I don't think so. And why is it that with all that security, the man was able to get away and no one caught him before or after he shot? If Albertson has power to heal, why did he just turn and run instead of helping Jena? And while we're on it, how did he heal that old man?"

Rachel could see what was happening. The event was hitting him. His emotions were beginning to erupt wanting to escape, needing to get out. She knew the best thing she could do was to let him go, to get it out, then she could be there to hold him afterwards.

"Why didn't the security guys around the stage protect Albertson? Why did they let a defenseless woman stand up for him? Why were Albertson's men at the warehouse so upset about the boxes? What was Ymir afraid of? What's going on? Something's not right!"

When he stopped talking, Rachel was ready. She could see it coming like so many others she had watched over the years. The anger, the pain, the emotions all build until they converge and an overwhelming sense of despair kicks in. Then they need the understanding and comforting. In that moment, when they sense their world about to crumble, that is when they need the reassuring arms of someone who believes they will survive. His eyes filled and overflowed down his cheeks as his hands began to tremble and his body became frozen. In Caleb's eyes, Rachel could see that he had run out of steam and slowly she reached for him.

She lightly touched his hand and then held it. With her other hand, she gently ran it up his arm until she reached his shoulders. Then squeezing his hand with the one hand and using the other to pull him to her, she wrapped her arms around him as if shielding him from the world. It was not long before he gave in and let go of the need to be strong. He wept bitterly with his chest heaving from deep gasps for breath.

Rachel held his limp body for an hour as he drained himself of the pain from not just this night, but also many others that had haunted him for years. His pain resonated with hers and she cried as well. So many times she had done this for patients at the hospital and yet this time it was different. This was more than a job assignment with no attachments, there was a deeper connection here. Not only did she believe in him, but she also felt something for him, she was in love.

# 22

From behind the two men, Rachel could not see anything. Taking a few steps to the right she saw the car in front of them with the trunk open. While the men talked, she walked over to the car and looked inside the trunk. It was empty. Suddenly the men spotted her.

"Hey! Where do you think you're going?" the lunatic screamed.

Before she could turn around, he grabbed her. The man in the suit held her while the lunatic taped her hands behind her back. Rachel tried to kick but they had her slumped over the back end of the car and she could not get leverage to lift her legs. After taping her ankles together, the lunatic rolled her over into the trunk. She landed with her back to the floor and her face looking at the two men. It was dark and the dim light from the trunk lid only shone enough to see their chests but did not reveal their faces.

"Do you still have your gun?" asked the man in the suit.

"Yes, sir."

Rachel watched as the lunatic handed his gun to the man in the suit. She squirmed to get free but was unable. She pleaded with them. "Please, don't do this. What do you want? Maybe I can help?

Please..."

They ignored her. The man in the suit pointed the gun at her.

"No! Please! Wait!"

"Good-bye my dear."

"No! Wait!"

There was a loud *bang* and a white flash.

"*WAIT!*"

* * *

Caleb watched as they placed Jena's body on a gurney and wheeled it down the hall into the morgue. He followed at a distance running as fast as he could, but he could not keep up, even though the man pushing the gurney was walking slowly. No one stopped when he yelled and no one paid any attention to what he was shouting.

"She's not dead! Stop! Don't put her in there, she's not dead!"

His heart was pounding and he forced himself to run as hard as he could. He thought of when he was young and on the track team drawing strength from certain thoughts to keep him running; but this was a prize greater than any medal he had ever won, and yet the strength did not come.

The more he ran the further away he got. In horror, he watched as the morgue door opened and smoke blew out over the floor as the cold air from inside mixed with the warm air in the hall.

"Jena!" he screamed once more reaching out his arms for

her.

"No! Please! Wait!"

What was happening? The image was fading but the words were not. His mouth was opened and those words were in his head but it was not his voice shouting them. The image disappeared as light filtered into his eyes. It was dim and cloudy and he felt as if his body weighed two or three times his actual weight.

"No! Wait!"

The screams jolted him back into the real world. It was a dream but the screams seemed so real. Sitting up in bed, his heart still racing, Caleb looked around to regain his composure.

*"WAIT!"*

*That was not my dream!* Throwing off the covers and leaping out of bed in one combined movement, he raced for the living room and Anna.

He found her on the floor next to the coffee table coughing, choking. Quickly he lifted her up and sat her on the couch where he had left her to sleep last night, then ran for a glass of water. When he returned, he helped her sip the water in-between coughs and sobs. A few minutes later, she was just sobbing. He held her as she had held him the night before, until she had calmed down and fell back asleep.

\* \* \*

Caleb looked up from the stove to see Anna rising from the couch. "Good morning. How are you feeling?"

"I've been better."

"Yes, I know, that couch is not the most comfortable. You were out before I could offer you the bed."

"Thanks, it was fine. I smell coffee."

"Breakfast will be ready in about twenty minutes. I've laid out some clothes on the bed for you. I thought you might want to take a shower and change. There's a robe hanging on the back of the bathroom door, as well."

"Thanks, Caleb, that's really thoughtful." She smiled at him and headed for the bathroom. "What time is it?"

"It's eight-thirty." Caleb smiled back.

Fifteen minutes later, Anna emerged from the bathroom wearing Caleb's robe with her hair wrapped in a towel. Caleb looked up at her as she paused in the small hallway between the bathroom and his bedroom. Her face was flush from the hot shower and her eyes seemed to twinkle. Probably because of the water reflecting off her face. It caused him to stare. She was beautiful.

"Everything okay?" Anna asked.

"Um, yes, its fine. Breakfast is just about ready."

Anna continued into the bedroom and shut the door. Caleb was just putting breakfast on the table when she came out again wearing an old pair of his sweatpants, tied tightly around the waist, and a large t-shirt. Once again, he just stood and stared.

"Caleb, are you all right?"

"Yeah, it's just that you make those clothes look fantastic."

Before he looked away, she removed the towel from her hair and shook her head, which allow her hair to fall over her shoulders.

It was then that Caleb knew there was something different about her. She was drawing out of him feelings he had not experienced before. Feelings he knew were deeper than what he felt for Jena or his first wife, Sally.

Both took a seat at the table. Caleb poured her coffee as she marveled at the spread he had placed before her; bacon, eggs, wheat toast, coffee, a glass of orange juice and a bowl of fresh strawberries. The place setting was real china and the silverware was his best. He wanted to impress and it appeared that he had.

"Thanks for last night, Caleb"

"I should be thanking you." Caleb hesitated not knowing if it was the right time to ask, but then asked anyway. "Was it the nightmare?"

"Yeah."

"How often does it occur?"

"More often than I would like. Each time it changes a bit and I see a little more than I did the time before. It's always about my sister being murdered, except this time it was me in her place."

"Do you think that means something, Anna?"

"I believe it does, but I'm not sure what yet."

They had not even finished their first cup of coffee when the phone rang. Caleb excused himself and took it in the bedroom.

"Hold on, Jeff, you're saying that Ymir called and canceled our contract?"

"That's right and all because of your screw-up."

"Well, I can't say that I'm very upset with not having the contract, but believe me it was not my intention to have this happen."

"Really? You sure you didn't just forget to check the boxes on purpose hoping it would cause us to lose the contract?"

"Now wait just a minute, Jeff. We've been friends and partners for a long time and you know that I would never do anything to jeopardize a contract knowingly."

"Yeah, like I knew you would never knowingly go through my stuff without asking me first!"

Caleb closed his eyes tightly. Jeff was right about that and the wound had not healed for either of them it seemed. "Jeff, you have to listen to me. Last night Anna and I went to Albertson's meeting..."

"You and Anna went, did you?"

"Jeff, listen, the drugs..."

"I'm not going to listen to this dribble. You've gone off the deep end, Caleb. You're allowing this girl to lead you into trouble and you're taking our company with you."

"It's not like that, Jeff."

"Oh no? Then why aren't you at work this morning?"

"I'm trying to tell you Jeff, last night Anna spent the night because..."

"She spent the night! Oh, I see what's happening, she got your attention because she's got you in bed! That's it man. You *have* flipped. You better start thinking about your future and the future of our partnership."

"Jeff, Jeff!"

While he listened to the dial tone, Caleb ran his fingers

through his hair, something he did each time he did not know what to do. He had hoped that Jeff would trust him and listen, but he realized that he had crossed a boundary that day in Jeff's office from which he could not recover. It appeared that their friendship and partnership would dissolve at the same time and he had no one to blame but himself. There was not even room to share it with Albertson.

Several minutes later, he returned to the table. Anna had cleared her portion of the dishes and was rinsing them off in the sink.

"I heard you shouting, is everything okay?"

"Well, no, not exactly. Jeff still doesn't want to hear about the drugs and now Albertson's people have canceled the contract with us. Jeff blames me. I don't think we're going to get past this one."

"Jeff will see that you are right once Albertson is exposed."

"I hope so. We need to get that vial to Dr. Claire and decide what to do next. Then I need to show up at work to show Jeff I'm not against him. I'm going to get ready."

"Caleb, before we head to the hospital could you drop me by my place so that I could change? I think I need to make an appearance at my office as well."

* * *

"I'll just be a minute or two," Anna said as she disappeared into her bedroom.

Caleb did not sit, he was too anxious. Instead, he paced around Anna's apartment. From the time they left his apartment until now, his mind tried to focus on what to do next. There was no way to do anything without bringing the police in on it. They had the vials and the report from the first vial that showed what it was. Soon they would have the second report that would link the two. In addition, they had the shipping invoice and the signed contract. This had to be enough to get the police to investigate further.

Anna appeared out of nowhere as Caleb turned to continue his pacing. It stopped him in his tracks. For the third time that morning, he stared at her. This time it was more than her face or her frame. She wore a simple blouse and slacks and carried her jacket. With her hair in a ponytail and light make-up, she was more beautiful than Caleb had seen before. The moment lingered and caused them to move to each other.

Face to face, their eyes peering into each other's and their arms wrapped around each other, they paused as if to check to see if it was okay to move forward. The longing and desire they had both tried to hide gave way to an unprepared passion. As their lips touched, their nerves exploded in a fury that sent a wave of chills through their bodies. Both pulled away and shook. Each saw the other's reaction to the kiss and they chuckled, and then tried again. This time the fury was in the kiss.

Two hours later, they had the second lab report, which as they guessed, confirmed the first, only this sample was much purer. After thanking Dr. Claire once more, they headed for Anna's office.

"Anna, I'll drop you off. You share what we found with Jane

and get the other report. I'll wait for you and then we can head over to my office and get the shipping invoice and contract. Afterwards we can go to the police."

Anna agreed.

Thirty-five minutes later, they were pulling up in front of the Merrill Lynch building. Caleb held Anna's arm, before she got out, and he kissed her once more.

"I'll pull around back and wait in the parking garage," he said.

She kissed him back. "I'll be down shortly."

He watched as she walked into the lobby and towards the elevator bank. It was not until she disappeared into the elevator lobby that Caleb pulled away. A mixture of fear and confidence came over him as he rushed to get into the garage.

* * *

"Rachel, are you okay? I heard about the events of last night at the tent meeting and I was worried when you didn't show up this morning."

Jane had met Rachel at her office door and did not invite her in. Rachel could not see inside her office because the curtains and blinds were drawn.

"I'm sorry for not contacting you, Jane, but I was unable to. The woman who was killed last night was Caleb's ex-wife. I stayed with him to make sure he was okay. However, we got the proof and had it analyzed this morning. Here's the report. It's the same stuff from last time, only purer."

Jane read the report quickly. "This is good. I believe the police will want to do their own lab testing though."

"I understand. Caleb and I believe that with the two lab reports, the shipping invoice and the contract, we can get the police to step in, expose Albertson and shut him down. We're on our way to his office now."

Rachel could see that there was something wrong by the look on Jane's face. She shook her head as if to tell Rachel not to speak. Handing back the report, Jane indicated for Rachel to get going.

Leaning in, close to Jane and holding onto her as if she was using her to steady herself while she fixed her shoe, Rachel whispered, "Are you okay?"

"I'll be fine," she whispered back. "Get going."

Rachel was not sure she had made the right choice by obeying her boss. Quickly, she walked to her office and grabbed the first report. Just before leaving, she glanced down the aisle towards Jane's office in time to see Jane leave her office followed by Michaels and another very large man. Something was not right, she could feel it and Jane must have known. *Why else would she try to get rid of me?* There was nothing she could do now except get back to Caleb. She waited until they were gone and then took the stairs down to the garage.

* * *

"So you didn't know who this other guy was," Caleb

clarified.

"No. I think Jane's in trouble, Caleb."

"You don't think they were all going to a meeting?"

"Maybe, maybe not, but that doesn't mean she's not in trouble. She's never acted this way before. Something's not right."

Caleb pulled his car into the parking lot behind his office and shut it off. "Okay, Anna, let's get the invoice and contract and go to the police. Once we're done we can go back to your office and check in on Jane."

"Thanks so much, Caleb."

Inside, they had made it as far as the kitchen before running into Jeff.

"So I see you brought your accomplice," he chided.

"Jeff, come on...enough is enough."

"What's going on, Caleb?"

"We're here to pick up the shipping invoice and contract with Albertson. We're going to the police with the information we have."

"The police? That's great. They're waiting for you."

"What? Jeff, what are you talking about?"

"The police. They just left here ten minutes ago."

"Here? What did they want?"

"You, my friend, and your cohort."

"Jeff, you're not making any sense."

"The police came here looking for you. It seems that while the two of you were otherwise engaged last night, someone murdered Albertson."

Caleb looked at Anna. Both were confused and shocked.

"You haven't heard the best part," Jeff continued. "They think the two of you were involved."

"What? And you believe them?"

"Well, it's no crazier than your story."

Caleb stormed past Jeff and into his office with Anna on his heels. Finding the invoice and the contract on his desk, he picked them up and waved them at Jeff.

"It's not crazy, Jeff, and we've got the proof. We have two lab reports that show the stuff in those vials *is* drugs."

Furious that Jeff would turn against him and that the police had the wrong idea, Caleb headed for the car with Anna.

"You know, Caleb, a lab report can be faked," Jeff said just before they walked out.

This caused them both of them to stop and look at each other again.

"He's right, Anna. The police might think we forged the reports. We need to get the vials!"

"I wouldn't drive your car, Caleb, they're looking for it."

Once again, Caleb gave Jeff a stern look, but he knew Jeff was right. The police probably were searching for his car, since it was there at the meeting last night and it is not at his home right now.

"We need to change vehicles," he said to Anna. Walking back to Jeff and swallowing his pride, Caleb requested Jeff's help. "Could you trade cars with me?"

"Caleb, two weeks ago I would have given up my life for

you. However, today, I don't think there is anything I could do for you except not call the police and tell them you are here. That's the only help you'll get from me."

Never before had Caleb seen this side of Jeff and it was too painful to bear. All he could do was nod his head as a sign that he understood Jeff's position. Instinctively, he started to raise his hand to shake Jeff's, but gave up the attempt when he realized that it would not change a thing.

As Caleb headed back to Anna, the rack of keys hanging on the wall caught his attention. *A van!* He grabbed a set as he walked out. Anna followed him to a van parked behind his car and they climbed in.

Things were getting out of hand. *How could the police think we were involved?* They rode in silence as Caleb pondered this question. Then it hit him.

"Oh, my God!"

Caleb sat straight up in the seat. Out of the corner of his eye he could see Anna staring at him and knew she was wondering what he was thinking.

"She was my ex-wife. That gave me a motive!"

\* \* \*

This time Dr. Claire met them in front of the hospital and escorted them to her office. Anna had called while they were on the way and Dr. Claire insisted she meet them.

"Quickly, hurry we need to get inside before we are seen,"

Dr. Claire said as she rushed them in through an employee entrance.

A few minutes later, they entered Dr. Claire's office. She went around her desk and pulled out two specimen bags and a piece of paper. Each bag held one of the vials and was marked with their analysis date as well as a report number that matched the one on the lab reports.

"I had Carol write up a sworn statement that she did the test on these two vials and I signed it as a witness, in case anyone thinks you are trying to create an alibi."

"Alibi," Caleb repeated, not understanding the significance of Dr. Claire's statement.

"You haven't seen or heard the news have you?" Dr. Claire picked up the remote for her television and turned it on.

It was muted, but on the screen behind the reporter was a picture of Caleb and Anna. Dr. Claire played with the remote and the volume came on softly.

"...It is believed that these two are either involved in the murder of Brian Albertson or they actually committed the crime themselves. Sources, who do not want to be identified, indicated that the two suspects attended last night's meeting and were heard saying they had real proof that Albertson was a fraud and would expose him as such. The two suspects are wanted by the police for questioning."

Caleb walked over to the television and turned it off. The three of them found a seat and sat quietly for several minutes.

Anna spoke first. "That's not what we said. How did it get twisted so..." Her voice trailed off.

"Who are these sources they're talking about? What's going on here?" Anger and confusion converged inside Caleb as he tried to make sense of what was happening.

The ringing of Anna's cell phone broke another moment or two of silence. "Admiral, I'm so sorry. I completely forgot!"

Caleb watched as Anna nodded her head in reply to whatever Admiral Garry was asking her.

"We've seen the news, yes. No, it's not like they say."

More nodding.

"Yes, there was a woman who was shot. It was Caleb's ex-wife. The man was trying to get Albertson."

Now Anna was shaking her head.

"No, we're at the hospital. We have proof of Albertson's involvement in drugs. We were planning on bringing it to the police."

Caleb could hear Garry telling Anna not to go to the police. He was excited. It seemed an unusual response for a lawyer.

"Okay, Admiral. We'll meet you outside."

"Anna, what did he tell you?" Caleb asked excitedly as he watched her close her cell phone.

"Admiral Garry thinks that going to the police now, with our proof, will be seen as an attempt to cover up the truth. They believe we killed Albertson because he caused your divorce and the murder of your ex-wife. He said to protect ourselves; we should hide until he and Fletcher can find out more information. They're coming here to pick us up."

"Let me take you downstairs in the staff elevator," offered

Dr. Claire. "We can wait in the break room on the first floor until your ride comes and no one will see you."

Caleb picked up the vials and Carol's affidavit and placed them in his coat pocket. "Dr. Claire, I'm sorry to get you mixed up in this, but I can't tell you how much we appreciate your help and the fact that you believe in us."

"Caleb, I want you to know that I made up my mind, it *is* good to meet you." She reached for his hand and held it in both of hers.

* * *

"How long will it take us to get to Blacksburg?" Caleb asked as he watched Anna change gears and pick up speed to merge onto I-64 heading west.

"It'll take about three and a half hours to get to my parents house. I hope that we won't have to stay long. In a day or two, Admiral Garry and Fletcher will find what they need to clear us and we can come home."

"I know Garry is a good friend, but I'm not sure leaving all the evidence we had with him was a good idea. What happens if the people who are after Garry and Fletcher find them before they have a chance to clear us and present the information to the police?"

"I've know Admiral Garry since I was a little girl, he'll be fine."

"I hope you're right."

Caleb leaned back in the passenger seat and watched as the

scenery around the car passed by. Although their lives were hanging in the balance and they had given total control over it to someone he barely knew, he had a peace that he could not explain. Whether it was the soft music from the radio or the silence or the comfortable ride, he did not know, all he knew was that he was beginning to relax and it felt good. So he closed his eyes and took it in.

An hour later, Caleb woke up and looked around, taking in his surroundings.

"Well, hello sleepy head. You're not much company on a long drive."

Caleb chuckled. "How long have I been out?"

"About an hour."

"I'm sorry. I must have been tired."

"It's understandable."

Caleb tried to be more entertaining for Anna's sake and decided to get her talking. "So, tell me about your parents." He looked out his window at the road passing by waiting for her to start, but she did not. He turned to look at her and saw the blank look on her face.

"Anna, is something wrong?"

Anna took several short looks at him and each time returned her glance to the road ahead. There was definitely something she was having a hard time saying. He waited patiently giving her the time she needed to think through what she wanted to say.

"Um, Caleb, there's something I need to tell you and it's kind of hard to say."

"Anna, the best thing is to just say it and..."

"My name isn't Anna!"

Caleb paused for a second and glared at her. "Wait, did you say...your name is *not* Anna?"

Anna looked at him with tears rolling down her cheeks. "I'm so sorry, Caleb. I never meant to hurt you or lead you on."

"You're not Anna Clark?"

"No."

"Then who are you? What's going on?"

"Caleb, my name is Rachel Gilbert and I work for A. E. Research."

"What! The same company that Michaels heads up and who's trying to kill Garry and Fletcher?"

"Yes, the same."

"What in God's name is going on?"

"Caleb, please listen and I'll tell you everything."

Caleb sat back and crossed his arms, unsure of whether he wanted to hear this or not. *One more deception. Would this never end?*

"When I was hired by A. E. Research, I didn't know Michaels ran it. He hired me to work in their Psychological Department under the direction of Jane. I didn't know what this was all about until I was too involved, and by then I believed I was helping to do something good. However, I had to do something bad to make the good happen. It was a hard decision, but in the end, I believed it would be for the best.

"A. E. Research is a government funded agency, involved in many different areas. One of these areas is The Connection. They use the information they gather to profile people to do tasks for which the government either can't be seen or doesn't want to be seen involved.

"Awhile back, they focused on Albertson and saw him as a problem that could have national repercussions if more people like him sprung up. My job was to pose as a match through The Connection and find someone who had the necessary requirements to expose Albertson for what he was. With Albertson being the reason for your divorce, the computer selected you as a match. When I found out that you had a contract to deliver his shipments, you stood out as the perfect match.

"I wasn't supposed to use my real name and I didn't think this would be a problem until I found out that I had to meet you. By then, I had to continue the charade to get you to go through with it. So many times I wanted to tell you, but I couldn't."

"So you lied to me."

"I'm sorry, Caleb. I know how this must look..."

"You have no idea how this looks to me."

"I know it must hurt."

"*Hurt*! You don't know the meaning of hurt. You think because you used me to get Albertson off the street that it justifies using me."

"No, I know it doesn't and I said I'm sorry. I didn't want to do this, but..."

"But you did it anyway! With no feelings for me or how I might react!"

"No, that's not true, I...I..." Rachel broke down and started crying. "I...worried about your feelings every day. I tried not to do this and I wanted out, but then something happened..."

"Yeah, you found out that I was your best hope at bringing Albertson down."

"No, you idiot!" Rachel screamed and jerked the steering wheel to the right. She crossed over two lanes of traffic cutting off an SUV and a tractor-trailer at sixty-five miles-per-hour. Pulling off the road, she slammed on the breaks which made the car skid twenty feet on the lose gravel before it came to a complete stop.

"Are you trying to kill us?" Caleb screamed back.

"What I'm *trying* to tell you is that I fell in love with you!"

They both sat in silence. Caleb forced his mouth into a thin line and Rachel wiped her tears as she tried to catch her breath and calm herself. When she did, she continued softly.

"What started out as a job with exciting possibilities, presented the one possibility I never thought of, but always wanted. I just never told anyone, not even Lauren. I wanted to meet someone who would believe in me the way I believed in him. That's what I found in you."

Caleb looked into Rachel eyes and saw the raw honesty in them. It was too much for him to bear. He climbed out of the car just as she reached for him and cried for him not to leave. He walked about ten feet away from the car and peered over the railing of the turnout at the hills below. Several hawks soared with their wings spread wide as if they were kites blowing in the wind. It was just beginning to get dark. He looked to the west to see the reddish-orange glow of the sun as it began to hide behind the mountains ahead of them and he felt its warmth blow over him.

*"What is truth?" Pilot asked Jesus.* Here, at this very moment, on the side of the road, Caleb found truth in the words of a woman he thought did not exist. Whether her name was Anna or Rachel, she had unlocked a door inside him that let out feelings from a depth he was not aware of consciously. For the first time ever, Caleb felt hope, real hope. He bowed his head and prayed as cars and heavy trucks rushed by.

When he finished, he walked back to the car. Inside, Rachel was weeping with her face buried in the side of his seat. He knelt outside the car and reached in, gently lifting her head. With his other hand, he wiped her hair from her face. He saw her eyes pleading for him to love her in spite of her deception. She said nothing. He stared into her eyes for a few moments before he spoke and when he did, it was soft and gentle.

"So, tell me about your parents, Rachel."

She closed her eyes and wrapped her arms around his neck and cried some more, only this time he was sure it was for joy.

# 23

Cautiously, Rachel stepped to the side to peer around the two men. In front of them is a car with its trunk open. The men are preoccupied with their conversation and do not appear to notice her. Quietly, she creeps towards the car. With each step, she studies the two men hoping they will stay absorbed with the topic at hand. Surprised and elated that she made it to the car undetected; she looked inside the trunk only to find it empty.

Not sure how she knew this, but aware that the men are guarding the car and deciding what to do next, Rachel wondered what it is they are guarding. She pushes down on the trunk lid to get a look at what might be inside the car and the action causes the trunk light to go out, which catches the attention of the two men.

"Hey! Where do you think you're going?" cried the lunatic.

Rachel's mind tried to process his question. *Where am I going? I wasn't going anywhere.* She released the trunk lid, which bounced back open and turned the light back on. *I was trying to...* Before she could finish her thought, several hands grab her around her waist and shoulders. Against her will, she is spun around and her upper body is pushed down into the trunk while her legs remain outside.

The man in the suit presses his weight against her lower half and holds her shoulders down with his hands and forearms. After positioning her arms behind her back, the lunatic tapes her wrists together. Rachel does not have enough strength to compete against these two, but she tries. She kicks one foot backwards and up towards her thigh hoping it might strike the man in the suit, but it's no use. Her position gives her no leverage and all she accomplishes is kicking off her shoe and causing the lunatic to tape her ankles.

In one swift movement, the lunatic rolls her into the trunk so that she lands on her back. Noticing the shoe at his feet, he picks it up and tosses it in front of her. The light from the trunk illuminates the area enough to see the two men up to their chests, but it does not reveal their faces. Even squinting does not help. Rocking herself and squirming allows her to reposition herself just enough to see better but still it is not enough to see who they are.

The man in the suit breaks the silence. "Do you still have your gun?" His hand is outstretched waiting.

The lunatic reaches inside his trench coat pocket and produces the handgun. "Yes, sir." He hands it to the man in the suit.

Rachel squirms and rocks some more expecting to see more. Her shoulder slides into a crevice in the floor that she cannot free herself from and she has to give up her attempts. Pleading becomes her only alternative.

"Please, don't do this. What do you want? Maybe I can help you. Please let me go and I'll help you."

Her pleas go unnoticed and unanswered. The man in the suit

ejects the clip from the gun and checks it. Satisfied, he replaces it and verifies that the safety is off before pointing it at her. All rational thought gives way to desperation and tears.

"No! Please! Wait!"

Fear has taken over and her throat tightens up, making it impossible to continue speaking. She lies on her back wanting a miracle, a savior, something, but nothing comes. In her disappointment, she leans her head onto her shoulder that is stuck. Because of the different angle, the light now shines just right. She wills her tears to stop so that her eyes can focus and is surprised that they obey. The man in the suit helps a little as he leans into his firing arm to speak.

"Good-bye, my dear."

The results of the last few seconds of movement reveal the face of the man in the suit and Rachel's eyes go wide with horror.

"No! Wait!"

Time slows down so much that Rachel can see the man's finger squeeze the trigger of the gun. A silencer muffles the bang and the sounds come in slow motion. Along with the noise comes the white cloud of smoke from the impact of the trigger hammer hitting the bullet and igniting the powder inside. Rachel adjusts her focus when she sees the bullet slowly leave the barrel of the gun and in that split second, she sees the eyes of the man holding it. *Michaels!* Trying to stop the inevitable, she screams once more.

*"WAIT!"*

\* \* \*

Within seconds, Doris and Walter Gilbert along with Caleb are at Rachel's side. Sitting up in bed, all she could do was gasp trying to control her breathing and the fear that had overcome her. Fifteen minutes and two cups of water later, she is finally able to speak, but her tears are now interfering.

"Would it help if I made you some tea?" Doris asked.

Rachel nodded her head.

Walter followed Doris out of Rachel's room and Caleb helped Rachel downstairs after her parents.

Pulling out a chair from the kitchen table, Walter offered it to his daughter. "Here Rachel, sit down."

Caleb helped her into the chair and then pulled up a chair next to her all the while holding on to her hands and trying to get her to talk. "Rachel, tell us about the dream. Was it like the rest?"

Her sobs had subsided enough that she could speak. "Yes, it was."

"Was it different at all?"

"Yes."

"Tell me what was different."

Rachel wiped her eyes as she explained. "It was like before, when I was in the trunk instead of Amanda."

"Oh, my God! It was that dream!" Doris stated in surprise. "It's back?"

Her parents exchanged glances as Caleb resumed his questioning.

"How was it different, Rachel?"

"This time I saw him."

"Saw who? Who did you see?"

"The man who held the gun."

"The one who shot Amanda?"

Doris pulled the sides of her robe together over her nightgown and tied the ends of the belt. She ran her fingers through her silver hair to straighten it before joining the others at the table, leaving the water to boil for their tea. Walter sat in his t-shirt and pajama pants gazing intently at Caleb. The mention of Amanda's murder caught both their attentions.

Caleb repeated his question. "Rachel, was it the man who shot Amanda?"

Rachel shook her head.

"It wasn't the man who shot Amanda?" Caleb asked confused.

Rachel shook her head some more. "No, it wasn't the man who shot Amanda; it was the man who shot me."

"You?" shrieked Doris.

"Yeah, me," Rachel answered, looking at no one in particular with her eyes bloodshot and swollen. "I was in the trunk and the man pointed the gun at me and pulled the trigger. Before I woke up, I saw his face."

"Who was it?" asked her father.

Rachel looked at her dad and then her mom and then Caleb. "It was Michaels."

"Michaels," repeated Doris.

Walter asked, "Tripp Michaels? That guy you used to date?"

Caleb tried to help Rachel out. "Rachel works for a company

that is run by a guy named Jason Michaels. Somehow the dream that she's been having about Amanda's death has been rewritten in her mind so that she has taken Amanda's place and it appears Michaels has taken her killer's place."

"How awful!" exclaimed Doris as she stood up to answer the whistle from the teapot.

Caleb tried to get Rachel to make sense of the dream. "Rachel, there has to be some meaning in this dream. What do you believe it's telling you?"

"I'm not sure. My mind's not fully functioning at the moment and I'm very tired."

"Okay, let's have some tea and maybe in the morning we can talk more."

The four of them sat around the table sipping tea while Caleb and Rachel filled in Rachel's parents about all that had been happening over the past few weeks. The discussion and the tea seemed to have the intended effect on the others who were getting sleepy, but Caleb was so excited that nothing took the edge off his anxiety.

After finishing their second cup of tea and finding a lull in the conversation, Rachel's parents headed back to bed. "Good-night you two, we've run out of steam," Doris said.

Caleb watched as they climbed the stairs and disappeared. He turned and gently kissed Rachel's cheek. "Are you okay now?"

"I'm fine."

"Well, then, I think you and I should head to bed also." Caleb rose and helped Rachel up. After walking her to the stairs and kissing her again, he started towards the living room where Doris had prepared the couch for him.

Rachel watched him. "I'm sorry about the couch, Caleb. Dad turned Amanda's room into an office after I left."

"It's okay, Ann...I mean Rachel. It's more comfortable than mine. I'm going to keep messing up your name, you know that don't you?"

"That's not your fault."

Caleb sat on the edge of the made up couch. He had been lying on top of the sheets not sleeping before Rachel had her dream. When he looked back at Rachel, she was staring at him. "Are you sure you're okay?"

"I'm fine, but I'm not ready to go back to bed." She walked up to Caleb and reached out her hands. "Would you mind if I sat here with you for a while?"

"I'd like that," Caleb replied as he reached for her hands.

He moved to the end of the couch and she sat close by him and brought her feet up next to her. She moved around until she found a comfortable position and then laid her head on his shoulder. It was not a comfortable position for him, but he did not mind.

"Caleb, I feel safe around you." She moved a little more and repositioned herself so that her head lay on his lap.

This was much more comfortable for Caleb and as he held her around the waist with one arm, he ran the fingers of his other hand through her hair. He remembered times he had done this with Jena, which made him realize he had left Richmond without finding out about arrangements for her. Rachel's eyes closed and he watched her chest rise and fall as her breathing slowed, indicating that she was falling asleep.

Caleb leaned his head on the back of the couch, wondering how long it would take Garry to fix this problem. He hoped he would be able to return in time for whatever arrangements were made for Jena. His thoughts of the events of the past few days played in his mind over and over while he held Rachel and massaged her hair. It occurred to him that there might not be anyone arranging things for Jena. Before he knew it, all his thoughts began to merge into a blur as his own eyes shut and his breathing slowed to match that of Rachel's.

* * *

The rays of the sun, shinning through the kitchen window, reflected off the mirror on the wall near the front door, right into Rachel's eyes as she slowly opened them. Something did not feel right and her mind was keenly aware of the fact that the sun had never shone in her eyes before when she woke up. Holding up a hand to block the reflection, she was able to see that she was in her parent's house, on their couch.

Slowly, her mind began functioning and the memory of the previous night came into focus. Still something did not feel right. The couch was not as comfortable as it used to be. Pushing up with her hand to sit up, revealed the reason for the discomfort and it shocked her so that she quickly sat up and retracted her arm.

The weight she had placed on Caleb's thigh when she rose to

sit caused him to stir and wake up as well. From the look on his face, he was as disoriented as she was, but then his eyes focused on her and a satisfied smile appeared on his face. She leaned in to give him a morning kiss, just as her mother came down the stairs.

"You two up already?"

Rachel smiled, as did Caleb and they both moved back away from each other.

"I hope you both slept well. Rachel, I didn't even hear you get up." Doris moved swiftly around the kitchen as she went through her morning routine. "I'll have some coffee ready in a few minutes and breakfast will be ready in about twenty."

"Thanks, Mom." Rachel placed her hand on Caleb's face and he covered it with his own hand. "I think I'll go upstairs and change." As she passed through the kitchen, she gave her mom a quick peck on the cheek then scaled the stairs.

Before going into her room, she noticed the boxes stacked on the floor outside Amanda's old room. A shoebox with pictures in it lying on top of the boxes caught her attention and she flipped through them slowly. Many of the pictures she had never seen before and she wondered who the people were with Amanda. Halfway through the box, she came across a postcard and pulled it out to see it clearly. On the front was a picture of a beach surrounding a three-story office building with the company's name on the top. After reading the back, Rachel gave up her desire to change and rushed back down to the kitchen where her mom was filling Caleb's cup with coffee.

"Mom, what are those boxes outside of Amanda's room?"

"Oh those," Doris said as she started to pour herself some coffee. "That's what left of Amanda's things from her room and her apartment in Richmond. I'm still waiting for your father to take them to the dump."

"Does the shoebox of pictures belong to her as well?"

"Sure. Why do you ask?"

Rachel held up the postcard revealing the back. "Because I found this in it."

Caleb and Doris looked at the postcard and then at Rachel.

"It's addressed, *My dear Amanda*, and it's signed, *See you soon, Jason*."

Caleb blankly stared back at Rachel and her mom headed back to the counter to return the pot of coffee.

"Yes, dear. That's the boy she was seeing before she died. Amanda met him through the Internet I think." Heading back to the table she asked, "Why are you so interested in it, dear?"

"What was Jason's last name?"

"Now I'm not really sure, I can't remember. Is it important?"

Rachel flipped the card around to show them the front. "It is when you factor in that it's postmarked from Jamaica and it's a picture of an office building belonging to the *Michaels Corporation*."

\* \* \*

Jeff could tell something was wrong besides the fact that Caleb was not at work again this morning. There was a commotion in the front office and his second phone line was ringing. The display on his phone told him that Tina was trying to get him even though she knew he was on the other line. She would only do this if it were important. However, before he could place his client on hold to check on what Tina needed, a man appeared in his doorway.

"Mike, I need to call you back. An important issue has just been brought to my attention. I'll call you as soon as I can. In the meantime, find out how many loads they're going to have and where they want them taken. I'll work out a price from that. Thanks, Mike, and sorry for the interruption."

Both phone line lights went out as Jeff hung up the phone. He knew Tina had hung up as well.

"Detective Thompson, I didn't expect you back so soon. I guess you didn't hear my receptionist tell you I was on the phone."

"I heard, but I like to check things out for myself." Thompson walked in and took a seat in front of Jeff's desk. "Have you heard from your partner this morning?"

"No, I haven't."

"Well, then, do you know where he is?"

"No, I don't."

"That's too bad, Mr. Birch." Thompson placed the tips of his fingers together and positioned them under his chin. "Tell me, Mr. Birch, do you know about the drugs?"

"Drugs? What drugs? What are you talking about?" As much as the detective irritated Jeff, the subject of drugs now interested him. There was no way the detective got this information from Caleb. *Could it be that Caleb was right?*

"We found a pair of jeans in your partner's apartment with a very thick honey like substance on the seat. We had it analyzed and found out that it was medium grade hash oil. Do you know what that is, Mr. Birch?"

Jeff was very familiar with the stuff. The buzz he got from it did not last long enough to satisfy him and he moved on to stronger things until LSD became his drug of choice. "Yes, I do."

"We also found a postcard for an Internet dating service called *The Connection*. On his computer, we found several e-mails between your partner and an Anna Clark. The interesting thing about Ms. Clark is that there are no records on her."

"The website is where Caleb met Anna. She is the one who said Albertson was trafficking drugs."

Thompson raised his eyebrows. "Albertson?"

"Yes, I assumed that's what you meant about drugs." Jeff sat back in his chair watching Thompson. He did not want to help Caleb, but deep inside there was a part that would always try to protect him. "Caleb told me that he broke one of the vials that we delivered to Albertson and that he had it analyzed and found out it was drugs."

Thompson glared at Jeff. "But you didn't believe him?"

"No, I didn't." Jeff became defensive. "I checked those boxes when I made the delivery the week before. I opened five different boxes and checked five different vials thoroughly, they were water not drugs."

Without changing his expression, Thompson continued to taunt Jeff. "And you would know what drugs are like wouldn't you,

Mr. Birch."

There was no way to answer without proving what kind of person Jeff was, so he lowered his head and answered truthfully. "Yes, yes I would."

"Did you know, Mr. Birch, that a highly refined concentration of hash oil is almost clear?"

Jeff looked up at him, surprised. Although he knew that the vials he had opened and tasted were water, he now realized that they might have been planted inside those boxes of refined hash oil and he would never had known. *Ymir had pulled a fast one.*

"So where is Mr. Prescott?" Thompson was now leaning over Jeff's desk peering into Jeff's face.

"He left here yesterday with Anna. They were talking about getting the vials back from the doctor that analyzed them."

"Doctor?" Thompson sat back in his chair. "What doctor?"

"I don't know the doctor's name. They left here in one of our vans, that's all I know."

"Well, Mr. Birch, I'll overlook the fact that you didn't call us yesterday when you should have, if you'll give me the make, model and license plate number of that van. Or would you rather be arrested for aiding and abetting a criminal?"

\* \* \*

By the time breakfast was on the table, Walter had joined them and the conversation had shifted from Jason Michaels to Tripp Michaels. Rachel was filling Caleb in on some of the details.

"So you're telling me that twelve years ago you dated a Tripp Michaels?"

"Yes. We dated for a while, but that's not what's important. The first time I saw Michaels, in Jane's office, he told me that he never used his first name for business purposes. Instead he used his middle name, *Jason*."

Caleb was not able to catch up with the pieces that Rachel was putting together. "Rachel, what are you getting at?"

"Michaels signed the postcard as Jason, his middle name. His relationship with Amanda was business!"

Rachel paused for a second remembering something important. Caleb could see that it was a painful memory from the fear that seemed to grip her face. "Rachel, what is it?"

She turned to face him and grabbed both his arms with her hands. "I remember Michaels being very angry when we split up. He said..." Another pause. "He said one day I'd pay for it!"

Rachel's eyes grew wide with fear and she began hyperventilating as she bounced in her chair. She realized something so horrible that she could not get it out. Doris rushed for a glass of water while Walter jumped out of his seat knocking the chair over and rushed to Rachel's side. Still holding on to Caleb's arms, Rachel caught her breath enough to yell.

"Oh my God!"

Doris handed the glass to Walter who tried to get Rachel to drink. She was so upset that she could not. Caleb knew if they did not do something quick, Rachel was going to pass out.

"Quick, do you have any ammonia?"

"Yes, it's under the sink." Doris retrieved a bottle from under the sink and handed it to Caleb.

Caleb opened the bottle and waved it under Rachel's nose. It was not as effective as what the hospitals used but it did the trick. Soon Rachel was coughing and then breathing normally.

After Rachel took several sips of water, Caleb tried to get her to talk. "Rachel, you said Michaels told you you'd pay when you broke up and then you remembered something, what was it?"

For a few seconds she stared into space and then, as she remembered, she cried.

"What is it, Rachel," Caleb prodded.

It took a few seconds for Rachel to curb her tears. "Jane told me that I needed to pay attention to my dream that it was trying to tell me something. My dream is telling me that Michaels killed Amanda!"

"But dear," said her mom, "I thought Michaels killed you in your dream."

"Yes, Mom. Caleb was right that in my dream I was replacing Amanda, but Michaels was not replacing the killer, he was the killer. My replacing Amanda was my dream's way of allowing me to see who killed her."

"Rachel, are you sure?" Walter was not buying this. "It was just a dream brought on by the stress you're under."

"No, Dad. It's real." She turned to Caleb for support. "You believe me don't you?"

Caleb nodded. There was no other explanation for this happening. He had learned from Pastor Reynolds' visit that some things cannot be explained, at least not in human terms.

"What about the postcard, Caleb? It proves Michaels had a connection to Jamaica and the drugs."

Walter walked over and picked up the chair he knocked over and sat in it. "This is getting out of hand."

"No, Mr. Gilbert, it's not." Caleb stood up and began pacing the floor. "Let's look at what we know. First, the lab reports confirm that the ointment Albertson was using is in fact hash oil. Secondly, there is a good chance, according to the article Dr. Claire gave us that it is coming from Jamaica. Third, we know that Albertson was selling it at his tent meetings. Fourth, Michaels has a tie with Jamaica. Fifth, Albertson was murdered and for a reason. Lastly, someone told the police and media that we are involved. There is a connection between all these facts and Michaels."

Walter nodded his head and quietly agreed that there may be more to this than he was ready to admit. Doris now sipped from the glass of water she gave Rachel without saying a word. Rachel sat with her head in her hands while Caleb continued to pace the floor. The silence was finally broken as Caleb wheeled around.

"Rachel, who else knew you were using the name Anna Clark?"

"Anna Clark!" Walter was looking at his daughter puzzled. "Who's Anna Clark?"

"Mom, Dad, it's a long story, but I used a made up name to meet Caleb."

Doris looked at Caleb and then Rachel. "Why would you do that?"

"Mom, please, can we drop this for now? Thank you."

"I certainly don't understand why you wouldn't use your real name..." Doris' voice trailed off.

Rachel continued. "Besides Jane, I only told three other people. I had to tell Lauren, Admiral Garry and Fletcher so that they would not blow my cover. But none of them would have told the police that story."

"No, I agree. If Dr. Claire wanted us arrested, she could have done it while we were at the hospital. Garry and Fletcher could have done it while we were with them. What about Jane?"

"Caleb, no! Jane was helping me piece this together and she tried to warn me when Michaels and that other guy were in her office."

"But she left with them," Caleb reminded her.

"She was in trouble Caleb, I just know it. It couldn't be her."

"Then who else knew, Rachel, and would do such a thing?"

Rachel stood up and turned away from Caleb. He knew she was struggling with the idea that Jane had betrayed her, but no one else knew.

"Obviously," Walter interjected. "This person you trusted set you up by pretending to be whatever she needed to be to get you to do her dirty work. Rachel, I've told you before you need to be careful about who you trust."

Caleb felt Rachel's pain. He knew deception well. If that was not bad enough, being berated over it did not help.

Suddenly, Rachel spun around.

"What is it, Rachel?"

"Michaels! Jane was reporting everything I did to him. She didn't sell us out, he did!"

"That makes sense," Caleb said.

Walter followed intently and worked through the logic as well. He realized he had misjudged his daughter. "Rachel, I'm sorry for what I said. I should've known better. But let me ask, why would Michaels use the name Anna Clark instead of using your real name when he leaked the story?"

"Probably because he didn't want the company to be exposed. He could say that I did this on my own when I met Caleb. They could cover up what I was working on." Rachel thought some more and continued. "Also, if he used my real name he might take the chance that Caleb would pull back and point the finger at me instead of sticking with me through this. He must have more planned if he needed to keep Caleb involved."

Doris finally finished her water and regained her ability to speak. "Why murder Albertson then? If Michaels wanted him out of the way why not let the two of you expose him like you were planning?"

Caleb took a seat on the couch and looked into space. "This isn't about a murder. It's about getting even." Looking up he could see the confusion in their expressions. "Don't you see? Michaels has used Rachel and me to chase Albertson. Then he has Albertson murdered and leaks that we are the killers."

Rachel came and sat next to him while he talked. Turning to her he added, "He's getting even with you just like he said he would."

"After all these years?" Rachel asked. "But why you? What did you do? And Amanda, what about her?"

"I did nothing, but Michaels needed you to find someone with a reason to chase Albertson, who caused my divorce."

"And your motive," added Walter, "was your ex-wife's death."

It all made sense except the murder of Amanda, but it was still conjecture and Caleb sensed that they were all aware of this. Silently they all sat. Caleb was processing everything they had said, trying to see if there was something they missed.

Finally, Doris spoke up. "Okay, now what? What do we do now? The police still think you two killed Albertson. You think they're going to believe that someone like Michaels took ten years to work out his revenge?"

"You're right Mrs. Gilbert," Caleb said. "We need to find a connection between Michaels and Albertson. There has to be a reason he chose Albertson."

Rachel hoped for the impossible. "I wish I could get into the files at A. E. Research. They have the largest collection of information on Albertson I've seen. During my research, I found out that even the police don't have some of the information A. E. Research does."

Doris got up to refill her glass of water. "How do you know that this Jason Michaels, from the postcard, is the same guy that runs your company? It could be just a coincidence."

Caleb and Rachel looked at each other. Had they jumped to conclusions? Their assessment of the facts seemed to hinge on the fact that the two were the same person. What if they were not?

"Mom, what else of Amanda's did you save?"

"Not a lot dear. What are you thinking about?"

"Do you still have her laptop?"

"Yes," replied Walter. "It's in my office. I'll get it."

A few minutes later, they all gathered around the kitchen table staring at the screen from the laptop. Rachel was doing several scans of the hard drive.

"What are you looking for dear?" Doris asked.

"If Michaels met Amanda through the Internet then maybe they passed e-mails back and forth. I spent a lot of time in the library searching for information and when Clark taught me how to use the system at A. E. Research, he showed me how to search for e-mail files." She scanned through files on the laptop for ten minutes.

"There! There they are," she cried out. "The last one is dated one week before Amanda died." She opened the e-mail file and found an image file attached to it. When she opened the attachment, she gasped. "It's him!"

It was clear by the way Rachel reacted that the reality of what they had just found confirmed the assessment they had made. It also revealed the reality that Amanda's murder had been a part of Michaels' revenge. Tears ran down Rachel's cheeks. Her parents wrapped their arms around her shoulders and cried too.

While they shared a family moment, which Caleb knew he was not a part of, he read the e-mail. It was dated May 25th, 1996 and it was an invitation to meet for dinner at the Athens restaurant in southeast Richmond on Saturday, June 1st, 1996, the day Amanda died. Caleb shut down the computer and as gently as he could, he interrupted the Gilberts.

"Rachel, I know this is bad timing." He watched as they all separated and wiped their eyes. "I don't want to seem insensitive and I know how much pain this must be bringing back to you, however, I think we should go."

"Go where?" Rachel asked after blowing her nose in a paper napkin from the table.

"Garry is missing one very important piece of the puzzle he's trying to sell to the police to save us. I think he needs this computer. I also think we need whatever information we can find at A. E. Research."

Caleb could see the fear in her eyes as Rachel asked, "How do we get the information from A. E. Research?"

"We'll figure out a way while we're heading back to Richmond." Caleb looked into the eyes of Rachel's parents and anticipated their feelings. "I promise you, I'll take care of her." Rachel leaned over and hugged him tightly.

Doris packed some sandwiches and coffee for the trip. Several hugs and handshakes later, Caleb and Rachel climbed into Rachel's Lexus. This time, Caleb drove.

# 24

"Okay, Admiral, we'll meet you at the elevator lobby of the garage's ground floor at seven-thirty." Rachel hung up the phone and replaced it in her purse. "The Admiral said to protect the computer at all cost."

Caleb looked over at Rachel. "In other words, don't get caught, right?"

"I think that's the idea, yes."

They had only been driving for about thirty minutes, so Caleb reasoned they had about three hours to go. He hoped nothing would hold them up. Meeting Garry and Fletcher at A. E. Research did not seem like the wisest choice they could make, but it gave them the help they needed. Fletcher had the expertise to get them in the building unnoticed if they needed it and there was no time to plan a second meeting to pass off the computer to Garry. This had to go well to protect all of them because if Michaels got wind of their movement, the results would be disastrous at best.

Since there was time to kill, Caleb decided he would appease his curiosity. "So tell me, Rachel, why did you break up with Michaels?"

Rachel did not hesitate to answer. "He scared me. I couldn't go anywhere without him drilling me on where I went and with whom. We met in an Industrial-Organizational Psychology class at Virginia Tech. and there was an attraction. At first, things went well; he was a Gentleman and he had goals and dreams. He was two years ahead of me in school and when he graduated with his BA, he moved to Richmond to work for his dad. We grew distant even though he traveled back and forth often while he was gone. When we talked, he wanted to know everything I did, even the small details. It was creepy. Months later, he went on a trip with his dad. While they were gone, his dad died. It took him months to get over it and that's when he started to change. I passed it off as grief, but he became obsessed with my being around him all the time.

"A year later he asked me to marry him and move to Washington DC. The CIA offered him a new position. I wasn't ready to get married and I wasn't finished with school. By this point, things were rocky and I wasn't going to commit with this kind of foundation. It was around this time that I met Joe Coffee at a party.

"Joe was energetic and fun, everything Tripp was not. We hit it off and started dating. The next time Tripp came back to Blacksburg to visit, I broke it off with him. Two months later, I found out that Joe was a drug dealer and I broke up with him. I was so disgusted with men at that time that I threw myself into school. After Amanda's death, I hated men. I haven't dated since, until you."

"What ever happened to Joe?"

"I don't know. I never saw either of them after that."

"Did Michaels and Joe ever meet?"

"Once, at a party. I was there with Joe and Tripp was friends with the host. That's where I saw Joe selling drugs to a buddy of his. I was furious. Joe tried to deny it, but I told him we were finished. I left the party and started walking home. Tripp followed me and asked if he could drive me home.

"During the ride, he apologized for his behavior while we were together. He said he understood how I felt and went on to explain why he was acting the way he did. It seems the promotion with the CIA not only required him to move to DC, but also to be married. He needed to fit in with the crowd that would surround him. I turned him down and the CIA followed suit.

"Tripp said he had finally gotten over the pain of losing that job and realized that he missed me. When we reached my house, we talked for a little longer. He wanted us to get back together. I told him no, that I was even more disgusted with him after hearing that I was just a pawn to gain a position. As I got out of the car, I added that we could never be more than acquaintances.

"His face got red, his eyes squinted and he clenched his teeth. That's when he said he'd make me pay."

"Man, did you ever see him again?"

"Surprisingly, no."

"Did you believe he would do something?"

Rachel shrugged her shoulders. "I never thought about it. I figured he was just angry and spouting off."

Caleb wondered how anyone, if they were serious about getting even, would wait this long to do something. He hoped they were wrong about Michaels. Just then, an image of Jena on the platform of Albertson's tent came to mind and Caleb gripped the steering wheel tighter.

"Caleb, are you okay?"

To curb his anger, he changed the subject. "When did your dreams start?"

"Those started a few weeks after Amanda died. It took me a while to get through all that happened back then and when I did, I went back to school to find out how to catch up. Two weeks later, after I tried to immerse myself in schoolwork, the dreams started.

"At first, they were just pictures of different events that Amanda and our family attended. Then they turned into pictures of faces and places I had never seen before and eventually they included images of Amanda with blood running down her head. We couldn't even have an open casket at her funeral because of her wound.

"Anyway, the images flashed in my mind in random order, not making any sense. They came every night and I always woke up screaming. When I could no longer do my schoolwork, I quit going, but the dreams didn't stop. Finally, my parents called the director of the psychology department at Virginia Tech and asked him what to do. After several sessions with him and a few others at the school, I was referred to Dr. Claire at the Sheltering Arms Hospital because she was an expert in this area.

"Lauren set up a treatment program that required me to move to Richmond. That was eight and a half years ago. Two and a half years later, I left the hospital with no more dreams. I believed I was cured, but Lauren wanted me to stay longer. All I wanted to do was get back to school, which I did that same year. A year and a half later, I finished my Master's degree and then enrolled for my Ph.D. A year and a half after that, I was doing an internship at the Sheltering Arms Hospital under the direction of Lauren. I finished the internship about three months ago and graduated last month."

Caleb looked at her, puzzled. "Then what made the dreams start up again?"

"I'm not sure, but I have a theory. The first one came the night I graduated. I thought it was due to the late night and the excitement of graduating. The next one came after I started with A. E. Research. I was concerned and intrigued by the fact that the dreams were now a sequence of events and not just pictures. Each dream brought me closer and closer to the actual event of Amanda being murdered, until I saw who did it. I believe my dreams were sent to protect me and show me the truth."

Caleb and Rachel started talking about how they believed that God, if he wanted to, could engage himself in people's lives in a way that only they would know what was going on. Their conversation ended when Rachel saw the time on the clock in the dashboard. It was coming up on five-o'clock in the afternoon and Rachel quickly reached for her purse.

"Caleb, I think I know how to get us into the building without the guards stopping us." She dialed her phone and a few seconds later began talking. "Clark, I need you to do me a favor."

Caleb could not hear what the person on the other end of the phone was saying, but from what Rachel had to explain, he guessed the person was not sure he wanted to get involved.

"Clark, just tell the guard that you are helping me with a system problem that will keep us there for a few hours. Ask him to put both our names on the list and then wait for me in my office. Keep the computer on so that it looks like you are fixing something for me. If anyone asks about me, tell them I went to the ladies room."

Clark must have agreed because Rachel thanked him and hung up. *Is everything okay*, Caleb wondered.

"With our names on the list the guards won't question my being there late." Rachel explained. "The only issue now is how to get into the building without the guards seeing us."

Caleb smiled. "A detail I hope Fletcher has covered for us."

Before they knew it, they were driving into Richmond against the flow of traffic that was trying to leave town. It was late enough that most of the heavy traffic was already gone. As Garry had instructed them, they drove around town making sure no one was following them. Each circle around town brought them closer to the Merrill Lynch building. They drove past it three times before pulling into the garage. Rachel did not use her parking card so that her entry would not show up on the security computer. Instead, Caleb took a parking ticket and drove in once the gate was up.

It was not long before Garry and Fletcher showed up. Rachel greeted Garry with a long tight hug that Fletcher interrupted.

"Sorry, guys, but we don't have much time. Any ideas on how to get in?"

Caleb looked at Fletcher with disgust. "I thought that's what you were going to do, get us in."

"I could if I knew the layout, but I'm afraid I don't."

"It's okay, Fletcher," Rachel said. "I've already got my name on the security list so they think I'm already in the building. What we need is for someone to leave the building through a back entrance so we can get in."

Rachel had her phone out and dialing again. "Clark, it's me. I'm here, but I need to get in. It's time for you to leave."

* * *

Clark left the computer on and left Rachel's office. He was careful not to turn out the light and to leave the coffee cup on the desk so anyone passing by could see it. Rachel hoped it would be enough to make them think someone was still working in that office.

The elevator door opened and Clark stepped out into the lobby. He tried to act as if he was not scared, but he was. He had always been a company man and did not like the idea of deceiving anyone, especially the security guards. As he stepped up to the guard's desk to sign himself out the guard looked up at him.

"By yourself, Clark?"

"Uh, yes. I, uh, fixed Dr. Gilbert's computer problem, but she needed to stay to finish what she was doing."

"Yeah? I'll make sure someone checks up on her later."

"I think she would appreciate that, thanks." Clark signed his name and time out on the late sheet the guard gave him. "I'm going to leave through the garage entrance. It's closer to my car."

"Have a nice night, Clark."

"Uh, thanks." Clark turned as fast as he could and walked to the door at the corner of the lobby between the building elevators and the garage elevators. The door closed behind him and he stopped to take a deep breath. A few steps up and one more door and he would be in the garage. For a second, he felt like James Bond eluding the wisest security in France and he lifted his chin and climbed the stairs.

Clark jumped as he emerged from the stairwell where several people waited. One man quickly grabbed the door while Rachel gave him a peck on the cheek and thanked him for his help. Two seconds later, they were all gone and he was alone. He had made it and now he had an incredible story to tell his tech friends over Happy Hour.

* * *

Fifteen flights of stairs had winded everyone, but they did not complain. Rachel led the way across the floor to her office and quickly took her seat while the others entered. Fletcher kept watch at the door.

Rachel logged on to the research database and entered the name Brian Albertson as the search criteria. Within seconds, the screen was filling up with names of files. The third file down had the word *Background* in it so she clicked on it.

The file opened and revealed a newspaper article about Albertson starting his practice in Richmond. Rachel scanned it and read the important information.

"It says here that Albertson started his practice here in Richmond four years ago. He apparently moved here from Jamaica where he learned his faith healing trade."

Caleb remarked, "That's stuff we already know. What else is there?"

Rachel closed the file and rescanned the list of file names. A little further down was a file named *Attempts* and she clicked on it.

"This is about the two attempts to murder Albertson. In each case, one of his followers saved him. The first happened in November of 2003."

"That's the meeting that Jena and I attended!" Caleb said. "I made her leave early and when we got home, we heard on the news that there was an attempt on his life."

Rachel kept reading. "The second one happened in December of 2004. It appears that in these two cases, no one was ever charged with the death of the martyrs."

"Is there anything there that indicates if there was an attempt on his life in Jamaica?"

"Caleb, are you thinking that these attempts were set up by Albertson's people?" Garry said.

"Not really, I was just wondering why someone would want to kill a faith healer, unless he really wasn't a faith healer at all."

Rachel scanned the list of files again. To make it easier she returned to the search criteria and added the word *Jamaica*. This time the search returned only those files that included the three words. It was a much shorter list.

"There doesn't appear to be any files pertaining to any attempts in Jamaica," Rachel announced.

While Rachel continued to scan the files and check out ones that seemed interesting, Caleb and Garry tried to come up with a reason for the murders.

* * *

Veiltek walked into Michaels' office followed by two other men. From his usual perch, Michaels invited them in without looking away from the window.

"Sir," Veiltek started. "The front desk guard has just informed me that Dr. Gilbert is in her office along with three other men. He caught them on the cameras we installed on that floor this past weekend."

"Well done, Mr. Veiltek. I guess you were right about spending the money on them. It did pay off." Michaels never changed his position as he spoke. "Who are the other men?"

"Mr. Prescott is one of them. We didn't get a good angle on the other two, but based upon their size and shape we believe they are Garry and Fletcher."

Michaels turned to look at the men for the first time. He was surprised that all four of them would be together in his own back yard. "My, they are bold. Gentlemen, it's time to go butterfly hunting. Remember, do this nice and gentle, no bruises or scars. We want nothing that can tie them back to us. Understood?"

All three men indicated they understood. Each checked their

handgun. Veiltek led the way followed by his two helpers and then Michaels, who was looking forward to seeing the look on Rachel's face.

* * *

"I can't believe with all this information there isn't anything tying Michaels to Albertson." Rachel sat back in her chair and let out a long sigh.

"It's not surprising," Garry offered. "Think about it, why would Michaels keep information on his own system that would incriminate himself?"

No one spoke. Caleb paced the floor near the window behind Rachel's desk. It was a short walk and he had made it at least ten times already. "Something just doesn't add up. Michaels must be tied to Albertson in some way." Whispering so that no one else would hear he prayed for help. "Lord, we are so close, help us find the answers."

"Caleb," Rachel said. "Why Albertson? What's so special about him that Michaels would set this up and then kill him? If he's trying to make me pay, why use Albertson?"

Stopping his pacing and staring at Rachel, Caleb had an epiphany. "Rachel, do you have any access to imaging software?"

"Like what police use to create suspect sketches?"

"Yeah, that's it."

"We do, but it's fairly limited."

"Great, do you have a picture of Joe Coffee anywhere?

Maybe in the database?"

Rachel searched the database to see if by chance there was a picture of Joe. Garry and Fletcher leaned over the desk to watch as Caleb stood behind Rachel staring at the screen.

"Oh, my God, there is one," Rachel said.

"Pull up the picture of Joe next to a picture of Albertson."

"Let me save you the trouble."

Fletcher and Garry turned to find three men with handguns pointing at their heads. Caleb stood up and Rachel looked up from her seat. One man stood back against the glass wall of the front of Rachel's office while the other two stood in front of Garry and Fletcher. Caleb did not recognize any of them.

"You were right about the microphones as well, Mr. Veiltek." Michaels walked out from behind the wall to the right of Rachel's office and then slowly inside. "Good evening, Dr. Gilbert, Mr. Prescott, Mr. Fletcher and Mr. Garry. It's so nice to see you all, together. I see you are working late Dr. Gilbert."

Caleb's heart sank; they came so far and were so close and now he knew no one else would ever know. His thoughts turned to Jeff and the fact that he would never be able to explain all this to him, or say good-bye. He knew Michaels would kill them.

"Mr. Prescott, may I say that you have a very analytical mind, I congratulate you. I believe that if we had not showed up when we did, you would have put two and two together and answered the million dollar question, who was Brian Albertson?"

Caleb felt his blood pressure rise as his disgust for Michaels ignited by the condescending way Michaels was talking to him. "He was Joe Coffee, wasn't he?"

Rachel spun around to look at Caleb with a shocked expression. Her action caused the front two men to shift their focus to Rachel.

"My dear, Dr. Gilbert, if I were you I wouldn't be making any sudden movements. My men are trained to react quickly. They may feel threatened and shoot."

As Rachel slowly turned back around, Caleb searched the room for help. There were no doors or exits out of the office except the one blocked by Michaels and his three thugs. They were fifteen stories up so the window was useless. He could not see Garry or Fletcher's faces so there was no way to communicate with them and even if he could there was nothing they could do without having these men react.

"Shocked, Dr. Gilbert?" It was easy to tell that Michaels was enjoying this. "Joe was an enthusiastic learner. After he recovered from his extensive plastic surgery in Jamaica, he took to the Rastafarian ways easily."

Caleb could no longer see Rachel's face, but he did not have to. He knew she was getting angry.

"I think it's time for all of us to take a ride. There's a place I'd like you to see." Michaels ordered the man against the glass to call for the car, which he did from a radio in his hand.

At the sight of the radio, Caleb got an idea. Slowly, he worked his hand to his waist where his work radio hung off his belt. As usual, it was off, but with any luck, it would not make any noise when he turned it on. It did not. He pressed the talk button down and locked it in place. With nothing more to do, he quickly prayed for Jeff. Having the talk button locked, prevented anyone from hearing Jeff, but there was no way to know if he was listening. He could only hope Jeff would be Jeff.

"So when did you make the switch with Joe?" Caleb wanted to give Jeff something that would let him know he was in trouble.

"I'm glad you asked, Mr. Prescott. It's nice to have someone appreciate your work. Two months after Dr. Gilbert broke up with me, I ran into Joe again. He was in trouble and needed to disappear, if you know what I mean. I realized that he could be useful to me so I hid him for a while and then sent him to Jamaica where I had some contacts that did very good plastic surgery work. So, nine years ago, Joe Coffee becomes Brian Albertson and learns a new career. It took several surgeries and then, three years later, Brian started his new career in Jamaica. I must say he was rather good at it, a born performer. Don't you agree, Rachel?"

Caleb gently held Rachel's shoulder to keep her from reacting and causing anyone any harm.

"The car's here, Mr. Michaels," said the man with the radio.

"Very good, Mr. Veiltek. Please escort our guests downstairs."

Michaels left the office and waited outside while one of the men led Fletcher out the door. The second man led Garry out. Veiltek waved his gun for Rachel and Caleb to move. Caleb pulled the chair out for Rachel and held her hand as they left the office with Veiltek behind them. Michaels brought up the rear.

\* \* \*

Jeff knew he sounded hysterical when he talked to Thompson over the phone, but he also knew that Thompson would go anywhere if he knew that Caleb and Anna were there. They pulled up in front of the Merrill Lynch building at the same time and had to stop quickly so they would not collide.

"Are you crazy? What do you think you're doing here?" Thompson was obviously not happy to see Jeff.

"It was the only way I could get you to listen to what I'm hearing," Jeff said as he handed the radio over to Thompson.

They listened for a short while and realized that Caleb and someone named Rachel along with two other men were being transported somewhere and were no longer in the building. Thompson yelled for one of his men.

"Find the frequency on this thing and get central to trace that line." Turning back to Jeff, Thompson started giving orders. "Mr. Birch, park your car over there. You ride with me. Anderson, you ride with Murphy and let me know as soon as you have a direction on that signal."

Jeff ran back to his car and parked it as ordered. When he reached Thompson's car, Thompson was calling for backup to be ready as soon as they knew where they were going. Jeff climbed in.

"What now?"

"We wait and monitor until we know where they are," Thompson replied.

Jeff felt a lump in his throat as he imagined what his best

friend was going through. He hated himself for not believing Caleb and tears came to his eyes as he thought about what could happen. *Lord, protect them.* Ashamed that he did not do more sooner, he hoped that Caleb would forgive him.

Thompson spoke quickly as the radio in his car came to life. "Go!"

"Sir, central advises that they are traveling eastward on I-64 about ten miles out of town."

Thompson screamed into his radio. "All units, subjects are moving eastbound on I-64 with a large lead. We have no descriptions of their vehicle so the signal is our only link. Stay on it. Let's move!"

Jeff closed his door as Thompson sped off. By the time they had reached I-64, Jeff saw several unmarked cars following them and three police cruisers with their lights on. Thompson had asked central to patch in the signal from the radio to his car so that he could listen as they drove.

"Seems like your partner was telling you the truth all along," Thompson commented in a calm voice even though they were traveling at speeds that made Jeff nervous.

Jeff could not respond. When the time came for his friend to need him the most, Jeff folded and he knew it. Silently, he continued to pray hoping they would not be too late.

* * *

"Since we have some time before we get to our destination, I thought I'd fill you in on a few details maybe you haven't figured out."

The limo rode so smoothly over the paved road that they could not tell how fast they were going. The tinted windows kept Caleb from seeing outside. He sat in the middle section of the limo next to Rachel. Facing them were Michaels, who sat in the seat across from Rachel, and Veiltek, who sat in front of Caleb. Behind them facing forward were Garry, Fletcher, and one of the other guards. The last guard sat in the passenger seat up front. All still had their guns drawn.

"By now I believe you have figured out how the hash oil was distributed during the tent meetings. It's funny how the police can be fooled by actually using water for a few weeks. But then, I found out a long time ago that the police can be manipulated very easily when I used them to blackmail your friend Joe into being Albertson."

"You know I never told you," Rachel said with disgust in her voice. "Your name fits you perfectly, Tripp."

Michaels laughed. "A joke! That's funny coming from you." His smile disappeared quickly. "Let's see how funny you think this is. It was Joe who met your sister that night in the restaurant."

Caleb grabbed both of Rachel's hands sensing that what they were about to hear was going to be the worst yet.

"I wanted to meet her myself, but every scenario I came up with had a chance of me being recognized and I just couldn't have that happen. Joe was perfect. Without any coaching he acted perfectly."

Rachel leaned forward. "What are you talking about?"

"Your sister, my dear, she thought we were meeting for dinner and had no idea who this guy was that showed up. Joe thought he was making a drug deal and didn't understand why the girl, whose picture he had, didn't know who he was. I, of course, called the police, anonymously, to tell them about the drug deal that was going down. Ready to be heroes, they raced there, and Joe, I couldn't have planned this any better, thought he was saving her from the police so he drags her with him as he flees. The poor thing though, had to listen to your sister bombard him with questions until he couldn't take it any more."

"Joe killed my sister?" Rachel screamed.

"Oh no, my dear, Joe's too weak of a man to do that, but he did tie her up nicely and deliver her to me. It was quick and I did use his gun."

Caleb held Rachel back as he felt her try to lunge at Michaels, who was enjoying this. Veiltek did not move but Caleb could see he was studying the situation in case it got out of hand.

Michaels looked at his right hand, which he had formed into the shape of a gun, as a kid would do. "I believe she recognized me just before I shot her."

That was more than Rachel could take and no matter how much strength Caleb used, he could not hold her back. She lunged with the strength of a tiger protecting her cubs with her arms and hands outstretched and aiming for Michaels' throat.

It was over in a flash, before anyone could do anything. Rachel's body fell to the floor of the car and the remaining three had cocked guns pointed at them. Caleb sat with his hands up and his heart pounding faster than he ever thought it would go. His eyes wandered to the floor.

"I warned her," was all Michaels had to say.

Veiltek motioned to Caleb with his gun, "Pick her up."

Slowly, Caleb reached down and gently placed his arms under Rachel's body and lifted her back onto the seat. Her head hung limp and blood was surfacing from the gash on her temple. Caleb pressed his hand against the wound to stop the bleeding.

"It's a good thing Mr. Veiltek is a professional. Any other man would have killed her with a blow like that. He knew exactly how much force was needed just to stop her, although she'll have a headache when she wakes up."

Caleb shot a hateful look at both Veiltek and Michaels.

"Keep the pressure on it, Mr. Prescott, the bleeding will stop soon." Michaels just smiled. "Trust me."

Rachel was out for the rest of the trip. Even the bumpy ride down the dirt road did not wake her up. The bleeding had stopped and Caleb had repositioned her so that she lay across his lap. He softly ran his fingers through her hair wanting so much to be anywhere but where they were. It was only a matter of time before Michaels would kill them out in this dark place so far from town. His senses picked up the smell of salt water. He knew, from the short time they drove, that they could not be at the coast. *It must be one of the fingers.* Caleb wanted so much to turn and look at Garry, but his fear kept him still.

The car stopped for a short while as the driver got out and

unlocked a chain before returning and continuing down a very narrow path lined with bushes and trees on both sides. The path opened to a field with nothing but a shed and a long pier that reached out into the water. A light mounted on the shed was on, though it gave little light. The crescent moon offered little light as well and the darkness seemed to swallow up even the sound.

When the car stopped again, Michaels ordered everyone out. Caleb was able to rouse Rachel, but she could not focus and kept one hand on her head.

Michaels led them to the end of the rickety pier. Caleb wondered if it would hold all of them.

"It's ironic that this story is going to end in the same place, and the same way, as it started." He turned and raised his arms, speaking to the river. "Here, at the edge of the York River, is where your sister died, Rachel, and it's where you will die as well."

He wasted his words on Rachel. She was still out of it and Caleb knew she did not comprehend what he said. He felt a little relief as he realized she would not understand what was happening to her.

When Michaels turned back around, he faced Caleb who was holding Rachel. "It's a shame she can't hear this, but you can, Mr. Prescott. I'll bet you're trying to figure out why you were dragged into this, aren't you? Well, let me explain it to you. I knew Rachel would never go after someone to ruin him or her. She wanted to reform everyone. I needed someone who had a reason to go after Albertson. When your wife returned to Albertson's tent meetings after the first time you went, we got to know her better. We counseled her that you were holding her back from becoming everything she could be. It didn't take long to convince her to leave you."

Caleb's blood was boiling and needed someone to hold him back now. Garry, who stood behind him, held onto his shoulder. Holding up Rachel also kept him from doing what Rachel wanted to do.

"Of course, your separation and divorce wasn't enough to get you committed to going after Albertson. There was too much goody-goody in you. So we had to take it a step further. We knew exactly what would send you over the edge, didn't we?"

With tears flowing down his face, Caleb dropped to his knees letting Rachel tumble onto the pier. All his strength left him as he realized he had done nothing to chase Jena away, it was not his fault. He cried as he pictured his soft angel ravaged by these wolves.

Garry bent over to help Caleb and Rachel stand. In a blink of his eye, the man watching him reacted and brought his elbow down on Garry's right shoulder sending him to his knees next to Caleb. Fletcher reacted as well and spun around to grab the wrist of the man holding the gun on him. He managed to disarm the man, but before he could do anymore, a bullet caught him in the left shoulder and sent him to the ground also.

Caleb looked up to see Veiltek's gun smoking. "Pick up your weapon you fool," he yelled to his man. "You four stay where you are. Don't move!"

"Mr. Veiltek, I believe it's time to get this over with. Give me fifteen minutes then finish them. I'll send the van for you."

"Yes, sir."

Michaels stepped in front of Veiltek and squatted down to face Rachel just as she was beginning to focus. "I'm sorry, my dear. This could have worked out differently if you had made the right choice ten years ago." He stood up and walked to the back of the pier. "Good-bye, my friends. Believe me, you won't be missed."

"Michaels!" Caleb yelled. "You won't get away with this. There are others who know."

"Could you be referring to your partner, Mr. Prescott? I'm surprised that by now you haven't realized that I plan to the utmost detail. Right now, because of your partner's background, the police think he was involved because of the drugs. When they search his apartment, they'll find several thousand dollars and a bag full of vials containing hash oil. They'll assume it was a pay off for the shipment he took. The fact that the contract got canceled because of your screw-up gave him the motive for killing you. No one is going to believe, Mr. Birch.

"Oh, and Mr. Garry, since you were so curious about the Cottonwood Lake problem, yours and Mr. Fletcher's bodies will join Barnes' body and be found floating in Cottonwood Lake. In case you were wondering. Gentlemen, proceed as planned."

Michaels turned and walked back to the car. Caleb heard it start and drive away. Rachel was not quite fully conscious; Garry was nursing his sore shoulder while Fletcher held his bleeding shoulder. Caleb was out of hope. By now, he figured Jeff had not heard what had happened or did not care. It was over and he tried to prepare himself for what was coming.

He reached over and wiped the hair away from Rachel's face aware of Veiltek's gun that followed his every move. "I'm sorry I let you down, Rachel. I'm glad I got the chance to get to know you." Caleb turned to look at Garry and Fletcher. Their faces revealed defeat. There was no last minute plan to get them out. In a few minutes, it would all be over.

"FREEZE, POLICE!"

Caleb looked up to see where the scream came from, but saw nothing but bright lights. Within seconds, Veiltek and his men were shooting into the trees.

"ROLL! ROLL! ROLL!" screamed Fletcher as he rolled off the pier.

Garry followed him and yelled as well, "ROLL!"

Caleb heard bullets soar over his head as he wrapped his arms around Rachel and threw his weight over the top of her towards the edge of the pier. From the corner of his eye, he saw Veiltek adjust his aim downward and look his way. Rachel was covering Caleb's body and he knew she would take a shot in the back. With all his might, he flung her off the pier just as a bullet caught Veiltek in the chest, which pushed him back by the force and caused his grip on his gun to loosen just as he fired. The bullet shot right past Caleb's left ear and into the shallow water next to the pier.

Quickly, Caleb rolled off the pier and fell the short distance to the water. Just before hitting the water, he thought he heard Jeff's voice.

"Caleb!"

\* \* \*

Caleb sat on the beach with Rachel leaning on his shoulder; both under blankets. Red and blue lights were flashing everywhere and there must have been thirty police officers scattered all over the area.

On the pier laid three bodies covered with sheets. Caleb scanned the area looking for Garry and Fletcher. Near the entrance, he saw a police officer putting Michaels in the back seat of a police car with his hands cuffed behind his back. To the right, he saw Fletcher being loaded into an ambulance and Garry standing over him holding his hand. They were fine.

As he felt Rachel stir, he turned and caught sight of Jeff talking to a police officer. Their eyes met. Caleb mouthed the words *Thank you* and Jeff raised his thumb indicating to Caleb that he had not lost his friend. Refocusing his attention on Rachel, he went to kiss her head and saw that her wound had already been dressed.

Caleb looked out on the water and saw the reflection of the moon. The motion of the waves that were reflecting the moon's dim light gave the appearance that the water was waving at him. In that moment, he knew he was no longer alone and a tear ran down his cheek. He looked up and whispered, "Thank you, God."

# 25

It was a cool overcast morning as Caleb and Jeff walked up to *La Portique*. Jeff was there for support. Caleb had a difficult task ahead of him and he needed his friend to help him go through with it. Without Jeff there, it would be easy to cave in.

Rachel was sitting at the same table she had sat at weeks ago when she first waited for Caleb. "It's good to see the two of you together," she said.

Jeff reached out and gave her a hug. "It's good to see you again, Rachel." He stepped back and reached out his hand to Caleb. "I'll be inside, buddy."

Caleb took his hand and felt the unusually tight grip. They had come so close to losing each other in so many ways and it caused them to vow that they would not take each other for granted ever again. "Thanks, Jeff. I'll see you in a bit."

When Jeff disappeared inside the café, Caleb turned and embraced Rachel. It felt good to hold her once more. They had not seen each other since the night at the pier, though they talked every day. Rachel's parents had come to spend some time with her. Mostly they were recovering from the ordeal.

Rachel wore the same perfume she had the day they first met here and it caused Caleb to remember how he felt then. He allowed himself the luxury of smelling the scent for as long as Rachel would let him. The warmth of her body, the softness of her skin and the beating of her heart comforted him once more. When she stirred, he pulled back and kissed her lightly on the cheek. He noticed the surprised look on her face.

"I couldn't wait to see you, Caleb."

"Same here, Rachel." He indicated for them to sit.

"It appears that you and Jeff have recovered."

"We've had a long talk filled with many tears and apologies. We were able to pick up the pieces and move on. I guess our friendship was stronger than we thought."

"I'm looking forward to getting to know him better."

Caleb looked away, towards the café. There was something that he wanted to say, but was not ready, so he changed the subject. "How are Garry and Fletcher?"

"They're doing fine. Fletcher's surgery went well and he should be up and around in a few weeks. Admiral Garry's a little tired. He's been spending a lot of time with that detective, Thompson. They found Hans and the four of them are making plans to go to Cottonwood Lake once Fletcher is able. Admiral Garry had to tell Hans that the police found what they thought was Mr. Barnes' body the day after they arrested Michaels. It was badly burned, so they're checking dental records."

"Any word on Jane?"

"I've tried to call, but she hasn't been in and no one is

talking at A. E. Research. Admiral Garry says there is still hope since no one has found her body."

Caleb checked out the café once more and still could not bring himself to share what he needed to. Again, he went off in another direction. "What do you plan to do now?"

"Well, I've contacted Lauren and she has found a place for me at the Sheltering Arms Hospital. Turns out, I'll be working with the new interns. She gave me some time to recover before I start." Rachel reached across the table and held Caleb's hands. "How did it go with Jena's funeral?"

"It was simple. I tried to reach as many of her family as I could. Some were hard to find. They had her cremated. I think she would have wanted that."

"Do you have any new plans?"

"As far as the business goes, Jeff and I are taking some time off over the next few weeks to plan for our future. We really need to define ourselves in more specific terms." He looked down at her hands and then added, "I've also met with Pastor Reynolds and will be returning to church. This whole event has shown me that God is still with me and does have a purpose for my life."

"That's great, Caleb, I'm so happy for you."

Once again, he looked at the café. This time Jeff stood in the doorway with his thumb up nodding his head. It was time.

"Caleb, is something wrong?"

"Not exactly, Rachel, but I need to tell you something and I'm not sure how."

"A wise man once told me that the best thing to do is just say it, remember?"

They both chuckled.

"Rachel, I have never felt before, with anyone, what I feel for you. We have connected in a way I never thought possible."

Rachel tightened her grip on his hands as he took one more look at Jeff.

"Rachel, I want to give myself to you wholly and I want you to do the same, however, I think we both have some healing to do first. I'm not emotionally there yet and I don't want to make another mistake. I want us to be sure that our relationship isn't based on this event. I think there are things we need to deal with before we can devote ourselves to a relationship."

Caleb felt Rachel's grip loosen and it took all he had in him to let it go and not back pedal. The relationship had to be based on their love and devotion and not the sharing of a traumatic experience. He released her hands and watched her sit back in her seat as a tear ran down her face.

Looking into her eyes, he saw an expression of hope as she nodded her head. "Caleb, you are the first man I've ever known that put aside what he felt to make sure a commitment would last forever." She wiped her tears away before adding, "Will we stay in touch?"

"Of course."

Caleb stood, as did Rachel, and they embraced once more. This time it was just long enough to part as friends. However, Caleb knew the scent of her perfume would linger much longer than the last time.

Before walking away, Rachel left him with one more encouragement. "We've both found something over these past several weeks that will carry us through this trial."

"What's that, Rachel?"

"Hope. We found hope." She kissed him lightly on the cheek and walked away.

He watched as she disappeared into the crowd that was just forming for lunch until at last, his tears clouded his eyes and he could see no more. This did not stop him from recognizing the hand that gripped his shoulder and he reached for it.

"Let's go home, buddy."

\* \* \*

Caleb logged onto The Connection for the last time that night. As he watched and listened to the introduction, his mind relived all that had happened. Though he would never want to go through this again, he was a least grateful to find himself and restore his relationship with God.

With one last keystroke, Caleb ended his short-lived experience with Internet dating by deleting his profile. After shutting down his computer, the sculpture of God giving Eve to Adam caused him to smile. He picked up his Bible and headed for bed, comforted by the knowledge that God is always offering a new life.

\* \* \*

Her parents had left and it had been a while since Rachel had been alone. She feared that it might be frightening, but instead she found it peaceful, resting and reacquainting herself with her apartment and her turtle. She would never forget all that Caleb had gone through for her or the way he protected her. He had showed her a respect she had never known before and it touched her. *This is the beginning of the deep relationship I have always wanted.* Feelings that she did not deserve it rose and she dismissed them. Caleb was not ending anything; he was making sure they would endure.

After a lengthy conversation with her mom over the phone, Rachel sat down in front of her computer and logged on to The Connection. She watched the introduction with disgust as she relived the ordeal of working for A. E. Research.

"Never again will I allow myself to compromise what I believe. My instincts serve me well and if it doesn't feel right, it probably isn't."

Not only did Rachel remove the profile of Anna Clark, but she also deleted the bookmarked link from her favorites list. The only thing she wanted to remember about The Connection was Caleb. She turned off the computer and headed for bed. In her room, the poster on her wall caught her attention; *Progress comes as we make day-to-day choices to continue towards our goal.* Rachel picked up her journal that she had neglected since her graduation and began a new page.

The night passed peacefully without a dream.

\* \* \*

The lights in the hallway went off one by one, the last one going off outside of Michaels' cell. For the past twenty minutes, he had been standing at the front of it, holding onto the bars and watched the counting of the other prisoners. He pulled and tugged at his orange jumpsuit hating the color and the feel of it.

As the guard came by each cell, he ordered the prisoner in that cell to back away from the cell door as he counted. Michaels was not used to taking orders from anyone. When the guard approached and ordered him back, he did not move. The guard did not even give a warning before slamming a nightstick down on Michaels' arm that was hanging through the cell door.

The sound caused the rest of the inmates to hoot and holler. Michaels quickly backed up and sat on his bunk, nursing his sore arm.

"Next time you won't forget," said the angry guard and he went on counting.

It took about thirty minutes for the cellblock to quiet down. Most of the inmates had drifted off to sleep, but Michaels lay on his bunk staring at the ceiling. His mind was his best asset and he used it to understand where he made his mistake. His father would never have let this happen. So, in the confines and silence of his current situation he began using his best asset once more.

As the night guard walked the floor and paused outside of Michaels' cell. Michaels stared back in defiance. Softly he repeated, "I will get even."

Other books by author Michael J. Senger Sr.

## Skies of Blue

## Unity 101 Workbook

## The Simple Truth

Coming Soon:

## Cottonwood Lake

The sequel to **The Connection**. Garry, Fletcher, Hans and Thompson head to Nebraska to find the secret about Cottonwood Lake.

www.ingramcontent.com/pod-product-compliance
Lightning Source LLC
Chambersburg PA
CBHW020836030726
47496CB00001B/259